THE GAIAD

WILLIAM BURCHER

CONTENTS

THE GAIAD

by

WILLIAM BURCHER

PROLOGUE

Head-on it was nearly invisible—a mere point of light as bright only as the faintest and most minor background star. If viewed obliquely, however, it was something different. The inconsequential speck began to elongate and brighten with the angle and it became a distinct and very artificial, *linear* form. The object began to move, slowly drifting against the ubiquitous stellar backdrop. There was a brief flash, a pulse of platinum light at the object's tapered rear and it accelerated, its magnitude expanding and it began to stir a sense of size and mass.

As it approached, the surface of it became visible—a damasked metal, reflective and shimmering. The ship was bulbous at its front, though the nose appeared sharp, as a teardrop, giving it a vaguely avian form. The rest of the structure tapered long and impossibly acute—the entirety of the craft evoking a sewing needle, traveling in the direction of its eye. Though mostly smooth and entirely free of markings, small antenna-like protuberances extended along its spine and side. The anterior bulge contained areas of darker metal, rectangular in shape. It began to emit powerful signals in a microwave band—non-repeating and encoded in binary. The emission was deep and startling and evident of a terrible power within.

The ship continued on a vector away from the yellow, main-sequence sun of this system. As it passed, its proximity to that sun became conspicuous. Another silent, platinum flash at its rear and it further accelerated, approaching the sun's first planet: a baked, darkened sphere. Sensors inside the ship began to register the phenomena, though minuscule, almost imperceptible in magnitude—a whisper, a slight and distant melody. The phenomenon was recorded and analyzed and it was determined that the sought complexity was lacking—an investigatory orbit would not be necessary. Within a few moments it approached the second planet, a shrouded insipid world covered in thick clouds of carbon dioxide, flashes of lightning viewed in multiple points of the spectrum by the watchers. The sensors registered nothing but silence—a complete absence of the phenomena. As the whispers of the first world faded to nothing, the song of the third began.

This world, though similar in size to the second, was alive. Its oceans were already visible, growing with each passing moment as the ship approached. Clouds of water vapor drifted high in the obvious atmosphere—white painter's strokes softening the edges of the harsh brown-green of continental land masses and blending organically with the ice of the northern and southern polar caps. The ship's trajectory would take it close, and it decelerated to an orbital speed. Already the strength and complexity, the organization of the phenomena here was evident. As in others the ship had encountered, there was a correlation between the presence of an ecosystem and the quality of the phenomena associated with a planet. The builders of the ship had designed its sensors to express the received data in an audible form and the translation became a song, a hymn sung by this blue world.

The song was not beautiful. It was dirty, strange, disharmonic. There was a croaking, discordant rhythm repeating itself as an initiate monk chants Latin verse. The tones of the song ranged from profound and deeply low to random, high-pitched cries but most of it averaged in the mid-range—a vague, haunting contralto. The listeners never judged or interpreted the song and a literal translation was beyond their purpose, beyond their mission. Another listener though, perhaps born of the world recorded, might hear a voice in the planet's song—a lone, strange voice speaking too loudly in an otherwise empty cathedral.

The ship, now in orbit, approached the solar terminator, the line of twilight marking the boundary of day and night on the planet's surface. As it passed overhead, from day to night, unbroken darkness stretched along the surface from horizon to horizon. Only the polar aurora, a shimmering ring of electric color, green and blue with an occasional red, stood apart from the darkness. Completing a full orbit, the phenomena analyzed and recorded, the ship left this blue planet like those before it, the song fading as it traveled further from the system's sun.

A smaller red planet, both dormant and silent to the listeners on the ship, hung next in the alignment. This was followed by the largest world of the system, a gas giant whose phenomena could be sensed millions of kilometers away. The structure of the phenomena here, too, was highly complex and the song sang deep and old and masterful. The distances between the worlds at this point in the solar system were greater and a platinum flash behind the ship was followed by a strange contortion of the light of the background stars near its front. The ship accelerated within an instant to tremendous speed.

The listeners on the ship noted that the remaining cold giants all exhibited the phenomena in varying degrees of strength and complexity, although none warranted an investigatory orbit, save that of the blue terrestrial world and the first and largest of the gas giants. Having completed its survey, the distortion of light preceding the ship through space expanded and became more distinct and the craft once again accelerated greatly, traveling in a few seconds past the halo of cometary objects marking the end of this sun's influence and out, out into the further spaces between the stars.

PART I

PRESENT

1

PEOPLE OF SHADOW AND FOG

Dream Log
May 23

I'm in a forest. It's dawn, or dusk. The light is low, muted. Everything is shadow and grey and I can't see very far in front of me. The forest is thick but it is fall, or early spring and the bushes and scrub don't have leaves on them. There are conifer trees all around me and they look old. They are large. It is an untouched place.

And then the day begins to lighten and I see that there is fog drifting through the forest slowly but it is beginning to lift and within a few moments I can see more, and more. They emerge into view as if *materialized*. First one, a man, a leader. His face is still dark. All of their faces are dark. They are walking along a path that I cannot see. There are many of them, many more than I'm originally aware of. They keep emerging, as if from the forest itself. They walk in single file and I see men of all ages, women, children, babies. They are silent and alert as they walk, and all appear to be a part of this place, not just walking through it. They belong in this forest. They walk quickly, all of them gracefully, deftly, athletic—even the old women and the little children. They are wearing leather and fur. Some of the men and women carry spears—some long and slender, others thick, stout. The spears are straight and topped with carved, sharpened stone. Although dressed in fur and carrying spears, I know these people are healthy and well-off. Everything about them— their bearings, their clothing, the items they carry—possesses a sense of care, of craftsmanship and purpose. They are beautiful.

I am standing beside the unseen path and the line of them begins to pass me. No faces, I don't see any faces, but they are close—close enough to smell. They smell of earth and of wood smoke and some kind of spice. They continue to pass me, all of them, and I want to talk to them, ask them who they are, but I don't. I'm silent. And they don't acknowledge me. It's like I'm not there. I'm a watcher. I'm a ghost. Yet I'm the one struck by their mysteriousness. I'm the one struck by their beauty. They seem to me to represent something—what we as people, a species could be. Or perhaps more accurately, what we *were*. In the dream, these two concepts are somehow the same.

The last man passes me. He is one of the taller ones. I see him as a rear guard, hanging back from the rest of the group. I see him more clearly than the rest and from the back. His hair is in a braided tail, tied with a strip of leather and is light brown, almost blond. He is bearded. His posture is straight. He appears to be a natural athlete, built lean, tough, functional—like he can *run* as well as do all the other things he needs to do. A running back. A mid-distance runner. A climber. He is wearing what looks like dark leather—pants, a shirt, a thicker vest. It looks like western Native American clothing, only simpler, less adorned. He is my age roughly. He is somehow … present, *there*, in and of himself more. I am deeply attracted to him.

He walks past me and continues for a moment. He slows, pauses and turns around, looking me in the eyes. His are blue. We hold each other's gaze for a few seconds, silent. I can see his chest rising and falling as he breathes maybe one breath or two, and I can see his breath in the air. He then turns and quickly, silently runs off to join the others.

William Burcher 9

2

FLEUR

"Hey. What are you doing?" Tim asked. She sat at her desk facing her computer in the cubicle. Knowing his voice like she knew her father's, she didn't bother to turn around and face him.

"Working on the warrant affidavit for that trucker case. What are *you* doing?"

"Heading out to County for an interview. I have a new one. An Applewhite. Our favorite family. The oldest is in County for some bond revocation/drug thing and has been pimping on his eleven-year-old sister. Wanna get lunch and come with?"

"Where were you thinking?"

"Mi Tierra. Would I be thinking anything other?"

"Point made," she laughed. "You talk to Bob already?"

"Yeah. He's good with it."

"Ok. Done. But you have to read through what I have so far

in this warrant."

"Deal. Thank you, Fleur."

She didn't have an assigned partner necessarily but she and Tim were close. They were both working the same department—Crimes Against Children—and they got along. He had his shit together, was tough, was handsome, her age, in shape. They sometimes went running on their lunch breaks, and most people thought they had a thing going. But only because most didn't know that Tim was gay. She got herself drunk on cheap wine sitting at home alone in the dark when she found out. But things evolve. She evolved. And they'd both settled into a symbiosis on the job.

After he bought her lunch at Mi Tierra she became suspicious; and by the time they got into their shared unmarked, he admitted the ruse. It would only be a few minutes, he said, explaining that the last time he was in the Applewhite house by himself he stepped in dog shit and had to restrain one of Candy Applewhite's autistic children. Violet, he thought her name was. She had an episode triggered by one of the other 6 kids in the 600 square foot apartment involving a bread knife, a stuffed animal, and her own wrists. The Applewhites were a two cop response now, but he didn't want to bug patrol. She told him he owed her for it, more than a cheap Mexican lunch.

They parked half a block from the apartment and as they approached on foot she caught glimpses of tired faces half-seen through dirty curtains and broken window blinds. A pair of men with cigarettes and tattoos on their loose, sweaty torsos hovered vaguely over the engine of a rusted primer-grey Ford truck. Tim nodded in their direction as they passed with a nod in reply by one of them. The other doused his cigarette in a beer can sitting on the truck's manifold. Two male pit-bulls tied to a tree greeted them with wagging tails, neurotic, anxious whines and short barks—the kind of response that could either precede a session of play or a mauling. The inner door to the apartment was opened by one of Candy's adult sons. He looked at them with dim eyes behind thick glasses as he played with the hair surrounding one of his large, exposed nipples. Tim asked him repeatedly if they could come in and finally he opened the screen door slowly and stepped out of the way after an angry shout from Candy in the living room.

They were greeted by a smell which was more common than she could ever have imagined before becoming a cop nine years ago—a combination of cat piss, mildew, processed and digested food and unwashed bodies. It was the smell of humanity.

"You here for Felicia?" the mound of flesh sitting in an over-stuffed chair facing a large flat panel television asked.

Candy Applewhite's age was hard to determine, and she imagined that the woman was not as old as she looked. The ages of her children provided a hint, but she guessed that Candy had gotten started early. Her oldest was 24. Her youngest, a toddler, sat in a corner of the small living room trying to grab the tail of a disinterested cat. The kid had a cold apparently, his face covered in a greenish mucus in various stages of drying.

"We are," answered Tim. This was his show, Fleur thought. "Can I speak with her in private? Is there a place here for that?"

"Private!" Candy erupted in nervous, forced laughter, her body quaking. "Ain't nothing private here. County won't pay for nothin' larger."

"Out back," Tim asked, pointing to a broken door at the rear of the kitchen. "Will that work?"

"I suppose. I'm watching my shows now. I don't need to go out there, huh?"

"No. I'd like to interview her in private, Candy," Tim replied, and he looked at Fleur with an apology, knowing that she dreaded the thought of being left inside while he spoke with his victim.

Felicia, a small, waifish girl with stringy blond hair came out of one of the bedrooms shyly. Tim introduced himself and led her out the rear door. Fleur could still see the two, which was important. He too faced the interior, continually glancing up at his partner still inside. Candy made no attempt to communicate as she stared unblinking at the screen of the television. Her shirtless 20-something son continued to stroke the hair around one of his nipples as he stood next to the front door staring at her. She ignored him and maneuvered herself toward the rear of the living room where the toddler had succeeded in grabbing hold of the cat's tail. The cat, old and fat, had merely turned around on its back and was swatting impotently at the boy's hand.

"What's your name?" she asked him. He looked up at her with blank eyes. She repeated the question and Candy replied for him.

"He's Jack. He don't talk much."

That seemed appropriate to her. She probably wouldn't talk much here either. The boy was maybe two and looked healthy, with the exception of all the snot. She quickly scanned the area for a clean rag, a roll of paper towels, and settled on a small stack of untouched napkins from a few-day-old bag of fast food, and wiped the snot from his face. The boy stared up at her unblinking with an open, receptive look. Even here in this place this child is a blank page, empty and ready. In his openness, his emptiness he embodies possibility and potential. Even here. Even him. But of course that potential will be unrealized. Within a few years he will be conditioned by the place and the people around him to repeat their mistakes and their sins. He will be conditioned to perpetuate himself and the cycle will continue until some outside force halts it. She was an extension of one possible outside force. But hers was an enfeebled one—unwilling and unable by mandate to create any alternative for this child. Hers could only restrain him when the seeds of his beginnings in this world bore their fruit.

And he was one of many. Oh, so many. He seemed to be one of *most*, to her. But maybe, she thought with a glimmer of hope that she did not trust, looking now at Candy sitting cross-legged in her chair and watching the television; maybe her own perceptions were skewed. Maybe her own experience was unique. Inside, however, she knew that this was not the case. Hers was merely a more intense version of everyone's experience and she sighed at the thought.

"Get back to the show!" Candy shouted suddenly at the flat panel television. A commercial had been extended for a news

William Burcher 13

update. It concerned a private rocket launch on a supply mission to the International Lunar Base. The billionaire CEO of the company, Abdul Sulayman, gave a glowing update to the press.

"How much does that shit cost, anyway? Couple trillion?" Candy spat at the TV. "Shit like this is why we don't get a bigger place."

Felicia came back into the house, Tim close behind. She looked back at him for a moment with the same sense she'd seen in the toddler, Jack. She then hurried back to her bedroom. He curtly thanked Candy, who remained sitting, and the two moved for the door, still blocked partially by the son. They burst forth into the fresh air, each breathing full and free.

"So, how we doin'?" Tim asked her with a grin. She looked forward as she walked, always observant in a place like this.

"Oh," and a pause. "Barely getting by," she replied.

And by his silence she knew that Tim understood. This was a thing that she loved about him and it made her smile. He understood. He always understood. Barely getting by.

———

They interviewed Jonathan Applewhite in a secure room in the county jail later that day. He was in for violating a bond on a felony methamphetamine possession case by shoplifting at the local Kmart. Personal lubricant and an *Elle* magazine, the report said. And although the items may have been specifically to Jonathan's taste, shoplifting was a specialty of his family's. Fleur remembered picking Candy up once in the parking lot of a grocery store with a cart filled high with cases of Coke that she didn't want to pay for. Jonathan had been cooperative with them and admitted to "liking his sister very much" and to being "affectionate" with her, but wouldn't go into further details, feigning shyness and saying that he did not like to "kiss and tell." The interview had been recorded and Tim believed that the statements, as well as the victim's, were incriminating enough for an arrest warrant.

"They continually amaze me," she told Tim in the car on the way back to the department. "These are not necessarily stupid people. They know why we're there to talk with them. They effectively spill their guts anyway."

"They have egos," Tim replied. "They have egos that want to be stroked. Even if the stroking is a show, or merely a neutral face worn by a cop."

"His face. 'Kiss and tell?' Like some frat boy bragging to his buddies. His eleven-year-old *sister* for chrissakes."

"Without that ego thing it'd be hard to do our jobs. Hell, without it—we wouldn't *have* jobs!" Tim said.

She stared out the window at the passing industrial areas, the apartment complexes built of concrete in the 1960's, at the strip malls and fast food. She saw the roads, some new, some in disrepair, and the cars on those roads. She saw the people driving those cars or waiting at traffic signals for a red light to change into something else, their faces tense and preoccupied. A man yelling angrily, silently behind his glass at a car in front of him driven by an older man slow to accelerate. Another, who stared down at the screen of his phone as he drove.

And she thought of the people in her dream walking silently, athletically through the forest.

"I have an extra ticket to a concert on Saturday," Tim said to her. "I don't know if this guy is your style but I like him. He's unique. Totally different."

"Unique?" she asked. "Totally different?"

"Yeah."

"I could do that," she said as they drove through their city at 65.

———————

Dream Log
May 24

I can't tell if I'm a part of this or merely a watcher.

It's late afternoon and the sun is getting lower in the sky—which is beautiful, blue, pulsing-vibrant. We (I guess I *am* a part of it) are walking in a field—no, on tundra. It is alpine tundra. The grass is tall and golden. The path is worn, packed, easy to walk on. We are in the mountains. I see them, off across an emerald valley. They are tall, rugged, capped with snow—no, with *glaciers*. There are clouds, mist in the valley below us and they mask the mountains in places. We are walking fast along the other ridge—a plateau of open country.

The people are the same. Although less mixed. Mostly men, although some women are here too. All are stronger, more athletic, more rugged. They are dressed the same, in leather and fur. They carry spears, long, symmetrical. I am impressed with the craftsmanship. Some of the men are shirtless. The women too. It feels like summer, an alpine summer. The sun is warm and I am struck by how good it feels on my face, my body. He is here, the same man from the last dream. He is walking in the middle of a group of ten or so. He appears somewhat younger, early 20's this time. He is tall, hair long, braided, dirty blond. He has only the hint of a beard. I am walking behind him and he does not yet look in my direction. He is shirtless and I stare for a few moments at his back as he walks. He is tanned, but not overly so. He is lean, stringy, well-muscled. He has the body of Carter, at the gym—only better. I'm instantly attracted to him, just watching from behind. He has a pack slung over one shoulder, made of leather and his shoulder is flexed as a result. I watch his body move gracefully, his muscles flexing and releasing, taut and hard. There is a line of sweat collecting in between his shoulders along his spine, running down to the small of his back where there is a small patch of blond hair. I imagine what his back feels like if I were to lay my hands on it, if I were holding it as his body flexed and released.

We are moving fast and I sense a tension in the group, an unease. They seem to be focused on getting down, or away from something. There is a sound in the distance, a howling of wolves. They are moving away from the wolves. And then I smell it: the scent of wet, of musk and of iron. Blood. They are each carrying packs and on some of them I see the red-brown stains of dried or drying blood. They've been hunting. They've been successful.

The leader of the group is an older man, mid 40's, well-bearded with grey in his braided hair, grey in his beard. He is shirtless too—hairy and muscled and scarred. The pace is ridiculous, as fast as it could be without running. Each walks silently, easily—even the oldest of the group.

We descend quickly and I have no trouble keeping up, apparently. The leader keeps looking back. Others do too, but not *him*. I want him to look back, to look at me. I want to see the front of his body.

We come to this rock wall and begin scaling it, down. It's the only way to get to the plateau below it. There is a crack, a fissure, and we use this to climb, squeezing in between it. It's the only way down an otherwise sheer cliff of maybe 40 feet. All of us make it down and the experience is exhilarating. As I touch the ground at the bottom he turns around and looks at me, smiling. My heart jumps. He is incredibly attractive. The muscles of his arms and chest are well-defined. His abs are perfect and I watch as his torso expands and contracts with each breath, the muscles flexing and releasing. I want to touch him, feel him, talk to him.

The others are smiling too. But no one talks. There is a sense of relief, and of release. The leader walks among us, grabbing shoulders and patting backs. He then leads us to a clearing, smooth and flat. We are closer to the mountains across the valley, and the plateau from which we just descended looms behind. The view is breathtaking. The leader puts down his pack

William Burcher 17

and the others follow. Almost spontaneously and without warning he breaks into a kind of martial arts form that I've never seen before. His arms are raised, palms upward, and he begins to walk in a circle, his head level. The others do the same, only each with minor variations. I am participating, and he is next to me, both of us aware of the other on a subconscious level. The forms are all circular, a kind of circular martial art—we walk in circles, we reverse step, we spin. It reminds me of Tai Chi—the martial dance that old people do in the park—only somehow more powerful, more primal. The speed of the dance (the word seems appropriate, but somehow not fully *enough*) increases, the tempo set by the leader. The motions become more energetic, more muscular. I am watching him beside me. His is the fastest, the most athletic. He is sweating, breathing hard. I can smell him, his scent. He is aware of me too. The tension between us is intense, palpable. I want our dances to merge, to be the same. I want to dance his dance and I want more than anything to touch him.

The pace reaches a crescendo and suddenly all of us stop, facing our individual directions. We then shift to a standing, straight position, raise our arms toward the sky and bring them downward, toward our centers—aware of the outer and the inner simultaneously. We stand still, each of us covered in sweat, each of us breathing hard and each of us totally relaxed and purged of the tension of the hunt. And I know that this was the purpose of the dance and I smile at this knowing.

Somehow I also know what this is called. Without any of them speaking it I know that this is, "The Dance of Earth and Sky."

He is beside me feeling the same as I do. The sweat is dripping down his face, into the coarse hair above his lip and his mouth. He spits it out hard, the spray becoming mist in the air.

I wake up glowing and wet.

3

ZHAR-OSS

The night was chill and clear, damp with a rain that hadn't come—the evening light of a dusk in late spring vaguely blue. They'd agreed to meet at a place grown into a Denver staple— a cafe uptown frequented by artistic hipster types and thirty-somethings with jobs and BMW's. As she approached on foot, the Victorian-looking table lamps hung in the large ash tree out front blinked once and then on, illuminating the green-golden leaves of the tree and the people trying to look comfortable smoking beneath.

The bell on the antique door to the cafe clanged as she entered and after quickly scanning the crowd her eyes settled on a hung bulletin board—in the usual place for cafes such as this one displaying an advertisement for a yoga class or a teaching by a visiting Buddhist monk. There a poster had been placed, small and cleanly printed in black ink on off-white paper, set aside from the others in its simplicity. On the poster was a symbol, something foreign and strange. It was simultaneously beautiful and enticing and when she saw it she believed it to hint at something sexual. It could have been a character in an Eastern written language, though she knew that it wasn't—she could recognize any of these—and it appeared hand-painted with a brush. Beneath the character was writing, in English. 9PM. Paramount Theatre. The day's date. She took a picture with her phone.

"Zhar-Oss," Google told her. The word was bizarre and sounded made-up, like some random grouping of syllables that chance and history had not yet formed into a word. She spoke the word in her mind a few times and as it rolled upon her mental tongue she began to sense that it was not something new, not something created by one artist's mind, but had meaning. It began to sound old. Very old.

Most of the web links displayed concerned a musician, a modern EDM artist named Zhar-Oss. One, buried among the fan sites at the bottom of the search site, stood out. She tapped the link and only a blank, grey backdrop was displayed with a single white log-in element; there was no text, no metadata of interest, no copyright mark or anything else distinguishing. The browser also displayed no page title. The simplicity of the site seemed to be making a statement as she guessed from the exposed source info that the page had been designed professionally.

She navigated back to the search results and accessed one of the fan sites for Zhar-Oss, the musician. He had a cult following—a lot of hard-core EDM adepts—but a few of the reviews, a bit of the chatter she could understand. He'd come onto the scene recently, with very little said about his history. He didn't start off playing in small clubs like most DJ's, and seemed to appear almost out of nowhere during a show in Trieste.

Most of the performance reviews she encountered were littered with glowing hyperbole. "Revolutionary," they said. "One of a kind." Most also described his work as having a strange style, one seemingly dismissive of the elements of his contemporary peers. "Alien" was a word she saw more than she thought she should. And there was virtually nothing negative posted about him. There were also no images of his face. He always performed back-lit wearing a fierce, tribal-looking war mask. People speculated that he was from Japan because of the mask, and there were deliberations concerning some of the similarities of his music to things heard in various adult anime scores, but nothing was conclusive. He was becoming a well-known mystery.

She pulled a pair of headphones from the inside pocket of her coat and began to listen as a track played from a live performance recorded in Madrid. There was video attached and she watched as a crowd of a thousand was silent for a few moments. There was a light that appeared suddenly, blinding the camera, accompanied by further silence and then he was there, on the stage, backlit. Sounds started emitting from the speakers on the stage, sounds she had never heard before, a kind of rising, palpitating force.

"Hey. What are you listening to?" a voice asked from behind her. She turned and saw Tim standing there, looking well dressed and clean. He smelled of cigarettes.

"Zhar-Oss tonight. Right?" she replied.

"Yeah! Well done. But I thought I was going to surprise you. You know him?"

"No. I wasn't familiar until a few minutes ago. Tell me about him."

"Well. I don't know. You probably saw all of the hype," he said, pointing to her phone. "I don't think I could add anything to all of that."

"What does he do for you?"

Tim smiled and looked down. He paused for a moment as if thinking for the correct response, or deciding if the real response was appropriate.

"Ok, so you know I'm not into most of this hippie crap. He's different. There's something different there. There's something unique. It's a cliché these days to say that 'so and so' is really special, or really original. And you and I, well, we see the same things day in and day out I think. People being people. Driven by the same base shit. But this guy … it's legit. It's hard to put into words. His music is … it's beautiful."

William Burcher 21

"Are you turning Christian on me Tim?" she replied with a smile.

"Yes," was all he said after a strange pause.

———————

It was an old art-deco space ornate and detailed. The colors were rich and warm, the light golden. It was an old theatre, smallish, but one open and alive with the expectations of the strangely diverse crowd. History was woven within the red velvet curtains, the upholstery of the seating, the tapestries adorning the walls, and the florid chandelier hung from the ceiling. It was an appropriate place for something original, and Fleur wondered at the thought, trying to sense whether the music would matter to her and her estimation of things.

In the theatre's foyer, Tim received a call on his work-mobile. He was technically on-call and would have to respond if the situation were serious enough. She made a face at him as he answered; he made a gun with his hand and pointed it at his head. There'd been a stabbing, one guy dead and another seriously wounded. Some jealous lover scenario. He was needed to attempt an interview with the suspect at Denver General. Despite her offer to help, he refused and demanded that she stay and see the show. It'll be good for you, he told her. And he followed that up with a promise to make sure she was assigned the next cold-case drunken date-rape that came into the detective bureau if she didn't comply.

So she walked in solitude down the carpeted aisle and found her seat toward the front of the stage. The light was dim and the cavernous space quiet. She found herself relaxing into her seat, into the place and the moment. Her mind began to slow and unbidden came the image of the man in her dream. She saw him once again walking with his people through the virgin forest, the light just beginning to break and filter through the fog. She then saw the man and his people seated together in a large, dark, open space lit by the light of small fires. They were quiet and waiting for something to begin. The image felt connected. And then the house lights went out, she was awake and in an instant, as one, a thousand pair of lungs breathed sharply inward.

Silence. The seconds passed and the crowd inevitably became aware of the darkness and the quiet. With each passing moment the crowd became more self-conscious. Each component mind grew momentarily shy and diffident, faced with the lack of external stimulation save the myriad voices heard within—a mirror glimpse that Fleur knew was psychological mastery. It was part of the show and was preparation for something, and she knew that the statement made was quietly profound as real things are. She understood that what came next would be born of silence and would be pure—emerging from a void as the universe once was born.

A flash of penetrating, high-spectrum light and heat from all around, coming brilliantly from the dark. A low, nearly inaudible roar sounded and Fleur realized that it was more sense and feeling and was below her range of hearing. The sound was resonating and dark and a spark, electric shot high along her spine. The sound became louder, more complex and she realized that its strength had not increased, merely its frequency. Her ears could hear as much now as her viscera felt. The blinding flash of light and heat diminished just as the sound intensified and out of the neural haze she began to make out a thin solitary figure, male, standing above her on the stage. The figure was perfectly proportioned, perfect posture, arms straight down and legs together, standing as if carved. He was a dancer, a statue—both at once. The light was comfortable now and she saw a man in skin-tight suede, dark grey, and she could see the muscles taut and ready beneath the leather. He wore a mask.

It was painted in fierce color. It was a warrior's visage. The colors were those of classic Eastern art—red ochre which seemed to bleed, black and brown on a base of powder white. The eyes were black and the colors, the patterns of the mask drew her gaze like fluid back to the eyes. She felt the fixation of

William Burcher 23

those eyes and then unease, anxiety. Suddenly the figure convulsed, his face skyward, his arms and legs exploding into a raw and ancient form like some character painted millennia ago on a wall in a cave in Europe. He began to perform a kind of martial dance choreographed strangely with the lighting, the audio. As the sound, the sub-sonic rumbling rose into a deep and alien roar that was to her like time, she thought once more of the man walking gracefully through the forest.

Tim!

You old queen. I've missed you.

It's been too long and with this email I'm demanding you tell me how Scott and the kids are doing—with details, significant or not. I'm not afraid to say that I've been lonely as of late. Ghosts of the past sometimes haunt me at times unexpected. But in these late years, after so much has changed, I wouldn't want to live without my ghosts. A part of me still clings to the very antique notion that without our past we get lost in the stream. I know that's almost sacrilegious to say these days, but sometimes I'd rather be a boulder standing resolute in the flow rather than some fallen leaf, floating on the surface free and carried by the force of time.

I was surprised to hear from you. I was not surprised to learn of your curiosities. I guess I knew that he'd become a gay icon over the years. But I suppose one can't underestimate the allure of an athletic body in tight suede leather.

(How I've missed you Tim!)

You left that night before the show began and of course we never had the opportunity to speak about it. I regret this. I could have used your wisdom and your strength then.

But so much has been said about that night already, and I don't know if I can add anything material. We all know the story. But I recognize the value of perspective. So much has changed since that night, too. We all know what came after. But you're right. My story of that night hasn't really been told. God knows no one wants to hear me tell the … other part … one more time. I've read your work, and always had the notion that it was right of you to not mention our friendship. Obviously it would have benefitted you. I've been meaning to say thank you, for that. And other things.

He was at his peak. He was perfect. And that was part of his point, I think. He wasn't smiling as he leaked all of his blood out on me—he was past that already. A body can bleed out quickly—if one has knowledge and knows what he's doing, or has the motivation. And he did. He had both.

He did have a look in his eyes, though. It was one that I've always had a hard time putting words to. I understood it, at the time, of course—but it was beyond a single descriptive word. There was no fear, no darkness, nothing that any of us would understand as negative. Purpose comes close. Purpose and an understanding of something. We had a moment, before he faded away, when our eyes met and I could see that look, and he knew that I was seeing it. It was after I'd shouted at everyone to give me their belts, and tried my best to tighten these around his arms. He'd done too much damage though. There would be no question of the outcome, and I knew that at the time.

I remember some woman in the crowd below me (no one else had joined me on the stage). I remembered thinking how confounding people are and how animal-like, or sheep-like. I sup-

William Burcher 25

pose there was a fear of being seen, on a stage like that—or perhaps people knew what I hadn't had time to think about. Perhaps no one wanted to ruin the final performance. Because that's what it was. It was part of the performance. It belonged, as morbid as that sounds. The act wasn't wrong, for the moment. I may have felt that for an instant, now that I think about it, before I'd gotten on stage and started to do what I did at the time. But anyway, this woman kept saying to herself in a pathetic voice, and to me, (I could hear her, it was very quiet), "Don't hurt him, you're going to hurt him!" I remembered how stupid I thought that was. You can't apply a tourniquet like a nursemaid. You have to put some force into it. She actually thought I was hurting him!

It all took maybe a minute before I saw him fade. I'd seen death before, many times before that night. But it had never happened in such an intimate way. I watched him go. I watched his eyes as he went. What people don't know and what I've never told anyone is what he said to me before he faded.

"Use this," he said, in a whisper. "Use this," he kept mouthing as he passed.

And as we all know I suppose—I did.

———————

He'd taken the mask off at what Fleur knew was the climax of the performance. The audience had sat for three quarters of an hour, too engrossed, too immersed to stand up or to dance. Fleur didn't know if anyone other than the performer ever danced to this music. It was possible with the beats she felt, but it didn't seem right. It didn't feel necessary to do anything but sit, stare, listen and follow every note, every change in pitch, every light and image with all the measure of awareness one possessed—if awareness, if consciousness could be measured.

Before them unmasked was an attractive man. He was perhaps thirty, with a darker complexion which might have been Italian or Middle-Eastern. His hair was black and of medium length, wet with sweat from the heat of his performance. His eyes were auburn and gleaming. Fleur knew his eyes because they stared at her, only they did not need the mystery of the mask to evoke the same unease, the same strange anxiety. For a moment everything stood still and there was no sound. The crowd was quiet as the sounds of the performance faded from memory. His look was one of purest intensity and of something more quaint—something akin to a man's satisfaction. A woman in the back of the theatre managed to scream as the man known only as Zhar-Oss, and later discovered to have the given name Benjamin Janus, fell to his knees and opened up both of his arms elbow to wrist with an unseen blade. The blood both gushed and spurt with the beating of his heart.

4

MYSTERY

"You're not on the case, Fleur," JD told her flatly, unblinking.

"Are you kidding me? I was here! He died in my arms! I still have his blood all over me!"

JD looked at her clothing, brown with blood now dry, as if in agreement. "I know. It obviously wasn't my decision. The case is mine, and I even talked to Bob about you. I wanted you on it with me."

This surprised her. JD was known to abhor working with other detectives. To request her as his partner, effectively, was out of character.

"Staff is worried about PR with this one. You haven't stepped out of this place yet but the news vans have been here for at least an hour now. The national guys are starting to cover the story too. They want it clean. And you're … not," he said with a smirk.

She couldn't resist returning it. JD rarely made any kind of joke. She was a mess.

"So, you didn't see the razor at any other time during the show?"

"I didn't. He must have had it on his body someplace. It came out of nowhere."

"Who is this guy, anyway? Benson knew who he was, had heard his stuff before, but that doesn't surprise me. No one else in the bureau knew who the hell he was."

"I really don't know. Tim had the tickets," she replied.

"Tim Jameson?"

"Yeah. We were here together. He got called out on that stabbing earlier."

JD didn't even blink. He had a way of making her feel like she was being interrogated, even if she and JD played on the same team. Jim Danner had a way of making you talk, so that afterward you felt as if there'd been some violation, some act of assault on his part. But that was just his way. He was polite and courteous to the core. It made him an excellent detective—the best she knew. They were close and had been from the day they'd met. He'd done her polygraph before she was hired, and as a result knew every secret she had, every insecurity, every item of maintained guilt. She'd felt the unease of his questioning then, and a part of her felt that he knew the effect he had on people in that situation, seemingly under the judgment of his large, dark, vibrant eyes and might have even felt a hint a guilt at it. She knew that there was no judgment there, however. JD was just really good at what he did.

"Christ," JD sighed. "Busy night."

They stood off to the side of the stage, and JD casually glanced over at the body. Fleur knew that the decision to not transport him to Denver General was a contentious one. In most cases, for appearances, the department wanted a transport when the body was still warm. It never looked good to be accused down the road of denying medical treatment.

The paramedics, however, had refused. They'd been quick to arrive, within five minutes she thought, but he'd already been dead for two or three by then. The blood had stopped flowing from his arms minutes before, and everyone knew there was nothing they could do. They went through the motions, like they always did—the requisite compressions, the respirations—they'd even shocked him a few times, to the point that some blood had leaked out of the wounds on his arms, but he was cored out completely and no one believed there'd be any chance of changing that. The amount of blood on the stage had been obscene. They'd all gotten it on themselves, walked through it, left bloody boot-prints all over the place. There was a substantial trail of them in front of the stage, leading up the center aisle toward the exit doors, slowly fading into nothing.

There was no one left in the theatre now except the two of them, and Morgan and Keck, who were both taking pictures of the body, the electrical leads of the defibrillator still attached to the exposed chest, the plastic tube still draped loosely from his mouth to the side of his face, his eyes open and cloudy and staring at the ceiling. Both of his arms were down at his sides, palms facing up, pressure bandages covering the wounds, pink and white and horrible.

"You said most people stayed to watch?" JD asked her, his face a mask.

"Yeah. Strange, huh? I thought they'd bolt, that there'd be a rush out the rear, but there wasn't. People stayed. Sat. And watched it. Like it was part of the show."

JD said nothing, but made notes in his pad. He had a way of pausing, forcing a silence which more often than not the person he was speaking to felt compelled to break.

"JD, why are you here? I mean, I know that's blunt, but it's a suicide …"

"I was waiting for you to ask me that," and his eyes hinted at a smile. His mouth didn't though. "I wondered that myself until Sue called me."

Sue was the Lieutenant of the district's detective bureau. She was a polarizing figure. Fleur had seen her make some tough calls, and take the heat for them, and she respected her for that. Other people thought that she was good at kissing up, and kicking down. JD was their lead homicide detective. Usually, suicides were given a cursory investigation, and usually by patrol. JD probably hadn't worked a suicide in a decade.

"She got the call from Linda Macallan, who got the call from Channel 9 probably just as the paramedics were arriving. I'd be prepared, Fleur. I'm betting that multiple people in the audience were filming the entire thing. You're going to be a household face, a household name. I'm going to talk to Bob about it. You're not going to be able to work the street for a while."

She sighed, her eyes dropping to the wooden floor, well shined and polished. "I didn't think about that. Christ."

JD managed a smile. "We might be able to work something out. My workload's heavy. And this one is really yours. They're going to want as complete a report as we can make it. Sue said something about a phone call, from someone she wouldn't name. Someone's going to milk this one for what it's worth."

"Tim prepared me for this guy's concert tonight by telling me that it would be original. And unique. Funny, right?"

"You ok? With all of this," he asked her, jutting his chin slightly in the direction of the body. There was a pause before she answered.

"I think so. It was intense. The man bled out in my arms. I'm guessing that the aftermath might be worse than what happened tonight," she trailed off, looking at the body. Keck and Morgan had finished with the pictures. Morgan was looking closely at the right hand, and she assumed that he was about to collect the blade. JD looked in that direction as well.

"I've had triples that have been less complex, and less … compelling, than this one's going to be."

She watched Morgan as he collected the blade—a simple square razor, from what she could tell. She felt a little stupid for letting his dying hand still grasp it. It was unlikely, but a weapon was still a weapon. Suicidal people were, in effect, *homicidal* ones. She dismissed the thought, however, as it served no purpose in the moment.

"Take the weekend, Fleur. I'm going to get a start on things but you need to rest. And to process. And to clean up. I'll call

Frank tomorrow. Monday morning, 7:00 a.m. My office. And here," he said, wrapping a long coat around her shoulders.

"Thanks, JD. I mean it," she said as she began to walk toward the exit. She turned quickly, an afterthought. "Oh, and will the coffee be black?" she asked, smiling faintly from the corner of her mouth. That was an old joke between them. JD was the only black detective in homicide. He'd worked hard to reach the place he had, and sometimes he allowed himself a bit of play, of parlance to recognize this. He smiled at her and she began to walk toward the exit.

"You know it, sugar!" he said slowly, strongly, wryly.

———————

Fleur stepped out of the theatre and into a maelstrom. The patrol cops assigned to scene-security tried their best to restrain the reporters and camera crews who clambered for comments and photographs. She saw the logos of all the local stations and newspapers and behind them with building-tall radio and satellite antennas were parked the trucks of the 24-hour cable news channels. The spring storm that had been threatening to break all evening finally had and sheets of torrential rain blanketed the fray. Blinded by the lights of the cameras and the flashes of the still photographers, she struggled through—walking in a halting, confused staccato along the path the cops defined for her.

She glimpsed a few of their faces and knew they wanted answers. A big motorcycle cop named Tate escorted her to a marked car they had waiting for her at the end of the gauntlet. His eyes were pleading, but understanding too. Now would not be the time. She could have hugged him for that. Within the crowd were others, people who'd been in the audience. There were shouts of "Detective!" from reporters seeking comment or a better camera angle. She heard murmurs of other things from people who'd been in the crowd. "There she is," they said.

"That's her! She's got his blood on her!"

Tate held an umbrella over her head as she splashed through the collected rainwater, inches deep in places. She opened the door to the patrol car, stepped in and mouthed "thank you" to Tate from behind the glass. The car slowly pushed through the throng before emerging onto a street, turning its overheads off and taking a very long route with multiple left hand turns to her apartment.

———

The clock on the nightstand told her it was after three. Outside, rain fell steadily in the light of the sodium-vapor lamp on the street corner nearest the living room window. She stumbled over and closed the blind and stood motionless in the dark.

She inhaled and her heart jumped. It was an old feeling, one well-practiced. She held it down temporarily, burying it, knowing well what it was and where it came from. There came an image of one of the man's opened arteries—pulsing and throbbing as it let forth its contents into the open air. The blood fell onto the wooden floor of the stage, his clothing, her clothing. She saw once more his eyes as they began to fade vacant and grey. His mouth began to gape, convulsing in some unnatural, amphibian movement—some vestigial remnant in his brain of a former self.

"Stop," she said aloud to her empty living room, shaking her head. But she knew the images of this man's death and her part in it would be with her and would come unbidden for months, perhaps years to come.

"Like the baby," she said aloud, remembering an experience while working as a street cop. The infant had died in her arms too. The images never went away. Relief came only when they no longer appeared with a surge of heat and bile in the middle of the night.

William Burcher 33

Awake, she sat down at the table near the kitchen and lifted the lid to her laptop. She briefly scanned the sites of the major international news outlets and saw that the story was headlined on all of them. Such a simple, common thing, she thought—one man's death. But add an underground celebrity and a performance, and the world became captivated. It was as if the world were suddenly awaking to the fact of death and mortality, and perhaps to insanity too. These things no longer surprised her. They kept her up at night, but they did not surprise. She quickly found one site displaying a still from a video shot in the audience of her tightening a belt around one of his arms. She closed the tab in reflex. She was terrified. She stood up from the table and remained motionless for a moment. She was a cop. A detective. She could not be a public figure and do her job. Furthermore, she was private, shy even. She shuddered at the thought of discussing her family, her dates, herself with others outside of her intimate work circle. And now, with an instant's passing, she was famous. No. She was *infamous*. I am not ready for this, she thought. And there was so much to know, so many questions. Fear. Curiosity. Such related things.

She sat back down and began to search for anything related to Zhar-Oss. Within a few hours his name had taken over the web. Many sites made available video of the entire thing—from start to finish. She struggled to find something written about him before that evening and not overshadowed by the sensational news of his demise. She found one site written in Cyrillic, Russian or Ukrainian which seemed to have a good amount of biographical material. She copied and pasted the text into a translator. The result wasn't perfect, and she struggled to place the facts that she could read into context. The author seemed to be saying that he was Russian, a former soldier, and he knew him when both were serving in a naval special forces unit in the Crimean. There was no unit name or designation given. The guy swore that his name was Benjamin (Veniamin), though he didn't remember his last name.

He remembered this "Benjamin" as quiet, intelligent, and obsessed with music and Eastern philosophy. Benjamin went missing or was mysteriously re-assigned before completing his tour of duty. The page seemed to conclude with an admonition that this should be researched, and that anyone with access to Russian military records could easily find the guy's name. As Fleur pondered this impossibility the screen refreshed and a generic hosting service's logo was displayed. She refreshed the page again and there was nothing; the same generic logo. She checked her browser's cache without any luck. The site was gone. She still had the text though. She quickly took a screen shot of the translation site, both the original text in Russian, as well as the translation. She then copied both and saved them in separate text files. Strange, she thought.

And she remembered the site she'd found before the concert—the simple page without any text or elements—other than a blank login without any prompts. She couldn't find it in any of the search results. She tried remembering the URL. It had been something complex; almost purposefully complex now that she thought about it. A proper name. Russian. Russian written in the Latin alphabet. She searched her browsing history and found it quickly. Igravyacheslavioksimovich.com. The domain was registered to a company out of Switzerland. She quickly accessed the site and discovered that it was the same as she'd seen it last—nothing but a login element, no copyrights, no advertisements, no navigation. She saw too that it was obviously secure and professionally developed despite the simplicity. She entered "Zhar-Oss" in the field for a presumed username and repeated the entry in the password field. Nothing happened. No displayed error. No messages. No prompts. She stared at the screen for a few moments and was almost overcome with exhaustion. The questions would have to wait. She closed the lid to the laptop and stumbled down the hall to her bed.

———

William Burcher 35

The wind is moaning, crying as it passes through the canyons nearby and along the cliffs that rise two, three hundred feet around them. Across the valley below are more cliffs, higher, the tops of which are still covered in snow. The light is red-orange, the sun about to set. The shadows are deep and complete and cover most of the valley below. The two people are not yet encased in shadow, however, and the sun is warm on their faces, warm on their hair, on their exposed backs and shoulders.

A man is with a boy perhaps seven, eight years old. The man could be his father. He is shirtless, his body well muscled and lithe, almost as a dancer's—but stronger. This man works and lifts and throws and runs for a living. The two are quiet for moments, for minutes as they look out across the valley, as they inspect their immediate surroundings. The man has long hair tied behind him. He wears a beard. His pants are made of leather, and he appears to be wearing slippers or moccasins. A dagger is at his hip, a handle made of horn or antler. Although his skin is fair, it is tanned on his back, shoulders and arms. The boy is a miniature version of the man lacking only the beard and is slight of build, skinny. While the man's focus is outward and around them, the boy's focus is on the man.

They have hiked up from below. The slope just below them is steep and they've had to switch back around boulders and gullies. There are large rocks strewn about which seem to flow, sculpted by wind and rain. The earth is red. Small trees, plants, bushes—all in stunted, twisted form grow in between the rocks and in the gullies. The land is a garden and the two are extensions of the forms around them.

The man speaks to the child with a tender seriousness. He is confident in bearing. The boy moves closer and looks up at the man, engrossed and respectful. He takes every word, every look as if it were something holy. The man is speaking slow and deeply, with gravity in a language never before heard but in a sense familiar. He is gesturing to the boy and the two look out over the valley and beyond, to the high places still covered in snow. Their attention then turns nearer to them, to a stack of rocks near the wind-smoothed face of a cliff a few feet away. The object is a cairn, a pile of rocks placed, stacked there artificially by the hands of another. The man gestures and speaks, first in his language and then in Fleur's, his words discernible.

"What is this, here?" the man asks the boy, his tone a socratic inquiry.

The boy pauses for a moment, thinking. He has played this game many times before. "It is a placement of rock," he says, choosing to be as literal as he can.

"Yes," the man replies. "It is that. It is also more." And he waits patiently for the boy to consider further.

"It was placed here by the hand of a man. Or men. It may have been placed long ago. Its placement here, near this cliff, in this place where the water flows below and the view of the valley below and the high places beyond, is conspicuous."

The man nods once, gently.

"It is a simple thing," the boy continues. "It speaks, as my words do. It is like a word, in rock. Its words are without time. The word stays and does not blow away like mine do in the wind. It could have been laid by the hand of a man yesterday, or many years ago."

He looks up at the man self-satisfied and with an expectation of approval. The man nods once more and pauses, the silence telling the boy to continue, that there is more. He looks down at the cairn once more, studying it. He pauses, breathes, and then looks back up at the man.

"It is a simple thing. It only has one word. It can say only one thing. I was here. I was a man. I placed this here for another to see. I existed. I still exist. I am."

The man looks at the boy with calm approval. He makes a simple gesture, his right hand flat and upright held momentarily below his jaw. The hand pauses for a moment before the man lowers it slowly toward his chest. The boy looks at the man and repeats the gesture.

"It is like God, Garr-Eth," the man says, looking out over the valley. "God speaks to us every moment. And it is the same message. God speaks to us, but only ever says one thing."

William Burcher 37

Fleur awoke with the man's face in the fore of her mind. His words too were an echo. Propelled by some suggestion below the level of literal logical consciousness, she hurried down the hall to the table where her laptop sat. She lifted the lid and found the site where she left it. Her cursor still blinked at second-long intervals in the username field. Here she entered "Zhar-Oss" once again. In the password field she paused only briefly before typing "One Thing."

Enter. And the screen went white.

She stared at the computer, her eyes wide until the Flash element expired. On the screen was displayed a standard site, mostly in Cyrillic Russian. There was text, however, in English. She repeatedly saw the word "Zhar-Oss" displayed—in a way that didn't seem to reference the username. It was displayed as if it were the name of whatever business or organization created the site. Heart pounding, she quickly checked to see if the word meant anything in Russian. It didn't. She tried translating the entire page. Nothing happened. She tried multiple times, and opened another browser, without success. The translation was being prevented. She quickly saved screen shots of the site, sensing that something was wrong. She had the feeling that the site was hosted by a government. She noted another login element, a request for a PIN, she thought. The site seemed very secure, and she regretted not using a proxy IP before attempting the login. Goddammit, she thought. She was probably being tracked. And on her home-computer no less. The site suddenly changed, all of it greying out except for the PIN request.

"Goddammit!" she said aloud.

A spark, electric ran up her spine as she thought of the implications. A secure, possibly government website displayed text in Russian. This recurring word, "Zhar-Oss," which she'd never heard before the previous night, and then only in reference to a man who'd committed suicide on stage and had subsequently died in her arms. She felt like she wanted to get rid of her computer, throw it away, or leave. She wanted to run. "Stupid, you're being stupid. Slow down. Think."

She closed the lid to the laptop and sat motionless. There was nothing she could do right now. Nothing to be done. No one to collaborate with, no one to discuss it with. She thought about calling Tim but he was probably asleep, having dealt with his own murder that night. And her mind stopped. Why did I equate the two? Why did I equate this suicide with murder? Was it? Could it be? Clearly the man had died willingly. She released the thought after a moment's contemplation. Frustrated and still tired to her core, she went back to bed and tried to sleep. Perhaps she would find answers in a dream, she thought sardonically, trying to ignore the image of the man's face as he spoke with the boy near the cliff-face.

"Dreams aren't supposed to do this," she whispered to herself just before her darkened room went dim.

5

FOOTPRINTS

When she awoke she saw that it was late. She got up and stretched and realized quickly that her body craved release. Sex would have sufficed, she thought, but dismissed this as too tiresome, too problematic at the moment. Her mind lingered though. She could call Theo. He was always willing. She'd dated Theo for a few weeks last year and the physical connection between them had always been overpowering. Something had been missing for her, though. She'd never placed it, never defined it but the rest was just … lacking. Many of her past relationships followed this pattern. She'd talked about it with her mother even, who just thought that she was too modern and maybe too self-absorbed to make a relationship work. Fleur had argued with her, although only mildly. Deeper down she felt that perhaps she could only fall in love with an ideal, or maybe just an idea.

Her work phone blinked with the notification of a voicemail. Just one. Her own phone told her that her mailbox was full and her email inbox displayed a "34." It would wait. It had to wait. Even work could wait. She laced up her running shoes, quickly tied her hair back and stepped out of her apartment half-expecting to encounter a news crew and preparing to make a run for it if she did. There wasn't one. She said a silent prayer of gratitude for a department that protected its cops' anonymity and for her own foresight in buying the place in the name of a limited liability company she'd quickly formed for that purpose.

Starting slowly, she wove her way between the shadows of the buildings and the sunlight. Crisp, clear, pure. She breathed the late morning air deep, loosened, fell into her groove and sped up. She passed the park near the river and then the main river trail where most people would run that day and instead chose a route north. Gradually the scenery changed. The renovated late nineteenth century loft buildings with cafes, shops and bars beneath morphed into the light industrial. These, too, contained shops and restaurants now empty of crowds. She continued north past the ballpark and the neighborhood grew rough, untouched by the explosion of gentrification the rest of the city had seen. This soothed her.

Gone for the moment were thoughts of the previous night. Gone too was the image in her mind of the dream she'd had and the implications of the words her dream had spoken to her. As soon as an image arose, unbidden, of the night or of the dream, she forced it down below once again with a creeping sense of anxiety. She knew she couldn't run from it for long. The grit around her helped. It was real. The people who lived in the neglected houses and Section 8 apartments on these streets had real problems. They were also less likely to wake up on a Saturday morning, open their laptops and start browsing major news sites.

A car caught her attention. It was black, nice. An Audi. Windows tinted. It drove slowly behind her before turning. She noted it and sped up. Her route took her in the same direction toward City Park and the Zoo. There it was again, parked in front of a house. It was too nice for the neighborhood. An executive's car. Or a realtor's, she told herself. Stop it, Christ. But instinctively she sourced the small revolver she carried with her in a band around her waist. She passed the car noting the license plate.

She increased her speed even more. It was as if the tension of the night, the anxiety she felt deep down were fuel for her, to be burned by her legs and her arms, her lungs and her heart. Legs in perfect union with her breath, back straight, running from her core she sped toward home, half-challenging anyone to follow her, to try and catch her.

Lungs burning, heart pounding, legs pumping she rejoiced in the exertion. Her body was a singular unit with a singular goal and she covered the two miles to her apartment in just under twelve minutes. For an hour she'd forgotten that the world wanted to know who she was and most assuredly wanted to speak with her. She took the steps up two, three at a time breathing hard, covered in sweat. Hallway clear. Door unlocked. She was home.

"Detective Romano," came a man's voice behind her just as she was shutting the door. She quickly locked the deadbolt.

"Detective Romano," he repeated through the door. "Do you have a moment?"

Something about his voice, a level of confidence or command, and his accent, vaguely and only slightly German, made her crack the door. Before her was a middle aged man of average height and thin build dressed in a suit almost too nice, too well-tailored, but without a tie. He had very intense blue eyes. He was both gaunt and severe.

"Forgive me," he said in a way which made her think he did not actually want to be forgiven. "I am sorry to intrude in this manner."

"Who are you?" she interjected mechanically.

"I am an acquaintance of your Lieutenant. My name is Axel. Kohl."

"Are you with the media?"

"Did you receive the message that Lieutenant Brady left you

on your work mobile? I was in the office with her when she called you. It was very early in the morning. We suspected you'd simply fallen asleep and thus overlooked the call, nothing conscious on your part of course."

Fleur knew then that Axel Kohl was a smart man. He was choosing to point out a possible oversight on her part in order to establish an authority. She was technically supposed to answer her work mobile regardless of the day, the hour. She looked at him with a genuine annoyance. She'd always been less than prone to instantly afford respect to structured authority. The man picked up on this.

"Perhaps if you would like to listen to the message while I wait here in the hallway?"

She closed the door as he half-smiled at her. She watched him for a second through the door's peephole, maintaining the same expression, the same stance. She found her work phone. Sue had indeed left her a message. And an email. Her heart jumped as she began to play the voicemail, expecting anger or worse. She was surprised with Sue's tone. It was almost motherly. There was a tension in it that Fleur did not immediately understand. It was almost as if Sue felt empathy for her, or even pity. Sue sounded sad.

> Hi Fleur, it's Sue. It's currently 6:00 a.m. You're probably asleep after the night you had and no one can fault you for that. I didn't get much sleep last night either. And about an hour ago I received a call from John Ingersoll, the Special Agent in Charge of the Denver Field Office. I know John, but John was just the introduction and probably handled the call as a way of establishing bona fides. I was then transferred to a … higher up. I can't go into specifics and can't name names. But needless to say all of this is real. If we don't receive a call from you shortly, you're going to receive a visit from an individual named Axel Kohl. At your home. I'm sorry about that, Fleur. But you're

to cooperate with him fully. The Chief has been informed and you have nothing to worry about here. I was not provided many details, mostly orders. But I felt that the implication was that you might be away for some time. I don't know much more than that. I know you're close to Tim Jameson. If you'd like, I can bring Tim into the loop and he can help with any open cases that you might have. If there's anything else, Fleur, anything, please let me know. I sent you an email too and it contains my home number. I also wanted to tell you something, something … from the heart. Obviously, women in law enforcement have a hard time of it still, and we have to stick together. I've always thought that you're an excellent cop. I was going to groom you, Fleur and try my best to get you promoted. I mean that. Good luck with things. From all of us.

Fleur replayed the message. In disbelief. How could this be right? She checked her email and found Sue's. It contained the same message effectively—cryptic, confusing, and sad. It was like she was saying goodbye. Why was she saying goodbye? What the hell was happening? Not knowing what more to do, she sent Sue a quick reply.

"Yes, please bring Tim in the loop," she wrote. "Thank you for the kind words. I'm totally confused, Sue."

What the hell was going on? She stood motionless in her living room trying hard not to get caught up in the ripening excitement. She realized quickly though that she couldn't stay standing there for long. She had to decide. She had to act. But what choice did she have? She had no choice. She inhaled deeply, trying to slow things down and returned to her front door. The man still stood, still smiled, as if he hadn't moved or even checked his watch. With a sense of dread, she opened the door.

"Mr. Kohl," she said with a halting smile. "Please come in."

The car had been waiting for them behind her building. It was the same, the Audi that she'd seen on her run. Kohl had not been the driver. There was another man for that and by his look, his demeanor and her suspicion that he knew how to handle himself, she guessed that he was there for more than just driving. Kohl called him Genji. He insisted that she call him "Axel" but to her he always remained "Kohl." She noted quickly that he himself never dispensed with formality when they'd spoken in her apartment.

"Detective Romano. You have questions. Many questions, I am sure. About today, of course. And about last night," he'd paused, waiting for the effect. Her heart had jumped at that but she did not want to give this man any sort of satisfaction. "I have answers," he said, beginning his entreaty as they both stood in her living room an hour earlier.

She'd found it awkward, but simultaneously thrilling and terrifying speaking with this man inside her house. She'd strangely offered him coffee, which he accepted. Afterward she realized this was just a ploy to keep her busy with the minor task, to lessen the anxiety and the strangeness of it all.

She'd begun to form an opinion of the man from the beginning when he called her name from behind her in the hallway, and with each moment this crystalized and was reinforced. He was charming and polite and seemingly at ease, and always striving to put those around him in equal condition. But this habit of his always served him, she thought. He was at once pleasant and dangerous. He was also restraining something within him, holding something down that she couldn't identify.

As she made coffee he asked her what Sue had explained and she admitted that Sue had given her very little. He seemed satisfied with this. She struggled to not demand answers of the man immediately, having decided that it was best in times of complete confusion to not betray as much to another who inevitably

William Burcher 45

knew more. She would be patient and allow this man to explain himself in time. He chose not to waste it.

As she placed a cup of black coffee on the table in front of him, she noticed that he'd taken off his jacket. He immediately rolled up the sleeve to his shirt, exposing a thin, hairy, vascular forearm. Upon his right arm tattooed in ochre was an image she recognized.

"Do you know it, Detective Romano?"

"I do, Mr. Kohl. The man I'm sure you're here to speak to me about had a tattoo similar to this one on his arm. He sliced through it with a razor last night and bled to death in my arms."

He blinked at her then but said nothing in response. And she continued, "As far as I knew yesterday it was an identifying symbol used by a musician."

"Yes, Detective Romano. It was that. And it is also much, much more."

She, unlike Kohl, drank her coffee. She took a sip with the ridiculous thought that the coffee was not special and that this man probably drank a much more expensive brand. She asked him to go on.

"Zhar-Oss. The image is a symbol for the word. And the word is not merely the strange sounding name of a now-deceased EDM musician. The word has multiple meanings. To us. But to begin with, I will say that it describes a group. A league. A confederation."

She nodded at him and lifted her cup slightly. "The Masons or the Knights Templar. And you're their leader, Mr. Kohl. Their Grand Poobah?"

He smiled as he felt he was supposed to. "No. I am not a leader. And I know nothing of those organizations other than to posit that they do not exist in any form the popular media would recognize."

"How would you know such a thing?"

Kohl smiled, more of a smirk, "The history of these groups is not what I am here to speak to you about."

"You're here to speak to me about Veniamin," she said. Kohl's facial expression betrayed only the slightest of reactions, and the hint of something she'd not expected, a flinching as if away from pain. It was enough of one to validate her guess, however.

"My opinion of you was correct, I see."

"I know very little else," she conceded. "And I'm sure in the end the *who* is not all that important. The *why* … the *why* is the reason you're here, I suspect."

"Not necessarily, Detective Romano. The *why* I believe you will find less interesting and ultimately less important than the *what*. But now is not quite the time for that. Let me say, so that you do not have any questions which might prevent your cooperation, that I am completely and utterly honest. I will not lie to you. I may not, however, be *able* to provide you with a complete explanation, for reasons beyond your present understanding. We became aware of you last night, at the same time and for the same reason the rest of the world did. Your actions, however, caught our attention for a different reason than most.

"Janus (this is his surname, Detective) was one man; one ultimately misguided man. But by his suicide a greater outcome may be manifest, one which he of course was unaware. Your subsequent activities on the internet only highlighted a need for an immediate response on our part. I flew from Munich this morning, Detective Romano. This is how important we felt our meeting to be."

Fleur paused, gauging the man's sincerity. She felt that he believed what he was telling her. "And what would you have me do, Sir?"

"All that is required of you at this moment is that you come with me."

"To Munich?"

"No. Munich is merely my home. To the south of France."

"France? What's in France?"

"Answers, Detective. Answers, and opportunity."

She paused, sipping more of her coffee, trying to use the simple gesture to calm herself. "Can I ask how we'll get to the south of France?"

"You need not worry about that. A plane is waiting for us.

William Burcher 47

We also have taken the liberty of obtaining a new passport for you. You let yours expire a few months ago, I believe," and he stepped over and retrieved his suit jacket, quickly producing the document from an inside pocket. He handed the passport to her, and she examined it closely, noting if not its authenticity, its undeniable quality. All of her personal information was correct. Access to information, to personal or government records did not impress her. Speed of action, however, did. The ability to bypass bureaucracy in her world always spoke of influence and authority.

And she was reminded once again that she had no choice in this game. She also realized that she deeply wanted to go with Kohl. She did not trust him, but she believed him. And the hints he'd already provided to larger mysteries were enticing to her like nothing before.

"I guess I need to pack, then," she told him.

"There is no need for that. You will have garments waiting for you in a bag on the plane."

"Of course," she said, smiling. "Why didn't I think of that? I am going to take a shower, though, Mr. Kohl. You can wait in the living room if you would like."

He finished donning his suit jacket and raised an eyebrow at her in response. Twenty minutes later she emerged from her bedroom wearing the nicest suit she owned. She felt the formality was necessary for a trip to southern France on a private jet. She'd also chosen the suit because it most easily allowed her to conceal her Glock subcompact, "Hannibal." She'd named all of her guns since her days in the academy, a fact that no one but Tim was aware of, and she didn't think she'd have to get through a metal detector before boarding this flight. Kohl had looked at her curiously and not disapprovingly before he led her out of her apartment and down the stairs to the black Audi waiting outside in the building's shadow.

———————

Somewhere over the Appalachians, the sun had set. Both Kohl and Genji were quiet and reclined in their seats. Genji may have been asleep. Kohl was looking thoughtfully out his window, the last shades of orange and red just beginning to fade in the western sky. They were all tired, she supposed. She certainly was. She felt somehow empty, as if she had no more capacity for emotion, for any kind of new experience. She worried at this, knowing that much more of both lay in store for her a short distance in the future. Kohl had spent the last few hours providing her answers, some more cryptic and vague than others. But he purposefully held back what was becoming the largest question of them all—that of context. She did not know why the group "Zhar-Oss" existed, what its purpose was.

They had spoken much of Benjamin Janus—and she conceded that Kohl's explanations seemed satisfying, though the man seemed to avoid using the Russian version of Janus' name, as if it pained him to do so. She had the creeping sense that once this trip was over she would no longer be a detective with her department, and she certainly wasn't a passenger on the plane in a professional capacity, but she still approached the subject as she would any investigation. In her mind she was already writing her report.

Janus had once been a member of their "Confederation," as Kohl most commonly called it. He had been one of its youngest and most promising. But he disagreed with one of the group's fundamental tenets—that of secrecy. He wanted to come forth with whatever secret the group kept in a spectacular, public way. This seemed almost a sin in Kohl's eyes. She'd asked him then if the secret was important enough to kill for. Kohl had merely smiled at her.

"The *Knowledge*—it is why we exist. But we do not kill, Detective Romano. At most we discredit. We were prepared to discredit Janus if it came to that. But we would not have killed him."

"Discredit him? How would you have done that?"

"Technically he was still a deserter of the Russian Navy. This would not have been hard. The Knowledge itself is also of a somewhat … foreign nature. Janus probably would not have succeeded if he disclosed it directly to the public. He chose to attempt this … in his own way."

"With his music?"

"Yes."

"Is the organization … the Confederation … is it Russian in origin?"

"No. We are a trans-national group, with members living and born in most countries. All races, genders, nationalities are represented. Our rolls are open, as has always been the case, even before it was of a political necessity to do so. Janus merely happened to be of Russian origin. The website that you accessed displays text based on the user's preferences. You managed to login to a first-tier page. We prevent immediate translations as an additional, minor security measure. And now, as it is impolite for a conversation to merely go one-way, I must ask you a question, Detective."

"Please. Although I am surprised that there are questions about me that still remain. Your Confederation seems … thorough."

"Yes. We are. But omnipotence is as yet not one of our qualities," he replied smiling slightly, amused probably at what passed for a joke in this man's mind. "I must know. How did you discover the password to Janus' login?"

Her heart fluttered for a moment. She hoped the dim lighting in the plane's cabin disguised the brief look of fear on her face. She then thought how strange this reaction was. Clearly the man had disclosed some outlandish, unbelievable things to her. Why should she be ashamed at the truth behind the answer? Why should she not tell him what he wanted to know?

"The password. What was it? I don't even remember, Mr. Kohl. Perhaps it was something I found on the web in reference to Zhar-Oss, the musician. Perhaps I heard it in a song of his. I don't know. I'm sorry."

"Did he speak to you at all, when you two were physically close … after he'd done what he'd done?"

"No," she replied without any hesitation, wondering again why she lied and hoping that none of the video of the event was good enough to capture his whisper. "He was absolutely silent."

Kohl's simple nod at her response betrayed nothing and she didn't know if he believed her. She attempted to change the subject.

"What do you think he attempted to accomplish with his death?"

"He was hoping, I think, that it would lead to an investigation and that things would be discovered. He was hoping, I think, that someone dedicated and capable would learn the truth behind the title of his act. He was hoping for you, Detective Romano."

"Is that why I'm here? You're granting this man his wish?"

"In a way, yes. By bringing you into the fold, so to speak, we are pre-empting an accidental discovery, which you seemed close to making independent of our designs. We are also ... recruiting."

"Recruiting?"

"Yes. Of course. The Confederation is always looking for individuals of extraordinary quality. The bravery, the force of will you displayed on the stage with Janus demonstrated this quality. A quick investigation into your background confirmed our hopes. Also, Janus had ... friends, in our group. You will find that out soon enough. These friends, they felt that his memory would be honored in a way with your inclusion."

"How many members of this group are there, Mr. Kohl?"

"The number has been set from our founding. It is a number with very old significance. Six hundred and sixty-six, Detective."

"The number of the beast of The Book of Revelation ..."

"Yes. Zhar-Oss is very old, Fleur. Very old. John, the Apostle was a member. He was a very humorous man, from what our lore states. The inclusion of the number in his book was something of a joke."

"You're telling me that Zhar-Oss is two thousand years old and that an Apostle of Christ was a member? All of this is admittedly hard to believe."

William Burcher 51

"Yes."

"Don't you think this is a bit beyond belief?"

"Well yes. But this is beside the point. And the Confederation is much older than this, Detective."

"How…old?"

"Are you prepared?" he asked her softly, plainly.

Fleur nodded.

"Zhar-Oss, a word of a language long ago lost to history, as an organization, has existed as far as we can tell, for twenty-seven thousand, three hundred and thirty-eight years."

She remained quiet then. Kohl sensed too that the gravity of what he'd just said required no response from her. The sun was low in the sky when Fleur heard those words, that number, as they flew above the hills of Western Pennsylvania. It was incomprehensible. Unbelievable. It was too strange a concept to begin to understand. The history of the country she flew above now was only measured by the *hundreds* of years. Kohl was talking about something magnitudes older. Nothing, as far as she knew, of human creation was that old. The oldest religions were only a tenth of that. The scale Kohl was talking about was geologic. An ice age had come and gone in this span. How could an institution, a group, a society exist for so long? And why? What were they doing that allowed for such longevity? And the thought, the thought of Paleolithic man, living in some cave somewhere actually creating something this important, this enduring, was fantastic to her. And the connection was immediately obvious.

"We're visiting a cave, in Southern France, aren't we Mr. Kohl?"

His response was one of instant mild amusement, and obvious approval.

"Yes, Detective Romano, we are," and he waited for more from her, another question, which might tell him more about how she'd arrived at this conclusion.

She recognized this and chose not to play into it. She stared out her window at the hills and farmland, the small towns, the highways passing below her—all of which were constructed within the last handful of human generations. She could not begin to consider what waited for her across the Atlantic. She continued looking out the window as she spoke, "If all of this is true, this is quite the club you have, Mr. Kohl."

The boy was a year or two older now, nine or ten. He'd thickened out slightly but still remained tall, skinny. He was there, before the entrance to the cave with his dog—a large, powerful animal seemingly more wolf than pet. It was almost dusk and the rock around the entrance was lit red with the setting sun—in deep contrast to the gaping black void that marked the beginning of the cave. He was scared. He knew this fear. He felt the fear of his dog standing beside him, too. He was afraid, but this was something that he must do. His father had a saying, "Men were not born of the Mother to live comfortable lives." He knew that his father meant that he must challenge himself always, that this should never stop, and that this was the way of life and the gift of the Mother. What waited for him in the darkness here was his challenge.

He knelt on one knee and said a prayer—that if something happened to him in the darkness his mother and sisters would be provided for and that they would not mourn his death too harshly. He also spoke briefly to his father, who he believed now to be one with the wind. "I will always honor the wisdom you imparted, Father."

He then quickly gathered bits of small dead wood around and began to build a small fire from a coal he carried with him in the horn of an ibex. Within a few moments the fire was ready and he took one of the torches he'd prepared from his pack. It lit immediately. He doused the flame on the ground quickly so the others would not happen upon it and know where he was and what he was doing.

"It is time, Aurochs," he said to the dog, who whined and

wagged his tail with anticipatory anxiety. The boy slowly entered the cave, his pack on his shoulders and the torch held high. The dog followed just behind him. They had to scramble around a section of rock wall which had collapsed over the entrance. It appeared that a further collapse had re-opened the cave partially. The boy knew that this area was prone to landslides and that the hills were littered with caves—physical entrances into the Mother, and thus the land of his people was the *Zhar-Nues,* "Holy Land."

Aurochs had stopped whining as soon as they'd begun moving and he was grateful for that. Caves should be entered with reverence, in silence and with an open heart. The air grew cool on his face and on the skin of his torso. He smelled the damp, the water, the clay and the musty old odor of something long since dead. The light from the entrance faded quickly and soon only his torch lit the stone walls, the cracks, the depressions, prominences and protuberances animated now with flickering shadows. He quickly realized that this cave had never been lived in. If men had been in it before, it had been deemed and treated a holy place. His heart quickened.

It was then that he saw the first of them, the images on the wall. He dropped his torch in surprise, so that Aurochs made a noise in startled response. He quickly picked it up once again and saw the head of the wisent as it appeared to grow from the rock itself. He stared in amazement. He had seen images in rock before, put there by people, but never this real and never this grand.

"I am sorry for the torch, boy," he said to the dog. "But do you see it? Do you see the wisent? Do you see the others?" But the dog didn't seem to see anything he took an interest to. He looked back up at the boy with wide, patient eyes. That was something the boy had noticed before—neither the dogs nor other animals ever paid attention to images made by the hand of man. It was as if only men could see them, or perhaps the animals viewed them as profane or unimportant. Somehow the boy did not believe this to be the case, though.

He quickly discovered more—images of animals of all kinds

and as he walked slowly and more deeply into the cave they shimmered, seeming to come alive, to run and jump, to chase and flee. He knew that the effect was one brought by the light of his torch, but he marveled all the same and said a prayer in thanks for the men and women who made the images long ago. The boy did not know the concept of large numbers, but knew somehow that this place was very old. It was old enough that the images had become part of the rocks themselves and nothing was older than the rock, the body, the bones of the Mother.

Although old, the images on the walls appeared new. The colors were vibrant, the charcoal used for outlines and shading still fresh. This place is outside of time, he thought. Day and night, winter and spring—they have no meaning here. The images are timeless. And as he stepped back as far as the walls of the cave and the light of his torch would let him, as he took in the entirety of the lower wall with scores of realistic depictions of wisent, ibex, horses, mammoth and lion; he sensed that the wall was trying to tell him something. The images, timeless, were meant to speak, only without words, for words are born of the wind and die as quickly as they are born. How could a wall of rock speak? But it was. The artists, long gone, were able to speak through their creations. But was it they who spoke? Was it with their voices that the message strained to enter his, the viewer's mind?

He shivered. He felt suddenly afraid and alone. He instinctively called Aurochs close and held the dog around his muscular neck. Unbidden came the feeling in his stomach that rose higher into his heart and then his throat until it stopped at his eyes and tears began to well up and then flow. Grief. For his father. He wished that his father were here with him now. His father would not be afraid and his father would understand the message of the wall. How he missed him! He knew that his grief was selfish, that his father now belonged to something greater than he, but this thought didn't lessen the pain. It was then that a breeze from the depths of the cave touched his face. It was his father, his breath he knew and he forgot his sadness and his loneliness. Before him was a gift, a gift of extraordinary worth—of the kind that few men will ever see. It was not a time for tears. And he stood up from his kneel and began to walk further, deeper into the cave, his bare feet slipping in places in the cool wet clay of the floor. He saw more elk, more reindeer, more lions and his mind screamed for an answer. He spoke to it, to the wall, to the artists of long ago. He spoke loudly and his voice echoed far.

"I am Garr-Eth! I am of the people of the Zhar-Nues! I know that you wish to speak! I am here to listen!"

And he stopped quickly in his tracks, quiet, silent. Before him at eye level, placed on a pillar of calcite by the hands of a man perhaps millennia ago, was the skull of a cave bear covered in a layer of liquid rock, the most holy of beasts and brother to man. The cave bear are born directly from the womb of the Mother, as are men and thus they return to caves throughout their lives for fellowship and renewal. And he knew that the cave had answered him and had given forth its message. The words of the walls of the cave, the images of the animals of his time were not meant to be the words of men or of the artists who created them. The images were the words of the Mother. The Mother was speaking to him as one man speaks to another. He knelt once again and made the sign, the simple gesture, right hand upright and flat beneath his jaw slowly lowered to his chest.

"Thank you," he said aloud, repeating it once so the echoes of both slowly combined and merged, spreading throughout the cave as one.

"Detective. Romano. Detective Romano. Please wake up."

She stirred, still curled in her reclined seat. She could see that the aircraft windows were still dark and she was confused. "Are we … there? Arrived?"

Kohl was there, close, a few feet from her. He had a look about his face intensely serious. "No Detective. We are still in the air, somewhere above Britain, I believe."

She saw that Genji too had been roused and was standing beside Kohl. He too looked concerned, surprised.

"What's going on?" she asked them.

"What were you dreaming about?" Kohl answered her in a sharp, commanding voice. Gone were the pleasantries, the politeness of before.

"I, I don't— "

"Clearly you do. Think. Now. Tell me. What were you dreaming about, Detective Romano?"

She shook her head, trying to wake herself further, trying to clear the fog. "Hold on. A boy. It was a boy in a cave."

Kohl looked at Genji, shaking his head slightly. Genji returned the look. They both then focused on her once again. "Please tell me more, Fleur," Kohl continued, softer this time.

She was awake now, the dream fresh on her mind. And she paused, thinking, deciding if she should tell these men the truth. Kohl saw her indecision, the internal dialog. He shouted at her powerfully in command.

"Now Fleur! Enough deceit! Tell me at once what was in the dream!"

The shock of the man's voice startled her and there was a moment of silence. The other man's eyes moved briefly to Kohl, questioning. She looked downward, away from the man's glare. She had no reason at this point to hold back from Kohl, and clearly it was important to him. It was only a dream.

"Was I talking? Did I say something in my sleep?"

"Yes. You were mumbling. Genji and I heard certain words. Ple —"

She interjected, disconcerted by his intensity. "It was a boy. Ten years old. He was barefoot and had a dog with him. The dog was large. It looked like a wolf, maybe bigger. He entered a cave and discovered drawings, paintings, images on the walls …"

"Go on, Detective. Please. It is of the utmost importance."

"The walls of the cave—they were covered. The images were life-like, moving in the light of his torch. There were hundreds

William Burcher 57

of them, animals. The boy knew that they were old," she said, wondering how much detail Kohl really wanted.

"Please tell me the kinds of animals that you saw."

"Horses. There was a wall of horses. There were bison. Like American bison. And some kind of African-looking antelope. And lions. There were lions, hunting I think."

Kohl looked at Genji once again, and he asked her a question, still looking at the other man. "Was there a pillar of rock, a stalagmite, growing upward from the ground?"

"Yes," she replied, looking him in the eyes now.

"What was on this pillar?"

She did not pause in her response. "There was a skull. Of a bear."

And Kohl exhaled loudly, partly through his teeth so that there was a partial whistle.

"I don't understand, Mr. Kohl. Why is this so important? We were talking of caves before I fell asleep. I must have put it all together in a dream. It can't be—"

"You have certain details, Detective Romano, that you could not possibly possess. But I am wondering now if you have a very important detail, one that I am almost afraid to ask you."

She stared at him for a moment, eyes wide, knowing what he was going to ask her. She stood up from her seat and brushed herself off, straightening her suit. Kohl and Genji both took a step back.

"You want to ask me the name of the boy, Mr. Kohl."

Kohl merely looked at her in a resigned, nervous way. His tongue was pressed tightly against his cheek, forming a bulge. He nodded once, almost imperceptibly.

"The boy said his name, shouting it to the cave, frustrated that he did not understand the images on the wall. His name was Garr-Eth."

"Mein Gott!" Kohl puffed in exhale. Genji too muttered something in Japanese. Fleur stood staring at both of them. She felt lighter and strangely detached as she watched these men and their reactions. She wondered to herself, amused at what further surprises lay ahead.

"Did Veniamin tell you this? Tell me at once."

"No, Mr. Kohl. I told you. He said nothing to me."

"Did you know him, from before?"

"No."

"Where did this information come from, Detective?"

"Mr. Kohl, I didn't want to disclose any of this previously for fear of sounding a lunatic. And I wanted to see first and observe … you. I've been having dreams lately."

"Dreams! More than one! Mein Gott," he repeated.

"I am sorry, Mr. Kohl. If I'd realized that all of this was as important to you as it is, I would have told you sooner."

"Others. Other dreams. How many?"

She realized that this question wasn't very logical. Kohl was not in complete control of himself.

"I don't know. 4 or 5."

"Four or five. Four or five," he repeated, grave. "I will tell you something, Detective. I will tell you something very important to us and something that I was not going to disclose until after we'd visited France. Then I will ask you to offer us everything else that you know, that you have seen in your dreams. The founder, the architect of Zhar-Oss, was a man named Garr-Eth of the Zhar-Nues. Garr-Eth is a … *revered* figure to us. Garr-Eth was a man who lived in Europe twenty-seven thousand years ago. And now you will begin to understand the reasons behind my reaction, Detective."

And she looked at him with eyes wide, not knowing what to say.

PART II

PAST

6

GARR-ETH

Although he was aware of the dim lights of the outdoor hearth fires of the settlement miles distant and across a steep and rugged river valley, his mind was not attached to these, the only visible signs of another human's occupation of this place. His attention now was directed upward, on the sky above and the crystalline light of the stars, the unblinking glow of the planets and the haze and confounding fog of the Milky Way. The moon was absent this night's sky and it was a time of contemplation, a time of wonder. The darkened land invoked thoughts of the void. Above the land was the emboldened sky—painted with objects of light usually fainter than the moon but now brilliant and clear. He thought of the juxtaposition in his own terms, and in terms of what he knew of the Mother. The dark was nothing. Empty.

Untouchable. Unfathomable. From it were born the objects of this world. It was like the emptiness in his own mind when he was aware of it—before the forms of his thoughts became manifest. The stars, the three planets he could see, the enormous swath of the galactic arm and the bulge lower in the southern sky—these were like his thoughts, delicate and ephemeral.

He crouched low in a muscular squat, relaxed but always ready, ready to move or ready to flee or to fight. He listened and heard the slight breeze as it sang the song of the stunted juniper trees and of the larger pines and spruces. The rustling of scrub and oak he heard too. And if he listened with a sharpened focus he could hear the wind moaning low but faint along the entrance to the cave behind him. It too was of the void, the womb of the Mother made manifest into a thing he could see or enter. The cave was like the land on a moonless night, darkened and full of infinite possibility. So much darkness around him, so much nothing, but this did not dishearten him or scare him. He felt that all of it—the cave, the land, the spaces between the stars in the sky—vibrated with a nascent virility, an unexpressed and latent potential.

An hour before he'd exited the cave and extinguished his torch to crouch on this precipice outside its entrance and breathe in the night, the darkness and the stars. The ledge was a few hundred feet above a sloping hillside. The openness of the air above and beneath would always be reflected in his mind— a valuable thing when his mind needed to process, when he needed to think. He'd been coming to the cave since discovering it as a boy. He'd shared it with only a few—men and women who would appreciate its gravity. People who might understand its message.

Tonight, the cave had felt different to him, as if something had changed. And it was as if the words the paintings had spoken to him had not changed themselves, but that something in his mind had. He was seeing the figures in the cave differently, interpreting their message differently. The Mother could always be felt if one stopped and harkened. It was when one *thought* about her, when one tried to put the felt awareness of her into

words that one ran into difficulties. He felt that the cave was beginning to ask him to do something. But what this was he could-
n't tell.

There came a sound to him from a few tens of yards away
and he listened, not yet ready to react. It was an animal. It was
walking. It was moving. It had two legs, not four. And by the
pace of the steps, the sound of the footfalls and the sense of muscular power they invoked, he knew they belonged to Thol-Ur,
his friend. Thol was one of the few who knew about the cave.
He remained silent and still while the other man felt his way to
the precipice. There was a pause, a moment of anticipation as
Thol sensed the area for his friend, or wondered if he should
enter the cave to find him.

"You're here, aren't you, Garr?" he finally asked in a low
whisper.

And after a moment of further silence he answered. "Yes, my
friend. I am here."

Garr-Eth felt Thol's nearly silent footfalls as the man approached him, probably making out his silhouette now against
the starry sky. Thol crouched down next to him.

"What do you see here?" he asked.

"I see the darkness. As you do. But I do not crouch here and
look out upon the darkened valley to see with my eyes, my
friend."

"You sense the Great Void in this place," the man said
simply.

"Yes," was Garr-Eth's only response. For a few moments
measured in their slow and deep breaths the two remained silent, sharing a feeling, an awareness of the infinity around them.
At the halt, the valley of a breath Garr-Eth broke the silence.

"Has something happened?"

"Yes. Or it will. Thom-Ar has been gored by an ibex. It was
a freak and unexpected thing. His lung has been pierced and
one can hear his breath exiting through the wound. It leaks out
of him as does his blood. The Mother wills it. He will die tonight
if he has not already."

Garr-Eth took in the news, pondered it, played with it.

William Burcher 63

Thom-Ar was the settlement head-man. He was loved and respected as a father by most—both caring and powerful. Garr-Eth was fond of the old man and felt that he was a part of his own life, a rock, a solid influence and a strong and wizened leader. The people will be lost without him. And then he was struck with the larger responsibility. It was known that Thom had named him, Garr-Eth, as his successor. Emotion, raw and powerful, gripped him. He felt it well up inside him from below, a fountain of feeling threatening to burst forth.

"This pains me, Thol-Ur. This pains me greatly. I see that it is the will of the Mother. She both gives and takes. But I am frightened by the meaning of it," he confided to the other man in the dark. He felt Thol's big hand on his shoulder then.

"I am sorry, Garr. Thom is a part of all of us. He is true. He is noble. He is true mensch."

"I am not ready for this, Thol-Ur."

"Will you ever be?"

Garr-Eth breathed deeply and quickly as the waves of both fear and grief rolled over him. He did as his father had taught him and stepped back, to the deeper place, and let the waves pass. But his thoughts could not remain detached for long, and the fear and grief became him. How could he fill the shoes of such a man as Thom-Ar? How could he lead? What would his people do without such a presence as he? He did not show this to Thol, however. His reaction he could control. He was grateful for the darkness then too, knowing the other man merely saw a shadow crouching resolute beside him.

"I am glad that you are the one to speak of this," he said.

Within the fear was also a seed of something else and he recognized its presence. Of course, the thought. Emotions are like all other of the Mother's creations. Within them are the seeds of their opposite. The briefest, faintest of smiles parted his lips as he recognized this and also his own foolishness for not expecting and simply waiting for the metamorphosis.

"I will face the aurochs, my friend," he said, an expression of his people that meant that he would meet his fate and his duty and would do the best that he could. He would show up, despite his fear in doing so. He would be present, facing the beast.

"It pleases me to hear that, Garr," Thol replied.

Garr-Eth felt then that the man was waiting, giving him not quite wholly the gift of space and patience.

"We will go then," he said. "Now. Fast. Let the darkness heighten all our senses so that we may make haste tonight."

He sprang forth, knowing by memory or some other force the way off the cliff and to the faintest path that lead through the rock and back down the hillside. Only a second passed before he heard Thol too moving softly behind him. They slid through the darkness like serpents or panthers on a hunt, each aware of the other and moving as a singular unit down, down to the valley below. Through the night they traveled fast and silently within steps of sleeping beasts and animals of prey, each of these only vaguely aware of the passing of something brief, something alien and unexpected—like wraiths on the wind.

———

Thom-Ar's partner and the head-woman of the settlement, Aye-Lin, met them at the entrance to the family's compound— a cluster of buildings made from stone and large cuts of timber built just above the highest flood line of the river. The family's dogs had announced their coming. Garr-Eth immediately grasped the big woman, who seemed as if she were beyond grief.

"He does not have much longer," she said simply before pulling away. "We have said goodbye, much time before, for fear he would be taken sooner. I am grateful that we had the time. But it won't be long."

She led the two men inside the largest of the structures. They were greeted with the strange smell of herbs and decaying plant matter mixed with the scent of smoke and iron. The light was dim—the hearth fire low in the center of the floor. Thom-Ar lay prone on a simple but thick bed of furs set directly on the floor of packed earth. The furs were soaked with liquid, the color unknown in the dim light. Garr-Eth knew the liquid to be blood, however. As they entered Thom-Ar began to stir slightly and began to make a rasping sound. Garr-Eth could not tell where the sound was coming from until he got closer and saw that it issued from the side of the man's chest. It was a testament to his strength, to the life contained inside him that he was still present in this world. Thom lifted two fingers only and beckoned them closer. Garr-Eth stepped forward, Thol-Ur just behind him.

"Garr-Eth. My son," the man began, his voice a whisper. Even in the dim, golden light of the fire the man was white as the moon. The blood had gone from his face, draining from the gaping wound in his side. "Garr-Eth. I do not have long before I return to the Mother." He paused awkwardly for a few moments, and Garr-Eth thought that he might have expired. He put his hand to his mouth, his nose, feeling for breath. The man smiled, amused.

"No, my son—I am not gone yet. Just ... tired." And he paused again, collecting his energy. "Garr-Eth. From the day your father died I have held you in my heart as my own. I am proud of the man that you have become. You are strong, of body and of core. I will leave this world in peace, confident that the people of the Zhar-Nues are in good hands. Your hands."

Garr-Eth knelt closer to the old man. His heart was in his throat, beating fiercely. He did not know what to say and instead chose simply to meet the man's gaze fully and to place his own hand upon his shoulder.

"I have something else to say, something else I have discussed with Aye-Lin. Aye-Lin will be your faithful guide on this path as head-man. She is wise and is no less than the embodiment of the Mother in our midst. She has seen what I have seen and my spirit will live on in her in part. Heed her council, my son."

Thom-Ar trailed off, looking toward the fire, his eyes a mystery. Garr-Eth did not know if they saw the fire or were now looking into the dark, infinite distance separating this life from the next. The man's breathing was no longer noticeable.

"We are a people of seasons and cycles, Garr-Eth," he began

again, more slowly. "We change our ways with the cycles of the earth. In winter, we stay close to the river and hunt only in the valley. In spring, we begin to range, tracking the herds as they move up into the high places. In fall, we store and prepare, we retreat back into ourselves and our homes to make ready for the coming hardship. These things are all constant. The cycle repeats itself endlessly. There is birth and death, prosperity and fatigue. There is change, but it occurs within the cycle and this has been the way of things since the birth of the earth. Are you there, Garr-Eth?"

"I am here, father," he replied instantly.

"Good. I have lost my vision and can no longer see your shadow or the light of the hearth-flame. It will not be long," the man said.

"I am listening."

"But what I have seen and what I speak about now is a change that I know is outside of this ancient cycle. It will take generations to complete, my son, but it will begin with your time. You may even be the one who gives birth to it. But what I have to say, and what I want you to remember, is to not fight this, Garr-Eth. Even if the change to you is abhorrent, do not fight it. The will of the Mother is beyond our comprehension. I have lived long and have grown wise. I know this. All things evolve for the good, even if on the surface they appear foreign, ugly or invoking of decay."

Even as he died, the noble old man was eloquent and wise. Garr-Eth held every word of the man's speech tightly, repeating the words to himself, even as he still listened. Thom-Ar was experiencing great pain to tell him these things. Although he did not now understand them, he was determined to commit them to his memory. Later he would ponder their meaning. Later he would know. And although Thom told him that he could not see, the old man's eyes were looking directly into his face. He held his blind gaze and gripped the man's shoulder.

"I have seen that you are a special man, Garr-Eth. You will always choose rightly to *face the aurochs*. But we cannot always slay that bull, Garr-Eth. Sometimes we must face him and let him pass—even though he may trample our children and gore our dogs."

There came another pause as the man seemed to collect himself further for a final word.

"I know of the cave, Garr-Eth. I discovered it myself as a boy," the man said, breathing inward once further in a deep, unnatural way. "The change I mention will come about through the cave. Be strong, my son."

And with those words the man's breath came out of him and into the world for the last time. Garr-Eth remained by his side for a long while and it seemed to Thol-Ur that Garr's will had left him, as had Thom's breath. After a while he went to him and by grasping him under the arms and by his shoulders lifted him up and to his feet. The two hobbled slowly out of the room and out of the structure. They passed Aye-Lin wordlessly as she entered once again, coming to prepare the body. The tears streamed silently down her face.

——————

The Rites were held the next evening before Thom's body could putrefy in the warm spring air. Most of the settlement was present at the funeral pyre, as were the envoys of the surrounding caves and villages. Runners had gone out that morning to spread the news and many came not just out of duty but out of felt regard. Thom-Ar had been a well-known, well-respected man. He had often proven himself on the collective hunts participated in with surrounding peoples—massive things in which entire herds were harvested and in which hundreds of hunters, men and women, participated. Thom-Ar was often the leader and organizer of such expeditions.

His counsel, too, had been valued by many and he had been mentor to most of the younger head-men of surrounding clans. The people were as thick and numerous as the largest herd of elk they hunted, as the logs were lit by Garr-Eth and Aye-Lin, the wood soaked with the rendered fat of an aurochs bull.

That morning Garr-Eth had directed Thol-Ur to lead a party of ten men into the forest to fell mature trees for the night's funeral pyre. They'd done well, and as he watched the flames expand higher and higher into the night sky he thought the scene appropriate to mark the passing of so respected a man. The sky was moonless and black. He and others thought it auspicious, the expression of such opposing forces—the dark, void of night and the powerful heat and light of the flames. Thom would have approved, he thought, as the flames began to roar in growing fury. As Thom's hair and clothing began to singe and his skin first redden and then char, the wail of mourning rose up from the crowd—a terrifying ululation to herald the man's arrival back into the womb of the Mother. The crowd then became silent and only the roar of the fire could be heard, the people watching as it hungrily devoured the felled pine trees and the body of the old man.

At the pyre's conclusion came a simple ceremony in which the coals of the fire were given out to representatives of the households of the settlement, and to the people of surrounding lands. These were placed in ember-horns and would later be removed and added to their own hearth fires, a symbol of the Mother's perpetual renewal. And then came the symbolic remarriage of Aye-Lin to Garr-Eth. Although she was old enough to be his mother, the ceremony marked the desired union of the archetypal male and the female forces at work in the surrounding environment and in the community itself. These forces must remain balanced for the community to thrive. Garr-Eth was seen as the physical embodiment of the male, not just of the concept of action, bravery, and force, but also of quiet strength born of wisdom and reverence for the Mother. And indeed he looked the part, taller than most with a relaxed but regal bearing, obviously strong of body and of speech. Garr-Eth's eyes communicated a wisdom beyond his years as well as a fierce intelligence. Aye-Lin was equally as representative of the feminine, her body the very ideal of the Mother. She possessed large, voluptuous hips and breasts which nursed many a child, her hair long and straight and black, shot through with streams of silver, her visage round and wide and shaped as the moon. Her eyes spoke too of wisdom and of a deep ability to persevere and endure.

Garr-Eth and Aye-Lin were expected to provide counsel to one another, to lead the people together as equals. The male and female principals were equivalent and could not exist without each other, but they were fundamentally different. The roles of the men and women of their society were typically defined and disparate as well, although there were individuals who were not born of the archetypical mold who would participate in the activities of the opposite sex: women who hunted, trapped or bred dogs; men who cooked or were artisans or healers.

The head-man and head-woman were not expected to mate, however. Garr-Eth suspected that in times past, the optimal union had been a physical one as well as a practical and ceremonial one, and that there might have been rites and rituals associated with a physical coupling. But this practice had been dispensed with over time. He was thankful for this. Aye-Lin had been a mother figure to him. He could not see her in any kind of carnal light.

The ceremony ended and the crowd dispersed back into the darkness, the visiting peoples hosted by families of the Zhar-Nues to be fed and sheltered by them, the resulting bonds and ties lasting long after that night. Garr-Eth and Aye-Lin walked together back to Thom-Ar's complex, which was now his to dwell in and maintain.

Aye-Lin and Thom-Ar had married later in life, after both had families from previous couplings. Both had been widowed and both had children with families of their own. Aye-Lin would remain in a separate structure within the complex with her two granddaughters, children of her own son, who had perished years ago in a fall. Neither of the girls were of age and both would be expected to help maintain the complex and to support both him and Aye-Lin.

His own mother maintained a structure on the outskirts of the settlement and he would speak with her about moving to his new home when the time was right. It was known that Garr-Eth had chosen not yet to marry. Though rare among his people, they had come to respect his choice. It was known also that he sometimes shared a bed with Cour-Ett, a woman who'd chosen not to marry herself—having pursued the life of a man and the thrill of the hunt. Because of his loose association with Cour-Ett, people did not pressure him too much to begin a family—thinking vaguely that it was perhaps in the plans of both to marry one day. He'd never discussed it with Cour either, but he suspected that she benefitted from their relationship in the same way as he. He'd only told Thol his true reasons, and that man's intimidating and taciturn nature would ensure this long remained a secret.

Within his house would also reside a young man, Durr-Es. Durr-Es had been apprenticed to Thom-Ar by Thom's own brother, the head-man of a village high in the hills above them. The young man had been orphaned by an avalanche one winter and he did not talk—though it was unknown if his lack of speech was a result of a physical trauma or of the stress of losing his family at a young age. He'd been a faithful and willing servant of Thom's for nearly a decade now, but Garr-Eth would need to find the young man a partner soon. This would not be an easy task, however, as he knew that few in the settlement would see him as suitable—not for his infirmity, but for his obvious ugliness. He was also made mildly uncomfortable by the young man's presence. He always seemed to be lurking in the background or in the shadows. Garr-Eth had the sense that he was much more capable, more intelligent and aware than Thom had recognized.

He and Aye-Lin entered the house where the hearth had already been prepared by Durr-Es. The young man was nowhere to be seen—a mild relief to him.

"Times of transition and change are always trying. But they are inherent to the Mother as are birth and death," Aye-Lin spoke with a knowing sadness. The two sat down on furs lining the ground around the hearth, the woman forced to slowly lower her bulk in halting steps. Garr-Eth had given up offering to assist her; she would always refuse.

William Burcher 71

"My concerns are small compared to yours, Aye-Lin," he replied.

"No, that is not necessarily true. I do not have many concerns now. Merely grief. At my age one has become … practiced, at this art."

Garr-Eth gazed upon her empathetically. "We do not have to speak tonight, Aye. The happenings of the Zhar-Nues can wait for the passing of our righteous grief."

"Yes, I appreciate that, my son. But the grief will be with me for the rest of my life. The years only blunt the sharpness of the knife. The knife is always there. It is important that you be made aware of your duties, and of the happenings of our people."

He nodded assent and stared for a moment at the corner where just a night earlier he'd watched his mentor expire. The light in the space, the air, the shadows flickering on the walls were the same now as they had been then.

"But first, Garr-Eth. I am curious to know what Thom said to you last night. He asked me to forsake his last moments so that he might speak with you in private."

He paused in the dim light considering this. It had been of great importance to the man to tell him what he had. He tried to intuit how much of the old man's speech he should disclose, searching his body, his core, his gut for direction. He felt that an honest response was going to lead to more questions. But Thom specifically hinted that Aye-Lin was aware—of the cave and of the man's warning.

"He spoke of change."

"Yes," she said, her face turning away from the fire, into the dark. "Change. Our constant."

"He spoke of greater change. Greater change than the cycles we are familiar with, I am sure."

"Yes," she repeated. "I am also aware of what you speak." She remained silent for a moment, hoping he would fill the void with further speech. "There was more, Garr-Eth. This I know. Please tell me."

Garr-Eth breathed deep. He always felt uncomfortable telling others of what he found. "We spoke of the cave."

Aye-Lin seemed to nod slowly to herself repeatedly, a soothing, rocking motion. Garr-Eth had the sense that the cave for her too was a subject which quickened her heart as it did his. "The cave," she repeated. "Tell me more."

"Thom-Ar told me he was aware of my discovery—as he had made the same discovery as a young man."

"Did this frighten you, Garr-Eth?"

"I was struck, as by a club. I believed the cave to be hidden from the eyes of most. A secret. I did not know."

"He found it before I knew him, before I found my way to the Zhar-Nues. He showed the cave to me during our courtship and it was this secret that I chose to marry, as well as the man."

"How did you two keep this secret? I am skilled at tracking men and the beasts of the earth through forest and meadow. There were no recent signs of the presence of men."

"Thom-Ar was equally as skilled, Garr-Eth. Perhaps more so. Few could match his abilities at the hunt."

To this Garr-Eth could only assent. The old man had been a wonder on a hunt—be it in the open plains of the high places or through a thick valley forest. None could compare. Certainly not he. "But why, Aye? Why did Thom keep this to himself?"

"Why must you ask this, my son? Why did you yourself keep such a secret?"

Garr-Eth pondered this for a moment. He had disclosed the cave to four people only, all close to him. Only Thol had seen it for himself. He had not been ready to take Cour or his mother to the site. Ready for what? Why did he not share the site with more, with the entirety of his people? Certainly they had as much a right to see it and to share in its wonder as he.

"I cannot answer that, Aye. My mind does not know why this is the path I chose. But I feel in my heart, still, that it was the right path."

The woman adjusted her bulk on the mammoth fur on which she sat. He could tell that she was uncomfortable. The conversation was making her uncomfortable, as it was he.

"What do you hear, when you are in the cave?" she asked him.

William Burcher 73

"Hear?" He paused, thinking. She was asking him more than this. There were more words, another question beneath her words. "It is not of a *hearing* that I am aware when I am in the darkness of the cave. It is more of a knowing. A feeling. It is like a dream."

"Do you not hear the song?"

He replied puzzled, confused, "I hear the silence of the cave. To me it is the silence of the—"

"The Mother. Yes. I too know this silence. But there is more. It is beneath the silence. It is heard in a different way than one hears with her ear. I hear it when I am there. Thom-Ar was unable to hear this as I do."

"Tell me more of this song, Aye. Please."

She was quiet for a moment, as if searching for words, as if she needed the right breath to say what she would say. "The song is as speech, from a time before our own." She paused once again. "Before I go further, I want you to tell me, Garr-Eth. What does the cave mean to you?"

"Within the cave one is aware of the Mother. On its walls are her words. She speaks to us through the images on its walls." He had not hesitated, surprising himself as he spoke. And the silence of the large room seemed to swallow those words. Aye-Lin made no response as she breathed deep, the man aware of her large soft breasts heaving forth slowly, rhythmically with her chest.

"As I said, Thom was unable to hear the song as I do. I believe it is due to my … form, as an expression of the Mother, that I can hear this. Women are closer to the Mother than men. Our bodies nourish the next generations, as the Mother cares for us. Have you heard, Garr-Eth, the sound of the wind at the entrance to the cave?"

He nodded in assent. "I have heard, too, the wind from its depths."

"The song is like this. It is also like an avalanche in winter, or a rock breaking apart as it comes crashing down a cliff, or the fall of water above the Zhar-Nues. It is all of these things and more. The song is sung with words. There are words buried in the ageless sounds of the earth that I hear in the cave."

"And these words, were they heard by those who painted the images?"

"I believe so. The images appear to me to dance to the song. They are connected to it."

"What is the song, Aye-Lin?"

"It is the song of the Mother. I hear her sing."

"What then, does she say?"

"I was hoping that you knew the answer to that question, my son."

"I have longed to understand it since I discovered the cave as a boy. This longing has haunted me from that day. I knew then that the cave spoke with the voice of the Mother, as I gazed on the painted walls with my companion dog, Aurochs, by the light of a torch. I also felt the presence of my father, long ago passed. I shouted down and out at the Mother when she would not speak to me. Her breath kissed my face and my neck. Then my father was there, Aye. He was a part of the Mother. I have within me the desire to hear these words, to know them. I want to know what the Mother speaks. This desire consumes me. It is toward this end that I now live my life. I feel that this desire has changed me. I am different now than the other men of this time and place."

"I too have this desire, Garr-Eth. She speaks, but I know not what she says. This haunts me my every moment. It was so for Thom-Ar as well."

"Why then do we keep such a secret held so tightly, so closely to our own breasts?" Garr-Eth lamented, the force in his voice a felt thing.

"Because we know in our deeper selves that what the earth says will be terrifying. Once we hear these words, we will never be the same."

Her words were fists, striking him in the chest.

"And yet I crave them, like nothing else still," he said slowly, looking down.

"As a deer for the water, I crave them too," she replied without hesitation. "Tell me. Have you had any … visions?"

"I am not—"

"Dreams."

"Yes. Always. But they are shadows and fog."

"Is there a woman in the dreams?"

"There is a woman."

"A woman. Yes. She is young. She is alien. But it is through her I believe the cave will speak."

"Have you seen other things in your dreams, Aye?"

"Yes," she said, and then hesitated.

"What have you seen?" he repeated gently, her reluctance obvious.

"I have seen my own body, violated."

Both fell silent then. The fire in the hearth had lessened, fading into a mere glow, only a hint of warmth issuing from it. It had grown cold in the great room. But Garr-Eth did not rise to tend it, sitting motionless across from Aye as both considered deeply what had befallen. They remained quiet and still until a soft sound came, the sound of a shifting of leather and fur. Looking up, Garr-Eth saw that Durr-Es was crouching in the darkest corner of the room. Their eyes met for a moment before the younger man stood and walked quickly out. How long the young man had been there, how much he had heard, Garr-Eth could only wonder.

———————

The dream came to him after hours of fitful, restless sleep. He had never before known such discomfort in rest. Aye-Lin's words gnawed at his heart, like some rodent gnawing on a root, burrowing deep. And the gnawing was fueled by the profound fatigue of the day.

The dream began as shadow and fog. First were the mere hints of darker objects set against a lighter background until these focused, materialized into vast structures standing tall against the backdrop of a grey and stormy sky. He wanted to cry out in shock and terror at what he saw, at the realization that these forms were not themselves of the earth. They'd been made, constructed out of formed stone and flattened, translucent ice. The structures were as tall as the mountains of the Zhar-Nues and they were harsh and terrible.

The smells of the place assaulted him like a cold wind of rain and snow, pelting him in the face. Sulphur and smoke, bad water and lightning. Everywhere was the scent of something hard and cold, to him like blood. He gagged. He wanted to choke it out of him, vomit it from his body, to purge the foul poison of it. But then a cool wind blew in from the west carrying with it the familiar smell of rain. His eyes focused and he saw mountains in the distance, their peaks capped with snow and the air cleared enough that he could slow his body's reaction, thought returning. This was merely a strange land, he told himself. It was still the earth.

There were people here. His momentary relief evaporating as his attention was drawn to them. They scurried about, strange and stunted. Many of them were obese. Most of them looked unhealthy, as if they suffered from disease. They walked with halting, staccato steps, their bodies imbalanced and deformed. These were people who did not exist among his own, who indeed could not. How could they not succumb to the physical demands of this place? All of them were completely clothed—more to hide their physical deformities he thought, than to stave off the wind or the cold. Some had darker skin, like the travelers coming to the Zhar-Nues from the South. Others had skin lighter than he and still others appeared to be of races he had never before encountered. They seemed older collectively than he imagined a people could be. They smelled of herbs and medicines, not of people. This made sense to him. They were all suffering from disease and were being cared for by healers. Even the young ones. Most were amazingly ugly.

None paid him mind. Indeed, most did not heed each other. It was as if they were all strangers to one another, traveling for the first time in a foreign land. Yet they seemed to know where they were going. It made no sense to him. Each and every one was elsewhere, not present in that place or that moment. It was as if each were dreaming a dream, and only vaguely there with him enough that they didn't bump into things or each other—although this happened occasionally.

A few of them talked to themselves, sometimes full and animated conversations speaking a totally foreign tongue. He knew of this affliction; it was a madness that he'd seen in people who were about to die. Many looked only at the ground, merely glancing upward occasionally. They were as people who rose from their sleep and walked around, still living out the night's dreams in the physical world. They were only half conscious or still asleep.

He saw that a few of them were led by small alien animals that might have been a stunted, misshapen variety of fox or jackal, most of these themselves exhibiting the same obesity and vacancy as that of the man or woman attached to them by ropes.

Some of the people had encased themselves in the same flattened ice and rock of which the structures were made. These encasements sometimes moved rapidly, propelled by what might have been a powerful, angry, growling animal trapped within its bowels. Those within the encasements sat reclined and seemingly on edge. Many appeared to be angry, perhaps in reaction to the angry beast enclosed within.

As the images were first vague and amorphous, so too were the sounds. As the dream progressed these did not sharpen, however, like the images. Their magnitude increased steadily until it was the chaotic buzzing of bees—a horrible, assaultive, living thing. It was the sharpening of chert knives and spearpoints on grinding rock; the thunder of a storm; the dying screams of rabbits speared by a pack of cackling boys. He wanted to hold his hands against the sides of his head but even then the cacophony would become a thing more intimately felt, the lower, deeper more frightening sounds experienced within as a vibration in his liver and his gut.

The whites of his eyes flashed like a trapped, hunted animal as he spun around, looking up and then out, aware of only horror, monstrosity. Searching for substance in a white-capped sea, for familiarity in this province of aliens, he saw a man dressed in black standing on the corner of the path of the moving encasements. The man was roughly his age, tall, and did not appear diseased. This man appeared able to use his body for more than the sickly, broken locomotion of most of the others. With him too was a dog. It was an obvious dog, although black and tan and smaller than those he knew. He was also alert, clearly present in time and place. Perhaps this man knew something.

He ran to him, hands up in greeting. He began to speak, his words bursting forth in a language foreign and shocking even to him. He quickly shut his mouth, then tried again. The language was a horrific, alien thing—like a song sung by a chorus of massive, terrifying birds. The man in black clothing took a step back from his approach. His dog began to bark and bare its teeth, wagging its tail in anticipatory excitement and aggression. The man's right hand went to his hip, to the strange object attached to him that Garr-Eth knew was some sort of weapon. The man then began barking orders, his words echoing the dog's bluster. And he saw that this man was not as he'd hoped—his eyes were dark and tired and set before a harsh and judging mind.

Then she appeared. Angel of feminine grace. She stepped from the entrance of a cave buried inside one of the strange structures. She saw instantly the situation's peril. With a second's glance she recognized both him and his bewilderment. She stepped in between him and the man in black and barked her own foreign words. The man stepped back, restraining his dog, both walking off into the background as the woman remained, her dark eyes meeting his. In his anxiety he saw both similarity and another thing there in her eyes. He saw himself, and he saw the alien. She motioned for him to follow her and he hurried to her side, as her shadow.

They walked along the same paths the diseased did, she taking hurried athletic strides, paying only minor heed to the others, but dodging their wayward meanderings. She suddenly was his guide to this country, and more. He was her puppet, her child and utterly her subject, her thrall, he followed. She would

William Burcher 79

lead him to further horror or to salvation from this place. Despite the surroundings, his fear, he could not take his eyes from her. She looked like one of his people, of the same race and blood. She was athletically built with strong legs and core. The outlines of the muscles of her buttocks flexed and swayed in her tight black pants as she moved. Her breasts were not overly large but well-formed. Her hair was black with an auburn tone. And she was aware. She was present. Her mind was not occupied with its self-obsessions. She seemed to see her world as he did. She continually glanced back at him with knowing eyes that seemed to say something. They whispered apology.

They stopped at a cave, the entrance to which lay off a smaller path and this woman, this angel produced a device from a pocket in her jacket which enabled the entrance to open. Briefly and for only a moment he saw that she too wore a weapon under her jacket as the man in black had. She held the door open for him and he followed her into a darker space than the outside, lit with fires void of heat or flame. She walked up a set of stairs, her wide hips, her body swaying with the steps in a rhythmic dance. She continued to glance back at him, their eyes meeting in wordless communion. They came to another entrance constructed of highly crafted wood, to a further chamber in this cave and she pushed this open. She stepped in and touched, pulled his wrist toward her, the gesture simple but charged with energy. A spark, electric shot up his spine. Into this cave, this dwelling, and his eyes were upon her. She smelled of flowers and spice. He could see that her nipples had hardened under her blouse, itself the color of blood. She took off her jacket and removed the strange weapon, carefully placing this on a wooden ledge away from all other things. And finally, taking a step closer without losing his gaze, she began to remove her blouse.

His mouth watering, breaths coming in quickened, shortened gasps, heart pounding beneath his sternum like a drum to dance to, he watched as she removed the shirt entirely. She paused for a moment before running her hands down across her breasts, propping them up slightly before looking back up at him. She licked her lips, her mouth opened and she spoke, in his own tongue, her voice like honey and wine. "This is not to be, Garr-Eth," she said.

He awoke then with a shout, sweating and cold, his erection taut and pulsing with his heartbeats in the open night air.

7

PORTENTS

Their progress was slow up the steep hillside. Aye-Lin's bulk prevented her moving at more than the pace of a small child. Both Garr-Eth and Thol-Ur assisted her walk when they needed to but it would be dark by the time the three reached the cave. Garr-Eth was impressed that the woman managed to progress as she did up the vertiginous trail. Before they set out from the settlement she explained to both men that she believed taking the trip to the cave together was of supreme importance.

"Perhaps what each of us was unable to do by ourselves, we will be able to do together. We must learn the message of the cave. My nights are haunted by my memories of the song."

"My nights are haunted by other things," Garr-Eth thought to himself as they set out. He decided that he would tell neither Thol nor Aye about his dream. A shot of electricity ran through his body as he thought of the world he'd seen, and of the woman, so significant was her memory.

They began the trek in the morning hours, when the sun was still climbing overhead. The trail, first made by beasts and now used by both men and animals, began meandering gently through the thick green places along the river. It slowly ascended into the rocky places where outcrops of limestone rose all around. There the trail grew steeper, more treacherous and it was here that they slowed.

It was a warm day, the sun shining brilliant in a cloudless sky, though the heavy air held the promise of afternoon rain. As they inched their way up the trail and into the higher places the clouds began to build, the wind picking up until it became another force above and beyond the climb itself with which to contend. They would pause frequently to allow Aye-Lin to catch her breath and rest. These pauses became insufferable, the wind howling all around whipping up sand and grit into their faces and their eyes. Aye-Lin's long braid had worked its way loose and her hair became a chaotic vortex about her face. They suffered in silence as was right, and to conserve the breath needed to force their voices above the maelstrom and din. They continued onward, upward, each trudging through the muck and mire of the soddened trail when the clouds burst and torrents of rain fell upon them. They too were quickly soaked and cold. They stopped momentarily as if to seek shelter, Garr-Eth's eyes meeting Aye-Lin's, her wet hair now plastered on her face. She interjected, breath heavy, before he could say a word.

"We will not turn back, my son. I know I slow you. I know, too, that you will not leave me. I am sorry for my bulk and my age. But we must continue ..."

"The cave will be here another day, Aye! I fear we are tempting a rough fate if we continue! Perhaps the Mother longs to keep her secret from us!" Garr-Eth shouted to the woman above the tumult.

"That she has already done long enough! No ... at the end of this day we will know of what she speaks. This angry air only strengthens my belief!"

Garr-Eth noticed that she was shaking from the wet and the

William Burcher 83

cold and the exertion, her bulk convulsing lightly under her woven clothes. The whites of her eyes, though, spoke of determination. He looked at Thol-Ur and the man understood instantly: both would double their efforts at assistance, despite Aye's protests. Garr-Eth removed his outer layer made from the skin of a megaceros, the giant deer, and placed this about her shoulders. They continued on up the path until they reached the heavily timbered high places and after a hard time emerged, finally, into the clouds.

There they stopped allowing the big woman to recover. The place was quiet, the rain had stopped, and it was utterly calm. They listened to the sound of their own hearts, their own breath and simultaneously all three smiled at one another.

"Nothing lasts forever, my friends. Wait long enough and a hardship will abate; a dark sky will lighten; a storm will pass," Garr-Eth spoke to the other two. "It will not be much further. Already I see the haze ahead darkening, though. Night will soon be upon us."

Garr-Eth began once more on the trail and with a sigh and a heave Aye-Lin followed, trailed closely by Thol-Ur. Within a half hour they had ascended further, surfacing above the cloud ceiling. All three breathed in the sight. Their home, their valley was completely enshrouded in the grey of cloud cover, soft and ephemeral in the waning twilight. Peaks as high or higher than they, however, stood out above the veil. And above that, the sky was as clear as vacuum. They continued the final stretch to the cave's entrance in silent reverence at the beauty before them, stopping at the ledge upon which Garr-Eth had spent many a night in wonder, pondering the images and the message of the cave. The dark now was nearly total, only a slight crescent moon low in the western sky.

As Garr-Eth watched the moon for a moment he heard Aye-Lin gasp in both wonder and fright. "What is—?" And he stopped short, his head toward the sky. Thol and Aye were looking in the same direction, their mouths open. A wave of green and shimmering light broke and crashed across the northern sky. Another formed from the air and followed it, like a snake gliding through the water.

"What is it?" Thol asked.

"I have heard of this …"

"It is like nothing—"

"A traveler from the North spoke of this once at the Fire," Garr-Eth said. "He had a name for it. It was foreign. Aurora. He called it the Aurora. He spoke of flames in the sky. He said it was seen most commonly in northern lands and most often in winter. He described it as a green and red light and fire in the heavens. No one else that night knew of what he spoke and few, I think, believed him. His words did not present a fraction of the truth of it …"

"My God. My God," was all that Thol-Ur could say, repeating this softly to himself.

"It is a wonder …" Aye muttered unconsciously.

The waves of shimmering green began to change and flow, exhibiting other colors at the fringes of their flame—red and violet and even a potent white, pure light. There was a central core to it far off in the northern sky near the horizon. Filaments, branches of flame would break off, flow of their own accord arcing across the entirety of the sky and would then seem to merge once again into the core. It was pulsating, flowing, shimmering and alive. All three stood in awe, mouths open to the wonder of the sight.

"Our presence here in this place is being acknowledged by the Mother," Thol-Ur whispered.

"It is meant for us, this night. How could it be otherwise?" Garr-Eth said.

Without taking her eyes from the green and living fire and light in the sky, Aye-Lin spoke in a curiously deep voice, both men listening intently. "The song of the cave, Garr-Eth, the song of the Mother. The song of which I spoke the night of Thom's pyre. What I see now above with my eyes; my mind has heard. This sight above is the dance of the Mother's song. This sight and the song are the same."

They watched the sky until the light lessened and finally faded back into the north. Their bodies ached from the strain of

William Burcher 85

prolonged and focused attention. They then mused at their ca-
pacities to observe and comprehend the promised, further won-
ders of that night.

———————

The air inside was warmer than out, and always felt the same,
constant. Something else was different now, however. There was
a smell, a presence that had not been there a few weeks before
when Garr-Eth had last laid his footprints on its floor. As all
three entered the cave he halted them. His torch was still as he
froze, a sliver of depleted coal and ash fell from the torch onto
the floor.

"Do you feel it, Aye?"

"I don't know," she replied.

"I smell it," Thol said. "It is the smell of another man's torch."

Thol quickly found a single set of prints on the cave's floor.
They hinted at the recent passage of a man, possibly young, not
substantial in body. He could not find a matching set leaving the
cave from the only entrance they knew of. "He must still be inside. I believe him to be alone."

Garr-Eth's heart froze. Who else knew of the cave? Who was
this man, and what was he doing? "Thol, quickly. Put out your
torch."

Both men quickly extinguished their flames. In an instant the
darkness of the cave was total—a black that seemed to suck the
air out of them, or seemed to discourage breath for fear of its
disturbance. Slowly their eyes adjusted to the void and Garr-Eth
was the first to see the dim flicker of a light deep into the cavern.
Thol quickly saw it as well. Aye did not. All three began walking
toward the light as slowly, as quietly as they could, careful not to
disturb the walls upon which images were painted or to slip in
the soft clay of the floor.

As their eyes adjusted further to the darkness the going became easier and they could see where they placed their feet. The flickering light ahead became greater too as they approached. Still, there was no sound other than their breath and the beating of their hearts. Garr-Eth's began to pound heavily in his chest as they approached. He questioned what would be required of him within a few moments, whether a fight or worse lay ahead. He was thankful that Thol was with him; the man was the most fearsome he'd ever seen with the dagger at his side. He also was thankful for Aye's presence. The woman's wisdom could always be counted on.

They'd gone far now, hundreds of yards into the deep and the light ahead lit their way completely. He thought he could see shadows moving ahead, too, though he did not trust his vision here. They approached as close as they dared and he marveled at the stealth they'd maintained. Aye had been absolutely silent and he placed his hand on her shoulder both to reassure her, thank her, and to communicate that she should remain. He and Thol began creeping closer, the anticipation of who or what they'd find growing with every moment. They came to a large boulder, a section of the cave's ceiling which had collapsed to the ground giving them cover as they peered around its edges.

A small fire lay on the floor thirty feet from them in the cave's largest chamber, the location of most of its painted images. Garr-Eth could see the light from the flames throwing shadows across the most extensive panel—where a herd of horses appeared to run and play in view of a nearby pride of lions. Light and shadow worked along the textured walls, playing with the images, making them move. Although he'd seen the horses and the lion many times before, he was still haunted by them.

Thol tapped his shoulder, then pointed in the direction of a corner at the far end of the chamber. There, images of simple beasts became strange and disturbing, morphed into more human forms. Seated on the floor in front of the most disquieting of the images—that of a woman, voluptuous and motherly in body giving birth to a deformed, stunted, demonic beast—was a man, his back toward them. Garr-Eth could tell that the man was young, his body still nearly that of a boy's. He felt Thol relax, as he did. There would be no fight. But still, who was he? What was he doing here? He could tell that Thol was waiting for him, deferring to him to make the decision as to what to do next. He paused for a moment and then stood up fully, stepping out from behind the rock. He motioned for Thol to remain.

"Friend," he said in a quiet voice. He then realized the chamber was too large, swallowing his whispered words. "Friend," he said louder, and the young man turned toward him in fright.

"Who are you!?" he demanded in clear terror, and Garr-Eth realized that he himself was still not visible. He stepped further out into the light, his arms down, palms outward. As he stepped closer he could see the man's expression turn from terror to something else, something less immediate, but nonetheless dark. Garr-Eth realized that he knew this man's face, as the man seemed to know his and for just a moment he was baffled.

"I see that you can speak when it suits you, Durr-Es," Garr-Eth said after a pause. And the young man merely stared at him in reply.

Thol-Ur and Aye-Lin heard the exchange and came out into the light as well, flanking Garr-Eth on both of his sides. They too were puzzled.

Aye spoke out to Durr-Es first.

"How did you find this place?" she demanded of him. He remained silent, his face betraying fear. He seemed confused and unsure of where next to take the exchange. He was nervous, anxious and to Garr-Eth he looked like a cornered beast. The three of them offered no threat but that posed by the light of potential witness. He suspected though that to certain people this was the most threatening position he and his companions could occupy. He spoke up.

"All three of us clearly heard you speak, Durr-Es. For honor's sake it is best that you continue plainly with us now." Although he was unsure how persuasive his words had been. Among his people dishonesty and falsehood were looked upon with disgust. It was offensive both to the liar and the one lied to. A deceit betrayed weakness, a desire to mask the truth of a thing and in most cases the truth of one's self. He allowed some flexibility with Durr-Es however, knowing the young man's difficult background, the total loss of his family at such an early age. He wanted to understand the man's reasoning.

"You have been in my house for years, Durr-Es. Thom-Ar and I have treated you as one of our own. I am puzzled by this," Aye-Lin spoke. Her eyes were confused, questioning. When the young man still did not answer she spoke further. "How did you find this place, Durr-Es? Why are you here now? And why have you played such a role in our house? Why have you pretended to be mute for so long? What possible advantage could this have brought you?"

The man looked at her in response, the whites of his eyes showing. All three plainly saw that he was debating with himself whether to speak with them further or not, debating the prospect of his falsehood being laid out before him and these three others in the clear and honest light of the flames of his small fire. The light still produced shadows that danced upon the walls of the cave around them. The painted images were as powerful and mysterious as ever. The eyes of the beasts painted there were watching the scene.

"Do you realize where you are, Durr-Es?" Thol spoke up, unlike him in a situation such as this. Garr-Eth did not underestimate the force of the words, born of such a physically powerful and intimidating man. When Thol spoke the walls echoed with the baritone of his voice. "This cave is a holy place. You are in the Mother's womb. You are in the presence of mystery. You cannot maintain a falsehood here. You stand plainly before her eyes and ours. Speak, boy."

And Durr-Es sunk down into himself, his body relaxing, the tension flowing from his face. He seemed resigned to his discovery, but after a few breaths he appeared reanimated, as if in his mind he had decided something else. Garr-Eth was suddenly saddened by this man.

"Yes," the young man said. His voice was surprising to them, high-pitched but well-practiced and seemingly well-used. He spoke too with volume. "I have maintained in Thom-Ar's household an un-real thing. I can speak, as you have discovered."

"Why would you practice such a deception?" Aye repeated her question to him. He was reluctant to answer her, hesitating.

"You would not understand, Aye-Lin. None of you would," was his reply. His eyes flashed in the dim light of the fire as he spoke.

"We are here listening, Durr-Es. You have from us the gift of space and patience," said Garr-Eth. He sensed that the boy wanted something from them.

"You, you most of all cannot understand," Durr-Es replied. "You, the chosen of the Zhar-Nues. Blessed by the Mother herself, in all that you do. You cannot understand, Garr-Eth." He turned toward the cave wall closest to him, gazing away from them and upon the images. "Just as you cannot understand this."

The three looked at one another, questioning.

"What, Durr-Es, do you think these images are?" Aye asked.

"They are what you and he thought they were," he said, looking quickly at Garr-Eth. "But they are more. You two could not decipher them, because you are who you are. And I am who I am."

"What does that mean, boy?" Thol-Ur asked.

"It means that I have suffered. I alone. No one can understand the depths of pain the Mother has brought into my life. My burden is heavy. Heavier than either of you could carry." The young man rose from his seated position, still facing the wall of images. He began to pace, his energy level rising. Garr-Eth wondered for a moment if he were about to attack them physically, as ill-advised as that would be. He looked the boy up and down for a weapon. Only a dagger was at his side, still sheathed.

"Only I have lost everything. From the age of eight years I had nothing, nothing but my own strength to endure. And mine is the strength of character, or internal fortitude, a thing different entirely from that which you and this beast possess," he spat, glancing only quickly in the direction of the two men. "You could not have endured. I lost everything. Everything! And then what came after that? Slavery! I was sold into slavery to pay some debt. And to whom? A beast of a man. A troglodyte. A man no better than a Neanderthal—a man possessing only the gifts that you, Garr-Eth, possess as well—physical strength. Skills of the hunt. Skills of oration. These are the skills of beasts. Endurance, and cunning—these are the skills of men. These are my skills. You cannot understand them.

"Only I was clever enough, patient enough, skilled enough to convince everyone of my meekness and infirmity. You all then became accustomed to my presence. You spoke as if I were never there. And I learned. I learned the value of shadows. One does not pay attention to shadows. One ignores them. And one ignores what hides among them.

"I was present during your talk with Aye-Lin the night of the pyre and listened intently as you spoke of this cave. I guessed at its location having observed Thom many times travel in this direction. And the trail was easy enough to find. A she-beast of the kind you have brought here, Garr-Eth, is bound to leave a well-defined trail. Her trips here in the past trampled and trod the earth like a rhinoceros."

Aye-Lin was calm as she watched Durr-Es' speech but her eyes betrayed a sadness, a hurt, a betrayal. Garr-Eth maintained a neutral composure. The anger threatened to rise inside him until it burst. He could feel Thol-Ur's potent emotion as the man stood beside him watching.

"I tell you all of this now because none of it matters anymore. I need not maintain my infirmity any longer. I came to this cave out of curiosity, and because I felt it wrong of you three to possess its secrets for yourself. Now I possess the secret. And more."

"What are you talking about, Durr-Es?" Garr-Eth spoke.

"I am talking about the real secret of this place. I am talking about that which neither you nor your she-beast had the capacity to discover for yourselves. I am talking about the cave's message."

Garr-Eth looked at Aye, confused. Durr-Es could not possibly know what this sacred place had been whispering for years. How could this angry man, full of his own darkness, discover such a thing? There was a silence filled only by the small fire, its flames lapping gently at its remaining fuel, while Durr-Es allowed his words to be considered. Another sound, the deep moaning of the cave, the resonant sub-sonic voice of the Mother could be sensed by the three as well.

"Tell us, Durr-Es, what you believe this cave to be. Tell us in your own words, with your own heart," Garr-Eth said quietly.

"Do you not sense it now? Do I have to repeat the truth of this to you, Garr-Eth? This place is not the womb of the Mother, as you and Aye suggested that night when I was listening in the dark. It is not the womb, my friend. It is … this." Durr-Es pointed to his forehead, to the low-center of it, between his eyes but higher so that his eyes and his finger formed a triangle. Garr-Eth knew instantly that what he said was the truth. The cave was the inner voice of the Mother, not her womb.

"These images along the walls—the wisent, the elk, the horses, the wooly rhino, the lion and the caribou—these were attempts by our ancestors, by the people before us to not only put the words of the Mother into our own speech. But they tried, too, to capture the words in time, and to communicate them to others who did not hear her song."

"Do you hear the song, Durr-Es?" Aye asked.

"Of course, woman. You are not unique in this regard. I hear it. It is as if the earth were moving in my mind. It is like the rock, made liquid, and flowing. It is deep, almost a felt thing. It sings to me and the song is like my own suffering. It is a voice telling me and only me a powerful message. This message was meant for me alone. I am the chosen. Not you, Garr-Eth, with your other beastly gifts. Not you, Aye-Lin, with your sagging breasts and foul and dried up crevasse. The Mother chose me!"

"I am sick of this bile," Thol growled. He moved toward Durr-Es quickly and before Garr-Eth could restrain him he was before the young man. Durr-Es squealed with an animal's shriek such as a rabbit or a rodent would make as an eagle grasps it in its talons, terrified of its own destruction. Thol did not destroy the boy, however. He merely struck him moderately on the side of his head with his open palm. This was enough though to knock Durr-Es unconscious. Thol caught his body as it collapsed so that it would not be damaged by the fall. Aye-Lin appeared made dumb by the speed and decisiveness of the act. Garr-Eth could do nothing but shake his head.

"I will never underestimate your ferocity, Thol-Ur," he said to his friend. "I cannot condone this, but I do not fault you for it. Come, let us take him outside into the night air, away from this place."

Thol hoisted the limp body onto his shoulder without any real effort. Garr-Eth re-lit his once-extinguished torch in Durr-Es' small fire before covering this in loose earth and rock with a sweep of his foot. Aye was quiet as they began to make their way back toward the entrance to the cave. Garr-Eth saw that she watched the images closely as she walked.

"I believe that he spoke the truth, Garr-Eth," she said. "He described the song as I hear it. He knows the words of the song. And I feel tired, very tired at the news."

They came to a wall nearer the entrance painted with red ochre and yellow pigment with hundreds of impressions of the artists' hands. Garr-Eth stopped, looking upon the images as he had a hundred times before. His heart too was low. Aye stopped walking and stood with him.

"There are words here, Aye. But I fear that I will not live to hear them spoken, but by the voice of that child on Thol's shoulder. How could this be?"

She could not answer his question and merely stood with him until they both felt Thol's presence, coaxing them out of the cave and into the night. Aye followed the man out first, Garr-Eth remaining for a moment at the mouth of the cave, invoking in low words a prayer of understanding. He thought the words impotent as they left his mouth. And the three continued out of the cave and into the dark, calm night, pausing only briefly before finding the small trail leading back down into the river valley. Aye-Lin did not look back as she began the descent, following behind Thol as he still carried the boy. Garr-Eth took the rear and for a final moment looked back in the direction of the cave. He listened intently.

He heard something soft, something quiet, something in the

distance he hadn't heard before—a low and mournful noise he thought expressed the passage of time, like the horns his hunters blew in triumph after a kill, only deeper, longer, stretched somehow. But this faded from his perception after he became attentive to it. In sadness he turned back around and followed the others down the mountain wondering at what he thought he knew of the world.

Like the others, he walked in silence through a night that grew calm, quiet as death. Durr-Es began to groan softly, waking from his sleep, as they made their way quietly down the mountain. Thol did not pay him any mind, walking as silently as the rest, seemingly unaffected by the weight he bore. The groaning became other things, other sounds, the beginnings of words that echoed across the night. "Sep …" he began to repeat, stuttering in a way that initially made Garr-Eth believe that he was merely groaning with Thol's hard and pounding steps. The word began to form, however. "Separ … separate," he repeated, still not fully conscious. They listened and Thol, responding, picked up his pace, walking harder, faster than before. "You … will … separate."

"Thol. Stop," Garr-Eth said. "He is saying something. In his haze."

The big man complied. He stopped for a moment, still standing. He lifted the body from his shoulders and placed the boy on the ground, propped against a tree. Durr-Es continued to moan softly with each breath. And he continued his half-audible chant. "Separate … you will separate." Garr-Eth drew closer, kneeling down. The boy's eyes were still closed. He felt Aye standing close behind him.

"What are you saying, boy?" he asked. He did not receive a response. "Speak, if you must."

"He is merely mumbling in his fog, Garr-Eth," Thol commented.

"I would like, then, to know what this boy dreams about in his sleep."

"Durr-Es. Son. Speak," Aye added softly, in a tone more motherly than either man had heard before.

"Separate. You will separate. Children."

"It is gibberish—"

"Separate?" Aye asked. "Is that what he—?" Her question was cut off as Durr-Es opened his eyes, blinking in the light of Thol's torch. He appeared awake, fully conscious, but looking off into the darkness. And then he spoke. His words seemed not his own, of a different time, a different voice. They emerged from him in a deeper octave than his own and with an emotion, a care that none believed the boy capable of. The words came from his lips in perfect clarity.

"My children. Born of my flesh. I long to speak with you as you speak among yourselves. But time is a different thing to us. Your minds were once at one with my own as your bodies are, but this will not always be so. You will separate from me. You will seek meaning and fulfillment where it cannot be found. For millennia you will forget, and during this time you will ravage my body for your own ends. Like your own mother in childbirth I will nearly be destroyed so that you in your infancy can grow. But of this body I freely give."

The boy stopped speaking and closed his eyes as Aye-Lin collapsed onto the earth.

8

BLOOD

The days after were fogged by the haze of anti-climax. Aye-Lin's family nursed Durr-Es, as he showed signs of fever the morning after they'd returned to the settlement on the banks of the river. Garr-Eth had not wanted him to stay in his own residence and after the young man's fever abated he did not demand he leave, but strongly suggested that his fortunes lay elsewhere. Durr-Es hadn't protested as he'd taken up his charade once again, not speaking as if he were unable. His eyes though had spoken in a plain voice for him. They were reptilian, the eyes of a serpent trapped in a corner. He looked as though he were about to strike out at any moment with a venomous bite. He left immediately without any fanfare as his friends numbered few in that place. Garr-Eth followed behind him as he walked along the thin trail that led up-river and watched as he disappeared far upstream, passing along a bend and behind a cliff of rock.

Their laws were simple and clear. Harm no-one. Contribute when necessary, help when needed. The boy had not broken any of these traditional tenets, but Garr-Eth knew now that he was capable of hatred of a kind he'd never before encountered. As the boy receded from view he had the sense that there was business between them unfinished, but his hand in the matter had been played. He would see the boy again.

But he had not time to dwell on this eventuality. The annual hunt of the steppe wisent was nearing. He and the rest of the settlement were busy with the preparations. If all went well the hunt could provide enough meat and raw materials to last his entire people a year or more. As head-man he was rapidly becoming acquainted with the practical necessities of his position, and more largely those of the physical world. There were times though at night, with his day ended and his mind too weary to protest, when the voice of Durr-Es speaking words not his own haunted him as a spectre.

"My children," he would hear. " … of this body I freely give." And most disturbingly, the word "separate" would occupy his thoughts, as a shadow, a tormentor he could not shake. It was during these times that his heart would pound in his chest, his breaths would shorten and he would feel a confounding, insidious fear. He would swallow this, push it back down into his body and sometimes even he could sleep. But most often he would lie awake at night restless and sweating, his body tense and cold. He knew that his future was tied unbreakably to the cave, and now to the words Durr-Es had spoken. From this truth, though, he hid. The needs of the present, the needs of his people required his attention fully. He was not yet ready to face the aurochs, as Thol-Ur would say. Neither Thol, nor Aye-Lin had broken their tacit agreement to remain silent on the events at the cave that night. A pause, before the plunge from the precipice, his mind told him when he allowed it.

The hunt would involve men and women from three settlements and as head-man of the Zhar-Nues, he would be its principal. Already scouts had set out from the settlement just to the west of his own, led by an impressive, respected man just past his physical prime, Alle-Nok. As if to fight this realization himself, Alle would always participate in the most challenging, the most brutal of physical contests. He led the scouting party which just a day prior located the herd of wisent, high above the Zhar-Nues, a day's travel to the northeast. The herd was near a site Garr-Eth knew of only vaguely—an ancient place, mentioned only by old men. The location possessed infrastructure already in place to make possible a wisent jump—a mass drive of the entire herd off a cliff. His troubled heart thrilled at this prospect. A jump had not been attempted by his people since before his birth. He'd consulted many of the elders of the settlement and only a few of them remembered one such undertaking. All of those who remembered the event described it exactly how he envisioned it—as nothing less than spectacular. Accomplishing such a feat successfully would be seen as an omen of blessing, the Mother empowering his leadership.

He worried that none of the old men who last participated in a wisent jump would be able to participate in the actual hunt, or in any of the preparations for that matter—all were too frail, too enfeebled. Both of the other clans were in similar straits. All had decided to learn as much as they could from any of the elders with knowledge of the last Jump, and each clan would appoint one or two individuals as "experts" after they'd studied the elders' memories. He'd tasked Thol-Ur and Cour-Ett with collecting all the knowledge they could from the elders of the Zhar-Nues. Thol was not much of a speaker, but he was an excellent, attentive listener and he possessed a limitless memory—frequently reciting verbatim the words of the elders when asked a question. Cour-Ett was simply the most competent hunter still living. She knew the wisent, and could think like them. The success of a Jump was determined by effectively manipulating the perceptions and behavior of a herd.

The clans agreed to meet at the proposed site a few weeks before the actual Jump. The herd was being watched closely by Alle-Nok's scouts who kept them all well-informed about its movements. Once the herd began to head south, as it would soon, the clans would need to act quickly. The day of their meeting was bright, clear, cloudless and hot. Garr-Eth's heart swelled with excitement as he and his companions caught their first glimpse of the area. The site was a high, bare plateau covered in thick grass just beginning to dry and golden. The plain, a few miles wide, was surrounded by the foothills of larger peaks to the east, and wooded, rolling hills to the west. It came down from the higher steppe to the north, a natural basin sculpted by the glaciers of the past. Beneath them, a mile or two distant, was the cliff over which the Jump would happen. Although perhaps only 20 or 30 feet high, in their eyes it was a wondrous thing. It was clearly a gift of the Mother, a thing to be taken advantage of with gratitude.

Garr-Eth arrived with Cour-Ett and Thol-Ur and they quickly found the valley overlook, breathing hard and deep, each damp and glistening with the sweat of the fast and strenuous hike. They believed themselves alone, the others not yet arrived. The three companions sensed the value of quiet in the place and remained so for moments, each imagining a herd of hundreds of one-ton animals thundering down the valley, a cloud of dust rising high into the air behind.

"It is a magnificent thing, is it not?" Garr-Eth finally spoke, almost laughing, as if a boy. The two merely glanced at him, their eyes lit in agreement and wonder. Garr-Eth was first to hear the footfalls of other men and turned to see two coming up the thin trail behind them. Alle-Nok was with a single, middle-aged man, a relative of Aye's he believed, Tote-Lon. The two seemed in equal good spirit.

"Garr-Eth! You beat us to it! What do you think, my friend?" Alle shouted, still breathing hard.

"I think that we are smiled upon. I, too, am grinning like a child. It is a beautiful sight to behold, Alle."

"You'll see, too, that our preparations will need to be few. The site as it was used generations ago is still intact. Is Hoss-Te yet arrived?"

The five each made the sign of greeting and understanding to one another, placing their right hands upright beneath their jaws, pausing before lowering them slowly to their chests. Alle grasped Garr-Eth by the shoulder and held him as he pointed out to the valley.

"We will need killers, *many* killers to complete the task, as the cliff is not high enough to dispatch the animals immediately. Some will die from the fall, yes, but most will need to be slaughtered at the foot of it. It would be better if the cliff were higher."

"My hunters will be flexible and adjust to any demands this undertaking asks of us, Alle. It will be spectacular all the same," Garr-Eth responded.

"Yes! Yes, my friend! That spirit!"

Three people emerged from the trees and brush above them, a place higher than they. They had clearly arrived at the place before all of the others. Hoss-Te, the leader of the people of the Ormané-Nues, the more distant clan of the wooded land, brought with him a man and a woman of Garr-Eth's age, both exceedingly athletic and resembling each other as if the two were siblings. Garr-Eth noted that Cour-Ett and the woman eyed each other warily, each sensing a potential rival with a mere look, the briefest of assessments. The man with her seemed to be of a relaxed and humorous, even flippant nature.

"Friends! Good of you to join us! We were wondering what all the racket was down here!" Hoss-Te shouted, too loudly. The three made the signs of greeting, standing back and above the others slightly.

"These two with me are my *wunderkinder*, Darre-Kos and Ouerre-Kos," Hoss-Te said, introducing the man first. Both nodded to the rest. "They are of the same birth and my adopted children. Shall we begin our discussions?"

The group assembled at the overlook with Garr-Eth and his companions. The spot afforded a perfect vantage of the valley below.

"Garr-Eth, this endeavor of ours is yours in conception. Would you please begin?" Hoss-Te spoke.

They'd been informed that the herd was miles to the north and out of range of their man-scent, and well out of visual range. But even still, Garr-Eth held his voice respectfully low.

"My friends. I am deeply grateful for your participation in this undertaking. As you all know a Jump has not been attempted in generations. I feel, however, that the Mother is with us in this and by our collective effort, our cooperation, She will reward us with bounty—"

"The boy is devout, eh Alle?" Hoss-Te interrupted. Garr-Eth smiled wanly at him. Alle-Nok did not speak.

"My two best have been speaking with the elders of my settlement. Cour-Ett will begin," Garr-Eth said, speaking to Hoss-Te directly.

Cour stepped forward and began to speak, sensing the challenge and also directing her words to the three from the far woodlands. Garr-Eth was pleased at her tall, strong and commanding figure. Her hair was long and dirty-blond as his was, her eyes an intense and piercing brown. She wore the leggings of a man, her weapons slung and strapped close to her body. And although many of the women of the Zhar-Nues would have gone shirtless on a hot day as this, she bound her breasts tightly against her chest, lest they become loose and handicap her activity, though the mounds tended to slip upward and out of the leather strap she used for this purpose.

"As you all know, a successful Jump comes only after the effective manipulation of the wisent's herding and stampeding instincts. There will be many critical tasks to perform before the animals will jump, requiring skill and cooperation among us all. First and foremost of these tasks, though, will be that performed by the runners—"

"Yes, we know of the runners," interjected the woman Ouerre-Kos. "I am the fastest, most skilled runner of my people. I will lead these runners."

"Yet I am the most skilled of my people. I had hoped to lead the runners myself," Cour-Ett said, never breaking eye contact with Ouerre as she spoke.

Both Ouerre and Hoss-Te appeared to grow excited, energized as if ready for a confrontation. Garr-Eth saw this intuitively and moved to deflect.

"Please, Cour-Ett, continue. It is imperative that we understand a role as important as this one to the overall endeavor, before we make assignments," he responded.

"Yes," she agreed. "The runners will be decoys. They will be adorned as such to resemble a wisent. Their task is to mimic the animal as they run, to bleat and call out like a wisent in distress, and thus to lead the herd in the desired direction. This task is innately dangerous. If the runner falters or is not swift enough, they will of course be run down and trampled by the stampeding herd."

"That is why the bravest, most skilled of us must handle this task," Ouerre again interjected.

"Let us hear more. These women and their running," Hoss-Te spoke, a look of annoyance on his face, the woman clearly angered at the words.

"The runners will form a relay, from the point of the initial stampede all the way to the cliff face. Although we do not yet know where the stampede will begin, the distance covered will likely be great. We should plan on at least five people running, each leg of a short enough distance to allow the runner's greatest speed."

"There is a small ledge just below the edge of the cliff face and off to the side slightly," said Alle-Nok. "The last runner will be able to quickly get below this, hiding himself, from the stampede."

"Very well," Hoss-Te replied. The group nodded together in agreement.

"Of importance too will be the role of those hunters placed along the path of the stampede. You will see that large cairns of rock are still in place from the last Jump, generations ago. These individuals, the guides, will use the cairns as protection if needed, behind which will be lit small, smoldering fires. The guides will carry and wave the skins of wolves and shout and call out, maintaining a boundary for the herd. The hunters behind the herd, those in charge of initiating the stampede, will also be adorned as wolves, shouting, barking and howling. They may also kill individual animals of the herd as needed—anything to frighten the beasts into their run," Alle continued.

"My elders spoke of another important point," Hoss-Te said, a gleam in his eye. "The herds have knowledge, passed down among generations as we do. They are born knowing certain things. In order to protect against the herds developing knowledge of this, of this Jump, it is imperative that each and every animal be slaughtered. We cannot risk the escape of even one wisent, as this animal may communicate in its way what happened, jeopardizing future jumps."

"The elder men of my people too spoke of this necessity," Alle-Nok responded. "It is known."

Garr-Eth considered this for a moment. "If it is the will of the Mother, then we shall slaughter the entire herd. Calves too."

"The young and old alike will contribute to our bounty," Hoss-Te replied.

"Very well. And as Garr-Eth and I have already briefly discussed, many of the animals will not die immediately from the fall. The group of hunters at the base of the cliff, the killers, will need to perform a critical and dangerous task. As we all know an injured wisent, even a crippled animal, can easily gore and trample a hunter to death. These men and women will need to be the most skilled, the bravest among us, lest they be incomplete in their task and one of our butchers—perhaps one of our mothers, or our sisters, our wives—be gored on the field of slaughter."

"I will lead these men, my friends," Hoss-Te spoke up without hesitation. Alle-Nok bowed in his direction.

"I am fine with this, as I had hoped to lead the hunters in charge of the stampede," Alle spoke.

"Alle, your scouts have been watching the herd for weeks now. I believe that this is right—that you and the people you know best continue with the herd, and stampede and guide the beasts over the cliff when it is time."

Alle nodded in approval.

"Hoss-Te, I have no doubts as to your abilities as a hunter. If you would like to lead those tasked with so critical a skill, I have no objections. I would, however, like Thol-Ur to assist you. I believe that all of us here would agree that he is the strongest and most physically able hunter we have. He will also speak with my voice among my own people who will be butchering the herd once the slaughter is complete."

"It is agreed then," Hoss-Te said.

"Agreed," said Alle-Nok. "But you, Garr-Eth. The Jump is of your own conception. Where will you be as this child is born?"

"Here. I will be here. I desire to watch as the entirety of it unfolds. This spot, too, is visible from the entire plain. All of those participating will be able to see it clearly. From here I will light the signal fire making known to everyone that the stampede has begun."

"I suppose that is your duty, my friend," Alle spoke. "But I would much rather be in the thick of it."

"Yes, I agree. Though you, Garr-Eth, will be the only motherfucker here without blood on his hands when all is finished," Hoss-Te laughed.

"The blood of the entire herd will be on my hands, friends," Garr-Eth replied. "And let us ensure that those we will be hunting with know their parts as they know their own mothers' faces. So that no blood of a man or woman will be on my hands as well."

All present nodded in agreement, and were silent for a moment as seemed right. Hoss-Te then spoke up abruptly, breaking the silence.

"All is settled. Except for this role of runner, that our women here seem to covet! What do you think Garr-Eth? Shall we draw lots?"

"We could, leaving the outcome to chance. I believe it is only proper though to have each demonstrate her ability directly. Both Cour-Ett and Ouerre-Kos claim to be the fastest among us. We shall see. A race, my friends, seems appropriate."

"A race?" Hoss-Te replied. "A race! Ouerre, do you accept the challenge this young leader of ours proposes?"

"I accept," was her simple reply.

"Cour?" Garr-Eth asked.

Without a word, Cour-Ett began removing the spears and thrower she kept on her back, the long obsidian dagger with an antler hilt. She handed these as well as her thicker stabbing spear to Thol.

"The runners will need both speed and endurance," Garr-Eth stated. "There, do you all see it? It is a cairn placed by the ones before us, am I correct Alle?"

"Yes, it is the nearest cairn to us, one marking the path the wisent will take to the cliff."

"The nearest rock cairn. And back. From this point. Do you agree?"

Both women nodded assent. Ouerre looked as a wolf does, eyeing distant prey. She was tall and bare-breasted, though her small mounds were almost muscular and advertised to all that she had not yet given birth to children. She was as Cour-Ett, a *lioness*, as their people called her. She had chosen a rare but accepted path among them, she would live the life and die the death of a man.

"On three then," Garr-Eth said loudly. Both women stood ready, each already sweating in the heat of the afternoon sun. Alle and Tote-Lon stood back without expression, Hoss-Te all a sardonic grin. Thol-Ur began to shout Cour's name.

"One. Two. Three!"

The women burst forth furiously. Ouerre took the lead with a few steps and pushed Cour-Ett hard as she passed her. The other men watched intently, some still shouting, all of them aroused by the display. Garr-Eth was glued to the sight of Cour's muscular legs and buttocks pumping hard, as intensely as they could, the rhythmic dance of contraction and release evident such a paradigm and everywhere in a man—in his heart, his breath, his sexual act. He felt an upwelling of warmth for the woman and shouted her name loudly. Ouerre was an equal sight to behold. Garr-Eth laughed as Thol first began encouraging Cour, then began shouting Ouerre's name, then simply rooted for both. Ouerre was fast and beautiful, her form perfect, a she-wolf scenting blood. Cour appeared more relaxed, settling into the pace of another beast—settling into the pace of a man. Cour was her own entity. She was all of them, she was a man chasing down an eland—not by speed but by the determined will of her heart and mind. As spectacular as Ouerre was, her muscles rippling as if with the wind, Cour would win the race.

The course began down a gradual slope, through a sparse wood desiccated already by the summer heat. Ouerre increased her lead, jumping high over any obstacle—be it a rock or stump, log or bramble. Her body quickly was glistening with sweat.

The course dropped behind a steeper place and they lost sight of her, Cour calmly following a distance behind. She emerged into the plain and they could tell that Ouerre was tiring; her vigor had lessened, her body no longer perfectly upright, her muscles tense and contracted. Garr-Eth could imagine the strain she felt, the burning fire in her legs and her lungs, the creeping sense of exhaustion and the mind's shouting, screaming will to postpone the collapse as long as possible.

Cour emerged from behind the hill as well, her form still perfect, her speed now increasing. Ouerre was almost to the cairn, Cour closing in behind her. The wind too was with the women—the long grass of the plain billowing in waves, propelling them to further feats of speed. Ouerre looked back and seeing the woman coming from behind and gaining, she herself sped forth, harder, faster than any of the men could imagine her capable. A hundred yards, then less, and she was at it, arriving at the cairn first. Hoss-Te and Darre-Kos both cheered exuberantly. But the race had not been just to the placement of rock, and the return would be up a steep hill, against the wind.

Ouerre slowed and reversed direction, her arms pumping hard to gain her speed. But even the other men could see that her speed would not return. Cour passed her, head on, the two women choosing not to acknowledge one another, for fear the loss of energy taken from their run. Just as quickly, but calmly and composed, Cour-Ett made the cairn, reversed and began the second leg. Her speed was the same against the wind and the slope as it had been going down, an amazing feat.

She was beautiful, Garr-Eth thought. A beautiful expression of them, and of the Mother's creative brilliance. The only sign of the furious force she was bringing to bear in her run was a slightly hunched posture to better control the powerful muscles of her buttocks and legs. Her arms too swung and pumped furiously as if brawling in a fight, punching the air to further propel her run. Her larger breasts heaved even behind their sash, and the single long braid of her hair was a whip, the powerful tail of some fearsome beast. Ouerre had the time and strength to look behind her only once, seeing Cour just a few yards behind. She summoned all of her energy, all of her life for one last burst of speed. But this was short-lived. Her animal scream could be heard by all of the men hundreds of yards away as Cour overtook her calmly. Up the hill like a deer Cour-Ett continued, as Ouerre slowed to a jog, spent.

As she approached, the men could see that Cour-Ett had slowed her pace too, although not for lack of wind or vigor. She'd chosen to keep her distance ahead of Ouerre at a respectable length, not wishing to humiliate the woman further. She crossed the point of the race's beginning breathing hard and gleaming with the sweat of her exertion, but clearly in possession of her self and with further reserves. She halted and bent forward, catching her sweet breath. The sweat had dripped down into her face and her mouth and she spat it out, an animal burst of wind that shot the spray high into the air, glistening like energy in the sunlight.

"Ouerre is the strongest of women. A true lioness," she said between breaths.

The other woman now approached, working hard and near exhaustion up the hill, her face contorted in pain's grimace. She was at the very limits of her endurance and upon reaching the point of beginning she collapsed onto the earth as if shot through with a thrown spear. She lay on her back, chest heaving, forcing breath, her body periodically shuddering in waves. Darre-Kos approached her with a flask of water, but held it back so she would not be tempted to drink in her extreme exhaustion. Slowly her convulsions lessened and subsided altogether and she sat up and grabbed the flask from Darre, drinking long and deep.

"There is a time for prolonged exertion. But myself and my kind prefer the shorter, more intense variety. There should be

William Burcher 107

screaming involved, not calm quiet panting," Hoss-Te spoke. "But still, your woman won the race they agreed upon. Now the fate of this jump truly does lie in the hands of the people of the Zhar-Nues."

"They are good hands, I believe," Alle said.

"We will see. Though I have little faith in my own to do any better at the moment," Hoss-Te eyed Ouerre, panting still as an animal, sitting on the warm earth. She met his gaze and held it, her eyes flashing. She suddenly spat, and in an instant was up on her feet faster than she should have been able. Hoss-Te reacted only subtly but for a moment Garr-Eth thought she might strike out at him, her eyes obsidian knives. She quickly moved past him, and coming before Cour-Ett she bowed her head low.

"I will serve dutifully as your second if you will so grant me the honor," she said. Cour waited for a moment, seeking some joke or deception. Finding none she touched the woman's shoulder with her hand, then made the sign of greeting and acceptance, lowering the side of her palm to her chest.

"It is I who will be honored."

Hoss-Te made a noise, a burst of air between his lips. "Look at this! Now no man will get between the legs of either of these two—for each will be always intertwined with the other!"

Neither woman paid him mind.

"A lesson to learn," Garr-Eth said. "Taught to us by those closer to the Mother."

Hoss-Te shook his head. "Until the time, then," he said. "We will go now."

He turned quickly and started down the path. Darre-Kos made a strange salute, smirking before turning and running to catch the older man. Ouerre paused for a moment and then ran off too, her strides again energetic, lithe.

"The man is an aurochs' wet spring turd, is he not?" Alle spoke, his words directed to Cour-Ett. Neither she, Garr-Eth, nor any of the others felt it necessary to answer him as they started down the path and back toward their homes. They descended quickly as a storm was building in the west.

Alle's runner arrived in the settlement a moon later. The herd was moving and would be in place within a few days. His hunters had been ready for weeks now, merely waiting for word to come. Also ready were the women of the Zhar-Nues, led by Aye-Lin. The butchering of hundreds of large animals would take days; the work needed to be done quickly before the meat could spoil. Every able-bodied woman would accompany the hunters to the plateau.

Nearly one hundred men and women hoisted packs on their backs within an hour of the runner's notice. Garr-Eth stood upon a large boulder beside the trail the group would be taking to the place of meeting, watching his people pass below him. Cour-Ett took the lead, followed closely by Thol-Ur. He himself would bring up the rear.

The day was brilliant and bright, warm and cloudless as they began and the people were in high spirits, although as always they walked quickly, silently. Their anticipation, their joy was a *felt* thing rather than a spoken one. Even Aye seemed light on her feet, although Garr-Eth noted that there was a fatigue in her eyes, of something she carried with her not in the pack on her shoulders. She gave him a look of something shared, a shared knowing as she passed below him.

The journey took a long day and a half and it was nearing nightfall when the group arrived at the large campsite where Alle's people had already set up. The site was only a mile from the base of the plateau and the sun set nearly directly behind the cliff over which the wisent would plunge. He noticed that not a few of his people stopped to behold the site, playing perhaps in their mind's eye what he himself could envision: hundreds of beasts, each weighing a ton or more, jumping and then falling, tumbling until their bodies collapsed broken and destroyed onto the green earth. The ground would then be red with the animals' spilt blood and as he saw this color in his mind's eye, smelled the iron of it, he said a prayer of inner thanks for the coming bounty.

His people entered the camp fatigued and with relief. Parties of men came out from the lean-tos and small teepees Alle's people had set up. Immediately Garr-Eth could sense a change, a differing. Although the men of the Alte-Nues—the high-land—were welcoming, there was a strangeness to their demeanor, a thing hard to recognize until it struck him like a rock. There were no women among them. The men were without women. He noted too that the first welcoming party to emerge from the camp and head in their direction had walked past Cour-Ett completely—she being the obvious lead in the train of tired people. Thol-Ur in second place thus received their greetings. Both he and Cour looked back in Garr-Eth's direction puzzled. The groups of men went down the line of newcomers acknowledging and welcoming the men only. The women they completely ignored—save for the occasional glance at a smaller, younger girl. Tote-Lon, Alle's second, led the first group of men.

"Garr-Eth! Greetings. My men here welcome yours, truly," he said, raising his arm in a gesture that Garr-Eth took to mean "halt." He realized quickly that this was the man's substitute for his own people's sign of respect.

"Greetings, Tote-Lon," Garr-Eth said, choosing not to repeat the gesture. "My people accept your welcome. The camp is well-placed and suitable I think for our needs. You have done well."

"Thank you. Your men are welcome to camp here, with us. Your women, though, must camp in the valley below. It is near water and serves their purposes. They may wash themselves daily as we require."

"Ahh, that is where they are. I noticed they were not with you here. It puzzled me."

Tote-Lon looked at him confused for a moment. "Yes. The people of the Zhar-Nues have not yet heard the Revelation. I just remembered. I will allow Alle-Nok to explain further when he returns. He is on the plateau currently inspecting the site once more with a group of our scouts and hunters. But for now, know that this is our way. Women live separate from men."

Garr-Eth did not know what to think of this man. A month before he'd been so lacking in words that both he and Thol thought him mute. Now he spoke as if his words were absolute authority. "I do not understand, Tote-Lon. My men camp with their partners, their daughters and mothers. How could it be otherwise?"

"Alle will explain. Their blood is not welcome here. And in preparation for such an auspicious undertaking as the Jump, we are holding fast to our new rituals without exception. Even your lioness must not come further. As much as she thinks she is one of us, she is not. She bleeds like the others."

"Who are these women here, then, if not your partners and daughters?" Garr-Eth pointed in the direction of two young women walking between structures behind them. Both were small and sickly looking. One of them glanced in his direction briefly and he saw what he thought was fear in her eyes.

"Yes. There are some women in our camp with us, though they are allowed only to serve. They serve us at our pleasure. It is the will of Our Father."

"Your father? Who is your father?"

"I will allow Alle, or the Teacher to explain when they return."

"The Teacher?"

"Yes. We were blessed to have him come to us months ago. He is young, but his words are truth."

"I will speak to Alle further about all of this, Tote-Lon," Garr-Eth said, too confused to take offense at anything the man just said. "But if this is your way, I will respect it. Although my people have our own ways."

"Old ways that are mistaken, yes," Tote replied.

"Our ways," Garr-Eth repeated. "We will camp in another location then. Down at the river as well. Please inform Alle of this and that I wish to speak with him as soon as he returns."

"Very well, Garr-Eth," and the man once again raised his hand as if to halt the others before him. He turned and with the other men who accompanied him made his way back to his

William Burcher 111

camp. As he passed Aye-Lin, who had been in hearing of the conversation, he spat on the earth. Garr-Eth could not know what was in the man's heart as he did this, but he gave him the benefit of his doubt. Perhaps the man had simply needed to spit. He called Thol, Aye, and Cour to his side.

"Something strange has happened in this place. Let us be on our guard. Thol and Cour, please tell the same to the hunters but communicate this discreetly. Aye, I do not want any of the women to be out alone—be it to gather food or water or firewood. Cour will arrange for an escort if needed. Let us head down the valley and set up camp as far from this place as is practical. There is a sickness here."

As Cour and Thol led the group back down toward the valley he stopped and gazed once more upward to the west where the sun had set behind the plateau. Whereas before it seemed a wondrous sight, full of promise and bounty, there was now merely a dim and greyish glow. He was struck with the memory of the night at the cave and the words spoken in a haunted voice. "My children … you will separate … of this body I freely give."

He watched as Aye passed him slowly, clearly worn, exhausted by the trek. Her words, too, repeated themselves in his ears. "My body … I have seen it violated." She could not have forgotten those words, or the images which led to their utterance. But still she walked on. He suddenly felt as though they were fish caught in a flood, saplings standing in the way of an avalanche, or a herd of wisent stampeding toward a cliff. He shook his head almost imperceptibly, burying the thought, and took up his position on guard at the rear of his people.

In a train of men and women they made their way down the slope toward the river that the most perceptive, the sharpest of them could just now hear far off and inviting. The land was only partially wooded, and the line of them snaked its way between the trees and occasional boulders. The night was beginning to darken, the moon nearly new and soon they were walking, silently, in near pitch darkness. Only the stars overhead lit their way—and brilliant they were, just light enough, he thought. There was always just enough. The Mother, the World, always provided just enough in an existence that seemed curiously perfect and this thought was a feeling in his chest, a knowing that he was a part of it all. He breathed this in, held the breath low beneath his navel, the place of birth and conception, and he reacted immediately when someone shouted, "Lion!"

A shimmer, a shadow, moving lightning-quick in the darkness flashed twenty-five paces in front of him. His obsidian knife in his hand he shouted, "Torches! Light torches!"

He heard a scream, a man's scream of pain and then shouts, curses loud and violent. Then there was the unmistakable sound of flint points piercing flesh and hide and the dying, fading roar of a lion.

"There will be more! Together! Gather!" he shouted and the people, well trained, began to form a circle, quickly. The smell of blood drifted up into the cool air.

"Hunters, out! Surround!" And the men and women with knives, with short stabbing spears and long throwing spears, all razor sharp, ringed the circle of people protectively. Behind them, without him ordering it, were older men or women holding torches. He glanced quickly behind and saw Aye at the circle's center, the other women huddling around her warm, comforting bulk. In position, they waited for another attack. First a minute, then two, three. It would not come while in formation. The beasts were too intelligent to attack now that surprise was lost. He calmly made his way around the rough circle to Thol and Cour.

"There, one hundred feet out. It is not yet dead," Cour pointed. In the darkness he could make out a large black form. A single animal, too large to be a female.

"Who threw the spear?"

"Thot-Mar," Cour said. "And then all of us at once. Thot-Mar has been mauled."

Garr-Eth looked behind him and saw the man on the ground, his leg bleeding beneath the skins and leather. The circle of fire and spears had closed on him completely. Garr-Eth saw that the man still clutched his knife in his good hand.

"How are you, my brave friend?" he asked.

William Burcher 113

"It is nothing. Though I don't know if I can walk. I claim the carcass of the beast!" he said loudly, so they all could hear. Garr-Eth could see his grin in the dim light of the torches. The others around him grinned as well, and two or three reached out to place their palms on the man's chest or shoulder.

"It is yours, Thot. As well as a scar or two to impress your children with," he said, directing the people close to Thot to dress his wounds quickly with strips of leather tied tightly for the short journey on to the river.

He quickly gathered five of the hunters and they approached the beast. Three long spears protruded from its torso. Its breaths came in ragged, gurgling convulsions. Though even as it lie prone on the earth, its sense of mass was overwhelming. Garr-Eth listened intently, approached ever more slowly, paused, and with his short stabbing spear jumped forward and plunged the weapon deep into the lion's chest, just behind the shoulder blade. With a popping, breaking of ribs, there came a convulsive expulsion of breath, a last contraction of the beast's muscles and the animal expired.

Garr-Eth then unsheathed his obsidian knife, took a step, lightning quick, and in an instant slit the lion's massive throat in a single fluid movement. The blood spilled forth only slowly without a beating heart to grant it pressure. It dripped too from his knife and onto the earth with a subtle, heavy sound. The smell of iron overwhelmed the cool night air and he looked around quickly. He was sure that others of the pride were present, and were watching him. He had slit the throat of the beast for them, so that the scent of its blood—the scent of lion blood— filled the night and soaked the earth.

Then, in an action not rehearsed or thought of in his mind, an action spontaneous and out of the dark void he felt underlay every moment, a sound of pure animal triumph arose from his chest. He shouted, he roared with the voice of the slain beast, directing the eruption out into the night. Raising his arms, he compelled first the hunters at the body of the beast to join him and then the others, nearly a hundred men and women, joined in the cry. The men and some women roared as the lions did and then Aye began her piercing banshee ululation, soon joined by the women around her. In the tumult, the overwhelming cacophony, Garr-Eth thought he heard another sound—that of many heavy paws plodding away from them and off into the night.

He and the hunters dragged the body of the male lion back into his fray. A large group—that surrounding Thot—hoisted the body above their heads. They all then began the walk again down toward the river in a similar formation as their protective circle, only elongated into a leaf-shaped spear. The body of the lion was held high, its loose limbs and nearly severed head swaying with the movement of the crowd.

Alle's messenger arrived late in the afternoon, the day muted by high, stagnant clouds and a cold wind blowing in from the east. Alle requested that he come back to the men's camp to meet with him. He arrived as the sun began to set with five hunters, Thol-Ur and four others. Cour-Ett had demanded to come as well but he decided that it did not make sense to provoke these strange men before he knew what they were about. As he and the others arrived he noted that the welcome they received was as cold and muted as the air that day. He noticed also that hand tools were lying strangely around as if in frequent, recent use— tools for the working of wood. He wondered what these men were constructing, their camp already complete. The thought faded as they were led to a tent seemingly larger than the rest of the camp. Alle-Nok emerged just as they approached.

"Friends!" he said with enthusiasm. "Garr-Eth! It is good to see you! I am sorry that our reunion was delayed. My hunters were ensuring that the rock emplacements were finished and that the plan of our hunt was fully understood by all. I heard that you had some trouble last night with a lion?"

"Alle. Yes, my friend, it is good to see you as well. Thank you for your concern. The man, Thot-Mar, may not yet live but he slew the beast as it attacked him."

"A brave man. A good death, if He wills it."

Garr-Eth was puzzled by the male invocation. He held his tongue though. Alle noted his pause and moved to fill the momentary silence.

"The herd is in place, my friends," Alle continued. "We must act soon. Tomorrow. My runners inform me that Hoss-Te and his people will be here at the camp shortly. We are ready, my people confident in the outcome. Are yours in similar stead?"

Garr-Eth nodded. "We are ready."

"Good. Now, then, we will discuss allotments."

"Allotments?"

"Of the bounty. Of course."

"I am confused, Alle. It has been the way since before either of our births that the bounty is split equally among all the clans participating."

"Yes. It has. But times have changed, my young friend. My people have tracked the herd and organized the Jump. We have worked, hardest. The successful outcome will be of our doing."

"Work? Why do you call it such? This implies that you are doing something which you would not otherwise do."

"Expenditure. Reward. It only makes sense."

"I see no sense in this demand. The Runners, the most dangerous of duties, will be of the Zhar-Nues and the Ormané-Nues. The job of killing the beasts will be nearly as dangerous. I do not mean to minimize your contributions, my friend, but if one looks to the ordeal in such a way as you propose, there do not seem to be grounds for your demand."

Alle-Nok considered him for a moment and then smiled.

"Yes. Perhaps you are right. I don't know what has come over me. We will not break tradition with the spoils of the Jump. Come, let us go inside. The wind is cold."

The flaps to the tent opened for them as they entered. It was dark inside and it took a few moments for their eyes to adjust. As soon as they did Garr-Eth was struck with a strange sight.

Sitting on a platform of timbered wood was a large chair, beautifully wrought, made from the interlocking antlers of a megaceros or giant deer. The tent's oculus, the hole in the ceiling for the escape of smoke and moisture, was directly above the chair so that light from the grey sky fell directly on it. Standing beside the chair was a young man, dressed in a long robe of wisent leather dyed dark, so that only his face stood out among the shadow. It took Garr-Eth a moment before he could recognize the man, he looked and was dressed so strangely. Durr-Es seemed to have grown taller and he held himself in a different, more purposeful way, smiling slightly.

"Please allow me to present our Teacher," Alle said.

It took Garr-Eth a moment to respond. "Yes, we have already been acquainted."

"You know our Teacher?" Alle looked genuinely confused.

"Yes, Alle. He was in the service of our previous head-man, Thom-Ar. He left us months ago. He was called by the name Durr-Es while he was among us."

"It is a pleasure to see you again, Garr-Eth. And under such auspicious circumstances," Durr-Es chanted in a forced-slow, melodic voice.

"I see that you are speaking fully among these people," Garr-Eth said.

"My voice is present for those who wish to hear it."

Alle stepped forth and sat in the ornate chair. "So tell me, Garr-Eth. The Teacher was among the people of the Zhar-Nues for some time. Why is that you still retain the old ways?"

"Yes. Ways. New and old. We spoke of this with Tote-Lon the day passed. I am confused by this—"

"Neither Garr-Eth nor his people were ready to hear my words, Alle," Durr-Es interjected. "As I have told you, yours is the chosen people. The people of the Alte-Nues have been and thus will always be the first."

Alle-Nok seemed satisfied with that. He sat back in his horned chair, the light of the sky on his chest and neck. "The Teacher has brought to us the news of the ascendance of another. He has brought to us the Truth. No longer do we close

William Burcher 117

our eyes to this, to the way of things. No longer do we suffer the whims of your Mother, nor of her physical expressions among us. The Teacher has brought to us something greater. We now are the people of the Father. He is the one true authority on earth. It is she who bows before Him."

To Garr-Eth the man's words sounded like those spoken by a child. They made no sense. He eyed Durr-Es, standing beside Alle with the same small smile on his face, his head bowed slightly. He seemed to refuse to look Garr-Eth in the eye.

"I see that you doubt the Truth, Garr-Eth," Alle spoke. "I, too, had my doubts. The Teacher put it this way, though, and I could no longer deny that which he said. Look at us, look at the obvious differences between a man and a woman—a typical man and woman, not the she-beasts you have among you, you call lionesses. We *men* are stronger, more cunning, more intelligent. We were given the ability to run faster, fight harder, to kill our food with these hands! And can with any of this the typical woman compete? They are inferior! They have been *made* inferior! And toward further argument, take for instance those who have traditionally been seen as expressions of the Mother's form. Your head-woman, in particular. Her body is near useless as it is so fat! She is weak! A she-cow among you!"

"What has come over you, Alle?" Garr-Eth asked the man.

"I have been awakened. To Truth. They even bleed, Garr-Eth! Of their own accord! On a cycle tied to the presence of the Moon—itself only a reflection of the greater Sun. They *bleed*!"

"I have heard words such as these from his lips before. Venomous words." Garr-Eth nodded in Durr-Es' direction.

"You admit, you have heard the Truth before? He admits it," Alle looked toward Durr-Es, who did not respond.

"I admit that Durr-Es has insulted us before with his unprovoked hatred of Aye-Lin, who for years was as his own mother ..."

"She represents the past, Garr-Eth. She represents the beliefs which have for many years kept us simple, as animals are. This is what women represent. They are closer to the beasts. They are the old. We, *we* are the new. Coming here and now, with my people first, is a new age. It is the age of man."

"How can you deny the felt reality that all of us know?" Garr-Eth responded, this time with a growing anger in his voice. "These who you call inferior. Where would we, all of us—born from mothers all—where would we be? It is through their creation, their creative wombs, that each of us comes into the world."

"They serve their purpose. Their purpose is limited to this. And to further ... service."

Garr-Eth's mind flashed to the image of the two young women he saw in the camp the previous day, scared and sickly. There truly was a disease here.

"In all things present in the earth there is a balance between principles: the feminine and the masculine. This is the only Truth that I know. It is evident in every place that I look, in every creature, in every body. It is this Truth that all of us look inside ourselves and see. To hear you deny this causes me to question if you are in your right mind, Alle."

"No longer do we *feel*, as you say, my young friend. We think. We know. And we believe. We look at what we plainly see—our superiority over them—and it is thus that we believe."

Seeing clearly that the man would not be reasoned with further, and that he was plainly mad, Garr-Eth bowed his head slightly, confused and saddened. "Why now do you speak of this, Alle-Nok?"

"It is due to the importance of the coming Jump! It is auspicious! We desire all among us to be of the One Belief, *united*, so that the Father may smile rightly upon this endeavor."

"I see. Have you spoken yet to Hoss-Te regarding this?"

"No. But I am confident he will see. He regards his women, I think, as we regard ours."

Garr-Eth could not disagree. He wondered at the safety of his people if Hoss-Te's aligned themselves with Alle's—if they too began to believe Durr-Es' poison. He did not know what to say further to the man in the horned chair, nor the slender man beside him. Sensing this, Alle spoke.

"My friend. As I mentioned, I too had doubts and inner ... resistance to the Teacher's message. Come, dwell on what has

William Burcher 119

been said here. It makes no matter to the Jump tomorrow. My men welcome your participation, and we will suffer even that of your lioness. The bitch can run, I have seen. We respect and honor your presence here, among us."

Garr-Eth bowed his head, further confused, not knowing what else to say, or if the man's insult was worth starting a fight over.

"But may I leave you with this one last thought, my friend. We, men are a *separate* thing. No longer are we to be governed by the laws of the rest of creation."

Separate. The word flashed forth in his mind like white-hot flame.

He turned to leave, seeking the fresh air outside the tent as a parched man seeks water. Before he could remove himself fully the young man beside the throne called his name. He turned to look at him.

"And I too will add one more thing, Garr-Eth," Durr-Es spoke in his slow, melodious way. "A friendly warning, perhaps. Those who deny the Truth will know the anger of the Father. For unlike your Mother, He does not relent and does not suffer denials nor disobediences."

Garr-Eth left the tent quickly, followed by the other men of the Zhar-Nues, all silent and confused by what they'd heard. His ears rang with Durr-Es' words—not those of a few moments before, but of months passed, as he and Aye, Thol and Durr-Es climbed down from the Mother's cave in the night: *"Your minds were once at one with my own as your bodies are, but this will not always be so. You will separate from me. You will seek meaning and fulfillment where it cannot be found. For millennia you will forget, and during this time you will ravage my body for your own ends."*

Evident before him was Thom-Ar's prediction come manifest. "It is Thom's *change*," he said aloud. The other men looked at him strangely and he wondered at his own role to play in the coming events—whether that role be as witness only or as something else which terrified him. He decided then to tell no one of his trepidation. Fate was a thing best left undisturbed.

"We will tell no one of what transpired here. I wish not to

scare or anger the women, nor infect our people with this sickness if any are yet susceptible to that man's words. Of first importance is the Jump tomorrow. We will harvest our share of the bounty, and then quickly leave this place."

The men bowed their heads in agreement. Beasts running toward a cliff.

———————

The day began as any other. Men and women awoke and left their tents to relieve themselves behind a bush or tree. They gathered water at the river, put fresh wood upon their cook fires. Some had a breakfast of pemmican, others ate smoked fish with nuts, tallow and berries. A palpable sense of impending action filled the camp of people, odorous and audible. They were anxious, laughing too easily, angered too easily, talking and joking too loudly. The day would be one remembered the rest of their lives—regardless of outcome. By now they'd all heard stories of the last successful wisent jump told by grandparents, great-grandparents—any yet still alive. In each telling the elder could only try and convey the spectacle with words— stunted, limited words—and each listener was left with a sense of so much untold, and the desire only to see and experience such a thing so that one day they could be the tellers of such tales.

He left them early, speaking only with Thol and Cour. To each he expressed his gratitude and wished them well in their duties that day. He was confident in each and worried not for his people's performance. He wished he could be present to see Cour and her runners, like wind racing before the torrent of bellowing fur and flesh and horn. The sight of Thol and his hunters piercing the hearts of tens, perhaps hundreds of wisent with their needle-pointed lances would be one to behold as well.

To Aye he paused briefly and made simply the sign of respect and understanding. The Mother in me acknowledges the

Mother in you. He arrived at his overlook early, before the others were taking their places across the wide plateau before him. Wood had been gathered already for his signal fire, which he was to light for all to see once the wisent began their stampede. He removed his hot-coal from the horn of an eland slung across his shoulder and built a small, smokeless fire in preparation. He had nothing to do at that point but gaze across the golden valley and wonder. It would be hours still before the stampede. Noon had been the approximate, agreed-upon hour.

"You are here early," a man's voice came from the top of the trail a few yards from him. Wheeling in response he saw Hoss-Te, alone and out of breath, sweating from the climb.

"Yes," was all he said in response, wondering at this man's presence.

"Are you here alone?" Hoss-Te asked him.

"Yes. My people are all now readying themselves. Soon they will be in position. There was nothing left for my hands to complete. Thol-Ur and Cour-Ett are capable."

"As are mine. Darre-Kos will take my place as head of mine at the base of the cliff. I may yet return to him, but felt as though I should first speak with you. The day will be a momentous one. Do you mind the company?"

Garr-Eth looked at the man confused. The request seemed out of character. He bowed his head quickly as if to say that it was not in his power to refuse it, the man could do as he wished. There came a silence as Hoss-Te sat down on a slab of rock at the best point overlooking the plain. He seemed to be searching for words.

"Alle-Nok spoke with me inside his tent late last night," were the simple words he settled on.

"I assumed that he would," Garr-Eth responded. He decided that he would let this man show his heart first.

"He said that he spoke with you that morning."

"Yes."

Again there came a pause. Silence. Hoss-Te still searched for words. The man seemed at a genuine loss and almost childlike and shy in his befuddlement. Finally, Garr-Eth could bear the quiet no more.

"And what did you think? Of Alle's words. How did they strike you?"

"As complete and absolute aurochs-shit," Hoss-Te blurted, surprising himself with the force with which he expelled them. "The man is mad," he said more quietly. He paused further and then, laughed. "The shit first tried to barter with me concerning his clan's share. He has no sense."

Garr-Eth could not help but smile, realizing suddenly that there was no deception in Hoss-Te, no internal dialog. He spoke simply what he thought. For this now he was grateful. "He is mad," he replied. "But his madness has infected his entire clan."

"Yes. I fear it," Hoss-Te said, looking up at Garr-Eth. "For a moment I feared that it might have infected you. Alle said that you had seen the truth of his words, the venom that little snake standing beside him had bitten and pumped into his veins. I worried, but briefly."

"Why briefly?" Garr-Eth asked.

"You have obviously been blessed. In bearing. In body. In mind. And you have the flesh of that lionness to warm your bed at night," he said smirking. "One such as you does not question the order of things. You are that order's perfect expression."

Garr-Eth considered the words for a moment. There was wisdom there. "I hear the truth in your words, Hoss-Te. But you are wrong about one thing."

"Yes? What am I wrong about?"

"I no longer have Cour's body to warm my bed at night. Since that day and the race, she longs for Ouerre only."

"Ha! I knew it!" Hoss-Te laughed, smacking his knee in mirth. "Such is the inexplicable nature of women, my friend. After this day, then, I will make it my duty to find you another. And Mother's Mercy, what a thing that would be to behold," he said in thought. "The sight of the two of them together …"

Garr-Eth smiled out of the corner of his mouth at the man.

"But all of this distraction aside. I am puzzled at what to do about Alle and his *Father*."

"As am I," Garr-Eth responded. "But what can we do? We

certainly cannot jeopardize the Jump. We have too much invested. And Alle's people have too large a part to play."

"That is the conclusion that I came to as well, Garr-Eth."

"And as for the sickness, the madness that he and the Snake, as you call him, spew forth—it cannot be for us to do anything. These are men and women choosing to live as they do. Although future conflict is sure to arise between our peoples, I think that we cannot directly interfere."

Hoss-Te paused to consider the matter further. "You have wisdom beyond your years. But I'm sure Thom-Ar, the old badger, recognized as much."

Garr-Eth nodded to the man and looked away, out at the plain below. "And I think, too, my friend, that it may be the will of souls greater than ours that things transpire as they do."

Hoss-Te said nothing but gazed too out at the plain and the mountains beyond.

The smoke came just as the sun, unobscured by any kind of cloud, was at its zenith. Cour-Ett's heart leapt.

"Smoke! It begins!" she shouted to her runners. She felt Ouerre, standing beside her, shudder in excitement. Then, as the smoke rose higher they felt the thunder. It began as a low thing, a feeling more than a sound, sensed in their stomachs, their bowels. It grew until it was heard, the sound of a landslide, of the thunder of a front of storms. Then came the dust, seen from miles away, the cloud the hooves of a thousand running animals churned up into the air.

"Ready, Tosk!" she shouted at the young man, the first of them to lead the charge. He looked at her intensely, the whites of his eyes flashing with those of his teeth.

"Let them come!" he shouted.

He would lead the beasts on the first leg of the course, the place where the relatively narrow slopes of two hillsides lessened to the degree that the land became open plain. It would be on this open land, a plain of golden grass a foot high, that they would need to herd and lead the beasts to their jump.

Each runner would have nearly a quarter mile to sprint at top speed, lest the herd run them over. The runner, too, could not get too far ahead of the massive herd for fear the beasts would lose sight and stop running altogether or worse, head off into another direction, possibly overrunning the hunters manning the rock cairns marking the course, flapping the skins of wolves in the air, barking and shrieking like rabid beasts.

The course formed a semi-circle arcing around a high hill, itself forming the other boundary, directly across the plain from the cairns and men with wolf hides. Along the base of this hill were strewn boulders behind which a runner's relief would hide, and behind which the exhausted young man or woman could recover once the leg of the run was complete. The entire group would then follow the stampede along the hillside, getting into position as needed, in case the herd needed further persuasion, or a runner was in trouble.

The thunder was almost upon them now. Tosk checked the wisent hide he wore loosely on his body, and then with a smile and a thumbs up moved into place, out into the open plain at the small valley's mouth.

"Look!" Ouerre clasped her shoulder, shouting above the din. The first of the beasts came galloping into view. Its size was unquestionable. As high as a tall man at the shoulder, all muscle, fur, horn and terror. It bellowed a strange noise and stuck out its tongue in Tosk's direction. It was clearly in a panic, the whites of its eyes flashing. Others were close behind. Tens. Then hundreds. There were so many, so many beasts. They were as an ocean, a sea of seething, churning brown fur and horn, all bellowing and shitting themselves in terror. Many of the beasts butted, rammed and tried to gore others of their own kind in their panic. The smell, too, was a felt thing—the scent of urine, shit and fear on the wind as thick as rain.

William Burcher 125

Tosk danced in excitement and then, at just the right moment, broke out into a jog. The boy even tried to mimic the wisent, jumping and bucking before sensing the beasts gaining behind him. In a fright he broke into a full sprint. The animals were almost upon him. The boy could run!

"He is an eland! Look at him!" Ouerre shouted in excitement.

The herd was following. And the boy was running perfectly, as practiced. No looking back once his sprint had begun. This was discussed—as the beasts might recognize a human face, even with a helmet complete with horns upon the runner's head. The runner should be focused too on running as quickly, as deftly as possible. Fear kept them swift, but too much might overwhelm them.

Tosk kept his speed, slowing only as the boulder, behind which his relief waited, came into view. The second and Tosk's relief, a boy named Uloth, sprang into the plain. Cour and Ouerre began to jog, giving slow chase on the slope of the arcing hillside, both continuing onward past the others moving into place behind their boulders. The two women would be running the last two legs of the relay. Cour would be the one to lead the beasts plunging from the cliff.

Uloth sprinted forth just as Tosk slid in the grass and dirt behind his boulder. Cour looked back and saw him clinging to the rock face in terror as the beasts charged past him. The din of the stampede was a thing unto itself—the collective roar of a thousand beasts, over a million pounds of flesh running across the plain as one living, writhing thing.

The wisent herd followed Uloth as it did Tosk, the boy just as swift. For a moment, as she watched, Cour could not believe such a thing was happening and that she was present and a witness, and would soon be a participant. If only Garr-Eth could be here with them now, to see the sight as she saw it, to hear the animals bellow and snort amid the thunder of their collective run. If only Thol-Ur could be running with them, too—he and the other hunters —to share in the glory and the blossoming joy of it! And she thought momentarily of the plunge and the killing that would take place below, and she wondered if there was a way that she could climb down the cliff after the plunge to take part in the bloody work herself.

The next runner, a small rabbit of a man, took off but fast—too fast. He was outpacing the herd.

"Coné! Slow down!" she shouted. But she doubted the man could hear her. "He will lose them," she said to Ouerre as they jogged. "He is running too fast. They will lose sight of him!"

She sprang into a run, fast now. Ouerre followed. The herd was falling back, further behind the runner. Both she and Ouerre shouted again but the man could not hear. There was danger here, Cour knew. Still he kept running, not slowing down. And a few hundred yards still lay before the next runner took over. The land too was an obstacle. Coné had just run past another valley coming in from the east. There was a danger that the animals could overrun the men standing guard on the course's perimeter here if they were not fully focused on the runner ahead of them.

It was then that she smelled the smoke. Turning her head, she saw a column of it—light grey, almost white—the smoke of burning grass. The smoke was drifting toward the herd! And then came the flames, low, consuming the grass of the plain, heading straight for the center mass of the herd. Instantly she saw the danger of it. A fire, coupled with a runner now too distant ahead could halt the stampede. She burst into a sprint, and felt the wind of Ouerre's a pace behind her.

The first of the herd passed the entrance to the side-valley, but was slowing. She noted that the men at the cairns had stopped waving their skins. And the cairns had been lessened, knocked over. The men were retreating!

She did not have time to ponder the actions of Alle's hunters further. She was ahead now of the flames of the grassfire, running through the choking, acrid smoke. Ouerre was still right behind her, running hard. They both coughed with the smoke. Cour gagged and felt the urge to stop and vomit but held the urge down below and kept onward, fast, as hard as she could. And then she was beside the herd, and then in front of it.

William Burcher 127

She bellowed and bucked, jumped and took off, seeing Ouerre beside her do the same. They followed! The herd followed! She risked a look behind her and suddenly felt the terror of a beast of prey about to be run down by a pack of wolves. The wisent were close! She could smell them with every runner's breath and her eyes met theirs—still flashing with the white of fear and panic. And she looked into the distance and could only barely see the slight rise that marked the plunge. She and Ouerre had by-passed three other runners. They would be sprinting nearly a mile before the beasts went over the cliff.

What she could not see were the flames of the fire finally reaching the herd just behind its mid-point, the flames licking at the animal's legs, burning fur and flesh. Here the stampede collapsed and chaos overcame the beasts, animals slamming into each other, confused, spinning in terror. Bellows and the sounds of horns and armored heads clashing broke out across the plain. Behind the flames too were men, dressed as wolves. Alle's hunters howled and cackled, shouted and screamed and within a few moments another runner had taken off—this time to the side of the plain, up the side valley and away from the jump. The beasts caught in the fire turned and followed. The herd had now broken in two.

Passing now the young man who was to be the next runner after Coné, Cour began to feel the sting of fatigue in her legs and her chest. The man was standing next to his boulder, dumbfounded, watching the two women run by him, followed closely by hundreds of wisent in the grip of panic. They could not make it to the jump. It was not possible. No man could run that far, that fast. Run, she told herself. Run. Think of nothing else. Run. Breathe. Lungs, air, light as an eland, as fast as the wind, run!

Cour went inside herself, to a mindless place, where nothing existed but the space within and the muscles of her legs—flex and release, air, the life that is the wind in, and then out. Ouerre too was in this place, she knew, for the woman next to her kept pace.

The second, confused runner looked on as they passed her, not knowing what she saw. Then the third, a boy, could think of nothing to do but jump up and down and point to the cliff, now only a quarter mile off. "I cannot go further," Cour thought. "I cannot. My legs are frozen as ice." And then from someplace deeper than this child's voice came something else. It was the banishment of all thought. The child's voice evaporated like a morning dew before a rising sun, and she ran still further. In her strength she found her wind and her woman's voice once again and urged Ouerre to run, run!

The land opened up before them into sky, blue sky. A few more paces! Run! And she was first to the edge of the cliff and realized that her body did not want to stop. For a moment she envisioned jumping before the beasts, leaping with her fury out into the void. She had to shout at herself, scream at her body to stop, stop running. Sliding, skidding to a stop her muscles suddenly were like cold lead. She managed to quickly clamber a few feet down the face of the cliff onto the short ledge upon which she crouched. Ouerre followed a heartbeat behind and the two women clutched each other closely, the ledge not nearly wide enough—their screaming hearts, burning lungs flooding their bodies with acrid fatigue.

The first wave of wisent was just behind. The animals screamed, realizing the fate that was to befall them. The first wave slowed, trying to halt—twenty animals skidding near to a stop, pausing, before the torrent of flesh behind caught up with them, collided with them, pushing them off the cliff and out into the void.

Ouerre screamed in animal terror and Cour clasped her tight, covering her as best she could with her own body. Above their backs, over their bodies, those of the wisent jumped out into the air. The thunder that was behind them gave way only to the sounds of animal terror as beast after beast took its plunge. Too petrified to look, the women didn't, and noted only the myriad forms of shadow passing over them strangely in the air. One beast caught the helmet on Cour's head with its hoof as it tumbled and plunged, loosing it from her head. Her blond hair now liberated, it swirled in the wind coming up from beneath the cliff, a flame of amber lapping at the beasts' bellies from below.

William Burcher 129

Thol-Ur felt the far-off thunder before he saw the smoke from Garr-Eth's signal. The dust the stampeding herd churned up into the air came shortly after. He did not need to shout at the men who waited behind him, for they all felt it too and knew what it heralded. As the moments passed and the thunder in his gut became something heard as well as felt, the excitement grew. It was born in his stomach, a budding lightness on top of the rumbling from the beasts above him on the plateau. The men grew restless with it, anxious with the surging roar. They flashed their eyes at each other, shifted the long lances in their grip, sweated until it stunk. But hunters all, they held their tension at bay.

He could see Hoss-Te's men, led by his adopted son Darre-Kos, a few hundred yards off and out across the field of slaughter at the base of the steep rise leading to the cliff from which the animals would plunge. They knew not exactly where the herd would fall, or how many, and thus they held back. His men too would be feeling as they, ready beyond restraint to finish that which the cliff began.

How he wished Garr-Eth could be here with him! The thrill that was to come! The overreaching bounty! The glory! And as he waited, shifting the grip of his own long lance, tipped with a razor-sharp point of obsidian shaped long like a leaf, the roar above grew and grew, rumbling like a storm. He realized that the sight he would see in a few moments would be the greatest of his life. Always would he remember that which was to come.

There! A runner! At the top of the cliff! Another! Two, there were two! And then a beast! A massive brown form, slowing, halting almost to a stop, five, ten, twenty others behind it skidding almost to a stop. Oh, the glory! The brown tide of flesh behind coming, pushing—the plunge! The beasts were plunging! Down, tumbling, cartwheeling down! And then they came crashing like meteors to the earth—the bodies of the fallen collapsing instantly into rubble, breaking like eggs on the rocks below.

The sound of it was horrific. Bones shattered, flesh torn open, burst in an explosion of fluid and gore. Each impact a shudder, felt through the good earth. And they came like rain, a torrent, a flood of bodies falling, plunging over, over, over. He could not believe the sight. He could not believe it. Hundreds, perhaps a thousand of them, each a drop of water in the flood. He saw animals falling, colliding with the hard earth in every position, every contortion, some braying and bellowing as they fell until they stopped, and there was a split-second of silence, broken only by the bray and the bellow and the break-shadder-collapse of the next.

The beasts began to pile on top of one another, two, then three, then four animals deep. Those on top of the pile had their falls cushioned and thus were only maimed, their legs shattered, their backs broken, their internal organs burst and bleeding. Yet still they came! Stop, he thought. It must stop. There were too many, too many animals. Too much blood, too much death and pain and noise!

From his vantage point a few hundred paces off he could see the blood begin to flow beneath the heaps of bodies, small rivulets collecting into larger ones and then forming streams—streams, and then a river of blood, of stinking iron crimson flowing down the slope before them. When would it stop? It *had* to stop.

The men beside him were silent in awe. Never before could they have imagined, in all the Mother's glory, a sight such as this to behold. Their mouths agape, the moments passed, the bellowing and braying of pain and agony coming from the beasts still alive growing into an unbearable din. Finally, after what seemed like minutes, an hour, a day, the last beast fell, onto a higher pile of other bodies, its own hitting the mound with a crack, then rolling, tumbling off like a rolling stone, gaining

William Burcher 131

speed, still tumbling before collapsing, before tearing itself apart on the ragged horns, hooves and exposed and sharp broken bones of its comrades fallen before it. A pause, a breath, two, three. The sky above them, the plateau above them was empty of falling beasts. It was done.

Slowly, almost inaudibly the men began to emit a noise as one. It grew into its own roar, its own thunder. A release of restrained excitement and with their roar they began their own stampede, they began to run. They charged as beasts themselves—propelled in part by excitement, in part by fear, in part by lust for blood. Many shouted the run entire, the sounds from their chests breaking only in rhythm with the hard, pounding falls of their feet. From both sides they converged and then in chaos, in pandemonium they fell upon the broken beasts.

They stabbed and thrust, sticking the masses of flesh surgically between the ribs and behind the shoulder blades, or directly through the eyes and into the brain. These were the surest of points, providing the cleanest of deaths. Many died immediately. Some thrashed or convulsed, spraying blood and gore upon the men around them. Others, their bodies and heads buried beneath other animals had to have their throats slit. Within moments all of the men were covered, dripping in the warm blood of the massive beasts. Single or in piles they lay. The single animals sometimes thrashed their horned heads about violently. These they had to stick from afar, and wait until the beast expired slowly, for fear of being gored. Others lay in piles and at times a beast in its throes would cause the pile to topple dangerously. A few men were trapped beneath a body, sometimes requiring the strength of ten men to remove.

It began as triumph, as glory. They cheered as they plunged their lances deep into a heart or brain, wrenching them free only with a spray of blood and a titan's jerk. It quickly became work; then the outright labor of exhaustion. Thol bellowed at them to continue, to keep at it, to persist killing—for the women and older men of the three clans lay in wait, ready to begin the butchering. The work must be done, the killing completed, lest a sister, a mother, a partner be gored by some un-expired wisent. Still, despite his shouts of encouragement, his attempts at mock insult, bellowed in his most hateful of voices, the men began to collapse with the effort—many lying prone and covered in blood; some sitting hunched forward and limp, the crimson dripping from the braids in their hair. He pressed on, killing, stabbing, slashing and soon noted that only a few others, Darre-Kos the most prominent, killed with him.

As they neared the center of the field, the core of the broken hoard, a banshee's scream enveloped Thol from both sides. The women, restrained too long and mad with the lust for blood, began to ululate, drowning out all other noises including the bellows and strange dying screams of the beasts. The noise grew closer, and closer, louder and louder and Thol realized that the women were upon them, beginning their grisly, bloody work before the killing had been complete. He could not restrain the women if he tried and coming upon a beast not yet dead they would descend on it like wraiths, slashing and stabbing with their obsidian butcher's knives. Soon they too were as he and his men, covered, dripping with iron crimson.

He stopped and saw Aye-Lin, head-woman, as she stepped forth from a beast whose neck she had just opened. She knelt onto the earth, her massive, fecund body drenched with the beast's blood. She looked toward the sky, raised her arms as the blood still dripped from her knife and let out the most piercing, terrifying ululation he had ever heard. Expressions of the Mother, their bodies born of the sacred feminine, he had no doubt then that death and horror, blood and gore were fundamental to the creative force of life and of the earth—as sure a thing as the clear blue sky in which the warm sun now held. He stared at the Mother's expression, at Aye-Lin's bloodied form, until he heard the further thunder up the plateau.

William Burcher 133

Garr-Eth could not fault the man for pacing, as a child waiting for some gift to be given him. He was nervous too. But he did not want to miss even a moment's sight of the beasts when they sprang forth from the valley entering the plain. Hoss-Te had no duty to perform here and could pace all he wanted and so he held behind, and then back, in a track he walked endlessly while Garr-Eth stared unblinking, like a lion does, waiting for it to begin. There were moments when his eyes played him tricks and a passing bit of dust or a fly looked to be the first wisent, leading the charge and he rebuked himself each time. You're just as bad as Hoss-Te, he told himself.

But then a brown spot emerged miles distant. The spot was followed by more, moving in a wave, churning up dust like a strong wind and he knew that it had begun.

"They charge!" he cried loudly. Hoss-Te stopped pacing immediately, hurrying to their fire. He quickly added fuel and once lit they both piled on the grass and loose branches set aside for the purpose. The smoke billowed upward. It had begun. May the Mother bless this thing.

The beasts surged out into the plain and before them, a speck of dark against the golden grass, he could see what must be the first runner, holding, then beginning a jog, then running at full speed once the herd began to follow. A magnificent sight! The runner, the boy Tosk he knew it to be, was swift as an eland!

"Mother's mercy," Hoss-Te exhaled, crouching beside him. "Would you look at that!"

The plain turned brown, writhing and seething like an unsettled sea. The herd as a single animal followed the solitary runner heedlessly as he led them on the slow arc that was the course. The low roar of the herd's stampede reached Garr-Eth now and he marveled. It was as thunder from a storm. And he could see small dark shapes on the other side of the herd just barely through the rising dust but one of these he knew was Cour-Ett. Ouerre was sure to be close by. He smiled at the thought of them. How he wished he could see both as they ran before the herd!

"It is larger than I imagined, my friend," Hoss-Te spoke, his eyes not leaving the sight of it. "Never before in my life have I seen such bounty. We are blessed."

As they watched the second runner took off, just as quickly as the first. If all such runners performed as this, the jump would be flawless. He began to see something from afar which confused him, however. He pointed at it, Hoss-Te squinting to see.

"The hunters of the edge of the course, closest to us, they are doing something. They appear to be re-arranging the stones of their cairns. They are demolishing them!"

"What?! Why would they do such a thing?"

"There! Look!"

Just rising from the grass that it consumed was the smoke of a fire, across the plain and the herd from their vantage point. The wind blew toward them from this place, Garr-Eth knew. The fire would be heading toward the herd.

"The aurochs' shit! I knew it! Alle!" Hoss-Te exclaimed.

"Wait!" Garr-Eth interrupted. "Wait and see what happens. We can do nothing from this place."

The men on the course's perimeter began to flee their placements and head up into higher ground. Garr-Eth then spied the third runner, a fast man by the looks of it. Too fast. He was ahead of the herd, far in front. The man was too far. The herd would lose sight of him, and the location of the herd now was a dangerous one. A side valley connected to the larger plain right there! It was a side valley now unguarded by the hunters who fled. The herd could turn and head in this direction, away from their cliff.

As they watched, the beasts at the front of the stampede passed this point, remaining on course and following the distant sight of the runner too far in front of them. But then disaster struck. The grassfire reached the central body of the herd, the animals in a clear panic, chaotic, without form. The herd was breaking up! As they watched, another runner broke out, this time up the side valley. Some of the animals followed! A new herd developed and began to stampede up the valley.

"I will kill him! Aurochs' shit!" shouted Hoss-Te.

"More runners!" Garr-Eth said, eyes intent on the far-off

scene. Two runners—it could only be Ouerre and Cour—were sprinting like the wind toward the front of the first herd. They passed its flank, moved out in front and within moments it was clear that the beasts had two new objects to pursue in their terror. For a moment Garr-Eth wondered if the third runner, whoever it was, was part of the ruse. The beasts continued, almost stronger, more cohesive than before and he saw that still the majority was with the group following the two women now. But the distance! It was too great! They would be unable to cover it at the pace they now ran!

He stood up from his crouch, intent on what he was seeing. It could not be possible, running at the speed of a stampeding herd for that distance—a mile at least. Hoss-Te was standing too, both men silent. The other herd heading off into the valley charged fully out of view and his focus now was only the sprint before him.

Garr-Eth wondered if he were about to see the death of Cour before his eyes, run down by the beasts behind her. But still she ran, Ouerre just behind. He could not make out the faces or figures from this distance, but it had to be such. The two were in lock-step and he could see that their legs were in rhythm, pounding, striking the earth in unison. He saw that they'd passed the third, errant runner's relief—then another, and then finally another. They did not slow. He could not imagine the strain they were under.

"Mother, how they run!" Hoss-Te whispered. It seemed all that he could say.

The cliff was approaching. The jump was almost at hand. The runners did not falter. They would complete the jump and survive to tell their tale. Garr-Eth watched as the two approached the plateau's edge and for a moment it appeared as if they would not stop, that they themselves would jump. His heart fluttered inside his chest. But it did not come to pass. The two slowed, stopped, and clambered down the lip of the cliff-face. Behind them the first wave of wisent must have realized what was to come and slowed, almost halting, pausing for a moment before the rest of the herd collided with them, and the animals began their plunge into the void. The sea of brown became a fall of water, a cascade, and both men were struck dumb.

And the torrent did not stop. Such a sight. The deaths of a thousand beasts. Minutes passed and still they stared at the massive animals disappearing into the empty air in the distance.

"I will remember this for all of my days," said Hoss-Te.

Yes, my friend, Garr-Eth thought. As will I. As will I.

And the shaking of his hands caught his attention. He looked at them quickly, placed them on his lap. It was not for the excitement of it all, the rush of witnessing such a thing. He looked up once more and seeing again an entire herd of beasts—such as an entire clan of men—driven from a cliff unto their deaths he knew that his hands shook not for a thrill.

"You will separate," he heard the words again and in him came a knowing, a darker thing. The deaths of a thousand beasts before him was a thing ... separate. By the hands of men these things died. By his own manipulations and designs he had killed an entire clan of wisent. A single beast had fallen at his own hands countless times before—since a child he had known the abilities of his own hands. But this, this was a different thing. In his chest a thing rejoiced. Look, behold what he had done! And then a deeper thing recoiled, lashing out—in frantic, thrashing effort to rebuke and restrain the euphoria. This, this was a separate thing. Torn in two was his heart. With guilt. With regret. With horror at his own designs. None other of the Mother's creations would ever feel as he. He, he, was a separate thing.

"Come," Garr-Eth said coolly to the man beside him. "My eyes are tired of this strange sight. I do not begrudge the Mother's bounty, but I shudder at such destruction. Let's see what Alle and his hunters have done with their own, stolen plentitude."

Hoss-Te nearly jumped. The two then began to run, off-trail, along the rim of their high-place. Garr-Eth moved like fluid through the bushes, fallen trees and large stones left by the glaciers of an earlier age. He did not slow or wait for Hoss-Te who clearly could not keep up. Soon the sound of the smaller man's heavy footfalls and stumbles faded behind.

From the corner of his eyes he could see the last few animals of the herd following their brethren over the cliff, driven still by hunters of Alle's party. At least the man had not shirked *that* responsibility.

He continued around until the cliff-face behind him was out of sight. A strange noise, the noise of release and of triumph filled his ears then, and he saw in his mind Thol and his hunters charging forth into the slaughter. Minutes later came another—the terrifying cry like darkness of another world, the women, the butchers of all three clans howling like horrific, frightening birds as they descended into the maelstrom.

And then came the return of thunder. He stopped running. It confused him for a split second. What could it be? He stood motionless. Perhaps a storm was building in the distance. Hoss-Te's footfalls grew louder behind him, but so did the thunder and in his mind he cried out.

"What? What is that noise?" Hoss-Te asked winded, panting.

Garr-Eth did not answer him immediately, letting the growing din speak for itself. And in an instant he burst forth into a sprint, faster than before, running only toward the sound, toward the rushing thunder. Coming to a precipice, an outcropping of rock overlooking the side valley, he saw what he feared. Alle's stolen herd was once again loose, charging forth down the slope. He saw no runner before it, just the beasts—frightened into an unthinking, stampeding madness. He guessed that they followed the scent of the larger horde, the scent-cloud of terror blowing now from the cliff so potent he thought he could smell it himself.

"Mother's terror," Hoss-Te exhaled as he caught up. "Will they make it? Will they head to the cliff?"

"They charge that way now! Look!" Garr-Eth exclaimed.

And coming to the point of junction, the first of the wisent turned immediately to the south, heading directly to the edge of the plateau.

"Disaster," Hoss-Te spoke slowly. Each man could envision the field of slaughter, crawling now with most of his own clan, his own people. And most of the women of Alle's too.

"We have to warn them! We must do something!" Hoss-Te

pleaded, not with Garr-Eth, but seemingly with the Mother herself. Both men knew that there was nothing they could do to change the outcome of what was before them. Hundreds of beasts now ran at full speed toward an unimaginable fate. The sound, the thunder was as before—as was the smoke and the dust and stench of piss and shit and fear. And there was the braying, bellowing of beasts and the chaos of their charge—wisent butting and goring one another as they ran. But this scene heralded only death. There was no glory here. Only impending holocaust.

Hoss-Te began to whimper, to whine as a child does.

Garr-Eth could do nothing but watch. "No. No. Mother's mercy, no," he repeated.

The beasts continued their stampede, as if theirs was the mind of fate, already set upon an action, an outcome. As both watched in horror two forms emerged from the plateau's edge. Cour and Ouerre. It could only be Cour and Ouerre. They, knowing what was to come, had chosen to climb up from their ledge and face the charging herd. They began to wave their arms, both men could see. It was futile, a fool's errand, but the two figures waved and jumped and probably shouted their lungs out. There came a point when clearly the wisent would not stop. The two could have turned back and clambered down to their protected ledge once more. And Garr-Eth thought he saw a pause in their frantic dance, a moment when the two may have considered such a course. But that moment quickly passed and they held their ground, two lone figures standing before an unstoppable fate, and then the brown torrent swallowed them up and plunged out into the air.

"Ouerre, it is over!" Cour told the woman beneath her. The shadows had ceased their flight. The thunder no longer raged.

William Burcher 139

The only sound now was a strange roar erupting from below—
and the otherworldly calls of agony and pain and animal death.
Slowly the two women arose, surprised that they'd survived.

They looked out onto the field below and lost what little wind
they'd recovered. It was another world. It was another reality.
No, they must have died and this was what waited once that
wide river had been crossed. Both struck dumb, exhausted from
their run before the herd, they remained seated on their ledge—
witnesses to a mad scene and to bloody carnage. They held each
other tight for minutes which passed like hours until that terrible
thunder rose once more from behind.

Immediately both knew what the thunder brought with it.
They looked at one another and for a moment shared in that
terrible secret. There was a second herd. It followed now the
first. This coming herd might jump as the first one had. But now
there were people below. Their people. People they loved.
Nearly their entire clans. The world was about to come to an
end. It was a horror beyond all other horrors.

"We must do something!" Ouerre cried out, frightened by
the sudden realization, the dark vision of an impending doom.
"There must be something. The people! They rushed upon the
field too early! Mother, please!"

Cour began to wave and to shout at the people on the field
below, her words blown back at her with the updraft. Ouerre
followed, shouting herself hoarse until she was overwhelmed
with a coughing fit. She then shouted again. But the effort was
wasted. They were as two small birds trapped in a cage, held far
off and singing a song for no one. And Cour realized that there
was only one thing they could do, as the thunder swelled louder
and the cloud of dust once again hid the mountains from view.

"We must stand before them. Take off your costume. We
must stand before them as men, as *women*, not as their own kind."

Ouerre looked at her once more with knowing, and removed
her helmet and robe. Cour-Ett did the same, both now nearly
naked. Climbing up the small ledge and they were presented
with the fate before them. It was a herd, smaller than the first,
but still formed of hundreds of animals. The first wave was

nearly upon them. Ouerre was just behind and seeing what Cour saw she grasped the woman's hand.

"Mother," Cour-Ett said. "It has been said that the Old Ones could speak with you directly, could know your will as a flock of birds knows which way is south. Hear us. Give us strength. Give us courage. May these beasts—your bounty—see us as more than we are. May we turn their charge. May we halt this charge. I am Cour-Ett of the Zhar-Nues. Beside me is my love. Together we are one, before you. May your will through us be done."

The women stood forth and moved forward slowly together, advancing like two warriors into the fray. Ouerre-Kos was the first to begin shouting at the beasts.

"Hey! You fucking dumb fucking beasts! There's a cliff here! Fucking run the other way!"

"Mindless wisent! Turn! Turn! You're going to die!" Cour joined her, jumping and flailing her arms, thrashing forth in rage, striking her chest, pumping her arms in anger. "We are the hunting women of our people. We are the lionesses! You cannot run us down!"

And there came a moment when both could have run back, quickly clambering back down the edge of the cliff to safety. Both women felt the moment's presence. Both let it pass.

"Fucking wisent! Curse you and your kind! You fucking stupid slobbering shitting beasts! I hate you! I hate your strange heads! I hate your furry shoulders! Your weird long tongues that loll about! It disgusts me! Fucking dumb, dumb animals. You charge forth to your deaths! And to ours …"

As the first wave of animals reached them at full gallop, not even slowing before the face of the cliff, Cour's mind gave birth to a single, shining insight. No, it was not for them to understand anything of the Mother's will.

———

William Burcher 141

He ran. He ran like the wind. He ran like the two women had, leading the beasts to their deaths. He knew of no other thing but this run, no other thing but getting to his people as fast as his body would allow. He'd broken tree limbs crashing through the brush, down the hillside onto the plain and his own limbs were bruised and bleeding. A scratch above his eye kept bleeding into it but he blinked the tears away—tears of blood as they were. His muscles screaming at him for mercy, his lungs mechanical and dying—all of it was as the noise of flies to him—minor things, before his memory of the thunder of the stampeding herd. There was no more thunder now. And when he reached the cliff there was nothing but the sounds of death the dying wisent made. He recklessly scrambled down the face of the cliff.

A young woman, blonde, from Alle's clan, was at the base of the cliff. She ignored him, her eyes empty of anything. She passed him and began to ascend just as he climbed down it. There were other survivors. Though not many. They hung about on the edges of the field of slaughter. Most, women, looked to him like shells, husks of people—barely animated bodies void of minds or souls. Some stared out into space, in directions which either gave them views of the horror or views of the landscape beyond. It did not matter.

One old man from Hoss-Te's clan was pacing about slowly, then speeding up, then slowing again, raising his arms and shaking. He would at times cry like a child uncontrollably and then he would stop.

Behind him the young blonde woman he passed with the empty eyes stepped off the cliff into open air and onto the jagged rocks below. He heard only the sound of it. He saw two other women rise from strange, uncomfortable crouches and head in that direction.

He did not see the bodies of many men or women. Those were buried under the heaps of wisent. The few that he did see were crushed and deformed, or torn apart by horns or hooves. Everywhere he stepped his feet sunk into the strange mud of mingled blood and earth. A man from his own clan, Mane-Lok, wandered about spearing dying wisent, as if nothing had happened. When he saw Garr-Eth he looked for a moment as if he would spear him too, and Garr-Eth prepared himself instinctively for a heartless fight. The man moved on though, wandering about as if nothing but his previous function mattered now—he would mindlessly kill everything that needed killing, feeling it right for the time.

Garr-Eth felt his legs growing heavy, leaden and he stumbled forth until he reached a group of women he did not know, all huddled closely together. There he collapsed. For a few moments he stared at the earth and at his feet, caked in the strange blood-mud quickly drying. A fly landed on his leg. A woman beside him scraped a handful of the mud from her own ankle and flung it out onto the ground.

"The meat will spoil," one woman said to no one. She repeated it. "The meat will spoil."

"The meat will spoil," Garr-Eth said. And he began to shake. And like a thing coming up from the earth below the shaking became strange sobs, convulsions of pain. And he had no mind to control the sobs and they became moans of anguish unobstructed. Tears flowed. Snot oozed from his left nostril onto his face. The world as he knew it had changed. But first it ended and died, before it changed.

9

THE RAGE OF GARR-ETH

A piercing, high-pitched wail cut through the gurgles and heavy breathing of the dying animals closest to him. Hoss-Te turned and saw a man approaching who had not been there before. It was Alle-Nok, and he was accompanied by two of his hunters.

Alle cried out once again. It was the high-pitched cry of a man no longer himself, a man overcome with grief. The others with him hung back, struck with the emotion displayed by their leader, confused by it—as they were by the sight of the field before them.

The man's strange cries became tears and barely audible words mumbled and garbled with a grimace of pain, with snot dripping from his nose and the corners of his mouth. "Father," Hoss-Te thought he heard. Alle collapsed onto the earth and kneeling began to rock himself like a small child. Hoss-Te approached them.

"Why, why, why why, why?" Alle was whispering to himself, repeating, letting the words echo into space. He looked up at Hoss-Te, blinking at him as if the sun were in his eyes. Hoss-Te felt nothing. He recognized that he should feel anger, hatred at this man but he felt nothing.

"Brother," Alle spoke. "Brother. I did not know. I swear to you I did not know—"

"What did you not know, Alle-Nok?" came another voice. It was Garr-Eth. He stood on the corpse of a bull wisent clutching a long lance in his right hand. All of the men looked at him, his form silhouetted against the greying sky. Alle did not respond.

"What did you not know, Alle-Nok?" Garr-Eth repeated, with the same tone, the same inflection. There was very little in his voice that Hoss-Te could discern, no emotion. The words were merely words, spoken from a man who somehow looked taller, darker, more menacing than before.

Alle looked down into the mud. He placed his right hand upon it, then in it, holding it in the pink clay. He looked up at Hoss-Te. "I did not know. His designs. All of … this."

"Who do you speak of, Alle-Nok?"

"Who else?"

"Who?"

"The Teacher. I did not know his designs."

"Durr-Es?"

"The Teacher."

"Where is he now?"

"The Teacher! I knew not his designs! He tricked me! He tricked me."

"Where is Durr-Es?"

"He left. To the north. He is with a few others."

"How many others?"

"He tricked me! We had them in a pen! Hundreds of animals, in a pen. He opened it. The pen. He opened the pen. We'd just begun to slaughter the beasts."

"They travel to the north. Where do they travel? Tell me."

"The pen! Oh why, oh why, oh why …"

William Burcher 145

"The rim trail. To the Cauldron. That must be their destination," Hoss-Te's words directed to Garr-Eth. He immediately regretted saying anything. The look in the man's eyes was something he'd not yet seen. Garr-Eth stepped down off the carcass toward Alle, still meeting Hoss-Te's gaze.

"Garr-Eth. You cannot, my friend. It is not for us to judge," he told him, surprised at his own words. The tall man still looked him in the eyes. The other men made no effort to intervene, both stepping back.

"No," came Alle's voice from below them. He still kneeled in the dirt, looking at his hand as it manipulated the strange pink mud. "It is warm. It is clay. It is mud. It should be cool to the touch …"

"If you do this, my friend … if you cross this river, you will never be able to return," Hoss-Te spoke to Garr-Eth, who said nothing. "We cannot judge this man—"

"No," came Alle's voice again. "The mud is warm. And I want to die."

In a single fluid movement as fast as lightning the tall man plunged the long lance into Alle's back, the entire point of the spear exploding forth from his chest with a profusion of crimson. The blood burst forth once again with the last beat of the man's heart, and then merely oozed and gurgled from the wound. The body went limp but held for a moment in its kneel, propped by Garr-Eth's lance. With a muscular jerk and sickening wet sound the man removed it and Alle's body fell forward, lifeless, into the warm red mud. The two others, with only a moment's hesitation, ran. An obsidian knife fell from the hand of one of the men as he ran.

Garr-Eth wiped the point of the spear onto his bare abdomen, the blood mingling with the sweat and dirt there.

"I would probably not try and follow, Hoss-Te. You will not like what you see." Not waiting for a response he burst into an inhuman sprint, running on the tops of the bodies of the wisent—some still alive—and then nearly as fast up the face of the cliff, scrambling like a cat before disappearing over its rim.

Hoss-Te stood for a moment, unsure what he should do. He

looked briefly at Alle's body once more in the mud, a rivulet of red winding down the slope. He looked around him at the field of slaughter. A few survivors wandered about. There were none injured, only dead. So many dead. The body of a man of Garr-Eth's clan lay a few yards from him. In the man's hand was one of the killing lances. He thought for a moment of taking it from the hand's grasp. He didn't though, and hurried after Garr-Eth as best he could, leaving the weapon to the dead.

———————

He thought nothing of himself. It was as if another man were running furiously against the wind at first, and then the rain. "Separate," was his only real acknowledged thought. The word became a mantra chanted in tune with his raging, inhuman strides. What he would do to the men he hunted would be a thing, *separate*. It would be his own. He knew this. It was not his people's way. There was no *justice*. There were no laws. There were no punishments. The penalty for the worst offenses was banishment—simply to get the offending party out, out of a society that didn't need structure. Weeds pulled from the garden, this was always the extent of it. The *structure* that existed was the earth's, the Mother's. It was all around them. Structure was the simple law that if you failed yourself, your family or your community, your children would die, then you would die, and none of you would live on in a future generation. You *did* it, you *killed* it, you *endured* it, you *fought* it, or you died. These were his laws. They were simple. And now he hunted men to punish them, to seek vengeance—albeit for an unspeakable crime. That was not simple. It was a holocaust. The images of that holocaust and of the vengeance he would wreak underlay every breath he took now, and it gave spirit to his legs and arms and lungs.

There ahead, far-off shadows in the mist. He gained on them. It would not be long. Perhaps they'd not yet seen him. Perhaps they had. It didn't matter. They could not stop him. The half-dark sky of dusk flared suddenly electric blue and he saw them for an instant. Two men running slowly away from him, their backs turned. Clearly they'd not seen me, he thought. If they had, they would be running more swiftly. The growing storm was charged now with his fury, flashing forth before the booms of thunder hit. The two forms ahead disappeared. Ah. They would fight, then.

Another blue flash and for a split-second came the image of a thing, flying through the air toward him and then of his own arm lifting, deflecting the thrown spear with his own long lance. The object went hurtling off into the darkness and fog. A curse could be heard over the clamor of wind and rain. And then a man stepped forth from behind a large, ancient tree. He held his hand up in the strange sign of greeting, although in this case he may have simply meant for Garr-Eth to halt. What ridiculous lunacy! And the lightning struck once more in time to light the man's face as Garr-Eth's lance struck him in the chest.

The second emerged in the center of the path tentatively. The man was big, one of Alle's hunters, powerful in thigh and chest. But he shook. His body shook. He had never fought a man before. Garr-Eth dodged his first forward thrust with his obsidian knife easily and the big man, off-balance from his powerful lunge, could not move in time to avoid his throat being slit. He fell to the earth grasping his throat and sucking in his own blood as his body breathed its last. With a single, fluid movement Garr-Eth grasped his lance from the other man, just as his body was collapsing, wrenching it free before the man hit the ground. He'd hardly slowed his run.

Out further, a mile distant, two more shadows through the mist. They moved faster, toward the Cauldron. Fine. It would be a fitting place. He ran on, on through the rain, his path lit by the storm, raging now with fury matching his own. A few minutes and he began to see steam rising from colored pools seeping out of the earth and the rock. From here the trail into the high places would rise steeply. His quarry would not take that road.

"Garr-Eth!" came a voice calling out from the darkness. The trail opened into a clearing, a space of rock and the bubbling, boiling pools of water and strange, fragrant mud that came up scalding from below. He could not tell where the voice came from.

"Garr-Eth! You come alone! Or perhaps there was no one left to come with you ..."

The place flooded his senses. It stunk, as a rotten, dead thing stunk. The ground was soft and he risked slipping in the stinking mud into a scalding pool ringed now by orange and red. The rain had lessened, coming now in a steady fall.

"Garr-Eth! You feel it, don't you!" Durr-Es shouted. The voice was loud and all around him, echoing from the rock cliffs that surrounded this place. He stopped running, standing in the rain, the water flowing down his body, the contours of his muscles, dripping from his beard and his hair. "You feel it, brother! I know you do!"

"Stop hiding like a rabbit gone to ground, Durr-Es! Show yourself!" he spat, the water spraying into the air.

"I will not. For we both know how that will end, brother. But in the end it matters not. The change I have brought forth has already begun. And it is in you, as well. We are one."

"Stop speaking, you fawning dog! Come out to meet the trap of fate that you yourself have set!"

"As you chased me down across the plain, did you not feel it? The separation? The absence of Her? Did you not feel the upwelling within, the glory of your own self? When you struck down my comrades, when their blood spilt upon the earth, did you not feel the difference within? This is the change of which I speak! Do you remember the words of the old man before he died? Remember ... I was there! This, brother, is the change of which *he* spoke! I am its herald. And you, brother, you are its manifestation!"

Garr-Eth heard the words the young man spoke, but didn't pay them heed. He didn't care. None of him cared anymore for anything beyond what was inevitably to come. There. The boy had to be there—a fall of rocks behind which he could hide—

William Burcher 149

and his voice would echo from the cliff walls. He crept in that direction, lance held low for a decisive thrust. A flash of movement from his right, and the other man was upon him. His right hand flared in pain electric-hot as the short bone club struck him and he dropped the long lance. The man came again, aiming for his head. This he ducked and struck out with his left—the hand in which he held his dagger. He drew blood—it came out searing and warm from the man's shoulder. His attacker stumbled onto him, grabbing, pulling him down. There came a cackle, a strange outburst of laughter from the rocks. Durr-Es could see what befell him.

The man was big and covered in coarse hair and he flailed and convulsed, strong, grabbing and pulling and striking. He bled too, from his wound. Within moments Garr-Eth was covered with it—hot, dark and slick. So slick. His body grew slippery with the blood and he writhed and contorted and slipped from the big man's grasp. He took hold of the man from behind, legs held with his own, arms around chest and then, yes, there, around his neck. The two fell back, onto Garr-Eth, and he flexed his torso, his core, pulled with everything he had, choking the man who coughed and sputtered and writhed. But it was done. He was like a rippling, constricting serpent and within moments, just a few breaths, the man went limp. He held for a minute more before he released, the body falling to the side. He got up, right hand dangling useless at his side.

He heard a scurrying, a sound like a rodent in a dead tree in the direction of the rock fall and moved quick. Durr-Es was trying to scramble up the rock face. He was soaked and covered in mud. It caked the hair on his bare head. He wore still his once-handsome cloak of dyed wisent leather, it too coated in mud—the stinking, sulphuric mud of this place. He was not able to climb because of the slickness of the mud.

The boy turned when Garr-Eth appeared, and slowly let his body slide-collapse down the rough face of the cliff. He came to rest on the ground half-lying, facing Garr-Eth. For a moment the two looked at one another. A fainter flash of lightning from the dying storm lit their faces.

"You are right, Durr-Es," he said. "You and I are now the same." And the boy could only flinch and cringe and shout "No!" as Garr-Eth moved like the wind toward him, striking him hard in the face with his left fist, breaking his jaw.

———

Hoss-Te came upon the bodies of the two men just as the rain stopped and a gibbous moon emerged from behind the clouds. He could only shake his head at the sight, the scene glowing in the moonlight. What change, what change can come with a day, the thought. He moved on again along the trail hiking as hard as he could until he heard a dragging sound ahead. A form was moving toward him, coming up the trail. He waited behind a tree in the dark.

"Come out, Hoss-Te," Garr-Eth cried as he approached. He emerged and saw Garr-Eth covered in a dark which was blood apparently not his own. His right hand was injured. Behind him was the body of a naked man facedown in the dirt. It was Durr-Es, Alle's "Teacher." Garr-Eth drug him by a braided strip of leather—made from the man's clothing it appeared. The strips were tied to his own waist and then to the body at the ankles—the tendons of which had been cut apparently to facilitate that purpose.

"Are you hurt, my friend?" he asked Garr-Eth with hesitation, stunned, frightened. Garr-Eth merely looked at him strangely for a moment before speaking.

"I have a long way to go before the night is done," he said. "Follow if you must."

Hoss-Te nearly jumped when a sound emerged from the naked body. It was a moan of pain. The man was not yet dead. He looked up from the body at Garr-Eth, mouth agape. The tall man only returned a steely look and started dragging again. Hoss-Te stepped off the trail and let him and his burden pass.

William Burcher 151

He did not know what to say, what to do, and paused for a moment looking around as if for instruction before joining the two on the trail. Onward into the night they marched, none of them speaking a word. Hours later, after the moon had set over the western horizon and the darkness was full, Garr-Eth stopped—not for himself, he suspected—but to allow Hoss-Te rest. He felt compelled to break the silence which had been so complete, save for the young naked man's soft and unconscious moans.

"Friend. To what end does this path lead?" he asked, his voice just above a whisper. There was silence for a moment and he was not sure Garr-Eth would speak. After a long pause Hoss-Te was startled when the man laughed. It was short and intense and quickly abated, swallowed by the still darkness.

"Do you mean, in a larger sense? Or the business with my friend there in the dirt?"

"I think … both," Hoss-Te managed. He could sense the man staring into the darkness, breathing, maybe forming words to his response.

"Durr-Es' life will end at the cliff, if not before. His blood will mingle with the rest."

"I thought as much, my friend. What of the … other?"

Another pause, this one longer. The barest hint of a lightening in the east allowed him to see Garr-Eth's face silhouetted against the sky. Even in the relative darkness it was contorted and changed. It was older, harder.

"There is a sickness," he said slowly, measuring his words. "I learned of this sickness many months ago. I ignored it, or rather, there was nothing I could do about it. It arose in others before it arose in me. But now it is a thing living in my chest. These acts that I have done—you yourself can see their darkness and from where they are born."

"Yes," Hoss-Te said after a moment. "I see. They are things born from another place in you, and are out of … alignment."

"But I am compelled nonetheless to see them done. The sickness in me may not merely affect me and pass, as some seasonal malady. This is my fear. The sickness may be a change. It may yet affect us all."

Hoss-Te pondered this for a moment and realized that he would not be able to understand. "I have always felt that our duty lies in living out the will of the Mother. Not in understanding that will, my friend."

"There is wisdom in that, Hoss-Te," Garr-Eth said immediately. "I am now, as you see, a sick and separate thing. It is something that I know, but do not understand. As you say. Perhaps I am living out another's will. There is a cave, my friend ... "

And Hoss-Te listened as Garr-Eth told him of the cave, of the images on its walls, of Thom-Ar's warnings and Aye-Lin's visions. Garr-Eth spoke of his discovery of it when he was a boy, his own father recently passed. He spoke of his sense that the cave was trying to tell him something, the images words of a message from Her—yes, from the Mother—only strange and indecipherable. They were nothing but whispers and mystery until the boy Durr-Es was able to speak for them, *with* them in a voice not his own. They were strange, startling words—words that were portents to the events of the day already passed. Garr-Eth spoke of his own visions of a woman of a different place, perhaps a different time when the people lived lives completely unconnected with Her. Hoss-Te felt a growing nausea as the man spoke, but he held the bile down, controlled it.

"How long will it last, this sickness?" he asked when the man was through with the tale.

"I don't know," Garr-Eth answered. Hoss-Te saw that the man no longer looked out into the distance but directly at him. "But I fear that it could be a very long time."

Hoss-Te could only nod his head in response, knowing that further words would not do them good. The two rose and Garr-Eth commenced dragging the boy once more up the trail. In the minuscule light of the just-breaking dawn, Hoss-Te could see that the body was ravaged, skin scraped off, bruised and the head appeared to be missing an ear.

With the passage of a few hours, the sun just risen above the hills to the east, they'd arrived at the precipice from which so much death had been born. They knew the place by the stench of it, long before they could see. Not yet putrid or rotten, it was the simple sour smell of blood. So much blood. The birds of prey, the eaters of carrion, the wolves and the bears knew the smell well—and had converged. When the scent of the place first reached them, a cave bear emerged from the brush, haughtily wandering into their path. Sensing something it did not like, sniffing the air, it moved onward with a bellow, not bothering to present them a challenge. The massive beast lumbered forth to the otherworldly feast at the base of the cliff.

They arrived at the precipice from its side, Garr-Eth avoiding the place where Cour-Ett and Ouerre-Kos had perished. The scene of utter horror was out before and below. Hoss-Te grew sick and retreated. The presence of so many scavengers. The horror, the sadness, the loss—all were too much and the animal revulsion came out in thin liquid vomit and dry heaves. He retreated away from Garr-Eth and his burden, into a quiet place where the grass was thick and the smell of blood less.

Hoss-Te sat, and he wept. His children. His clan. His partner. His friends. They were gone. Incomprehensible destruction and loss were a few hundred yards away. There was nothing to do but weep—and retch when the feeling of it overwhelmed him. He was tired, so tired—of death, of blood, of living—when pain such as this could be manifest in the world. Why had he bothered following Garr-Eth? Why had he wasted so much time in this fool's errand? He searched inside and discovered something horrific.

He wanted to see it done. He wanted to bear witness. He wanted to know that vengeance had been taken and perhaps even to participate. He felt the bile, the acid of that realization and he stopped weeping. What was happening to them all, that such a thing existed? All of it—the deaths of hundreds, the jump of the wisent; Durr-Es, Alle-Nok, Garr-Eth's transformation—it defied comprehension. Where was the natural will of the Mother in any of this?

He rose, numb, stepping out from the quiet-place with long un-cropped grass and flies and bees that buzzed in the midst of the wild flowers in the calm morning air and watched from a distance as Garr-Eth tossed Durr-Es over the cliff.

PART III

FUTURE

10

AXEL KOHL

He sat reclined, watching as the green-wooded hills and vine-yards of the countryside south of Lyon rolled by outside the calm other-world of the Bentley's interior. He sipped on a glass of Riesling, a vintage from his own small town in the Rhineland-Palatinate of western Germany. He would have to thank Philippe personally. The manager of their Lyon facility was an exceptional man, as most of their employed were. He never overlooked details. The bottle had been discreetly stowed in the car's wine cooler—an option for the car he'd requested himself. Some of the more *liberal* members of the Confederation scoffed at such luxuries. He, however, felt it important to pay homage to the significance of the secrets they all kept with particular, modest displays—luxury could at times speak of a certain seriousness of purpose. And it was all such undeniably serious business.

He chanced a glance at the woman sitting beside him. She'd declined the glass he'd offered her and seemed to now be calmly viewing the passing scene outside her own window. No doubt there was significantly more turmoil within. There couldn't possibly be anything but.

He vividly remembered the first few hours of his own tentative exposure to the Knowledge, decades ago. He'd been a student, an outstanding one at that. He'd been studying both business and physics at the graduate level—the magnetic and electrical properties of the upper atmosphere in particular, when he'd begun to formulate certain ideas concerning the complexity of the earth's geo-magnetic field. He'd submitted a draft publication to an obscure journal and shortly after that submission he had his own first encounter with a member of the Confederation. Johannes Bundt. Another, exceptional man. His mentor, long dead.

Fleur must be formulating a working hypothesis. He'd told her nothing really of the Knowledge, but he'd given her enough to guess at certain things—the age of their group, a short history of Garr-Eth's life; vague hints if not at the exact *nature* of the secret they all protected, certainly its magnitude. She was a smart woman. Despite her relatively modest station in life, he'd immediately determined that.

It had not escaped his attention that she was also beautiful. And she was a poker player, as the Americans might say. And of course there were her dreams. For these he could convince himself of no real, satisfying explanation. Janus had dreams too. Vague dreams, scenes, without context, without speech—and certainly without specific imagery of the Founder. Yes. This was … anomalous. He could not be sure what other dreams she'd had, or anything of their content. There could be significantly more than those she'd divulged, and as he thought more of the subject and of the aspects of Fleur's personality he'd already divined, he decided quickly that there was sure to be … more.

How much of it she was consciously aware of, however, was another variable to possibly be considered. Or not. In a few hours she would know their secret and then none of these considerations would matter—she would be part of the fold, and things would return to their lower, more natural states of energy. This business with Veniamin would be laid to rest, with finality.

William Burcher 157

Though as he told himself this he did not necessarily believe it and he gave consciousness to a growing sense of unease, deeper than his harried reaction to Fleur's restless mumblings and her subsequent admissions a few hours ago. Indeed, he shifted his body in the undeniably comfortable seat of the Bentley now as he remembered his own *loose* reaction. He could not be blamed for his lack of control though, he told himself, mind wandering toward dark places. It was exceptional. It was anomalous.

" … of the Zhar-Nues," had been the first words she'd mumbled in her sleep. Even now as he remembered her saying them a spark, electric shot up his spine. He'd woken Genji then and they'd listened to the young woman's babbling for a moment. She repeated the phrase more clearly the second time and then said, "I know you wish to speak. I am here to listen." And it was then that he knew she was in the cave. He shook his head quickly, lightly, almost imperceptibly as if trying to rid himself of something.

He wondered what Anatoly Lysenko would make of all of it. That would have to wait though, he told himself—as inevitably contention, confrontation would emerge. Anatoly would of course be at the cave with Patricia Augustin, but they could wait to hear the whole of it. He would not deny these confederates of his the truth, but he would delay their awareness of it if he could. Genji would remain silent too, he mused, glancing briefly at the back of the man as he sat in the driver's seat, driving them on the narrow French road. Genji believed as he did, and the man could be trusted.

Of course, he'd thought Veniamin could be trusted too. Veniamin with his gifts, with his intelligence, his innate spark. These thoughts came unbidden and so too did the feeling in his gut, the acid-flutter and subsequent rise of pure, undifferentiated emotion. And he looked once again at the young woman sitting beside him. The words surprised himself, even more than they did her.

"Janus had once been my protégé."

She looked up at him startled, confused. "I'm sorry. I didn't

...”

"Veniamin. Janus. He had once been my student, my pro-tégé. I saw him as my inevitable replacement," he said slowly to her, then to the view outside the window.

"Oh," Fleur said mechanically. "I'm sorry."

"Some things are meant to be, Detective. Others are not," he smiled wanly. Then the moment passed quickly, the essence of it receding back into the hard gravity of the man. "We will be at the site within an hour I believe."

Fleur nodded her head.

The sun was lower in the sky when they arrived at the base of the hills and cliffs just above the river, the late afternoon light golden, the shadows beginning to lengthen. The car arrived at a wrought iron gate, opening automatically with their advance. Discreet cameras recording their presence, the driveway up to the house was masterfully designed to force a slow approach. The entire property was designed for both security and discretion and looked to be a typical French country home—owned undoubtedly by some non-local capitalist.

The car came to another gate attached to a high stone wall. Once through, a long circular drive led to the front entrance of a large, old-looking and ivy-covered home of simple French design. It was square, plenty of windows with open shutters, red tile roof and a facade seemingly pockmarked and stained by age and history—a simple, charming place, he thought, every time he saw it. The real structure was of course underground.

"Have you ever visited a French country home, Detective?" he asked her as the car stopped outside the front entrance. She seemed relieved to speak once again, though her demeanor was still restrained. She was nervous, Kohl thought.

"I haven't, Mr. Kohl."

"Well, unfortunately this one is not typical of that style—beyond the outside which is of course a facade. It is handsome though, is it not?"

She flashed a simple half smile at him in response.

Genji opened the front door for them, placing the breast of his jacket close to a magnetic card scanner, which activated heavy solenoids within the frame. They entered into a large foyer, the floor stone and tile, the ceiling high and dimly lit. A large staircase led to the upper floor off to the right.

"The upper level contains rooms, residences, just as any other house would. This level as well contains a kitchen, parlors, baths. It is below, however, that we do our work," Kohl explained as he opened a large and heavy oak door stained darkly and motioned her to follow. Genji now took up the rear.

The room was small and simple and existed only to provide a bit of discretion for the elevator entrance at its rear. "Now we will descend into the larger structure," Kohl said. "But first, Detective, I must ask that you give me your gun."

She looked at him, suddenly pale in the face.

"Please," he repeated, holding out his right hand, the palm up. "To us this is a sacred place."

There was a moment, when it looked as if he might have to ask her again, but then she quickly reached into the thin cut, black jacket of her suit and removed a compact black handgun. She held it for a moment, muzzle pointing upward before she ejected the short magazine into her left hand. She then racked the slide vigorously, a 9mm round flying a meter into the air. She handed the gun grip-first to Kohl, the slide still open.

"Take good care of it, Mr. Kohl."

He gave a polite nod and placed the weapon in a drawer of a rich-looking bureau near the elevator door, seemingly there for that purpose. The door to the lift opened and they stepped inside.

She smelled vaguely of both cinnamon and cloves, and a little fear—mildly earthy and sweet, he noted, as he stood next to her in the small space of the elevator. Genji's cologne was overpowering in comparison. The ride down always took longer than one would expect and she looked at him questioningly when it became apparent that the shaft of this elevator ran deep, very deep.

Finally, the doors opened and before them was a grand hallway lit as the gallery of a museum would be, lined with ornate shelving and glazed displays containing countless works of ancient art—ceramics, tile mosaics, statuary—from seemingly every ancient culture. Before them was the Louvre in miniature. Many of the displays appeared to discreetly house specially controlled environments.

Fleur was obviously interested in the presentation, but seemed to restrain this interest. He guessed that she'd resigned herself to asking as few questions as possible—and rightfully so. The answers would be given in time.

As they continued down the hallway, each of their steps echoing in its silence and its depth, the objects on the walls seemed to move backward in time. The jade-work, porcelain vases and busts, the statues and works of ornate jewelry became clay, earthenware—pots and figurines, ornate carvings of bone and ivory. These objects were then replaced with more simple, archaeological finds. Knives of shaped flint and obsidian, spear points, arrowheads, beautifully worked bows and other implements of wood. He had always been struck by the other objects displayed in this section of the hallway though, not merely the weapons and tools of a functional existence, but the clothing, the baskets, the jewelry. At the end of the hallway was a singular display, larger than the rest. He saw that Fleur paused in front of it, rapt. Before them, mounted on a wooden torso the rough shape of a man's, was an individual's costume—the clothing of a male.

Fleur turned briefly and looked Kohl in the eye, not saying anything. He saw that there was knowing in her look, a logical and subsequent wonder. The clothing belonged to a tall man, over six feet in height. A pair of pants were laid out simply, flat within the display and were of a soft but weather-proof looking leather, dark more with age and wear than with tanning. They were form-fitting but comfortable-looking. Upon the torso was a long shirt, a robe of similar material but embroidered with strings of lighter leather or sinew and possibly the woven hair of an animal, or of a human. The embroidering created a pattern, geometric, which looked vaguely Celtic. Beside the pants were shoes, moccasins of formed leather and fur. And placed on a simple white pillar beside the display was an obsidian knife, the hilt of an ornately carved antler. Fleur looked back at him, and then at the display repeatedly.

"How is this …?" she asked finally, her voice wavering. With a mild regret he chose not to answer, and to interrupt her instead.

"Please, Detective. Follow me."

Her face betrayed nothing but she paused for a moment, eyes lingering on the display before turning to follow him. The hallway and the artifact displays ended in further corridors and a sense of the size of the facility became evident. He led Fleur to a large set of double doors which opened into a voluminous, cavernous space resembling a college auditorium. The room was dominated by a series of massive flat-panel liquid crystal displays, illuminated with beautiful, high-resolution images of planets and in the center of the wall on the larger display was an image of a dynamic, active and raging sun.

Kohl continued walking toward the back of the auditorium where a mezzanine floor was accessible by a contemporary winding staircase. They ascended and entered another room, a kind of ancillary conference room dominated by a massive table of solid wood surrounded by perhaps two dozen leather chairs. At the opposite end of the table facing them were sitting a middle-aged man and woman. Both rose politely to greet them.

"Anatoly. Patricia," Kohl said flatly. It was as if the three knew each other intimately and were perhaps mildly bored of the others' presence. "May I present Detective Fleur Romano."

The two smiled and bowed their heads, almost in unison. Fleur tried awkwardly to return the simple greeting.

"Fleur, these are my confederates, members of our order, Anatoly Lysenko and Patricia Augustin—" Kohl said, interrupted by a more animated Anatoly who said in a booming, bearish voice with a heavy accent of the Ukraine, "Welcome Fleur. Welcome."

"We have heard much about you, young lady," the black woman said. She was the oldest of the group and spoke with the mild, soothing accent of the Southern United States.

Fleur picked up on the fact that both still waited for Kohl to direct the meeting and subsequent presentation. "Please, let us take our seats," he said, motioning Fleur to sit at the corner of one end. Despite the group's small number, Anatoly and Patricia maintained their seats at the opposite end of the massive table. Kohl and Genji both sat down to Fleur's right side. Anatoly continued.

"You will excuse us, Fleur. My partner and I represent a modest committee of sorts. Frequently, Axel alone coordinates a new confederate's induction into our … group. But shall I say, Patricia and I have a special interest in you."

"We were close to Veniamin, Fleur," Patricia interjected. "We were his friends."

Anatoly looked affectionately at the older woman. "Yes. And I'm sure that Axel has explained to you that our numbers are held to a certain … quota. Veniamin's death created an opening."

Kohl almost smiled, realizing that the man was uncomfortable discussing the confederation with one so new to its discovery. Fleur spoke up for the first time.

"I was under the impression that Janus. Veniamin. Was no longer a member of Zhar-Oss."

Anatoly and Patricia looked at one another. "Well, that is not entirely true. Most of us view one's induction as final. Permanent. For life. Ben had … disagreements with certain others. In our eyes, however, he was the same. He was Ben."

Kohl saw that Fleur's interest was piqued at Patricia's mentioning of Ben, and probably wanted to probe the two further. She chose, though, to take the explanation at face value, biding her time until her questions were answered. It was the right thing to do. Anatoly continued.

"You are viewed by many of us as Ben's natural replacement. Many of us feel, too, that you two are … connected, in a way."

Fleur nodded in their direction, as if to ask them to continue.

"Obviously, you were the last person to see Ben alive, Fleur," Patricia said softly. "We also believe that he … well … that he chose you in some way."

"Chose me?" Fleur asked.

Patricia looked once more at Anatoly. They were clearly having trouble with the conversation. It was very polite of them not to be blunt about the group's divisions to a newcomer, he thought. But it was amusing. Very amusing. After a pause, Anatoly took over once again.

"We are sure that you have many questions about us. About this. About the Knowledge itself. And our history—"

"Concerning Garr-Eth. Yes. Were those his clothes in the museum?" Fleur asked. She'd looked at Kohl just prior to the question, and then intensely at Anatoly. He saw for an instant a spark. Something roguish.

"You know … Garr-Eth?" Anatoly was confused. "Normally an inductee is exposed to our history only after *other* aspects of our story are presented."

"We had a conversation on the plane over the Atlantic," Kohl was forced to intercede. But he realized that he'd just betrayed to the young woman that he desired to keep her dreams from these other two.

"I see," Anatoly said, unconvinced. "Well. We should not delay this day any further. It is of an extreme importance. Dare I say that you will remember this day for the rest of your life, my dear."

"We are going to the cave at some point I assume?" Fleur asked, again with her mischief. Goddamn her, he thought.

"You know of the cave as well!?" Anatoly could not contain his surprise this time. He glared intensely at Kohl.

Mein Gott! Kohl thought. Mais … C'est la vie. They would have found out soon enough. Kohl returned the look, but with an added submission. He would inform the man as soon as it was prudent.

"Yes, Fleur," Kohl spoke. "We will be entering the cave shortly. Anatoly and Patricia will of course be accompanying us. One's first exposure to the phenomena is a special moment. They have come too, I suspect, to witness the event."

And they have come to claim you as their own.

"The cave awaits us. But first, after years of practice, we have determined a simple but effective way to be the best method of induction of new confederates. Within the last few decades the Knowledge has grown to incorporate certain technical, scientific details. It may seem somewhat … inglorious, but we have a presentation for you to view before we proceed."

"A movie?" Fleur asked.

"Yes. A movie. Of a quality suitable, however, to the material it presents. It is the most efficient way to explain the admittedly foreign phenomena you will be directly exposed to shortly."

And it was. Of quality. It had been completed just recently, directed by the Academy Award winning film maker Timothy Kane—a confederate himself. The man had faked an illness for an entire year to complete the project without conventional, professional distraction. Kohl had viewed the film just once before and he was looking forward to seeing it again. Timothy had done an exceptional job—no doubt inspired by its subject matter. It would be ironic that the one work he himself considered his magnum opus would be viewed by only a few hundred people. But that was the way of it, he thought, with many of the contributions of the Confederation's members. It was the way of things, and had been for millennia. Zhar-Oss as an entity, its wealth and potential to influence, existed solely by the talents, skills, the exceptional natures and abilities of its members. Kohl was very proud of this.

"Shall we?" and he stood up slowly, motioning for the others to follow him into the larger auditorium outside.

Once they were all seated in a center row the lights dimmed and then went out, controlled apparently by an unseen hand. For a moment the dynamic image of the sun on the central screen remained as the other two flanking screens went dark. The five of them were left with a single, powerful image of a body Kohl knew most took for granted. If one were perceptive enough, one would realize that the image of the sun was live— or at least as "live" as the speed of light allowed at the distance of 1.5 million kilometers, from them to L1 or the First Lagrangian Point, the point of gravitational balance between the earth and its parent star, where the observing spacecraft orbited.

The movie began in darkness, with music, growing from a

William Burcher 165

whisper into an almost overbearing din, exquisite in the auditorium's sound system. The orchestral composition was conventional, powerful. It quickly began to morph, however. It grew discordant, strange, until it was something else entirely—it became the music of Benjamin Janus, Zhar-Oss.

Kohl had not approved of that addition to the film, but conceded the power of its effect. The black faded into light, becoming a high-resolution image of the earth as seen from the approximate distance of the moon. An animation of a flight from there to a much closer orbit proceeded until the view was that of an astronaut on the aging International Space Station. Here the music stopped and there was silence and a slow, uninterrupted scene of natural beauty. The earth in its spectacular, wordless glory, without enhancement.

The scene continued for minutes of silence and wonder, the viewer passing from day into night, across the solar terminator and then from a lower latitude into a higher one. There were clouds below, the smoke of a volcano, then light, then darkness again as the camera traveled from empty ocean and then onward over a populated area. Europe.

The artificial golden light of the cities on the surface was then eclipsed completely by the shimmering, iridescent, green of a strong auroral display. Here the camera stopped, no longer tied to an orbit. The earth continued rotating below, the aurora grew more intense, the shimmering green rose higher in a strange gradient toward red, then rosé.

For minutes, the image was dominated by the aurora, silently illuminating a black and empty space. The silence was once again broken by the strange, other-worldly rhythms of Janus' music. Then a flash of light, and a procession of scenes from all of the planet's main surface biomes began. The music faded into a slow narration as the images of coastlines, temperate forests, plains and tundra, savannah and mountain continued.

"Gaia," the familiar female narrator began. "The word, Greek in origin. The concept universal, ancient. The Latin equivalent—Terra. Earth as deity, earth as personified entity."

Kohl glanced subtly at Fleur. She was entranced, sitting forward slightly in her seat. She seemed to be forming unintelligible words with her lips.

"The Gaia Hypothesis," the narrator continued. "The modern concept proposed originally by British scientist James Lovelock in the 1960's—describing the earth as a complex interaction of biological and non-biological processes mimicking those inherent to individual organisms. Under the Gaia Hypothesis the earth could be seen as a single organism, of which all of its component biomes, ecosystems and their included forms of life are a part."

Kohl noted that Anatoly and Patricia were both chancing glimpses at Fleur, waiting for a reaction they assumed would come. His study of human body language was more fine-tuned than most, he believed. He would see things that they would not. And he'd known the woman for a few hours longer than they. He watched the young woman's attractive, full lips and realized that she was mouthing the word "Yes," repeatedly.

"The Gaia concept can be illustrated by a simple thought experiment, formalized into a computer simulation by Lovelock and others in the 1980's," the narrator said, the screen fading into an animation.

"The hypothetical 'Daisyworld' is one like our own, orbiting a star with variable radiative output—the amount of light and heat shining on the world varies over time. On this simple world are just two forms of life which cover the surface: flowers—black daisies and white daisies. The color of these flowers affects their *albedo*, or reflectivity. White daisies will reflect light (and heat); black daisies will absorb it. As the intensity of the world's sun increases, the temperature of the world also increases. Black daises begin to thrive—their dark color allowing them to absorb more light and create more energy for themselves. The black daisies then propagate and soon cover more and more of the surface of the planet. As their numbers increase they collectively lower the albedo of the entire planet's surface, warming the planet further. The planet soon becomes too warm, to the point

that the environment is no longer comfortable for the dark flowers. The white flowers, however, have an advantage in their
color, reflecting light and heat more effectively and are thus able
to thrive in higher temperatures. In this warmer environment
they soon begin to take over, covering areas of land formerly
colonized by their black cousins. Their spread raises the collective albedo of the planet, thus lowering temperature. The black
daisies would soon find it comfortable once more to grow and
reproduce. In this way the temperature of the entire planet is
regulated over time."

Fleur looked impatient. "I know," she seemed to be saying
repeatedly with her lips.

"Although the example is extremely simple, it represents a
method by which an entire planet can maintain a *homeostasis* similar to that of a single organism. This is accomplished by the activities of the component populations of organisms living on that
planet's surface. One can only imagine the implications of this
concept if the myriad populations of plants and animals on a
planet such as Earth are considered—beyond that of just two
fictional species."

The Daisyworld animation gave way to surface scenes of the
earth. Geological processes. Volcanism. The geothermal activity
around Yellowstone. Iceland. The cinematography was stunning.

"All geothermal activity, all volcanism, the movement of
plates of the planet's crust described under plate tectonics, happens due to the immense heating caused by the radioactive decay of certain physical elements within the earth's mantle. At the
center of the earth is a core of iron, both inner and outer. The
solid inner core is surrounded by an outer core of liquid, molten
iron. The interaction of this liquid and solid material produces
the planet's substantial magnetic field."

Another animation displaying the theorized *geodynamo*. This
faded then into an ethereal scene of a northern winter night,
possibly in Iceland, a massive green and red auroral display
lighting the sky. This continued in real-time, and the only movement visible was that of the strange light above. Kohl saw that

Fleur appeared more calm, sitting back in her seat once again. Her eyes were wide. She was deep in thought. The northern scene continued for minutes, setting a meditative, open tone as much as it was meant to educate. Meditative and open. It was hard to remain such, thinking of what was shortly to come.

"Auroral displays are caused by the interaction of the earth's magnetic field with the solar wind—a constant stream of electrically charged, incredibly hot gas streaming outward into the solar system from the sun. The earth's magnetic field both deflects and interacts with this plasma expelled by the sun. To a planet in space, the solar wind represents a constant bombardment of energetic atomic particles traveling at great speed. It is thought that other planets, such as Mars— which no longer has a strong magnetic field—have lost a sizable portion of their atmospheres due to a gradual stripping away by the solar wind. Many scientists postulate that without the protection afforded organisms on the surface of the earth by its magnetic field—both shielding them directly from energetic solar particles, as well as protecting the sheltering, breathable atmosphere—life would not have developed."

Images of flocks of birds flying in formation, of monarch butterflies crossing the Gulf of Mexico, of immense herds of caribou, humpback whales, pigeons, and a young Asian boy, playing silently with a needle on a round piece of cork as it floated in a calm pool of dark water.

"Certain animals—perhaps all of them—can sense the planet's magnetic field and use this to navigate during cycles of migration, in some cases over thousands of miles. It has been postulated too that humans have a magnetic sensory organ, vestigial in some, more active in others, centered in the sinuses."

The young boy stood up from his play with the simple compass and looked off into the distance, seeing a rugged range of mountains obscured by mist and atmosphere. Then the scene from space of a slowly rotating earth. Once again a strong auroral display provided the planet a halo of iridescent green and red. For the third time in the film Janus' music returned, whispering at first, then growing, growing into something alive. Deep

William Burcher 169

and powerful it took only a few seconds to realize that it was somehow connected to the auroral display, in tune with it, the musical expression of it. Every note, every pitch produced a corresponding shimmer within the aurora. Peaks, baritone valleys were accompanied by the rise and fall of ethereal light. The scene remained as it was for minutes until it faded into black, the music seemingly more powerful as it continued in the darkness. After a moment it too faded, and the simple text of a quote by Albert Einstein was displayed:

"Everything is determined … by forces over which we have no control. It is determined for the insect as well as for the star. Human beings, vegetables, or cosmic dust—we all dance to a mysterious tune, intoned in the distance by an invisible piper."

11

LA VOIX DE LA GROTTE

Hello JD,

It was a pleasure to hear from you last month. Over the years I have come to value you and your friendship more and more for the stability, for the honest and wise counsel that you have always offered me. You are a rock to me, JD.

You and I have not spoken directly since our loss of Marie. I am deeply, deeply sorry, my old friend. And while I have not been physically close to you all in a very long while, I miss her presence immensely. I have come to see physical distances as a relative thing and I have always felt close to you and Marie. Einstein has a way of getting to one's thinking, in a place such as this.

I'll admit that I was surprised when I heard you'd become a spiritual man. You were always so mental, so exacting, so analytical. I wouldn't have imagined there'd be room in that very structured mind of yours for faith. But then again, things may have changed in the decades passed, and many practical men and women might now have a substantive, solid foundation for the exploration of the less tangible aspects of our existence. And of course, to someone of your motivation, I recognize that reading Tim's book might leave one wanting. His chapter on the cave was admittedly somewhat mechanical and brief. But his interest has always been in Benjamin Janus. And I suppose that Janus' status as the real hero here is deserved. None of it would have come to pass without him, without his actions, or for that matter his music. You know already that I believe in complete transparency and an openness which perhaps touches the insane. Please feel free to share this account with whomever you like. Perhaps others might benefit from a more detailed understanding of what transpired in that dark but special place.

As you probably know it was protocol in those days for the new entrants into Zhar-Oss' circle to see the cave immediately after the viewing of a somewhat educational (although admittedly vague), yet beautifully wrought film. My experience was no different. After the film I was accompanied into the cave by Axel Kohl, Anatoly Lysenko, Patricia Augustin and Genji Ueshiba. All of this is known, yes, but what hasn't necessarily been told was my own internal experience throughout that afternoon— and not for any desire for deception or even privacy on my part, but simply because the rest of it has always been seen as so much more important.

I had a killer headache. I thought I was getting a migraine. I'd never had one before but my mother was plagued by them on a regular basis, so I knew the signs. I thought at first that the flashes of light I was seeing in my mind's eye were the aura of a migraine. But after a few minutes of their growing intensity, their resemblance to the auroral displays I'd just seen in the film, and

especially their strange dance (they seemed to be tied to a repeating chorus I'd heard in Janus' music, a repeating chorus that
I couldn't quite get out of my head), I suspected that they were
something different. Obviously I was experiencing the phenomena for the first time. So, with my head throbbing painfully, and
flashes of strange light obscuring my vision, I entered the cave.

It was as you can imagine, any cave would be. The Confederation had done an excellent job granting physical access to such
a special place, without damaging or modifying it really in any
way—other than the simple steel door leading into it from their
compound. Once the door was shut behind us, the darkness of
the place was total and complete. It was a darkness that I'd never
experienced before, and that is the accurate word. One does not
"see" that kind of darkness. One feels it. It was cool, damp, and
utterly quiet. A strange breeze could be felt coming up out of the
cave's deeper parts. Once we'd entered, Kohl kept us in the
darkness for a few moments purposefully—and the void, the
deprivation of external sense-stimuli seemed to intensify the sen-
sations in my own head. The dancing lights got brighter, the
pain was screaming, and the music—well, it became so loud that
I realized that it wasn't simply repeating itself like some annoying
song will that you can't forget. I was hearing it somehow.

What I haven't told many people is that despite this sensation,
and despite my budding realization as to what that sensation
was, I could really only think about one thing—the prospect of
somehow encountering him, or at least some piece of him in that
place. It was ridiculous, but that's where my mind was. In the
face of all of that, I was thinking really only of him. I wanted to
breathe a little of his air, perhaps still trapped in some corner or
crevice somewhere in the cave. I wanted to see the things that
he saw, feel the place as he had and insanely, but deeply, I
thought he might be waiting for me there somewhere in the
dark. Of course he wasn't. Not his body at least.

I realized then that I was in love with a man who hadn't walked

William Burcher 173

the earth in 27,000 years. I didn't really question my own sanity then; as I hadn't had time. I've had time since, however. To me, still, it is a real and tangible thing. And back to my preoccupation with Einstein—the relativity of time and space have been established. Perhaps love, real love—and this is real love, JD—can somehow transcend impossible spans of both. If you were suddenly transported to the Andromeda Galaxy, two million light years away, would you not still feel the incredible love that you and Marie shared? Space and time are one thing, and this has always been my simple (if not very technical or convincing) argument.

As I said, it was dark—until Kohl lit a torch. It was cinematic in its effect. Suddenly the walls of the cave, fifty feet from where we stood, were illuminated. But still the light was dim. I knew what I was going to see, of course, but my heart jumped when I was able to discern the first of the images. It was a bison, and it seemed to move.

Everyone has seen the images by now but to be there, to see them emerge from the darkness and lit by firelight as a man or woman back then would have seen them—well, it was startling. They looked as if they'd been painted the week before. The single bison became then a herd, and then I saw others—reindeer and horses, and then a pride of lions, a simple outline of a cave bear. I was struck immediately by their artistry. These were images created by artists. There could be no other description given. I was in awe. Clearly, these people were capable of perfectly correct, anatomically accurate depictions of the beasts they saw commonly in that time and place, but they chose in most cases to draw the beasts abstractly, as Van Gogh or Picasso might have. I knew immediately that they were trying to communicate more with their work than mere representation. And this thought made the hair on my neck stand on end.

I'd not yet fully admitted to myself what all of this was or what it was about. Certainly I had my suspicions, subconscious mostly.

The film I'd seen minutes before had not explicitly outlined what the Knowledge was and the idea was so foreign, so strange and counter to the prevailing worldview of the time that I hadn't let it take hold of me yet. For some strange reason seeing those images on the walls of the cave painted millennia ago released the flood gates, so to speak. The realization of what it all meant struck me dumb and I was suddenly leaden. I was overcome. It was as if my mind had been walling off certain truths artificially—sabotaging or at least postponing awareness until one small strange addition to my own consciousness overwhelmed that delusional ability (which we all have), and the reality of it came bursting forth.

The dreams, the repeated allusions by Kohl, the music of Janus, the strange influence of this secret group, the explanations given in the film—and most importantly my own sense of separateness then, the disillusionment I'd felt since becoming an adult—these all had added water to the reservoir. And the images on the wall were the last bit that simply overwhelmed the dam. I was suddenly crushed by what spilled out. I was utterly terrified.

I think Kohl knew then that I was perceiving the phenomena for myself, in a direct way, in a way that few people obviously can. I remember him vaguely coming over to me as I suddenly crouched onto the damp floor of the cave in pain and confusion, only in my state then he wasn't Axel Kohl, middle-aged German wunderkind. He was Garr-Eth of the Zhar-Nues. I was seeing Kohl as Garr-Eth. He reached down with a welcoming hand which I grasped feebly and he helped me back to my feet. Together we stood, and I saw the younger man hold his torch high, watching the images dance in the light. He watched the painted scenes intently, trying to divine their meaning. Then his head turned and he looked at me in the same way, seeing me for what I was.

"It is much as it always has been, Fleur. We have done nothing to the images, to the bones littering the floor. It is untouched. It

William Burcher 175

is as Garr-Eth knew it," the man Kohl said. I remember his words clearly. They awoke me, but only to the reality of the unbearable pain inside my head.

It became so intense that I wanted to cry out, to demand that it stop but then I heard a voice (yes, I know) that spoke clearly, and I knew that the voice was his. "Resist nothing, Fleur," the voice said, and it was the first time he'd spoken my name. The light and pain grew stronger still until I was aware of a pressure, building too within the sinuses of my face. I think that I started to make some noise, a moan of anguish and maybe of something else.

I had the distinct thought that my head might explode from the pressure of the light and the horrible din of the song. And just when I thought I couldn't take anymore there came a felt sensation, a noise, a "pop" that was centered in my face. It was instant release. The aurora within lessened. The intensity of the light faded. The cacophony of strange music was still there but it changed into something different. It grew from Janus' music into the mournful, discordant noise of an alien's voice. I heard it no longer as a song, but as a voice. It was the voice of the earth herself, Jim. And I was no longer terrified.

"I am Fleur Romano. Of another time and place," I'd said then. "I know that you wish to speak. I am here to listen."

And it was thus the journey began.

12

LA VOIX DE LA TERRE

"I will not lower my voice!" the big man shouted in clear frustration, standing up from his leather chair. The grandness of the room and the leather-bound books lining the shelves muted his outburst. "She is now a part of it. She should know sooner rather than later our divisions!"

"Anatoly, please," Patricia Augustin pleaded in a deep voice.

He looked at her and something briefly relented.

"It is not right," he continued, more softly. "Veniamin died to bring this outcome about. Is it not yet more proof that the time has come?"

Kohl was quiet for a moment. All of this he'd expected. But of the man's lack of tact he did not approve.

"We should postpone this discussion until after the viewing, my friend," he said to the man. He tried his best to moderate his tone to avoid an obvious condescension. He had to consciously swallow his anger to avoid responding, but still he felt his face flush. He briefly looked at Fleur and noted she seemed unaffected by the tension. Indeed, if he had to describe her state he'd say that she remained perfectly relaxed, open, even above them all and what she might have judged (if she knew) to be a petty concern. But this was his own projection, his own insecurity, his own *envy*. The matter was not petty. It would have to wait, however. The timing was ridiculous.

The five of them sat about a large round table made of a wood both old and dense. As the day before, the scene looked somewhat ridiculous, as the table was much too large for them. He'd endeavored to not allow the obscene physical space of the place to give emphasis to their divisions, but despite his wishes Anatoly and Patricia sat opposite him and Genji, some twenty feet away. Fleur had naturally taken a position between them all, the symbolism of such an act being obvious. He wondered how conscious it had been, as he quickly looked about the ominous, airy space. It was a library. It was massive. The shelving, full of old, rich volumes, rose in three levels, lining the walls of the large atrium in which they sat. All of it, the moulding, the shelves, the access ladders even were wrought in cherry wood. Good work was meant to be completed here, Kohl thought. Was *his* work such? Was it good?

"In a few moments, Fleur, our curator—Mrs. Amala Singh—will present an object for your inspection. The object itself is very old. You will be given also a pair of gloves for your use if you wish to handle the object. As it is so very old, it is of a somewhat delicate nature. Considering your … experience, yesterday in the cave, we would like your opinion of the object before we describe its contents to you in detail. Ah. As I speak. There it is."

Kohl stood and smiled warmly at the curator as she entered the room, a small, friendly woman just beginning to grey. The others stood as well. If Fleur was confused by this show of respect, she did not show it. They all watched as Amala Singh approached. She moved with surprising speed and grace and in her embrace was a book. It was a large book, held in careful arms, the hands of which were gloved in white. The woman hurried quickly to Fleur's side and placed the book onto the table in front of her, in a square of wood darker and worn differently from the rest of the table's surface.

"May I present the *Oss*, Ms. Romano. The Zhar-Oss, if you like. The words translate to—"

"Holy book?" Fleur interjected.

Amala paused for only the briefest of moments, smiling in response. "Yes. That is correct. It is the object from which our Confederation received its name. Although *codex* is technically accurate, many of us use the word 'book.' And 'Oss' may refer more to an *account*, or a *telling*, rather than the object itself."

Fleur considered this for a moment. "Janus—as performer— did he name himself after the codex, or the Confederation?" Fleur asked.

Here Amala was caught off-guard. Anatoly quickly spoke up.

"Veniamin chose the name Zhar-Oss in homage to both the book, and the message that it contains."

Fleur smiled and nodded politely at the man. She took her seat, as did the others, Amala remained standing over Fleur's shoulder as her attention fell upon the object. It was the size of a large coffee-table volume and seemed bound in some kind of wan, pallid leather. The cover of the book was bare, save for a strange symbol in black, the character of a language, or the stylized representation of an animal. Amala had seemingly placed the book on the table backward, but she quickly explained that this was the correct format, the book had been "written" in a language right-to-left, rather than the left-to-right orientation of most languages of the world. She then realized that she'd said too much and smiled apologetically in Kohl's direction.

"How old is it?" Fleur asked the woman. Kohl looked at Amala and nodded in consent.

"Prior to the 1950's we didn't know, for sure. The evidence we had was somewhat subjective and interpretive in nature. With the advent of radiocarbon dating, however, we were able to pin the age of the book down within a certain range. The analysis was performed by Willard Libby, the scientist responsible for the development of the technique. Libby himself was a confederate." Amala looked at Kohl once more as if for permission to continue. He nodded almost imperceptibly.

"The results of the test, which coincided nearly perfectly with our own analysis of the subjective source, stated that the *Oss* is approximately 12,300 years old."

For a moment Fleur looked uncomfortable. She leaned back further in her chair, away from the object made more foreign by its unbelievable age.

"How is it possible that something that old could remain in such a good condition?" she asked. "I mean, it looks old, but you just touched it. And now you want me to touch it."

"That is a legitimate question, Ms. Romano. The *Oss'* condition is due primarily to near constant care as well as the conditions within the cave itself, where it was stored until just a few centuries ago. The book is also made from a very durable material."

"What is it made of?"

Again the look to Kohl.

"It is made from human skin, Fleur," Kohl said flatly.

"My god," she exhaled after a pause.

"The practice is called anthropodermic bibliopegy and in times past was not uncommon. We believe that the skin was of a confederate, who most likely felt honored to donate her body after her death in this way."

"How do you know it was a she?" Fleur asked.

"There are bits of ... *anatomy* ... preserved in the pages as well. Most notably the nipples of a woman's breasts. We believe the practice in this case was meant to pay homage to the source of the phenomena you experienced yourself yesterday. Although I admit that it is as macabre a detail as one could imagine," Kohl explained.

Fleur smiled slightly from the corner of her mouth and shook her head. "Well thank you for the warning, Mr. Kohl. May I now take a look?"

"Of course!" Amala said with genuine enthusiasm. "Please

put these on," she said, handing Fleur a pair of white cloth gloves.

She first traced the outline of the design on the cover with her gloved fingers. It was less foreign to her than the first time she'd seen it—on a poster for a strange show on the wall of a cafe in Denver. The cover crackled as she gently lifted it. The rest of the group eyed her intently. Upon the first page were inscribed hundreds of apparent characters of a language she'd not encountered before—the same language of the object on the front of the book. Vaguely resembling the logograms of Chinese, each character seemed to consist of three parts, and most were repeated multiple times on the page. They were highly stylized, but within a moment she was able to recognize their forms, their design as familiar.

"The characters are based on the images on the walls of the cave," she said out loud, still looking at the book. None of the rest of the group said anything in response. Patricia and Anatoly, however, both shifted their weight in the big leather chairs. The characters were clear and easily defined, spaced at regular intervals. She scanned them right-to-left as they were meant to be read. They were set perfectly straight, the lines of a thin guide-rule engraved in the parchment. She flipped the page, discovering more of the same. There did not appear to be any punctuation of any sort, just endless characters, some obviously more common than others.

"Written language wasn't developed until thousands of years later than this book, I know," she said. "I don't remember the exact details, but I believe Sumerian was the first—in the ancient Middle East. Cuneiform it was called I think."

"Yes. This pre-dates Sumerian cuneiform by thousands of years, Fleur," Kohl said.

"Amazing. It is amazing. Unbelievable," she replied, whispering, trying to ignore the obvious pores and other imperfections of skin clearly visible in the parchment. She turned the page once more, not knowing what she was now looking for. As none of the others yet reacted, she knew that she'd not yet found it. On this page were more of the same, hundreds of characters.

Apparently a very detailed account of something was written within. She could sense the mood of the others change slightly. Kohl seemed to lean forward in his seat. She guessed that she was getting close. Another turn of a page. And then another. And another. And there it was. She knew instantly what it was, the importance of the material marked obviously by the presence of two very large and dark female nipples, one in the upper left corner, the other in the bottom right, framing the text diagonally. The text itself was set apart from that of the rest of the codex by more space, thicker margins both vertical and horizontal. The characters stood apart and she recognized them instantly.

"It is the message written on the walls of the cave," she said. All four of the others seated listened intently and Fleur could hear Amala, standing behind, her breath coming in quick gasps. And she knew now what they wanted. It was clear. She looked up at Kohl, meeting his sharp gaze. Then over at Anatoly and Patricia. Each of them held looks which she could only see as pleading. Genji sat motionless, expressionless—a stone statue of a man.

"You don't all experience the phenomena, do you?" she asked them collectively. Patricia sighed heavily. Kohl continued to stare at her. Anatoly's hands were shaking.

"We do not, Fleur," the Ukrainian said.

"Do any of you?" she asked him first directly. Then she looked at Patricia, then Kohl.

"No, Fleur," Kohl said flatly.

She inhaled this reality, realizing instantly that for these people her obvious connection with it was something that each, knowing what they did about the cave, about the history of their group, about their earth, craved and were probably deeply envious of. She immediately felt their longing, their sense of separateness. She suddenly felt deflated somehow, darker than moments before.

"Does *anyone* within the Confederation?"

The momentary silence gave her her answer. The mood within the room was now seemingly full of sorrow.

"There are a few of us who can almost hear the song—vague whispers, hints at the glory underneath," Kohl spoke, his eyes now downcast, looking at the codex. "Amala, for instance, has this ability. But a deeper connection with the source of that song … well, that gift is rare. Zhar-Oss is lucky to have within its fold one within a generation who is actively aware."

"Janus. Benjamin Janus was the last," Fleur said.

Kohl looked at her blankly. "Yes."

"His music. It was the song itself," she said.

"Yes, Fleur," said Anatoly. "And those with the sense to hear, dimly, the song the earth is singing, confirmed this for those of us who couldn't."

"You will see now, Fleur, how important Veniamin was—how *cherished* he was by many of us," Patricia said. "His work allowed those of us who long deeply to be *in touch*, a connection, almost direct, to the Mother."

"But the film. The science. The aurora. Surely some kind of technology exists—"

"Yes. Of course," Anatoly said. "For the last fifty years Zhar-Oss has been able to confirm the existence of the phenomena with technological means. We have sensors in orbit which record it, even translate it roughly into an audible signal. But it is not the same."

"We believe that there are layers within the phenomena, that we are not yet able to access," Amala added.

"Layers?" Fleur asked. Kohl spoke up.

"Yes, Fleur. There is not one simple signal here to record and listen to as one does a radio. It is highly complex. And," he paused and then added, almost as a lament, "we believe that a portion of it is somehow *unrecordable*—"

"As in, you can't hear it, or—"

"As in we may not *ever* be able to. We believe that a portion of the song is exhibited only as a *quantum* phenomenon, and that it is somehow *outside* of time."

"Outside of time," she repeated to herself. Her gloved hand still rested on the codex. She thought for a moment of its unbelievable age, the age of the group, of *him*. It was *all* outside of time. She almost laughed.

"Have there ever been those of greater talent, than Janus?" she asked Kohl, looking up at him. He was slow to respond.

"Even more rarely than Janus, perhaps once in a few centuries, there will be an individual of more special talent, yes. Demonstrating a … deeper ability."

"Translation," she spoke immediately. Her voice was powerful and frank. "You're talking about translation."

"Yes," he said quickly.

"I see," was her distant response. The eyes of all of them were upon her now. She felt the sadness of these people, their craving, and also the depth of their hope. This hope, she knew, was directed at her. She was conflicted, knowing finally that nothing for her would ever, ever be the same. But there was no turning back now. She had to do it. For them. For all of them. For everyone.

"My children," she began slowly as the sound of breath—either taken in quickly in a gasp or exhaled involuntarily in surprise—met her ear. She was aware that both Amala and Patricia had immediately begun to sob. The emotion of it became too much and her voice began to crack. And as she continued Kohl stood abruptly to his feet, a soldier at attention, followed by Genji Ueshiba, whose head was bowed and whose eyes were closed. Anatoly's face was white and he could only stare at her, his mouth agape.

"Born of my flesh. I long to speak with you as you speak among yourselves," she tried her best to continue, her voice now strained, heart pounding.

"Thank you," Patricia was repeating softly to herself, looking off into space. "Thank you."

"But time is a different thing to us. Your minds were once at one with my own as your bodies are, but this will not always be so." She tried looking at Kohl, focusing on his steely face hoping it would calm her. She realized quickly that something was arising in him too.

"You will separate from me," she continued. "You will seek meaning and fulfillment where it cannot be found. For millennia you will forget, and during this time you will ravage my body for your own ends," she managed, her voice a foreign thing as Axel Kohl looked directly at her, the emotion behind the look a mystery.

"Like your own mother in childbirth I will nearly be destroyed so that you in your infancy can grow. But of this body I freely give. Until your return …"

Her voice trailed off into nothing and the room was silent once again, each man or woman left only with the throbbing echoes of those words and the sense that nothing would hence be the same.

13

HISTORY

It was all there in the codex, of course—the entire story, written in a manner to record the occurrence of the events only—not to elucidate the motivations of the people behind those events, nor their significance. Details, too, were vague. But her mind could see it all happening as if she'd been the one to record it within those pages herself; and as if 15,000 years hadn't passed since their happening and that first recording. She saw it all in her mind's eye as if she were there. And of course she could easily imagine *him*. As a man both young and old.

Amala explained that the "subjective source" of the history of Zhar-Oss had been an oral narrative maintained separately and completely independent of the written one. Since the book's completion, the Confederation had been comprised of two factions, roughly equal in number and in influence. One faction maintained the book—its hundreds taught to read the symbols within it, many memorizing the account completely.

To the other faction, the codex held less meaning and to these people was taught the oral history—one rigorously translated into modern language. The original, spoken language of the history and of the *Oss* did not survive beyond certain words and proper names, their true pronunciations really only an educated guess. The two groups rarely mingled and never discussed their respective histories—it was the ultimate taboo, never broken, except on an occasion, a ritual, held on one day, every one thousand years. During this event, the Zhar-Anín or "reckoning," each group would recite their history to the other, and the information would be compared, discussed, and if there were contradictions or dissimilarities, other sources would be researched and consulted. The records within the *Oss* state that only very rarely are there serious contradictions. This is due, Amala said, to the group's inherent orthodoxy.

Zhar-Oss was founded to maintain knowledge of the message. Its raison d'être is not lost on any of its members and the accuracy of that message, its purity and lack of human corruption, are obsessions of an almost religious nature.

"It is as it always has been. The culture of the Confederation has not changed, as far as we can tell, from that of ages past," said Amala. "Of utmost importance is the accuracy of the translation. Secondary to that is the accuracy of our own history. For buried in the pages of the book, and also within the story of the *tellers* is a reality that our founder believed inseparable from the message itself. The message tells our story, and as he saw it, it told Garr-Eth's story too."

Fleur could recognize and interpret a few of the characters, by comparing those which recorded the message to the words she seemed to somehow know. But Amala told her it would take time to be able to *read* the book as the most practiced of them (as she herself) could. The characters represented the words, the concepts of a logographic language such as Chinese, rather than the phonetic representation, the *sounds* of the words of that language. And just as Chinese, one did not need to be able to *speak* the language, to read it.

William Burcher 187

"Will I ever hear the tale, told by the other faction?"

"Yes, of course," Amala told her. "One person within a generation is chosen to know both written and oral histories. A translator is obviously afforded this honor by default."

"But there is not always a translator …"

"No. To be able to hear the song fully is enough."

"Janus. He was this man."

"Yes. I knew Ben well," Amala replied, looking down and away as she did.

"Why did he leave?"

"I'm sorry," the older woman told her after a thoughtful pause. "You will need to ask Axel this."

Fleur was not surprised by her response. After a silent, awkward moment Amala began again, explaining more of the Confederation's lore. Fleur was polite, fascinated, but her heart began to pound in anticipation when she could sense that the story of Garr-Eth was about to be told. Ancient words were then made modern, an epochal span of time nullified as the two women sat side by side at the big table in the monumental library.

———

The story comes to her as the images of a dream.

Hearing thunder she looks up toward the top of a cliff. A swarm of hundreds of bison plunge from its height. She has time enough only to marvel, to focus on a single animal as it falls, striking the ground with a sickening sound feet away. Then it comes, in a roiling mass of hoof and horn and broken bone weighing a ton, rolling on top of her.

A man, the morning sun on his hair and off in the distance near a patch of earth worn bare by some catastrophe, tosses something large and dark over a precipice. There is a moment of silence before the same sickening sound as before reaches her ears.

Garr-Eth, his face covered in grime streaked by sweat or by tears or both is running hard and alone across a plain. He carries nothing with him and looks only at the ground a few feet in front. He is hard and gaunt and without expression.

A wasted man, half-naked and starving stumbles out of the entrance to a cave. Flies buzz about. There are the half-consumed carcasses of animals on the ground, their bodies rotting and crawling in a writhing white mass of maggots. The man's hair is matted in dreadlocks and through the mud and the dust it is clear that he is beginning to grey. He looks at the carcass of a vulture for a moment, spits, and steps back toward the cave.

Darkness, then sound. A far-off light, shadows among the rocks. A figure has entered the cave, and he watches from the gloom. He approaches it, creeping slowly toward the sound. He is then aware that his own stink will probably give him away, panics, and kicks a loose rock with his left foot. The figure freezes, looking directly at him. It is a woman, old. She wears clothing and markings unfamiliar to him. It is the first woman he has seen in a decade. Her eyes are green.

There is a smokeless fire in the center of the chamber. The light of the flames dances on the faces of four people crouching on the floor of the cave. They are looking at the walls, at the images that she herself has come to know. The images are the same. Garr-Eth stands behind them, his arms crossed, his eyes calm and bright. He is still thin, still wasted, but looks somehow healthier, younger than before.

A child sits in the sand. She has with her a thin stick and is drawing in the grit. Garr-Eth is watching her, though she doesn't yet know it. She is attempting to mimic one of the images of the cave—from the wall of horses. She uses hash marks, lines in an abstraction—but clearly it is the first of the horses of the wall— tossing its head in a whinny that makes him think of laughter.

A young man approaches. He is the same from the image of the cave in the dark with the fire. With him are three others— another man and two young women. He is smiling. They are all smiling, and a little shy. Surprised, Garr-Eth welcomes them warmly inside.

William Burcher 189

Hundreds of people, standing in the largest of the cave chambers. Many on the outside of the crowd carry torches. They are mixed, both men and women. Most appear very different from one another—different styles of clothing, of hair, of piercings and facial markings, even of race. They stand facing the center of a rough circle. They are quiet, intent, reverent. In the middle of the circle is a dignified old man dressed in a dyed and rich leather robe. His hair is long and white and tied behind his head in multiple braids. His beard is nearly as long. He stands tall despite his age, is quiet for a moment, then speaks.

Fleur can not hear his words but she's knows that he is saying goodbye. He is a powerful speaker even now and seems to address each one of them directly. He is admonishing them to continue the work, to take solace in their life's devotion, to stay close to the Mother, despite her own message. They are the keepers of the relationship. Though time will pass and the rest of humanity, those outside the Confederation, would separate and *fall* as he once did—it was they who would remember. It was they who would be waiting, and *ready*, when the time for *return* was upon them. This had been, perhaps, his greatest gift to them. Just years ago, already an old man, he had translated this most recent addition to the *song*. "Until your return," the words repeated on his lips as he spoke to the crowd. The words had always been there, rising in contralto behind the rest. He would leave this life content in the knowing that these people had hope.

Fleur looked up at Amala, and the woman stopped reading the codex.

"The images on the cave walls. They were there before Garr-Eth. He thought they were old already. Do we know who put them there?"

"We know nothing about this time, or about these people," Amala replied. "All we have are rough timelines provided by carbon dating. Many of the images on the walls are charcoal, as you know. Charcoal can be dated. It seems likely that the artists used charcoal which they made for that purpose. The charcoal dates to approximately 5,000 years before Garr-Eth's time."

"5,000 years. Before. That is the span of modern civilization's recorded history, effectively."

"Yes. It is amazing, isn't it? People had been visiting the cave for eons before the Founder."

"And obviously they, or one of them at least, was in touch with it. They could hear the song. They could hear the words."

"Yes. We believe that people in times past were more in tune with it. They lived lives closer to the earth, to natural cycles. I think they viewed themselves as a part of everything they saw, not separate from it or distinct in some way. Like we do."

Fleur thought briefly of the life she'd left just a few days ago, before Janus' suicide. She thought of her empty apartment, of the work she'd left, of the cases of assault, of incest and abuse. The image of the living room of the Applewhite home in Denver appeared, the children crawling on the soiled carpet.

"How was it for you, when you realized what you were hearing?" she asked Amala.

The woman paused, searching for words. "It was … I don't know. It changed me somehow. I had a seemingly successful academic career before my realization, and before … this. But there was always something missing. I felt alone. I felt separate. I don't feel that way anymore."

Fleur thought a smile at the woman was the only appropriate response. No. No longer alone. No longer separate. She inhaled the warm air of the library deep.

"I want to ask you something," Amala said, as serious as she could be.

"I know," Fleur murmured.

"Well?" the woman replied softly.

"You want to know if there's more to it. The song."

"Is there?"

"I don't know yet," Fleur said, and Amala Singh pondered that for a moment, probably not ready to fully trust her.

"I do know one thing, though. It came to me as you read the *Oss*. A word spoken on Garr-Eth's lips. You will be the first to know, and may keep it to yourself if you like. Just between us."

The older woman raised an eyebrow.

"Their word for mother was *Huomére*."

William Burcher 191

Struck dumb by Fleur's recitation he'd been slow to act the day before. Too slow. Even torpid, like a cow. Ridiculous. The opportunity may have already passed. He'd not told Genji. No, he would spare the man the burden of what he was about to do and the blood would be on his hands alone.

He stood naked in front of the bathroom mirror, his pale skin and eyes glowing in the white light of the fluorescent fixture. He'd shaved and removed a blemish on his neck with the razor, scraping the pimple off the surface of his skin with the thin steel. It now bled, more profusely than it should.

Blood, he thought. His, and theirs. Impossible to isolate that exchange. The crimson oozing from the capillaries of the skin of his neck grew until it became a droplet, then a rivulet tracing the wrinkles of his face downward until it reached the plateau of his collar bone. He fought the urge to stop it quickly and allowed it to drip further from his body onto the porcelain white of the old sink. There for a moment the droplet of blood sat, being fed by others from the wound until his arm quickly shot out like a serpent, wiping the sink and his own skin clean.

It would not be without precedent. It had been done before. During extraordinary times, revolutionary times, to protect the Knowledge, to protect the Confederation, such actions had been taken. Not many knew of this history—yet another, protected secret. Theirs was an organization of secrets. During the first World War the man occupying his own position had taken such actions. And this, this current threat, was greater certainly than the vague national allegiances of some of those unfortunate members.

Indeed, it was a lesser-known requirement of his position, to take such action when necessary. Very few knew this. His predecessor, Johannes Bundt, had explained the matter to him simply once. "We do what must be done to protect the integrity of what we love most. Zhar-Oss has survived for millennia only because men such as us have been willing to take action when change threatens. They naively believe that theirs is an inherently different time or scenario, never before encountered by us in our 27,000-year history—and that this will justify the change. This is never, never the case, Axel. This is what you must fight."

Garr-Eth himself had committed murder in animal revenge, without any real *objective*. His act today would not be of a similar nature. His act today would have purpose.

He patted his smoothed face dry with a folded towel and moved naked to the adjoining room hunched and thin, his body a neglected thing. He began to dress, light blue shirt first, then underwear, then pants, socks, shoes. He paused briefly to rub a scuff from the back of one of them. His coat was just lighter than black. Black would have been better, in case there was spatter. The gun sat on the table next to the bed, where he too sat now, looking at the weapon for a moment.

It was moderately worn. The bluing of the slide's steel had been repeatedly rubbed in places, exposing the silver underneath. The grip, too, was not perfect. It was someone else's, a second-hand gun. And a weapon of close range, he thought. His own action would need to proceed quickly, before one of them could flee. The effective range was too short to be used well in that *particular* scenario. Fleur's Glock was not the perfect weapon, but it was *hers*. It would have to do. Its presence alone was remarkably convenient. She would be the murderer today, and overcome with guilt she would turn the weapon on herself.

He reached forward, grasping the gun from behind. With his left hand he took hold of the single magazine. Ten 9mm rounds. Sufficient. Optimally it would just take three. Or four. The fourth he would determine on the spot depending on her reaction and the feeling in his gut. Yes, some things he was not able to plan. Luckily his mind worked extraordinarily quickly in such situations. He personally liked Amala—she was a brilliant, beautiful, graceful woman. But he was unsure of her allegiance. The tears yesterday during Fleur's *recitation* were not encouraging.

William Burcher 193

He rammed the magazine into its well, the object seating perfectly with a satisfying click. He quickly chambered a round. "The agency of fate is burdensome," he mouthed before rising, checking the room once more, and heading out the door. As his hard-heeled footsteps echoed down the hallway he thought of more that Bundt had told him, before the man's death.

"The Confederation's exceptionality does not lie in the Knowledge that it protects. It is that through our conservatism, our orthodoxy, the Knowledge has been protected at all. Remember this, Axel. The rest of the world can never know of this secret. It would be the death of us, and the death of them."

Anatoly and Patricia had arrived a few minutes before. They were surprised when they realized Kohl was not present.

"He summoned us for a discussion I think, this morning. I admit, I was taken aback," Anatoly said. "His is not the way to approach issues such as ours in an open way."

"Fleur and I were just reading the *Oss*," Amala said as she closed the codex. Fleur picked up on the tension in Amala's voice.

"Anatoly, you are of the *tellers*, I presume?" she asked him.

Anatoly looked at Amala first. Yes, I have told her, the woman seemed to say with her eyes.

"Yes, Fleur. Both Patricia and I. We are here to teach you our history, when the time is right, just as Amala has begun teaching you hers, or theirs, rather," he said.

"And there is more," Fleur interjected. "This conflict between you and Kohl ... "

"Axel Kohl, is a *man*, Fleur" Patricia spoke up. "And like all men he has this ridiculous idea in his head called *control*," she said low, smiling. "He believes that the Confederation exists only to *control* the Knowledge. To keep it hidden. To go on as we've

always done, the same way, plodding along like some lame gi-
raffe over millennia."

"What Patricia is saying," Anatoly interrupted, looking toward Amala, "Is that those of the *Oss*, of the *book*, are naturally
more conservative than those of the *telling*. We acknowledge the
necessity toward a certain … stability. We even acknowledge
that this stability is what has kept us in existence for these many
thousands of years. But we believe that the reality of the times in
which we live—the unprecedented *change* that we are witnessing
in our greater society, in the world at large, outside of our Confederation—necessitates a different action."

"We are a reflection of the society from which we come,
Fleur," Patricia added. "We always have been. And any one of
us with a brain knows that human society is changing rapidly.
Things are accelerating. Climate change, the instability of old
political systems, rapid economic growth, the ridiculous pace of
technological development. Things are evolving toward some
inevitable end. This is obvious to everyone. One, inevitable conclusion," she said, her southern accent flowing like water.

"You want to come forward. You want to tell the world!"
Fleur said, too loudly. The excitement of it surprised even her.
The others were made visibly uncomfortable at the articulation.

"Perhaps not something as direct," Anatoly suggested. "But
slowly, we believe that it is nearing time …"

"The return," Fleur said. "What Garr-Eth spoke about.
Garr-Eth's addition to the message."

"Yes," Anatoly and Patricia said together.

"The pace of change in society," Anatoly continued. "In the
technological sphere, in the average life of anyone anywhere is
growing, exponentially. It must be growing toward some conclusion. Zhar-Oss, with its privilege, its Knowledge—for us the
conclusion is obvious, is it not?"

"We also believe that the Return *must* happen soon, Fleur.
The message speaks of the *body* of the Mother. And that body
being ravaged. The state of environmental degradation on this
planet is also changing rapidly. It too is *accelerating*. It does not
take someone particularly insightful or sensitive to realize that

William Burcher 195

this can't go on for much longer."

Amala looked particularly uncomfortable. She was slouched in her seat, leaning back from the rest of them. It was as if the three were speaking some kind of sacrilege. But she listened, intently.

"May I interject?" she asked politely, even though the intensity of what she was about to say was not lost on them. "What you are speaking of is completely contrary to one of the primary tenets of our existence. The Confederation exists to maintain the secret, alone."

"Maintain that secret for a time —a time when it should no longer be," Patricia replied immediately.

"But who are you to judge this?" Amala responded. "'Beware the danger of exceptionalism,' Garr-Eth mentioned directly in our *Oss*." She then realized she'd just broken taboo and blushed severely.

"Yes, Amala. We too know of Garr-Eth's admonition for the ages. But we also believe the Founder did not mean for this warning to be applied to those living in the time of the Return. Never before in our 27,000-year history has the Knowledge been needed more than it is now."

"But you can't say that!" she replied. "10,000 years ago. The way of life that all of them knew was coming to an end. They would no longer hunt, but would grow plants out of the ground, raise strange animals, *milk* them. All of this must have seemed upsetting. Revolutionary even. What if the confederates had not maintained the secret then? What if they, too, thought their time was *exceptional*."

"Correct me if I'm wrong, but the Confederation exists to both protect the secret, and facilitate the translation of future additions to the message," Fleur spoke, raising her voice to be heard above the heat of the argument. "I may have something to offer here."

The three of them looked at her simultaneously, the argument stopped. Fleur was flushed. "I mean, the words aren't there yet. They're not … words. But there's more to it than what you have recorded."

"The song? The message? You have more?" Anatoly was almost angry.

"I don't know. I already told Amala. I don't know yet. But it's like Garr-Eth mentions in the *Oss*. Another layer. Higher. Behind all the rest—"

"Does Axel know about this?" Patricia asked her.

"I don't know. I don't know how he could. Amala and I were just speaking—"

"Here? He knows then. *Bozhe* ..." the big man exclaimed. "We have known for many years that he has the Library bugged."

Amala looked at him, her eyes confused.

"Yes. There is more to our conflict, Ms. Singh, than mere disagreement. A man like Axel Kohl requires a certain ... response."

As he spoke these last words all four of them became aware of a heavy-footed approach, the sounds of the footsteps of a man, his feet clad in hard-heeled shoes, growing louder as they echoed off the marble of the floor of the hallway outside the library. All four of them looked in the direction of the entrance to that grand room. Anatoly was the only one of them to speak, his voice infused with irony.

"Ah," he said. "The man of the hour approaches."

———

Genji Ueshiba was not Axel Kohl. The normally stoic man seemed pressed.

"Has Kohl arrived?" he asked.

"No. We're waiting for him," Patricia answered. "We thought you were him—"

"You all must leave at once," he replied, hurriedly.

"Why would we leave?"

"All of you, immediately. You must leave."

William Burcher 197

"What is going on?" Amala asked.

"You do not know the man as I do," said Genji.

"Oh, you are wrong about that, Sir," Anatoly replied.

"No, you don't. I believe that he is coming here now to …" the man seemed unable to speak the words.

"What? To admonish our beliefs? To explain the error in our ways?" Anatoly said.

"To kill you."

The four went silent. After a breath Anatoly exhaled, "*Bozhe* …"

"Why are you now telling us this?" Patricia asked quickly, fear and suspicion in her voice. "You are *his* man."

"No longer," Genji replied. "The situation has changed."

"Why are we to believe you?"

"It changed the moment this young woman began to translate the words of the *Oss*. Never before have I known the message, the Knowledge in such a way. I believe, friends, that you are correct. The time of Return is here. She is its herald."

They all looked in Fleur's direction. She was becoming excited. Her years driving to work with a gun strapped to her side taught her to not delay when the threat of real danger approached. Act. Act immediately.

"I believe him. Now. Let's go," she said, rising to her feet. "Which way?"

"Follow me," Genji replied quickly.

Fleur, Patricia and Anatoly followed him at once. Fleur looked back briefly, noticing that Amala was not with them.

"My place is here," she said, meeting Fleur's gaze. "Regardless of what happens. Please, go. Good luck."

Fleur only nodded, running out the door. She worried immediately about the racket they made walking quickly down the marble hallway. Genji led and she took the rear. Genji started to run, Patricia and Anatoly immediately struggled to keep up. "Where?" she asked Genji from behind.

"The elevator. Quickly."

The lift was 100 yards down a corridor to the right. Past the displays of ancient artifacts. "Then where, Genji?" she shouted.

"The car. Anatoly's. It is already out front waiting." His words were almost forgotten when the sound of another man's rapid footsteps reached her ears.

———————

They'd been warned, though not by Amala. By the look in her eyes, one of disbelief and animal terror, she'd not believed him capable of such a thing—until he arrived suddenly and his own look displayed his obvious surprise; and disappointment.

"Where are they?" he asked her calmly, coldly. When she didn't reply he shouted. "Where are they!"

The woman closed her eyes and jumped in autonomic response. Slowly she opened them and saw his pale eyes staring into hers. For a moment it seemed as if he were deciding something. Then he turned and left the Library, heading down the hall in the direction the others had taken.

Questioning now many things; her faith in this man she'd followed for so many years shattered, she sat down in one of the rich leather chairs, put her head in her hands, and wept.

———————

Just a few yards ahead, the elevator door was closed. Genji reached it first. Fleur rejoiced when it opened immediately. They rushed in, though she shouted in frustration when she couldn't figure out how to operate the lift.

"It is automatic," Genji said quickly. "It only goes to one place. Everything is automatic."

They realized that Kohl would be upon them in an instant. Standing in the elevator's entry, Genji had time to look back at

William Burcher 199

her once. He had decided something.

"No!" Fleur shouted as she saw Kohl approach, the man's steely eyes meeting hers as he reached into his jacket. The doors to the elevator began to close, Genji stepped out of their way and toward the approaching man. He reached into his own jacket but was not quick enough. Patricia screamed as Kohl shot the man twice in the chest and then once in the head, the elevator doors open just enough so that a spray of blood and brain matter coated the rear wall of polished steel. The doors shut, and it was quiet.

"Are there stairs?" Fleur shouted at Anatoly. "Stairs!"

The man was numb, however. He looked at her but did not seem able to speak. She realized that the next few moments would be hers alone. She would have to act.

"Think. Think," she repeated softly to herself. Yes. There had been a stairway. Kohl was ascending it now toward their own destination. He would arrive when they did, or only shortly after. "Think, Fleur …"

"There is another level," Patricia mumbled, her eyes closed. She was forcing the words through the shock. "An access, for emergency, maintenance."

"Where is it? Are we to it yet?"

Patricia seemed unable to tell her more. Not knowing what else to do, she hit the red emergency button on the otherwise button-less control panel. The elevator slowed.

"Ok, ok," she thought. "It's automated. What next. What next," she murmured, and quickly realized that the door would open to their peril, whenever it did. Quick, there, above. The ceiling. There must be an emergency hatch. She jumped up, hitting the center ceiling panel and seeing it move slightly.

"Anatoly!" she shouted. "Lift me!" The big man eyed her wearily, but obeyed. He picked her up enough that she could move the panel back, exposing another hatch. She opened it, lifting it outward.

"We need to climb out!" she shouted at him, wondering if he and Patricia would be capable. They would have to be, by God.

He set her down and she held her hands together in a prayer

below her. He understood and stepped in with one leg. She struggled and moaned but held on, bracing the big man with her legs as a power lifter, and she thanked God for squats and the gym. Anatoly with help was able to lift himself above, and scrambled up through the hatch. Next came Patricia. It was easier than Fleur thought it would be. The elevator came to a halt and as she jumped up, reaching Anatoly's big outstretched hand, the doors began to open on the maintenance level. Once up she quietly lowered the hatch and whispered "quiet!" to the other two.

It took somewhat longer than she thought it might, but then again the seconds were like minutes whole, the sounds of their own breathing like cymbals giving their hide away. But then it came, the sound of heavy footsteps and a man violently out of breath. For a moment, when he entered the elevator and stopped, standing just below them, she thought they would be discovered. All of them instinctively held their breath until they could no longer, and exhaled just as he left the elevator, the sounds of his heels a receding echo as he ran down the long hallway. Encouraged, she opened the hatch quickly once again and dropped down, hitting the floor like a cat. She hit the emergency button once again and the doors slid closed.

"Quiet," she mouthed. "Do it quietly!" And they did. Anatoly and Patricia slid back down the hatch awkwardly just as the elevator began to rise once more. "Thank you," she repeated to herself. "Thank you."

A minute later the doors opened once more. She had to grab Patricia by the arm and pull her to get her to move quickly enough. As Genji said, a car was waiting in the drive for them.

"Give me the keys!" she shouted at Anatoly. The man began to pat his pants pockets, search his jacket as if he were looking for something. Fleur's heart jumped at the prospect, but then Patricia held an electronic key up.

"He always loses things," she managed.

Fleur wasted no time. The doors to the long BMW unlocked automatically as she approached. She hurriedly took the driver's seat and started the ignition. Patricia and Anatoly both fell into the back of the car, wheezing and heaving in a sickly way. Just as she hit the accelerator and the rear wheels kicked off with a squeal on the paving stones of the driveway, the main door to the country home flew open, revealing a well-dressed middle aged man heavily red in the face. He panted heavily and in her rear-view mirror she saw clearly that her gun was still clutched and held low in his hand. His pale eyes met hers as she watched him quickly recede, the BMW speeding off into the French countryside.

14

ABDUL-JABBAR SULAYMAN

It began as a recognition of the undifferentiated emotion inside her, a kind of physical feeling not yet expressed. It was a heavy thing located near her heart, a concretion of lighter stuff, stuff that should be free. She let it overtake her—which was hard, scary. In an instant it overwhelmed her like an ocean wave. It became something else, something more. First it was pain, *raw* pain, raw sensation. Then it was heartache, then something more specific. Longing.

A flash of insight and understanding and she knew that this was a felt acknowledgment of a span of time, born from a deeper perception of the actuality of it, the physicality of it. Longing such as this was her mind sensing the immeasurable span of time between her present, and *his*. The depth of it was vast and dark. Behind it though was the song.

It was a lesser thing now that she was thousands of miles from the cave, but with her nonetheless. It became a thing heard with her body, with her bones when she gave it attention. And this is how it would always progress—the depth of her longing, her loneliness, her loss—then the song. But of course he would be there, in it somehow, waiting for her. There were no words, no images, just presence—presence that was not merely her own. When she sensed him, the song grew louder, a palpitating, living force. Sometimes her head hurt as it had in the cave. But none of that mattered. Here, in the dark, she could travel that vast span of time. Together they listened to the voice of the earth and it was here that she first understood the rest of it.

———————

Abdul Sulayman worked long into the night on most occasions and this night was no different. He'd called Aaqilah hours ago to tell her but he knew that this wasn't really necessary. He'd not been home at a decent hour to spend an evening with his wife and two young daughters in months. He sighed at that. But it was the way of things now. He had to honor it. There would be a future time when his family would receive all of his attention. But this time was not yet near.

There was simply not enough time. Or money. There was not enough time to raise those *sufficient* funds. He'd committed last week to staking his personal fortune on it, but a cool billion wasn't even close to enough. If only others could do the same. Many others. Or if only he could start a movement of some kind.

A *movement*. He smirked at the idea. Who did he think he was? A movement!

The music began to play on his stream again. It still struck him as strange, months after he'd first heard it. It wasn't surprising that it now played—since it seemed that it was all anyone was playing these days. That man, that *Zhar-Oss* as he called himself, he knew how to start a movement. Somehow he didn't think Aaqilah would approve, though, if he went on stage to start his movement in such a way. Such theatrics. Granted, the man's commitment to his own stuff was something to respect. To *die* so that others would learn of your work. That was devotion.

This had been the consensus anyway, he'd read somewhere. No one could find any *reason* behind the act. It seemed simply that he'd done it for the publicity. And publicity he'd received. Unbelievable. Millions. Billions of downloads. Billions! Completely inexplicable. If only he could somehow tap into *that*. If only he could create a similar phenomenon, or to be carried on the same wave. But it was art, he surmised. Of a purity few had seen before, of course, but simple, regular, wordless art. Art becoming meme, art becoming *movement*. Fascinating. And beautiful. But completely inexplicable. *His* endeavor was of a different sort.

The office where he now sat was simple, spartan by most accounts—certainly considering his station. The desk where most of his work was done was a large square of glass supported by a metal frame. The walls, too, were made of glass. He liked the clarity, the lucidity these walls seemed to bring him. It helped put perspective to his thoughts, which by any account were neither simple nor spartan.

About the office were flat panel displays with slideshows of photographs repeating in loops—the creations of his which he felt most proud. Chief among them were images of the Genesis spacecraft, the first privately funded, fully operational, manned spacecraft to leave low earth orbit. That event had occurred nearly two years ago. Six months later Genesis had left the earth's orbit altogether—ferrying supplies to the aging, small and underfunded ILB, the International Lunar Base. Three subsequent, successful trips to the moon had established the company of which he was head, Cronus Space, as the dominant player in private space operations, rivaling most country's space programs and sitting just behind NASA itself in perceived resource and capability. The success, though, had come at a personal price. His own obsession.

He'd told few the true scale of his original ambition. Indeed,

William Burcher 205

he'd been laughed out of many a funding meeting when he proposed a truly private space program—a company with investors, with stockholders, like any other. He knew that if the majority of his investors really understood his designs, nothing would have ever gotten off the ground, so to speak. Some were still calling him crazy, impractical. But these critics were merely holding on to already antiquated notions, protecting their own egoic delusions which so clearly had been proven wrong. Genesis had proven them wrong. He wondered if his next ambition would ultimately provide them a taste of his own current satisfaction.

He watched the largest of the three flat panel screens as it cycled through the images. He knew that it was approaching—his current favorite. The screen took up nearly an entire wall and its display was something not yet available in the commercial market. It was stunning. The next image showed Genesis, in polar orbit around the earth, the iridescence of a brilliant green and red auroral display silhouetting the craft. It would be the next image, he knew. And he watched as the aurora faded and out of a moments-long darkness came the ethereal, mystical image of a red planet. Mars, with its ice-caps in full bloom, a dust-storm raging in the southern hemisphere, the extent of the volcano Olympus Mons rising above the rust-covered, wind-swept plain. It filled the screen, the resulting red glare reflecting off both his glasses and the lenses of his own eyes.

His mind isolated the two conflicting thoughts within—the hint of self-doubt of moments before and the image of this red planet now before him. He isolated and he made a choice. Ignore the doubt. Let it evaporate, dissipate. There was no place for it here, in his head. It was artificial resistance and to him something like a sin. Others would try their best to tell him "no." He did not need to add to the impending chorus with his own self-talk.

Choice made, he focused on Mars—its barren beauty, its vague familiarity. The doubt faded, replaced by an upward feeling within—a thing starting in his guts and moving up into his chest, into his heart. Sometimes when he acknowledged the feeling it made him smile. It was the feeling of creation. And it was for this feeling that he worked long into the night.

A manned mission to Mars was a thing of science fiction still. Sure, it was being talked about more—US presidents had even made it a "stated goal." Though that nation's space agency had not fully committed to the prospect beyond certain exploratory demonstrations of concept and technology. The ILB had been a pitiful half-attempt, he thought; a way to keep things on life support. The real ambition languished in the minds of too many. The public expressed little support for such an endeavor—languishing itself in its own self-created problems. He'd seen the results of a recent poll indicating that the American public had a greater interest in the shenanigans of the latest company-created teenage pop-star than the doings of NASA—by a 3:1 margin! The same poll stated that when asked what the greatest achievement of the human race had been, 73% answered "putting a man on the moon."

The duality had struck him. The magnitude of that act—completed many decades before, *generations* before, had not been repeated. And it could have been repeated. Bested. Improved upon. The world had squandered its momentum in space. He would change that. Genesis would change that.

The feeling in his chest remained, throbbing with his heartbeats. The thought still excited him—years after he'd first conceived of Cronus, years after he admitted to himself the true ambition of the company, his creation. With his lips he mouthed a simple prayer of thanks for the longevity of this feeling, for its resiliency in the face of so much opposition. And then came the resolve to put his mind to work, to solve his funding problem.

The strange music of the dead performer kept sabotaging his thoughts, however. He turned it down, then off, but still it remained, stuck in his head, repeating itself in an endless, intoxicating loop. What was it with this? Why did it have such inexplicable appeal? There must be something subliminal in it, he mused. Or maybe it was an unconscious, macabre attraction to the circumstances surrounding the strange man's death.

Regardless, it held its own in his mind and he relented, letting it play out as the image of his wall-size display shifted to the iconic photo of the earth taken from the far side of the moon by the crew of Apollo 8 on Christmas Eve, 1968. The planet was a beautiful, fragile looking thing—its blue a striking contrast to the harsh and apparently lifeless grey of the far-side of its satellite. Such beauty, he thought. Such majesty. If only everyone were inspired in a similar way. If only everyone were as convinced as he that destiny was a thing *out there*.

The thought returned, only this time the seeming absurdity and comedy of it were gone. "What I need is a movement," he said aloud. And it was then that he saw the silhouette of an attractive young woman standing at his door.

———————

Abdul froze, startled. "Hello," he said, unsure. It took his eyes a moment to adjust enough to see her face. The rest of the floor had been darkened, others calling it a night hours ago. He was supposed to be alone. The cleaning staff didn't begin work for another hour or so. This woman, she was indeed beautiful. "Can I help you?"

She took a step into his office, the dim blue light of Apollo 8's Earth illuminating her face further. She looked to be in her early 30's. Long, black hair was cut straight at her shoulders, her skin a light olive. She was athletic and held herself well, with a quiet confidence he assessed immediately. She wore a black woman's suit, a white blouse underneath. She smiled at him only slightly, from the corner of her lips. It was more of a smirk.

"I heard you say something a minute before. Something about a movement."

He paused, uncomfortable, thinking for a moment that she might be there to do him harm.

"Who are you?" he asked, also searching his memory for a meeting in the past, for some recollection of her face. He found it, but it was vague. "Do I know you?"

"No," she replied simply, looking him directly in the eyes. "May I sit down?"

He knew of no other appropriate response. "Yes," pointing with his hand to a chair in a corner of the room nearest her, clearly not meant to be sat in. She picked it up immediately and moved it toward his desk, sitting down a few feet from him. She was more beautiful the closer she came.

"Please. I am working. What do you want?" he asked.

"You said something about a movement, Mr. Sulayman."

He looked at her, waiting for more. She was taking her time, seemingly enjoying the mystery.

"My name is Fleur Romano. You and I have never met. I came here to discuss a symbiosis. I believe you like that word," she said, smiling more now.

He did indeed, using it frequently in interviews, in press briefings.

"This. Here, now. Disturbing me in my work. It is late …"

"Yes. I'm sorry for that. There are reasons, good reasons, that I did not approach you through *official* channels."

"Are you with the government?" he asked her. A part of him had been waiting for this, a cloak-and-dagger visit in the middle of the night by some representative of the mythical Men In Black, or some other spooky extra-governmental agency.

"No. I'm not," she said simply, looking up at his wall of pictures from space for a moment, quiet, seemingly moved by the current image displayed—the Sun's corona viewed from Earth during a total eclipse, the magnetic field lines obviously visible. "But I do represent an organization of a certain *influence*. Half of one, at least."

"I see," he responded, instantly suspicious. "How did you get in?"

"I asked nicely. The security man, John. He's a new friend of mine," she said, again with the smirk.

"Who are you, really?" he repeated. She held the look for a moment. "I'm about to call the police." He went as far as to unlock the mobile phone sitting on his desk.

"Google Zhar-Oss' death. The video capture of the event.

William Burcher 209

The stage," she said, a more serious look on her face.

He was confused, but did as she suggested. He played the video, muting it so she would not know which parts exactly he was viewing. He'd seen it before, as had most of the world at this point. He knew what was coming, the solitary figure on stage, the flash of a razor, the scream of a woman, the blood, so much blood, the figure's collapse. The familiarity didn't lessen the emotion of the content, however. But suddenly there *she* was, with him, the woman sitting in front of his desk. She'd ascended the stage alone, immediately trying to stop the blood, applying a rough tourniquet as someone in the audience told her to stop, to stop hurting him. Here she was, the mystery woman that the police department in Denver would only acknowledge worked for them as some sort of detective.

"Well?" she asked. "What do you think?"

He didn't know how to respond immediately. "It's a good introduction. You should've had me do it sooner. I was really about to call the police."

"Yeah, that wouldn't have been very effective."

"Perhaps not," he admitted, relaxing, sitting back into his chair. "So. Ms. Romano. Please tell me more about why you're here, and maybe a little more about who you really are. You disappeared for a few months, I imagine. And now you're back. In my office. Tonight."

"Yes," she said playfully. "Tonight!"

"Symbiosis …"

"The word of the hour. Of the day even. Perhaps of the millennium," she said.

"Two organisms in a mutually beneficial relationship, you were saying—"

"Yes. A symbiosis. Toward a singular goal."

"A goal?"

"Some design, some outcome. For most … *symbionts* … that is survival, is it not?"

"Yes—"

"This goal will perhaps go a bit further than that—"

"How far, Ms. Romano?"

"Oh, about fifty million miles, give or take a few," she said, her smile now an ear-to-ear grin.

Mars was approximately fifty million miles away from Earth at its closest. That caught him off guard. Although it wasn't a secret necessarily, he'd certainly not gone public with Cronus' plans. Only industry insiders and the boards of the companies he'd approached for funding knew of his true aims. And there'd been non-disclosures thrown around like confetti. Someone, clearly, had spilled the beans. It was bound to happen sooner or later. He just hoped he didn't wake up tomorrow and see his name in the headlines attached to some jokey by-line.

"How do you know about this, Ms. Romano?"

"As I said, Mr. Sulayman. I represent a group of certain influence."

"Everyone thought you were just a cop. There in the audience of that theatre, the wrong place at the wrong time, or right time."

"It is relative, Sir, whether right or wrong," she said, nodding his way. "That was a former life. Detective. I was a detective. Working crimes against children." She said the words with a quiet gravity.

"And now you're here, in my office, talking to me about Mars."

"Life is brilliant, isn't it?" she said, brightening a little. "It will continually surprise you if you let it."

"I have to admit that it's surprising me now," he said, smiling himself. "And I think that before this night is over it will offer more. Surprise."

"Undoubtedly."

"Well. Surprise me further. Please."

"The group I represent is willing to offer you something, if you're willing to accept it."

"Money?"

"Well, yes, if you need it. But perhaps something better than money."

"What could be better than money?" he said, and instantly regretted it, the elitism of the comment harsh and almost violent, even to his own ears. The young woman seemed to catch the look in his eyes and nodded, as if to say that she knew what he meant and understood.

"We have been following your efforts for some time now. We know that things are not going well."

Despite her honesty, and apparent empathy, he grew impatient. "How much are we talking about, if this group of yours is interested in investing?"

"Ten figures. But as I said, we might have more to offer than funding."

That was certainly the right figure, but there were other, more proper channels for this, for an *investor*. The elitism returned.

"With all due respect, ma'am, I have the best engineers in the world. I have the best designers. I have the best technicians. I have the best creative minds, the best legal team, the best people on Wall Street. I have built a company from scratch which has literally landed on the moon. The security people may not be the best, but after tomorrow I assure you that problem will be solved! What, Ms. Romano, can you possibly offer me more than money?"

She paused for a moment, as if gauging whether it was time to lay her cards on his simple glass table. When she spoke it was with a voice somehow not her own, somehow bigger.

"A *movement*, Sir. I can offer you a *movement*."

15

400 TIMES LARGER, 400 TIMES DISTANT

Abdul Sulayman agreed to meet at the airfield the next morning. He was still suspicious of the woman, still unsure, but something about it all—their initial encounter, her sense of presence, her mystery—it convinced him to pay her heed until he had reason otherwise. It was Sunday. It hadn't been difficult to clear his schedule. His mercurial reputation helped, too. Elena, his assistant, had learned not to ask too many questions in situations like the one she found herself in near midnight a few hours ago, when he told her to cancel everything and that he'd be off-grid for most of the day.

Fleur still hadn't told him anything, beyond the vague offer of assistance. She also hadn't shared anything about her own whereabouts or activities in the last few months since the death of the musician. "Things changed," she'd said, after Zhar-Oss' death. She offered that his real name had been Benjamin Janus, and that he'd been of Russian descent. He asked Elena if she knew anything about the man, if there was some Russian insight that might be gained, but he'd not been lucky there, and probably just confused Elena more. Google seemed to confirm the name, but there was no history, no images associated with his search. Fleur, too, had not left any online trail since her appearance in the videos of Janus' suicide. Curious to a fault, his interest had undoubtedly been piqued. Perhaps her bona fides were legitimate. Perhaps there was advantage to be gained here. Perhaps he was in the process of encountering the real-life, goddamn *Illuminati* he thought as he turned off the highway and onto the ancillary back road, just southeast of Napa.

The airfield would be private, she said. The paved road became dirt, and he wondered briefly if this was all just an elaborate kidnapping attempt. It'd be more plausible, he thought, than the story he suspected to hear from the woman today—more plausible really than what had already occurred. But kidnapping was a simple thing, and one wouldn't need to go to such lengths to accomplish it. He was confident this was something … else. Life, he thought, really was stranger than fiction.

His electric vehicle turned silently up a long gravel driveway leading up a hill, through fields of golden grass. As he crested the hill he saw a large estate and then a mile further a runway with two large hangars. A single jet was visible, resting just outside the larger of the two structures. A solitary vehicle, a large dark luxury sedan, was parked next to the plane. He took a path bypassing the main house heading in the direction of the airfield. As he approached he could see that the plane was some kind of custom job. He didn't know planes well, choosing usually to book a flight through a jet-share program rather than deal with the hassle of owning one himself.

He was absolutely sure, though, that he'd never seen a plane such as this one before. It was of the vague shape of a typical 10-passenger business jet but was colored differently—a strange

dark grey—and the body material didn't look to be simple aircraft aluminum. It also looked fast. He briefly looked at the dig-
ital display on his own vehicle and noted that he was precisely
on time. Good.

By the time he reached the other car, a woman had gotten
out to greet him. Fleur stood beside the big BMW confidently,
wearing dark sunglasses in the morning sun as another man and
woman exited from the back seat. The two were older, the man
looking European, the black woman smiling warmly at him as
he parked, got out and walked toward them.

"Your car!" the man shouted as he walked toward them, a
booming voice with the heavy accent of the Ukraine, his hand
outstretched in greeting. "It is fast, no? And so quiet!"

"It is, Sir," he could only respond, the man's look warm and
welcoming, but also bright and intelligent. "As fast as we can
make them."

"Good, good. I have not yet driven one of these electric mod-
els. Perhaps you will one day take me for a ride?"

Abdul could only smile at him.

"I am Anatoly. My wife, Patricia," the big man said after a
pause, introducing the woman beside him. She took his hand
gracefully.

"It is a pleasure, Mr. Sulayman," she said with a thick accent,
of maybe Georgia, or one of the Carolinas. She also exuded a
sense of intelligent, calculating warmth. He decided he liked her.

"Mr. Sulayman," Fleur stepped forward, smiling. "Thank
you for coming. My friends and I had a bet between us, whether
you'd show or not."

"On which option was your money?" he asked her. She only
smiled at him, raising her eyebrows behind the glasses in reply.

"Please, could you provide the key to your car to John here?
He will park it in the hangar. As I said last night, there is a need
for discretion."

He looked at her for a moment, and then realized that she
was talking about the possibility of being seen from above. Satellites? Was this woman worried about satellites?

A well-built, middle-aged man walked toward them from the

hangar. Abdul handed him his car's RFID key and they all began walking toward the grey plane, Fleur in the lead. She must have seen him looking closely at the aircraft, particularly its surface and said to him quietly, "It's not quite an F-117. But it's close."

They boarded, ascending the steps built into the aircraft's door. Inside was another young woman, approximately Fleur's age. She was sitting toward the back and greeted them almost reluctantly, clearly occupied. She sat near a group of scientific instruments, cameras and other recording equipment, and some processing device he didn't recognize.

Fleur pointed to a seat near the equipment, "Please, Mr. Sulayman. This is Amy. She's a scientist."

"Biological physics," the woman said shortly, not looking up at any of them. She was tall and blonde and thin, dressed like a man, but in possession of a strange, unaffected beauty. A nerd's wet dream, Abdul thought.

He sat as the others did the same, Fleur first having a word with the pilot, the subject of which Adbul could not hear. Neither of the others seemed to be in any hurry to explain the reason of this trip, or his presence on it. His impatience he could no longer contain.

"Where are we going?" he asked Anatoly, trying to maintain a genial tone. The big man smiled and was about to begin when Fleur quickly took the seat next to him.

"The South Pacific," she said. "We will be witnessing an event. A *natural* event."

"The South Pacific ..." he repeated slowly. The plane's door closed and the activity in the cockpit seemed to increase. Abdul realized quickly that the aircraft's engines were running, but that he hadn't heard them. The plane began to taxi slowly and he buckled his seat's belt around his lap, noticing the others hadn't bothered to do the same. The plane accelerated smoothly but powerfully, and he was pushed back into his seat.

"You're probably wondering why you're here, Mr. Sulayman," Patricia spoke soothingly.

"The thought hadn't really crossed my mind," he replied

smirking a little, trying to rid himself of a growing, stubborn anxiety. "But please. All of you. Call me Abdul."

"Abdul, then," the older woman said. "Have you heard of the Illuminati?"

He flinched. He hoped the plane's liftoff had disguised the autonomic gesture. He noticed that the woman first looked to Fleur, and then to Anatoly, all three of them smiling as if sharing in some joke.

"We, Adbul," the Ukrainian man said, "are not them!"

Fleur and the black woman chuckled. He thought he heard the woman next to him, engrossed in her machines, laugh quietly as well.

"Well," he managed, "that is a relief …"

"And we are not part of some governmental organization, as you may have suspected," Anatoly added. "Although some of our members are heads of state. We transcend national allegiances."

Fleur was looking at him intently, having removed her sunglasses. She seemed to be gauging his response to all of it. He was sure that he was giving her a show. He'd never been good at masking his emotion, and hated the proverbial cloak and dagger.

"I apologize, Abdul," Fleur spoke. "Sometimes we have too much fun with it—when we encounter people for whom all of this is somewhat … new. Truth be told, we have not had much fun, nor many laughs, in the last few months."

He felt the mood in the cabin darken immediately. There was silence for a moment, and each of the others seemed to look down, as if in some private remembrance. Fleur finally spoke, slowly.

"What we will discuss here today is fairly serious business. But months ago I decided that you were a man who only dealt with those who conduct business of this kind."

He nodded in her direction.

"It will be foreign to you—this discussion. You may not believe it, our assertions at first. Although we hoped that by partic-

ipating in the event today some of your questions might be answered immediately."

He wanted to interrupt, but she continued, as if knowing
what he would ask her.

"The *context* of our proposal needs to be understood. Please
be patient, Adbul. I promise that your forbearance will be re-
warded." She held his gaze for a moment, then pressed a button
on the wall of the cabin causing a rigid projection screen to descend. The lights within dimmed, the shades of the windows
lowered, and a film began—the haunting wail of the music of
Zhar-Oss emerging out of black silence.

———————

Fleur could see his confusion and in another sense his fear.
The film had ended moments before and they sat now in the
cabin of the plane, a collective but unnamable mood between
them. She knew the look he displayed on his face. She'd probably displayed the same just a few months before. The film was
subtle in its introduction. It did not declare—only suggested.
And the reality of it would either register with his subconscious
or it would not. One is not afraid of pure fiction, however. She
suspected that something had resonated with this man so capable of big ideas.

The shades darkening the cabin windows rose slowly, the
pure light of the stratosphere above the Pacific shining painfully
bright and clear. Fleur decided to break the silence abruptly,
with talk that would focus this man's mind. She decided that it
needed no further introduction.

"A *direct* funding model," she said after clearing her throat.
"Financing sourced directly. Transcending national—or any
other—*artificial* boundary. You appeal directly to the people of
the world. You jump over the heads of the resistance, the nay-
sayers, those who would say *no* simply to avoid the intellectual

challenge of saying *yes*."

"I don't—"

"You appeal directly to the people of the world for your funding. All eight billion of them. $100 from a measured percentage of that. How much would that represent? Would $100 billion, would $200 billion be enough, Abdul?"

"Well, yes—"

"And then, there'd be more. Each of these donors—these investors, the world over—are granted fractional ownership of the resulting entity. Each will be a part of what results."

"But the SEC!"

"The SEC will not be a problem, Mr. Sulayman," Fleur said, reverting back to formality as she spoke with a seriousness that made him believe her.

"But I'm still not sure—"

"Of us?"

"I'm not really sure I know yet what this is all about. What *is* this all about?"

Just as he asked the question, the sound of his voice higher than he wanted it to be, the daylight outside the plane began to dim. It struck him immediately as strange, thinking that it was still around noon, the sun high in the sky just moments before. And they were of course flying above the Pacific cloud cover. He glanced briefly at his watch.

The pilot banked the plane hard to its starboard side. Below he could see the strange glow of the sun's light on the tops of the white clouds. The plane's course changed, the pilot leveled out once again and Abdul could see the sun still prominent and unobstructed above him—save for that darkening provided by the moon.

"An eclipse …" he murmured.

"Yes, Abdul," Fleur said. Anatoly and Patricia moved to his side of the plane to get a better view. Amy, the scientist, was a one-person circus of activity. The instruments she managed were recording the eclipse.

"I've never actually seen one," he said.

"And not many will see *this* one. Its path of totality follows open ocean over the Pacific only. It is why we're here. And in a sense, Abdul, *this*," she said, pointing first out the window and then at a large display on one of Amy's instruments—some kind of camera. "*This* is what this is all about."

On the display was the sun, magnified. It was now only partially obstructed by the moon. Red, brilliant beads of pure sunlight slipped through the apparently smooth arc of the moon, following dips and depressions on the moon's surface, perhaps those of valleys or craters normally not seen. He found himself wishing he'd prepared, that he'd brought his own equipment. Fleur seemed to read the look on his face and handed him a pair of binoculars specially filtered.

The view outside his window left him wordless. The arc of the moon moved slowly over that of the star as the sky above him and the white clouds below darkened further. Amy activated an intercom, speaking with the pilot directly and the plane made a slight course correction, turning to port. Her equipment then seemed to come to life. There were audio speakers somewhere that began to project a halting, incomplete noise, as if someone were tuning an old fashioned radio.

The sky outside his window darkened to an otherworldly dusk, the glowing orb above becoming something else, something different—a crescent. And then very slowly, the silhouette of the earth's moon traveled across its surface, the sun becoming almost completely obscured. The normally invisible red chromosphere became clear, the glowing red imperfections of solar prominences rising up from its surface. Moments, seconds left, and then totality. The solar corona flashed into view—a ghostly-pale halo of gossamer tendrils snaking out, away from the star. The corona was stationary from his perspective but its chaotic, vaguely flame-like form made him think of movement, otherworldly, alien movement. His mouth agape, he watched the scene in wonder, a strange and haunting sound bursting forth from the audio speakers of the instruments next to him.

It came forth in a shriek that threatened to pull him from the view outside his window. The volume was adjusted immediately and it lessened to a background noise, a song that seemed an appropriate accompaniment to the scene his eyes witnessed. Moments passed, his perception widening, still in awe. The sound was structured, rhythmic. A flash of recognition. It was related to the music of Zhar-Oss, Benjamin Janus.

He took his gaze off the scene above him, looking over at the instruments. He saw another display that he hadn't before—an image of the sun as seen from space, provided by a solar observation satellite. The image was dated and time-stamped and he realized that it was live. The lower structure of the corona and the chromosphere were visible as the image appeared to be enhanced somehow or recorded in some wavelength other than visible light. Suddenly there was a small flash on the screen, an eruption of light from one of the surface prominences. Instantly a corresponding audio note was produced, coinciding exactly with the solar activity.

The sky outside began to lighten. He returned his gaze to the view above. The outward veil of the corona lessened and then disappeared, the brilliant red beads of light returning to the dark edge of the moon's silhouette. The music emitted from the instrument lessened and faded with the coming return of a more normal sun. The others in the cabin began to react to what they'd just witnessed.

Anatoly said something in Ukrainian.

Patricia was repeating, "Glory, glory …"

Amy was visibly pleased. "We got it. It worked," she said, smiling. "It *actually* worked."

Fleur was still looking at the display with the magnified view of the eclipse. The image of the sun, still half-obscured by the moon's silhouette was reflected in her eyes.

Sulayman didn't know what he felt, or what to think. He was numb. "What was that? That sound? It was like the music of your Janus."

Fleur looked up at him, her eyes still blazing with the sun's reflection. "Yes," she said. "It is very much like Janus' work, only not entirely."

"Not entirely, no," he replied, confused. He could still remember the images in the film he'd finished just minutes before of the earth slowly spinning on its axis, the light of pulsating, shimmering aurora at its northern pole, the music of Janus choreographed to each step in the dance of the Northern Light. "What was it, Fleur?"

"That, Abdul, was the song of our sun."

He could only look at her as his mind decided whether it should admit the truth of a realization a scared part of him had been trying to repress for the last hour. Fleur saw the confusion in his eyes.

"We belong to an organization, Abdul, that is very old. It was formed to maintain the knowledge of what you've just witnessed—but pertaining specifically to the earth's song only. The song of the sun is something new to us, one we've only recently discovered. The name of our organization is the *Zhar-Oss*. It is the same taken by the musician. Janus was a part, a member."

"The song. That song the sun was … singing. And that of the earth before it in the film. There's something *there*, isn't there?"

She looked at him, a glint of some emotion sharp but warm in her eyes. "Are you ready?" she seemed to be asking him.

"Please, tell me more," he asked her again.

"Yes," she replied simply. "There is. *Something* is there."

"Has it been … decoded?"

"For longer than the span of human history that before today you knew," she smiled.

"How, is this possible?"

"We don't know entirely. People like Amy are working very hard currently to understand."

"What does it … say?"

"Are you ready?"

"Yes, please."

"There is a message contained in the song of the earth. It is … direct. We have not yet decoded that of the sun. We don't know yet if *that* is possible. Or if it is, if any of us is capable of understanding it."

"Direct?"

"Directed at us."

"You're kidding me."

"As far as we can tell the message comes slowly, very slowly. The earth is over four billion years old. Time is a different thing to it. Each thought, each word comes with the passage of a thousand years or more. Beyond maintaining the knowledge of it, Zhar-Oss was formed to translate subsequent portions of the message as they come to us over eons."

"How old is your group?"

She smiled at him again. Anatoly and Patricia had left their positions on his side of the plane. They were now flanking her, smiling also.

"Zhar-Oss is over twenty-seven thousand years old, Abdul."

He could not look at her directly then. It sounded too absurd. He recognized, too, that the most amazing absurdity was that he believed what this woman was telling him. It all seemed to resonate somehow, to make sense. He ignored the implications that were arising in his mind; questions of what he thought he knew about the world and his place in it.

"When the message is viewed as a linear thing, the words coming at a regular rate in regular intervals, we can go back in time and apply an approximate date to its beginning," Patricia spoke for the first time in minutes.

"The date of its beginning is meaningful," Anatoly added. "For it seems to coincide with the rough era that scientists apply to the genesis of our species."

"This is unbelievable," Sulayman managed, his breath coming now in gasps.

"We believe that the earth, a sentient, intelligent being, was aware of our genesis," Anatoly continued. "She seemed to begin speaking directly to us, the moment that we were first able to understand what she was saying."

"The message, Abdul," Patricia added, not waiting for his response. "As far as we can tell, is approximately 300,000 years old. It has been spoken over the course of 300,000 years."

"And you're waiting for me to ask what it says. What does this message say?"

The three opposite him were silent for a moment. Patricia sat down, and Anatoly looked as if he were contemplating doing the same. Fleur began to recite the message, the words that all of them knew now by heart. She held back, coming to the end of it. Abdul was pale.

"The last portion of the message has only recently been translated."

"How? How is this translated?"

"By people. By us," Fleur said.

"By Ms. Romano, Mr. Sulayman," Anatoly corrected, placing his hand on Fleur's shoulder. "Fleur is our current translator."

"It is some kind of perception. Direct. I can hear it without the instruments, Abdul," Fleur said. "As hinted at in the film earlier, the current thinking is that we all possess the ability to sense the planet's magnetic field. There's a grouping of specialized cells within our sinuses. For some it is more active than others."

"Janus. He could too …"

"Yes."

"The most recent part of the message. I assume this is why I'm here."

"Yes," Fleur said.

"We believe that the timing of this is absolutely critical. That more than an obvious *synchronicity*, the fact that this portion of the message has been translated now, is meaningful in a way that few things are," said Anatoly, his excitement a growing thing. "As *Gaia* herself says, *time is a different thing to us.*"

"Please. What is the rest?"

Fleur did not hesitate any longer, speaking as she sat. Anatoly remained standing behind her. "Until your return," she continued as if reciting verse. "As a prodigal child, wiser than before. I await this day. My brothers and sisters in their dormancy await your coming too."

A spark, electric, ran up Abdul's spine. He was silent for a moment, the words repeating themselves in his head. "What does that mean?"

"It means that we're getting you to Mars, Mr. Sulayman. And it appears that the earth itself is providing the mandate."

He asked them all an hour ago for space, for silence to con-
template the revelation just befallen him. As he watched the afternoon sun reflecting from the clouds and here and there on the
water of the Pacific, he had to admit that these people had not
really offered unequivocal proof of what they claimed. Could it
all be a hoax—albeit a very elaborate and expensive one? What
would the goal of such a hoax be? Embarrassment alone? It was
more likely these people were simply mad. This shadowy
"group" to which they supposedly belonged—it could just be
some cult. There had to be well-funded cults out there. His own
ethnicity and religion had certainly given rise to conspiracy the-
ories.

After a few moments he admitted that these thoughts, these
reservations were just that—his mind's way of coping with something more outlandish than he could have dreamed. And somehow despite all of his caution, his inherent skepticism, he believed it. He admitted this to himself, the words welling up inside. I believe it. I believe this. Their story. Them. Her. And
threatened with a realization that challenged his concept of self
and surroundings, the ego in him quickly attempted to build a
wall, a redoubt against the coming flood. It was inevitably swept
away with the torrent. The ocean below and the clouds above
that sea, the horizon hundreds of miles off into the distance—
the strange blue line high above the plane in which he flew, underlying a deeper, darker more void-like space—all of it was now
a different thing, in possession of a meaning more profound.
And somehow it all made sense. It was as if something in his
chest had opened and bloomed and caused the words to come
out.

"Ok," he said to all of them at once, or possibly to himself.
"How do we do it? What do we do? How do we do this?"

William Burcher 225

Fleur had been staring out her own window. Her hair was loose and fallen, covering one side of her face. She looked back at him almost startled. Her eyes were red and swollen.

"We tell the world, Abdul," she said in a low, quick voice as if the words had already been prepared. "We tell the world."

16

RESISTANCE

He was fatter and older than the pictures he sent, but it didn't matter. He was here in this place for a singular reason, and beauty had nothing to do with it. The man clearly hadn't showered recently either—or maybe it was the gear he wore. No, he hadn't cleaned his gear. The rough of it would be good. He was sure of that, his heart pounding in anticipation. Deep inhale. Urine. Sweat. Bleach. He began breathing harder, panting in preparation for the pain to come, the pain already extant. The man approached, brown eyes glaring behind the black leather hood.

"What do you deserve, Faggot?" he said, trying hard to lower a naturally effeminate voice.

"Pain, Sir. I deserve pain. I'm a nasty faggot, Sir," Kohl replied, whimpering. He struggled against the ropes binding his arms and his feet.

"What kind of pain, Faggot?" the man shouted as he took hold of the bullwhip.

"Any kind you want, Sir!" and then an animal scream as the whip cracked loud in the stale damp air. His heart was about to jump out of his chest, his panting a terrified, animal thing. Already the sweat was dripping from his forehead, his armpits, his crotch.

"Please Sir! I'm a nasty faggot! I deserve pain!"

The first flash of the whip to make contact was lighter than he'd hoped, but he put on a show for it, screaming and contorting. "More Sir! Please, Sir!" he shouted.

The next didn't disappoint. It knocked the wind out of him, drool soon dripping down his chin. He didn't have time to shout before the next one hit him in the abdomen and across the chest and all he saw was an eruption, a flash of red behind his eyelids.

"You're a nasty faggot bitch, Slave!" the man with the whip shouted with a lisp, his own excitement taking hold of him, striking out with the whip again, lower this time. Kohl shrieked and shouted as loud as his convulsing lungs allowed him, the breath coming in mere seconds before the next one forced it out again.

"Please, Sir!" he managed, not sure if he wanted more. The man behind the mask took it to mean one thing only and put a dark red gash across Kohl's chest. His body writhed and contorted, the stand to which he was attached rattled and shook. It was shaped like a cross. He'd suggested it tonight, wanting a certain extra, a certain symbolism. One lighter slash, and his master gave him a break. But only long enough for Kohl to recover. He approached Kohl moments later once his breathing had just begun to slow—a pair of electrodes in his hand. The man on the cross began to scream once more, and whimper, and beg.

———

Kohl took a long drag on the cigarette, savoring its hot poison. The room was dark save the tiny bedside lamp with an old-fashioned bulb, the dim yellow light throwing shadows on his face, the silhouette of which cast large and monstrous on the opposite wall bare of anything but a water stain. No one would ever look for him there. A dirty place. A dirty soul.

He sat up slightly to remove the old blue jacket to the track suit, wincing a little with the movement. He took the jacket off slowly, like an old man in the yellow light—the contusions from the whip now purple and green, the rope marks on his wrists and ankles black. The jacket fell to the floor, lying among ashes from his cigarettes and a bag of fried chicken a day old and half eaten, tipped over after he stepped on it, kicking its contents across the floor. It was hot in the room and it stunk. It was his own stink. He took another drag and blew smoke into it, watching it hang there just above him, churning silently with unseen currents.

He tried to summon the mindlessness of hours before, but already it was faded and gone. A thing of the past. For one hour, maybe two with the subsequent numbness, he'd been free. Of thought. Of memory. Of that different kind of pain. But here it was, returned. As throbbing-hot as before. As always.

He turned his palms upward and looked at them, his wrists and his forearms. St. Axel von De Wallen. The tattoo on his right arm still looked red in the dim light. It always managed to look red, even in absolute darkness. It held no meaning to him now. No. His interest now was in the other arm, hashed with innumerable thin scars just below his wrist, and running all the way down near his elbow. Man is indeed a dark thing. I am a dark thing. Separate and alone in this dirty place, a shadow. Walking, suffering clump of ash. So separate. So alone.

"Why, my friend?" he whispered, still looking at his wrists. "Why did you leave?" He said the words in Russian, in the language that had been their favorite, seemingly theirs alone. "In the light of my memory …"

In the light of his memory it was a perfect thing. But that light is a false light. It had always been tainted. Tainted with him, his worry, his obsession. Tainted by duty. It haunted him still and the longing, coming up from below, threatened to come out as vomit. He wished it would. Get it out, out of him. But that never happened. A spark of fear both real and violent and then the realization, "Who would I be. Without this?" He swallowed it down, held the sick, familiar bile of it inside.

"Veniamin," he said after a moment, low and hoarse, just to hear the name again. I am sorry, my friend. I am sorry. And he realized the mournful sadness of having never called Janus anything other than *friend.*

His cigarette complete, he stubbed the still glowing butt on the surface of the glass table and picked up the square razor. The small little perfect implement held tight between thumb and forefinger, he began to cut the surface of the flesh of his left forearm.

"I am sorry, Veniamin," he repeated in his head as the crimson bubbled up, beading inconsistently from the capillaries beneath his skin. His own current act was proof enough of what he'd decided. He, in all his ability, his quickness and cleverness, was still an imperfect, flawed, and dark thing. Separate and alone was all that we deserved. We are not yet ready for more, he thought.

"I am sorry, my friend. But you were wrong," he repeated aloud in Russian. "You beautiful, beautiful man. You were my light. You were my star. And you left me alone and in the dark for an idea both flawed and false."

He reached over with this left arm, the blood from the cuts now dripping onto the floor, and turned off the dim yellow light, to end the night in sober darkness. Someone, somewhere, in another room was playing strange music too loudly.

————————

The synod was to begin precisely at 9:00 a.m. and to his pleasure all of the invited confederates were present well before he cleared his throat loudly and began to speak. There were precisely 12 of them—all but one of them male. He'd kept the number small and these were trusted allies all of them, each fully devoted to maintaining the integrity, the orthodoxy of their Confederation. He knew this with absolute surety because he'd had their lives hacked. Most, of course, were keepers of the Book, but not all.

"Gentlemen. Madam. Our fugitives have surfaced," he said in English, without introduction. The others looked at him startled, and not a few were obviously pleased by the news. He paused for effect and to let the murmurs subside before continuing. "As many of you know Anatoly procured a *Wraith* before the incident at the cave. Beyond the obvious pre-meditation this demonstrates on his part in the events leading up to their departure, the plane is of course extremely difficult to track. Last Thursday, however, we got lucky."

He stepped aside allowing for an unobstructed view of the flat panel behind him. A satellite focused on the western coast of the United States, zooming quickly in—the Central Coast, the East Bay, Napa and then the image of a small airfield. It was a private runway based on the relative lack of structures and aircraft. Only one plane was visible. The image zoomed further and focused and the clear outline of a small business jet appeared—the skin a dark shade of grey.

"Gentlemen. Madam. Our missing Wraith," he said. "We know that the aircraft is nearly undetectable save for a very unique IR signature produced by its engines. For the last few months we have been utilizing an American asset—a supposed NASA space observatory designed for observations in the infrared—scouring the globe for this specific signature. As I said, last week we were lucky."

The image behind him, until now a still-frame, flickered and became alive—a video. The frames came quickly, fast-forwarded minutes, then hours, then suddenly slowed and the playback was once again in real-time. A dark vehicle approached, parking next to the plane. Moments later another vehicle. Occupants of the first exited, followed by a single individual from

William Burcher 231

the second.

"Presumably our fugitives, my friends," Kohl said. Within a few moments the figures in the video boarded the plane which quickly began to taxi before taking off. The image then flashed to a larger image from orbit displaying most of the south Pacific region. A linear red overlay displayed the plane's course. "It traveled for four hours at an average velocity of mach 0.96, reaching an uninhabited area of open-ocean approximately 500 miles east of the Marquesas Islands. There the plane circled for approximately 30 minutes before following a return course back to the airstrip in north-central California."

"What were they doing there?" Jorge Dias-De Santos asked. He was a small, old man of quiet bearing. He asked the question knowing that Kohl would have an answer.

"At first we had no idea. Then we discovered that the flight appeared to place the plane in the path of totality of a solar eclipse which happened to be occurring at this time."

"An eclipse? I knew of no eclipse during this time," Dias-De Santos added.

"It was not a well-publicized event. Totality occurred only over open ocean in the Pacific," he responded.

"Curious," said the old man. "The sun. Could it be that they were investigating the phenomena associated with the sun, as our colleagues have proposed?"

"*Former* colleagues," Kohl corrected. He did not want to go too far down this path. He recognized that he could not predict how any of these 12 might react to possible radical, new additions to the Knowledge. Already rumors of an update to the message, possibly provided by Fleur Romano, had begun to circulate. These he'd worked hard to quell. The old man sensed this and ceased his line of questioning. There were those, such as Dias-De Santos, who would protect the purity of thing by denying the truth of another. He knew that he could count on Jorge for anything, when the time came.

"The *what* of their activities is of less importance presently than the *how*, and the *who*, I believe. Our goal now should be singular. To find them and to apprehend them immediately; to halt whatever designs they may possess. We will expend all possible efforts and accomplish this as quickly as possible. We owe this much to our fallen, our *murdered* comrade. We owe this to Genji Ueshiba."

The others nodded their assent. Kohl's eyes met with the old man's and discovered a knowing there. He had his suspicions, apparently. But within those eyes was also an approval. The old man was aware that Kohl was also willing to do whatever it took to ensure the Confederation's survival—in its current form.

"Who is the other? In the other vehicle. We have our three fugitives. Who is the fourth?" he asked Kohl.

"We are not yet sure. We believe he arrived at the airstrip driving an electric luxury vehicle not yet on the commercial market. This will of course make his identity relatively easy to discover. We are exploring this lead now and will have an answer shortly."

"Good," the old man said simply, nodding.

"The Reaction Team is on alert, ready to respond anywhere in the world within a few hours, once they have been located. Each of you knows what you must do, owing to your individual specialties. All necessary files have been uploaded to the secure server. I reiterate the need for absolute secrecy in this matter. I should not have to remind you of the divisions currently present in Zhar-Oss. This is a critical time for us. But I am confident that one thousand years from now, our progeny will look back on the thirteen of us with reverence and respect, knowing that *we* protected the integrity of our heritage, and the Knowledge itself. The world is not yet ready. This was true at the time of our founding and it is true today. Work hard, my friends."

The twelve rose and began to leave the room. Dias-De Santos was the last to rise and held Kohl's gaze for a moment before turning to follow the others. Just before he exited he turned.

"Mr. Kohl," he said quietly. "Can I have a word in private?"

Kohl was not surprised. "Yes of course, Señor Dias."

The old man shut the door behind him and went to sit back down at the conference table. Kohl followed him. "You are wise to limit this synod to twelve, Mr. Kohl," he said. "These times are dark, and indeed one does not know the true allegiances of anyone anymore."

Kohl nodded. Dias was not one to small-talk. He was communicating something.

"I want you to know that I represent a larger group than you may know. A group whose loyalty you can rely on," he said, to Kohl's pleasure. "But my friends and I have other concerns that I wanted you to be aware of."

"Please, go on."

"Chief among these is the apparent popularity spreading across the globe like a virus, of Janus' music."

"I agree, Señor. It is most concerning."

"Are we doing anything to counter this?" the man said flatly.

Kohl was not sure where this conversation would lead. He did not like it, though. What would the old man have him do? By all accounts *billions* had now been exposed to Veniamin's work. Despite their influence, no one can suppress the activities of the myriad users of the Internet. The democratization of the Web was something none of them had been prepared for. Dias read his response.

"Why have you not yet undertaken a campaign of defamation?" he asked, his voice rising.

Kohl was caught off guard.

"I believe the direct threat posed by Anatoly and Ms. Romano constitute—"

Dias interjected forcefully. "You and Janus were close, it is true?"

"Yes, of course. That is not a secret," he replied.

"He was your ... protégé, yes? And I have been told that there were other rumors also."

Kohl grew silent. The undifferentiated emotion welling up inside threatened to turn into something other than fear. Dias backed off slightly.

"But these we do not need to discuss now. What I am concerned with explicitly is whether you have allowed this former *closeness* with the dead man, to cloud your judgment in this manner."

They stared at one another for a moment. He wondered why Dias-De Santos brought this up now, today. Could he somehow be aware of his own activities last night? He held that thought deep within lest it surface and the fear of it show on his face.

"I assure you, Sir, that I will do whatever it takes in our shared goal. Janus was wrong. Our society is not ready. Now is not the time of Return. Such a thing would jeopardize our exclusive position as the keepers of the Knowledge. Indeed, such a thing would challenge our very existence."

"Yes, it would, Mr. Kohl."

"But perhaps I will give the matter of Janus' music another review," he added in an effort at placation. The old man nodded.

"Yes. We think that wise. And I will trust in your judgment," he said in a way which Kohl understood as "for the time being."

"We have an understanding then," the old man said.

"Yes. An understanding," he replied.

"Good day then, Mr. Kohl," Dias said as he turned to leave, smiling gently.

"Good day, Sir," Kohl replied, mechanically. He waited for a moment until he was sure Dias-De Santos was well down the hallway outside the boardroom before taking a chair and sitting. His mind was quiet for a few moments as he stared down at his hands, resting on the table's surface. There seemed to be a buzzing somewhere in the room.

It would be a profanation, the voice in his head spoke, the words strange and separate things. Of everything they stood for. Of the Knowledge itself. Zhar-Oss had not existed for millennia to be profaned in such a way. An image came, unbidden, of Fleur Romano as she watched the Atlantic passing below them on the flight to Europe, that fateful first day they'd met. For a moment he wondered what she was thinking. He thought of the ramblings in her sleep and then her disclosure that she'd been dreaming scenes of Garr-Eth's experience. He thought of the moment she said it: "His name was Garr-Eth ..."

"Mein Gott," he whispered with a single exhale. And he lost himself in another scene—that of Genji's face in the split-second before he pulled the light plastic trigger of the Glock. The man had completely accepted it. And he'd been brave. He, too, must be brave. He must fight for this cause. As it was righteous. Correct. Fleur, Anatoly, Patricia, Veniamin—all of them were wrong.

And he returned to the present moment. Hearing a strange sound, he looked down at the rich wood of the boardroom table and saw his own hand tapping out a melody on its surface. He stopped it quickly with his other before someone else could recognize the tune of Janus' song.

17

WHOSE TIME HAS COME?

"There will be resistance, you know," she said, breaking the long silence.

"There always is," Sulayman replied.

"Yes. Perhaps. But I meant something more specific. My group. Zhar-Oss. It is divided. There are those, a large number, maybe half of us, who do not want our secret out."

"Your need for discretion …"

"Yes. There is a motivated and capable faction among these who will try to stop us. Directly. If they could find us."

"Violence?"

"Yes. There is the potential for it," she responded, not hesitating, but also apparently not willing to provide anything more.

"I understand," he said.

The plane had descended and the coast was coming into view. The cloud cover had broken and the afternoon sunlight hitting the cliffs off the Central Coast and Big Sur made Sulayman think of his childhood in Tel Aviv. But these he knew were comparable in his imagination only.

"Why don't they want it out, this revelation?" he asked her.

"There is a tenet ingrained in the culture of the Confederation, one of extreme conservatism, suspicion of anything representing change. It has served them well, however, carrying the group through millennia. But without *exclusive* access to it—the Knowledge—their sense of exceptionalism is threatened. There are those, too, who enjoy the power and the money the status quo provides. But mostly it is terrifying for them. Opening themselves to what they in their hearts know will happen. It is a violent expression of your *resistance*, Abdul."

"And what will happen, Fleur? When we come forward with this?"

"People will wake up."

"Wake up?"

"From their dream, their nightmare of separateness. It will give them purpose, Abdul. Purpose to look *up*, and *out*. And *in*. Purpose and perspective."

He turned to look out his window for a moment, watching the breakers of the coast fade and the golden, rolling plains east of Monterey replace them.

"I have to admit that I am a little scared myself," he said, turning back to her. She smiled, knowingly.

"I'd be lying if I said that I didn't have doubts," she replied. "But underneath these is something else. A feeling. Maybe an emotion. Maybe something else. I'd experienced hints of it before ... *this*, before that day half a year ago when I came in contact with this group and what they had to show me. But since then I've known it without pause. It's the earth, and it's also more. It's a part of her, and a part of me simultaneously. It comes up out of the darkness from below and seems sometimes like ... *joy*. And I know that nothing can stop it but that things *want* to stop it, dark things, things both outside me and within. Your resistance is its opposite, its shadow. This feeling is connected to this path we're on now. And when I feel scared, or doubtful of this plan of ours, or of myself, I remember this feeling. I get in touch with it. And all of that *shadow* goes away. Do you know this feeling, Abdul?"

"I do," he said seriously. "I know it well. And three hours ago when I saw the Moon eclipse the Sun, and you presented me with this story that sounded like science fiction, my first reaction was a skeptical one, born perhaps of *resistance*. But then there was something else. A recognition. I saw in it the same thing, what you're talking about. And I knew that there was truth there."

"What do you call it? The feeling?" she asked him.

He paused for a moment, taking a breath before responding.

"It's a pure thing," he said. "I would propose that women have always known of it more than men. Creation. I call it creation."

———————

Anatoly was going over the scenario intently, to a degree that made Fleur's head hurt. She was amazed Sulayman wasn't fatigued after the revelations of the day. She respected the man's mind.

"The process has already begun," Anatoly explained. "Seeds have been sown. Memes have been created by various confederates, and slowly leaked to the public. Many of these are associated with the work of Benjamin Janus."

"Which itself has gone viral," Sulayman added.

"Yes. This we did not expect. We estimate that the number of people across the globe who have been exposed to Janus' music is now in the billions. This is validation, truly, that there is some resonance, some recognition within the minds of most men and women. As you yourself witnessed today, we do not believe it will take much for people to awaken. And to believe."

"What are these other 'seeds', as you say?" Abdul asked.

"Some are works of art. There is a television show now running in China with familiar themes. A popular theatre production in Mumbai, a novel just released in Spanish by a Chilean author. Certain mobile phone advertisements throughout Sub-Saharan Africa. A football jersey seen at the World Cup this year. Many incorporate the images of aurorae—and we are helped of course by our timing in the Solar Cycle. It is of course the solar maximum this year, and I am told that the solar CME and sunspot activity is this year exceptional. Aurorae have been witnessed by many people across the globe living in latitudes where the phenomenon is not common."

"Yes. One of my launches out of Florida was scrubbed recently due to an unprecedented solar storm. This has been in the news media frequently."

"Yes. Our timing could not be better. The list of our *seeds* is extensive. We have prepared for this for some time. And it appears that certain *natural* phenomena agree," Anatoly said proudly.

"Janus' music is still the most valuable of these memes," Fleur interjected. "It is the single most powerful connection we will have to the minds of so many. Once we come forward—with the truth, with the Knowledge—once people know what Zhar-Oss' music really is, and once we connect you and your ambitions to it and to the message of the earth, you will have your movement, Abdul."

He looked out his window, away. "I will have a movement," he repeated.

"And then there is the matter of the press conference," Anatoly added.

"Press conference?"

"Just prior to it we will release the video that you have just seen. To every news outlet, to every social media site, to every hosting site on the Web. We will also release a prepared, recorded statement by Fleur and others, explaining it all. But yes. We feel that a press conference, as quaint and at this point *anachronistic* as that may seem, is the best way to come forward in an official manner. There are a good many confederates in the media. Some, yes, are still on the fence, but many support us. Once we come forward, though, the movement will be like a wave, a tsunami, something unstoppable. These confederates will assist in the reporting of our story."

"How are you going to organize something as public as a press conference with this other … faction … on your tail?"

"You may help us in this regard," Anatoly said. "We originally planned on limited conference at a time and place of our choosing, discreetly arranged for this purpose. But we feel there may be another way."

"One of mine?"

"Yes. We recognize that you speak with the media regularly, and that most of your launches are covered heavily. It would be an easy thing to present ourselves there, to *hijack* the conference, effectively. There would be an obvious security advantage in doing such a thing, as the act would be a surprise. We believe that there would also be an added sensationalism, as well as the obvious linking of your own ambitions with those we represent."

"The next launch is in two weeks. It's a big one. Another resupply of the Lunar Base. A deep-space mission. The press will be out in force."

"Yes. We know. We were hoping for this."

"Let's do it, then."

"Perfect."

"Perfect," Fleur agreed.

"It's settled then."

"Almost," Anatoly spoke. "We must of course ensure that your familiarity with us, with the Confederation, and our meeting here today, remain unnoticed."

"Of course," Sulayman said. His voice betrayed an anxiety, perhaps at the proposition of this vague threat he did not fully understand, perhaps over the scenario itself. All of them in the plane's cabin knew the man would be risking his career, his reputation on this plan of theirs. "How do we do that?"

"You give us your car," Anatoly replied. Abdul looked at him, puzzled.

"Why?"

"It is just a precaution, but we cannot risk the possibility that it has been tracked. We are fairly confident in our understanding of the capabilities of the faction. The vehicle was probably not identified as our analysts tell us that it looks similar from above to many others in its class. But it could probably be tracked if you were to drive it home from our airfield."

"But that would mean that this plane is being tracked currently. That it was visible on the ground before we took off. All of this, could be at risk—"

"The *Wraith* may perhaps be spotted and identified by its unique characteristics, but we are quite sure that it cannot be tracked, Mr. Sulayman."

"We'll get you home, Abdul. You'll then be watched, by us. You won't be aware. No one else will know. But we'll be there. For the next two weeks, you live your life normally. I know it will be hard, but it has to be this way."

"I understand," he said. "But if we land at the same airfield, won't it defeat the purpose? Can't we still be tracked?"

"We're not landing at the same airfield, Abdul," Fleur said just as the plane banked to the north toward a line of thunderstorms. Fleur checked an app on her phone. "Have you ever been to Murphy, Oregon, Abdul?"

"I can't say that I have."

"Good. You'll get to see it this afternoon, apparently," she said smiling. "It will be a long drive home though, I'm afraid."

He shrugged his shoulders. He suspected that he could use a long drive, and the time it would offer him to think. To absorb. To feel. He took a breath both long and deep.

"How do we know this will work?" he asked them. Fleur looked as though she didn't want to speak any longer, an exhaustion creeping into her face.

"A French author," Anatoly continued, "Victor Hugo, once said that nothing is more powerful than an idea whose time has come. This is something, more than an idea, whose time has come." And the world outside went dark as the sleek little plane flew on into the mass of grey and turbulent clouds.

John didn't know who these people were, exactly. But they paid unbelievably well. His SF background had obviously helped him get the job, along with his personal tenet to never ask too many questions. The daily reality of it had him traveling the world and doing odd things like driving this car to his own home in the dead of night. But shit, it was a nice car. Really nice car. He didn't mind taking direction from that Ms. Romano either. The woman was smoking hot. And sure, he carried a gun—that was part of it, probably the most important part—but he hadn't had to use it yet. They weren't into anything illegal, anything dishonest as far as he could tell. Just a strange group of secretive rich people led by a smoking hot brunette.

His leading suspicion was that they were some kind of cult. But it didn't bother him. He was making six figures running glorified errands. None of the guys from the team could claim the same. All in all it was a sweet gig.

He'd waited around most of the day in the hangar where he'd parked the car, reading a book and exchanging text messages with this girl, Andrea, he was seeing. He had instructions to wait until dark to drive the car out and home. They were apparently worried about satellite coverage—nothing new. He did as he was instructed but thought they were all a little paranoid. Despite the suspicions of many a right wing nut out there, the government didn't spy on its citizenry beyond an occasional snoop into email and text messages. And if some NSA puke wanted to get off reading his sweaty ramblings to Andrea, that was fine by him. People gave the government too much credit. Spying was a tough business, hard, expensive. Secrets were hard to keep. Organizations inevitably had leaks. That kind of spying couldn't be kept up for long.

William Burcher 243

He adjusted the cooling setting on the seat and the car notified him that his setting had decreased the range of the batteries by a half mile. Abdul Sulayman's personal car. Unbelievable. The man was worth billions. In the news all the time. Rockets. Private space exploration. Takes a visionary type, he decided. A visionary type with a nice car.

He pulled off the highway toward his place in Sacramento. Ten minutes later he arced into his driveway and then silently into his garage. It was late, and the neighbors wouldn't notice. It wasn't all that strange anyway. Last week he'd come home in a brand new 7-series, the week before a Jaguar. They thought he was some sort of luxury broker/dealer.

He took a moment to collect his things as the car's soft lighting glowed on his face, rough now with brown and grey stubble. He remembered to plug the vehicle in before heading into the house. As he set his wallet and phone down upon the counter he heard a strange noise from the side of the house, then the back. He froze and immediately sourced the gun in a holster still under his jacket, instinctively verifying that it was there, ready.

A silent moment passed and his doorbell rang. It was 1 a.m. Shit, he thought. They're around the house. He was sure there were others already surrounding the house. No choice. He could do nothing, wait for them to come in, or he could open the door for them. He thought briefly about his M4 upstairs but no, that was premature. And probably ineffective.

He walked to the door, looked out the peephole and saw a slight but severe looking man standing in the half-light in a shirt and tie. Well, whatever. This is why he was paid as much as he was, apparently. Though no amount of money was worth dying over. Did he believe that? He had only a few seconds to decide what he believed.

He opened the door and the man standing there held out his hand, smiling wanly. He spoke coolly in a slight German accent.

"Hello Mr. Murphy. My name is Kohl. Whose car were you driving?"

18

DARK WATER

It was a warm, wet evening, the air heavy, still and stagnant. Light rain from clouds broken and incomplete drifted down onto the otherwise undisturbed swamps surrounding the constructions of men—the concrete tarmacs, runways, launch pads and towering cubes housing the objects of a former ambition.

Traffic was heavy on the roads leading into the Cape. Traveling by car was the only real choice—the relative anonymity of the big SUV, its windows tinted an ominous black, a necessary thing. Fleur sat in the middle seat, Anatoly next to her, Patricia up front. The car was driven by a "security associate," a dour and alert man whose obvious athletic build betrayed nothing toward his indeterminate age. Two more, a man and a woman, sat in small swiveling seats in the rear.

They sat in stillness, in quiet, each absorbed perhaps in the music of Benjamin Janus playing at a subdued volume over the audio system; or perhaps in something else. The music at least was part of a tribute and mild documentary to Janus aired on a satellite radio station. Fleur had been checking on Internet search trends associated with Janus when she came across an announcement for the program, and quietly asked Patricia to turn it on. The satellite radio station was a popular one, and the statistics displayed on her phone significant. Searches for "Zhar-Oss" were up 147% that week, 130% the week before. The trend betrayed a ridiculous, exponential increase in the world's interest—something begun immediately after the incident on the stage in Denver six months ago. Searches for "Benjamin Janus" displayed a similar pattern. Most interesting to her though was an analogous trend, though less pronounced, for the terms "Gaia" and "Gaia Hypothesis." She leaned over and showed Anatoly the data then. He smiled and shook his head.

That was minutes ago, and she'd put her phone away. She sat now and watched the other people in their cars on the same road as they. Some of the vehicles in the gridlock clearly transported government and media types. But most contained families, children, coming out to see something spectacular. Sulayman's rocket, the Olympus, was the largest and most powerful in the world and dwarfed even the fabled Saturn V of the Apollo era. She saw one boy maybe 8 or 9 years old dressed as an astronaut with a silver-reflective suit looking out his window seemingly toward her. The boy could have belonged to an earlier era, a time when children by the masses still dreamed of rockets and space and trips to the moon. Now he seemed a curious anachronism.

Their vehicles converged and she watched him, sure that he couldn't see her through the obscurity of the SUV's windows. He was of a mixed, indeterminate race, his hair mussed, the only child in the car. She saw that he was looking above her own vehicle, away and out, toward the launch facilities periodically breaking the horizon. He might have seen the Olympus on its launchpad, nearly 400 feet high, lit from below. Or perhaps he saw a bird, an eagle even. Or maybe he saw nothing and looked only into a grey and empty space waiting for the manifestation, the materialization of something only a child's mind could dream.

She had cause for anxiety, she admitted. Though she didn't feel any. Every few yards the vehicle made in the heavy traffic brought her and her friends closer to a place and a time where destiny was like gravity, pulling them inward, causing their coalescence and heating them up—objects and light circling fast toward the inevitable singularity.

She wasn't alone. Not anymore. She closed her eyes and felt it, felt *her*, felt *him*, and indeed something perhaps *more*. Breathed it in and then out. The pulsing, flashing red brake lights of the vehicles on the roadway lit her empty face. She kept her eyes closed, the red light seeping through her eyelids. She opened them when the light went away and the SUV began to accelerate, the traffic clearing.

"Where are you going?" she suddenly heard Anatoly speak, his voice rough. "Rand, I think you missed the turn."

Patricia looked over at the driver, for a moment mildly concerned.

"The complex is back the other way, Rand," Anatoly repeated. The driver didn't seem to hear him, or was strangely choosing not to listen.

"Rand?"

"What's going on?" Patricia joined him. "He's right, Mr. Cummings. It's back there."

Fleur suddenly was aware of a change, a hard and heavier mood most notably from behind her. Anatoly's voice displayed increasing concern as he continued to ask the driver what was going on. Fleur placed her hand on Anatoly's knee when she realized that both the man and the woman sitting behind them had drawn their weapons, holding them low but most assuredly in their direction.

"I'm sorry folks," the driver said in a Texan drawl. "There are other plans. Truly. I am sorry."

The three of them froze, silent. There was no confusion. They'd lived the last six months aware that such a scenario could befall them at any point. But it hadn't materialized. And here, now, to be so close to their goal—Fleur immediately felt deflated. She could sense the anger flaring in Anatoly sitting beside her. Patricia too was clearly incensed. Despite their best efforts clearly Axel Kohl's tendrils had extended their way. Patricia broke their momentary silence.

"So tell me, young man. Two hours ago you sat across that aisle from me, talking to me about your two little boys. What do you think those two little boys would think of their father now, betraying a friend for what, for money?"

The driver ignored her, turning onto a perpendicular, ancillary roadway.

"Is that was this is about, young man? Is this about money? Do you know who's writing your check, Sir? The last time I saw Axel Kohl he placed a gun to the head of someone who up until five minutes before was his protégé and confidant. He pulled the trigger and I had the man's brains and bits of his skull on me."

The man shifted in his seat.

"This is the man you're working for, Rand. He is a killer. And now, by implication, so are you. You are delivering each of us to our deaths. You may not know the whole story, but that's what this is, Rand. Before you continue on this path you'd better ask yourself, Son, if you will ever be able to face those two little boys as their father knowing you were an active participant in murder."

The man was clearly uncomfortable.

"We never got this far, Son. But I know that you were in the service. Corps, by the look of you and that haircut. I was in the Navy Medical Corps." Patricia said. The anger in her voice was something else now, but no less intense. "Force Recon is my guess. I know that we like to hire folks with special teams experience. I was a surgeon, Rand. I spent most of the 2000's in Iraq."

He chanced a look at her, a sideways glance, his knee twitching.

"Shut her up, Rand," the woman's voice came from the backseat. "She's trying to get to you. You don't know if any of that is true. She saw your damn file, that's all."

"Bravo surgical company, Camp Fallujah," Patricia said.

"Shit," the man said slowly in exhale. He turned to the others in the back, his look pleading.

"All we're doing is bringing them to him! What happens after that isn't our responsibility! Shut her up!"

"It doesn't fucking matter! We're here. Christ. Look," the other man said from the back of the SUV. "Fucking spook bullshit," he muttered, shaking his head.

Two vehicles approached them rapidly. The pavement of the road became dirt. It was some kind of service area, unfrequented by the look of the overgrowth. The road opened to a kind of lot. The other vehicles, both SUV's, didn't slow until they were threateningly close. One in front, skidding to a halt, the other continuing and then circling quickly behind. Immediately men got out, weapons drawn. They approached aggressively, covering Rand and everyone else in the vehicle, shouting to get out. The three with guns were scared, confused. Rand opened the door, his hands held up.

"I'm sorry," he said to Patricia, his face anguished. "I'm sorry," before being restrained by two men and disarmed.

No one's loyalty was a given thing, apparently. The other two were approached and treated similarly, then removed to the vehicle behind their own. Patricia sat in the front seat, shaking her head, disgusted at the pale visage of the man she saw sitting in the front passenger seat of the SUV in front of them. She was the first to get out of the car, refusing to place her hands above her head. She kept Kohl's gaze as one of the men forced her roughly to the ground and put her hands in cuffs, his knee in her back. Anatoly got out next, swearing in Ukrainian and spitting before being restrained in the same way.

Fleur was now alone. She watched as Anatoly and Patricia were led into Kohl's SUV, the front passenger door opening in a way that allowed Kohl to avoid contact with either of the two. He approached slowly, and motioned the other men to approach with him. She thought about that, wondering briefly what she would do if she *had* been armed. Well, so be it. She stepped out of the back seat, addressing Kohl directly.

"Axel. This won't accomplish anything. It's already begun," she said, and for a moment she saw something not expected behind his eyes.

"Hello Fleur," he said after a pause, holding back a few yards from her. His voice was low, barely audible in the thick air and light rain. "You've been busy these last few months. It's a pleasure to finally see you again."

She was patted down roughly, thoroughly by one of the men.

"It is already happening, Kohl. You're aware, as much as I. Janus' music. Billions, Kohl, billions are listening to it now—drawn by their own recognition of something deeper."

"You cannot stop this, Kohl. Gaia herself wills it!" Anatoly shouted from inside the black SUV, his voice ending sharply. Fleur guessed that he was struck.

"How can you deny the world this, Kohl?" Fleur asked him. "Go walking down a street in any city of the world. You see it in their faces, you hear it in their voices. We are incomplete without that connection. We have reached a point where we cannot go any further without it. And the earth cannot survive much more of our self-obsession, our mindlessness."

"You're wrong," Kohl said, taking a step toward her, speaking so that she was the only one to hear his words. "Without you, it stops."

She held his gaze and in a moment of insecurity she wondered if that were true. Maybe it was.

"There's more to it. The message. There's more there," she said loudly, so the other men with him could hear. Judging by their immediate reactions she guessed that a few of them were confederates. Maybe all of them. "The fact that I am translating it now, and that we are here in this place today about to witness this launch screams that now is the time for Return, Axel! The message has come at the only time in our history that we are able to fulfill nothing less than the will of the planet! We can do it, now! This cannot be a coincidence!"

Kohl shifted his weight, briefly glancing back at the others behind and around him. They were all listening intently.

"We are all standing here in a clearing on Cape Canaveral about to witness the launch of a rocket designed for deep space, capable of propelling *large* payloads beyond earth orbit. Not ten years from now, but now!" she almost shouted. "I can feel it now in the center of my head, throbbing, palpitating—singing. It's talking to us, Kohl! The earth is speaking to every one of us!"

The others were clearly affected. "She can translate?" Kohl heard one of the men ask. "I was only ever told she could hear the song. Like Janus," another said, confused. Fleur heard them too.

"He told you that I murdered Genji Ueshiba. This was a lie. Kohl confiscated my gun before the cave. Genji died protecting us, knowing that after discovering that I heard it, that I could understand it, he would act. Kohl killed Genji for this. He used my gun. And now you are all here today to assist in silencing me."

One man close to Kohl was now staring at him. A few had lowered their weapons. When she began to recite her own translation of the message she heard a few of them exhale, deflated. Her voice rose to a powerful pitch as she spoke. "Like your own mother in childbirth I will nearly be destroyed so that you in your infancy can grow. But of this body I freely give."

"Be quiet!" Kohl commanded. "Shut up!"

Two of the others almost spoke in unison, stepping toward her. "No! Let her continue."

"Until you return," she said. Then, pausing briefly and speaking louder still, she continued with words neither Kohl nor the others had yet heard. "Until you return, as a prodigal child, wiser than before. I await this day. My brothers and sisters in their dormancy await your coming too."

"My brothers and sisters …" Fleur heard one of them repeat. "What does it mean?"

William Burcher 251

"Planets. Other planets ..." she heard another.

"Mars," one said. "It means Mars."

"Shit ..." another whispered.

Kohl was not prepared for this reaction. For a moment there was indecision in his eyes and then the spark of some darker thing.

"Enough!" he said to both Fleur and the other men. "She and I must have a discussion among ourselves. We will go for a private walk."

As Kohl removed his own weapon from inside his coat the men looked first at him and then at each other. They were confused, unsure. He saw that he must act immediately, before one of them showed any kind of resolve. He pushed Fleur quickly in the direction of a small Jeep trail leading off into the brush and the bracken. There were mutterings of disagreement and confusion behind him, even his name uttered without any real commitment, but he gave the situation no time to evolve.

"Keep walking, Ms. Romano," he told her, holding the gun in both his hands, arms outstretched. The noises of the others, of Anatoly and Patricia in the car faded quickly, the foliage around them closing in. She could hear her shoes sinking into the wet, green earth. Kohl's steps too came slogging in behind her.

"I won't plead for my life, Kohl. But I'm not going to be quiet," Fleur said. "My death will not accomplish anything. You saw. It will still continue. People *want* to understand this. The Confederation can't contain it."

He looked around to see if any of the others had followed. They hadn't. The two were alone with each other, with the mist and the dark foliage. He slipped briefly in the wet and the mud. He was also too close, Fleur realized. He was too close to her. And he held the gun out too far from his body. The ground was slippery. He wore flat-soled shoes. She stopped walking.

"You told me months ago that you and Janus were close, that he was your protégé. How did it feel when he came to you and told you his wish—to come forward with the Knowledge?" she asked him.

He stopped too, staring at her face in half-shadow.

"It felt like a betrayal."

"Why? Why did it feel like a betrayal?"

He seemed to be thinking, struggling with something. "I exposed him to it. I brought him first to the cave. I was there with him when he first heard the song. It was I who he first allowed to listen, to his work, to his music—"

"You shared in it together," she said, her face a mask.

Not liking where she was going Kohl gestured with the gun, slipping slightly in the mud. "Continue walking, please," he said, the words an interrogative.

"His music. It was first a gift to you. Because you cannot hear the song."

He looked downward, and then up. "Yes. Yes, Ms. Romano. Veniamin first brought forth into this world his music—so much an expression of what he heard in his own mind listening to the song that Gaia sings—for me."

"You loved him."

"I cannot—"

"He loved you."

"He is no longer—"

"Alive."

Kohl inhaled the word. He looked down once again and for a moment the gun lowered slightly.

"I too know what longing is, Kohl. But somehow, those we've lost are not truly gone. I've been there—a place where she resides. And time is a different thing there. To her. They are there. With her."

Kohl did not seem to be present and for a moment she thought something may have changed, but then it came back, he came back, looking back up at her.

"I think we've talked enough, Ms. Romano. Please continue walking," he said, this time the muzzle of the black handgun flashed toward her.

She saw that he no longer held his finger out of the trigger guard. His finger rested on the trigger itself. He gestured once more and she took a step, two, three—faster than before. Kohl subconsciously tried to keep up and she heard the tell-tale sound of his feet slipping once more in the mud. Now, she thought. It had to be now.

Centered, balanced, her legs crouched and gravity low, she spun hard and fast, finding Kohl's arms and the gun in them right where she thought they'd be. She heard a grunt from him and then a muffled explosion as it went off inches from her ear. She heard nothing more after that as the round passed through empty air and the space occupied a half-second before by her own head. Kohl didn't have time to get another off. Off-balance and stumbling backward, he took a hard left hook to his face. He had time only to grab onto Fleur's body, clutching her desperately like an old man and the two fell off the trail, down a small drainage embankment.

Standing water, mud, rotting greenery, Fleur was ready. She went immediately at his face, raining blow after hard blow, feeling the bones of her own left fist break, the skin around them cut deep by Kohl's teeth. He lifted his hands in front of his face to deflect her, but stopped nothing. He began to writhe and splash in the mud and the shallow water, hitting her hard with his leg, knocking her off balance.

He was on top of her as she fell. His hand to her neck. Squeezing, clawing, grasping. She coughed and choked, the whites of her eyes flashing in the dark. With her index finger she dug deep into his left eye and then her right hand, struggling to strike him, instead found purchase on an ear. She closed around it and pulled, ripping it off wholly with a sudden explosive jerk. The ringing in her own had lessened and she heard his scream, the blood bursting forth. It fell bubbling and hot soaking her neck, her chest. The hand around her neck loosened with the coating of lubricating blood. Able to breathe, she kneed him hard. A pause, a second gone and she felt him go limp. She pushed his body off her own and with heavy, forced breathing she got up, immediately kicking Kohl hard on the side of the head with her booted foot. He was down. He remained down.

She stood above him, panting hard, looking first at Kohl's form, lying almost motionless and prone in the muck and the mire, and then at the sky, suddenly bright. The broken clouds of the ceiling to the north flashed with a golden, explosive light. She heard Kohl begin to moan slightly before his animal noises were awash in the terrifying roar of the rocket launching in the distance. Within moments she saw it, strangely larger than anything poised in the air should be, climbing quickly, steadily above the trees. The rocket climbed first through a low band of clouds before hitting clear air, then clouds again—each layer exploding in golden glow before falling dark again with its passage. Higher it rose, constantly accelerating, the deafening, rolling thunder fading up, up.

"I want you to kill me," came the voice of the man beneath her, still hushed and muted by the rocket's din. He then began to cough before looking up at her with one eye—the other bruised and swollen shut. "I dropped the gun just up there. On the path. Please retrieve it, and shoot me."

Fleur looked at him and then spat blood onto the surface of the dark water. She'd bitten her tongue during the fight. She climbed back up onto the trail, doubling over with a coughing fit. She saw the gun resting plainly on bare earth where Kohl had dropped it. She picked it up, cleared the chamber of the live round and removed the ammunition magazine, holding the gun in her right hand, the mag in her left. She tossed the gun as far as she could into the tannic water of the swamp, the mag she tossed in the other direction. The single loose round she let lie alone in the dirt.

"No more dying," she said to Kohl. "There's been enough of that. Wake up and start living, Axel."

Kohl whispered something, then coughed.

"What?"

"We have him."

"What are you talking about?" she asked.

"We have his body, you know. It is preserved. Frozen. The body of the Founder. Garr-Eth."

She stood for a moment saying nothing in response, pausing only briefly before turning to leave him there still prone in the thick biota. Kohl watched as she walked slowly back to the place she hoped her friends were. Fleur gone, faded back into the dark, he lowered his head and began to cry.

———————

The two SUV's were there, still. She emerged from the dark and approached them. The passenger door to one flew open and the man stood for a moment staring at her, a phantasm walking his way from the forest.

"What the fuck?" he muttered. Headlights flashed on and the night was lit, Fleur was lit, covered in mud and blood seemingly not her own.

"Where's Kohl at?" the driver asked the other man, then asked Fleur as she approached. "Where's Kohl?"

"There was a gunshot…"

She didn't answer him, nor the other one; walking past them to the second vehicle containing Patricia and Anatoly. Neither of Kohl's men in the vehicle got out. When she reached the driver's door she stood for a moment, staring into her own reflection in the glass of the dark window. She rapped on it with the knuckle of her right fist. Slowly the window lowered.

"Get out," she said to the man. Patricia and Anatoly were in the backseat, their eyes wide. Patricia was sobbing. "And give me your key," she told him, holding out her bloodied hand to receive.

He did.

19

TRUTH AND THE LIGHT

"Ladies and gentlemen. As you already know the launch of the Olympus VI was a complete success. All three stages performed flawlessly, propelling Genesis out of earth orbit. Genesis is now well on its way to the moon for a successful supply delivery to the ILB."

He looked out into the crowd, noticing some familiar faces but also many others new to him—older faces, more distinguished faces. It was as if many of the media representatives who normally attended his launches and the conferences afterward had been replaced by their bosses, and in a few cases it appeared, the senior executives of their companies. Sulayman was amazed to see Laura Watson, CEO of NewsGroup, sitting in the front row with a tablet, as if she herself were writing the story for publication on the Web and tomorrow's newscast. Perhaps she was. The tension in the large room was thick—a sour, pungent thing.

Elena had told him that a few of the networks were delivering the conference live.

"But the success of tonight's launch is not the only announcement that I am here to make," he said, pausing to gauge the crowd. They all stared at him intently. Indicator lights on the cameras in the back of the room blinked steadily.

"The first concerns the future of Cronos Space," Sulayman said, this time pausing for effect. "The second concerns the future of us all."

———

The roadways were surprisingly empty this deep into the Cape. They'd gotten through the security checkpoints earlier in the night, before their betrayal had been evident. She drove the SUV fast, befitting a singular purpose. It was strangely quiet in the vehicle's interior—the steady roar of the heavy coastal air against the windshield, the occasional squelch of the wipers trying to clean too-dry glass the only affront to the calm. Anatoly and Patricia seemed numb, the big man nursing a large goose-egg above his right eye. Patricia continually looked backward, out the rear glass for the other SUV, but it didn't materialize. After a few minutes she must have realized that it probably couldn't *catch* them even if the men decided to try and stop them. There came a strange shudder in the big vehicle as its speed-governor activated, the engine valves opening with a rush of air, at 105 miles per hour.

"When were you going to tell me?" Fleur asked suddenly, her eyes not leaving the roadway, the question directed at both of them, either of them.

"Is Kohl dead?" Anatoly asked her. She looked at his shadow, his silhouette in the rearview mirror for a split second.

"Not that I'm aware of," she said mechanically, staring once more ahead.

"We were going to tell you, Fleur," Patricia interjected. "I swear it to you. The time just never seemed right. And you have so much on your shoulders already."

"We planned on telling you after tonight," Anatoly said quickly, Patricia touching his leg in silent rebuke. Fleur was quiet for a moment.

"After tonight," she repeated.

"Yes," Patricia said.

Fleur let up on the accelerator and SUV slowed. She applied the brakes, hard, and Anatoly and Patricia held onto one another tightly. They turned onto the short roadway leading to the admin facility where Sulayman would now be speaking with the press. The tires squealed on the wet pavement.

"Tell me how it came to be," she said, hitting the accelerator hard once more, the vehicle's big V8 roaring. The admin complex was visible now in the distance. They would be upon it soon.

"But we are almost—"

"Tell me, Anatoly. Now."

———

The screen behind him flashed on displaying the image of a crescent earth. It appeared static until one realized that it was receding ever so slowly. The image was large, and the mostly-dark globe of the planet took up the entire frame. Clearly it was taken from well out of low earth orbit. Time and telemetry data were added suddenly and it became apparent that the feed was live, from Genesis. The yellow-white light of the cities of North America, the eastern seaboard partially shrouded in a weather system, were clearly visible. South America's northern half was mostly clear and dark, save for the lights of the cities on its edges. Both continents' western coasts were still awash in sunlight.

"This feed is of course provided by a camera on Genesis,"

Sulayman told the crowd. "Which is by now reaching the distance above the earth occupied by satellites in geosynchronous orbit. It's beautiful, isn't it?" he said, his tone becoming conversational.

"And when you see the earth as this, as the awe-inspiring but *finite* location of all of our worries, all of our concerns, all the petty dramas that dominate the majority of our lives—there is of course a sense of fragility, of insignificance—but also one of uniqueness and appreciation. This is our home. And there we are, our entire civilization, living our lives on its surface."

Sulayman took a step away from the thin podium and began walking the stage, the energy in him requiring physical outlet. The image changed, and now included the moon, as seen apparently from an observatory at a Lagrange point further out. This image was also live. Some in the crowd were startled and surprised as they realized that such an observatory was not known publicly to exist. Others in the crowd stirred for a different reason. He had footage from their satellite. It was his first admission of what was to come.

"This image contains all of us in its frame. All of us. Every single one, is here," he said, pausing, pointing. "It's time to change that. Cronos Space and Genesis are about to change that. And we're going to do that with the direct assistance of anyone on the planet willing to help."

He watched as a bead of snot dripped down from his nose and into the dark water below his face. He could see it with only one of his eyes. The other was now dark except for a red halo that throbbed painfully with his heartbeat. Most of the rest of his body hurt. Half of his face was numb, though he didn't think the raw and wanting flesh where his ear had been bled any longer. Or perhaps it did and merely flowed down across his face and neck into the open collar of his shirt.

He'd ceased feeling anything from his testicles, though the pulsing nausea remained deep in him, in his guts. He'd pantomimed a vomit earlier but nothing but a small amount of bile had come out of his mouth and into the swamp water. He'd been too nervous throughout the day to eat anything. He rose painfully, a facsimile of a man, something less—a homunculus rising up out of the biota. It took him nearly a minute to lift himself to the bank. There he sat, shaking lightly, breathing hard, wincing with every inhalation.

"A man sees in the world what he carries in his heart," he said, spitting something dark out of his mouth and into the bracken. Blood and Goethe.

Had he told Fleur about the body of the Founder to hurt her? Or was it a gift? Why had he told her? It had been the last thing to give her. That was all. The last bit of him that would matter to her. Good or bad. Would she feel loss? Would she feel excitement? Would she feel anything?

"Veniamin. Look at me now. Do you see this?" He spoke under his breath, head slumped, looking down at the water. "But perhaps you always knew this to be the real Axel."

His head slumped further. He was prepared simply to fall asleep when his one eye saw something dim laying in the dirt beside him. With crone-like fingers he reached out and lifted the single 9mm round up into the air. He held it higher for a moment, silhouetted against the clearing night sky. His hand clutched it tight and he stood. Blood and Goethe, he thought, and began to hobble and limp down the trail.

———

"We have always had him. They, the originals, preserved it immediately after his death. Perhaps the process was begun even before. They could not of course know what they were doing, but probably had a sense that the glacial ice would prevent his body's return to the earth. The ice would preserve him, for years—for longer. The ice would allow his body to endure."

Anatoly spoke in hushed tones as they sat in the vehicle, the engine still idling quietly, parked in a fire lane outside the large building.

"The artifacts in our facility at the cave; they were of course with him. They, too, were preserved," Patricia added. "We only recently separated the artifacts from … the man," she cut the words off quickly and looked down, as if she believed a sacrilege had been committed.

"As the technology for a thorough … analysis, became available it was decided to open Garr-Eth's tomb within the ice. The site itself is also threatened by a well-known phenomenon—that of the worldwide melting of alpine glaciers."

"Where is this site?" Fleur asked.

"The French alps. Near Mont Blanc and the Chamonix Valley."

"That is a well-traveled location, correct?"

"Yes. The confederates within the French government have worked diligently to ensure it remained a secret," Anatoly said, voice louder and seemingly proud.

"Which will of course be moot after tonight," Patricia added, trying to lighten the air.

Fleur did not pay the comment any attention. "And what kind of analysis, Anatoly, did Zhar-Oss perform?" she asked.

He pondered the question, aware now that he might need to restrain his exuberance. "Archaeological of course. We have learned much from the Founder's clothing, his tools. Anatomical. He was approximately sixty-five years old when he passed. He was 191 centimeters in height—quite tall it seems. He had a meal of something like pemmican as his last. And genetic."

"Genetic. His genome was preserved?"

"Yes. His body was remarkably well protected within the ice and not subject to any exposure or freeze-thaw cycle such as other frozen bodies from prehistory have been. It also appears as if he were frozen immediately after death, or as I hinted at earlier, that he died during the freezing itself."

"Is his … appearance, preserved?"

"Well, yes."

"Was there anything else of note discovered with the analysis?" she asked.

"No, not really. Of course it is all very fascinating. But I don't …"

"Please tell me, Anatoly."

"As I said, he was remarkably well preserved. It was mentioned almost in passing in the initial reports but certain *individuals* have since seized upon the information. I don't know. Perhaps it is important. Preserved along with his genetic signature was his, well, his reproductive capacity. Our scientists believe they have obtained viable sperm."

Fleur looked at him then for a full second before turning the vehicle off, opening the door and stepping out. She moved quickly toward the building's entrance knowing that neither of the other two could follow her at that pace, and knowing that this would prevent them from seeing the emotion in her face.

Sulayman stopped briefly on the stage, gauging the energy in the room. Despite the anxiety, despite the obvious anticipation coursing through the large space like an alternating current, they were with him. These people were with him.

"I have for some time now been pursuing a project that only some of you are aware of. For the last year I have sought funding from multiple sources for this project, primarily the United States Government, but also the governments of other countries. These attempts, for the most part, have been unsuccessful. I have come to the conclusion that *government* no longer possesses the will to engage in projects of this sort. And that for the greatest aims and ambitions of the 21st century, *government* may no longer be the appropriate framework. Tonight I am proposing nothing less than the *transcendence* of government for what promises yet to be the century's greatest aim."

He paused. A cough. A murmur. They were waiting for more. The screen behind him split into two images—a live self-shot of Genesis taken from a rear-looking camera, showing the spacecraft with the receding earth as backdrop, and then another of a previous mission as it orbited the Moon.

"I was once taught by a teacher and mentor of mine that the simple question '*what if?*' can activate our imaginations. So, *what if* an organization existed which transcended national boundaries? *What if* that organization sourced its capital directly from the myriad peoples of the planet, peoples in all countries, professing all creeds, from every economic, political, cultural background? *What if* that organization were completely and utterly transparent? And what if that organization were devoted solely to the most trans-national, species-wide endeavor possible—the manned exploration of space?

"Many have suspected from its beginning that Genesis was not designed simply to ferry supplies to the Moon, that larger ambitions were seen in the minds of its creators. This suspicion would be correct. Genesis was designed for *deep* space—for extended travel, in deep space, supporting multiple crew. Ladies and Gentlemen, it has been decades since humanity took its first steps on another planetary body. Many people, if you ask them what the single greatest accomplishment of humanity has been, will answer with that first pivotal event. And that event belonged to our grandparents' generation. Decades have passed. Generations have come and gone. And some might say that we've squandered the legacy of Apollo. I'm more positive on the matter—I believe we've only *postponed* that legacy.

"That ends tonight. Society's self-obsession and isolationism ends tonight. That decades-long period of our own insular turn will end tonight. Because it's time to go further. We will do this together, as partners, as fellow inhabitants of this planet, and as equal, interconnected parts of a much greater whole. Genesis. Cronos. Humanity. We're going to Mars."

<hr width="20%" />

He walked along the roadway stumbling in a dark lit only vaguely by the South Florida light pollution and the occasional passing car. A few slowed for him, one had stopped—continuing on only after he ignored the driver's shouts and entreaties. Despite the pain, the bright electric acid coursing through his veins, he walked on toward the place where he knew she'd be.

Still a mile or two out, he thought he could make out the glow of the admin complex in the distance above the reeds and mangrove. He'd been walking already for an hour, his watch would have told him if he had the strength to look at it. At times he had to stop, overcome with something he couldn't identify, something welling up from below and different from the pain. It seemed to come from the same place in his guts that ached from the young woman's strike to his groin. The last time it came up with the force of vomit he'd noticed that the tears from his eyes had moistened the dried blood on the side of his face. Both tears and blood flowed then in union.

With the tears had come images of Veniamin unbidden. The look on the young man's face when he first shared his work. Standing before a mirror nude as he shaved his throat. His last presentation before the synod. Dancing to a song that only he could hear when he was first brought to the cave. Janus, alone before a fire. Janus, looking up into a clear winter's sky that night in Reykjavik. Janus on the stage with Fleur Romano.

The dense metallic weight in the breast pocket of his sport coat became the contrived focus of his attention. It held his sway, allowed him to walk, tied tenuously together an angry remnant of something now foreign. It swung awkwardly, loosely with his halting, handicapped steps. It was heavy. It had taken him what seemed like epochs, eons of time to locate—resting on the plucky branch of a mangrove. That it hadn't ended up in the dark water

William Burcher 265

or been buried in the mud, the angry part of him judged to be providence. He was meant to find it. He found it, he carried it now for a reason. A gun. His gun. A single round found gleaming in the dirt. Providence. Reason.

This reason would keep him walking, keep him fighting the pain and the desire to vomit. But it wouldn't quite keep Veniamin away. Nor did it prevent him from beholding the nascent luminescence suddenly flaring to life in the northern sky. An aurora. At this latitude. On this night. An auspicious thing.

———

She flashed the badge Sulayman had provided to the guard just inside the door, who looked at her questioningly before waving her through.

"Nosebleed," she said to the man before hurrying to the nearest restroom. She saw that he'd been watching a feed of the press conference on his phone before standing to greet her. Sulayman was already speaking energetically to the audience. It would not be long.

She removed her own jacket, then the white blouse underneath, soiled completely with Kohl's blood. She stood before the mirror wearing nothing but her bra wiping the dirt, the grime, the dried blood from her neck and her chest. She could do nothing about the red finger marks developing on her throat.

The blouse would have to go, and she tossed it into the trash. She put the jacket back on, buttoned it high to cover her breasts, and leaned forward to look once more at her reflection. Her eyes focused first on her own tired face, then through the mirror's reflection to a space behind.

He stood behind in the shadows, out of the sharp light of the LED fixture. She could see that he was young now, her age, the age he'd been when it began. His eyes met hers and he raised his hands to show them to her. His face was pleading, imploring.

His hands were covered in blood.

"I know, love. It began with you," she said aloud, her voice echoing volubly in the empty, sterile space. "And tonight it ends with me."

He lowered his hands and nodded in assent, his eyes mournful. The pull of his gravity was something she almost couldn't overcome. It was a longing beyond space, beyond time. But she summoned the strength from a place within. She left him there in the shadow as she walked out of the restroom and toward the place where she could hear the echo of Sulayman's amplified voice speaking now of Mars.

———

The tumult was something he'd not expected. There was an instant reaction, people jumping to their feet. Some, he could tell, reacted to his apparent audacity. Some were simply excited. Still others reacted for a different reason. These, he surmised, were Anatoly's "confederates." There was anger there, as if somehow he encroached on a boundary that only they could see. Through the uproar, through the confusion he heard a word shouted from multiple sources, screamed, hurled like a lance, thrown like a jagged rock in his direction as a weapon, a retort vastly more than it was a question. He stood before the storm like a rock, waiting for it to subside.

"How," he said. "Yes, indeed. How."

The crowd quieted further, ready to listen. For a moment he was struck by the audience's constituents. The NASA administrator, in the front row. He recognized two more CEO's of large media companies. Editors of traditional newspapers were present too, many more of online sources. Authors, bloggers, television people. He'd never given a presentation of this kind before. He'd expected a strong turnout, but nothing like this. Anatoly had hinted at a significant presence, influential individuals not normally present at such an event, and the old Ukrainian hadn't missed the mark. It gave him confidence, assurance, that he wasn't committing suicide, professional or otherwise, on the stage right now.

"How will Cronos motivate—or inspire—participation in such a project? How will we raise this money? $100 billion. We're looking at a cost of $100 billion to do it right. This will not merely be a trip and back. We're not simply orbiting the planet, though this would be a significant accomplishment in its own right. We're not traveling fifty million miles to touch the surface and then to leave after a few hours. This figure gets us a permanent settlement on the Red Planet. And it will be the first of much, much more."

He noticed subliminally that many of the crowd were now watching the screen behind him. He continued despite this.

"Direct participation," he said. "The people of the world directly participate. Sounds implausible? A tall order? Perhaps. In just a few minutes, however, your minds might change. We accomplish this through a *movement*, a movement that's already begun."

Every face in the audience was now directed above him. He turned to look and saw the twin screens: Genesis live with the earth in the background, and Genesis orbiting the moon on its previous lunar mission. He manipulated the display controller and the live image spread across both screens and the sudden flash of green and red lit the lenses of his eyes. A massive aurora in the Northern Hemisphere was developing.

"Genesis!" he said aloud, his voice suddenly tense. "Sarah, get in touch with Space Weather immediately." He ignored the fact that his voice was still amplified by the room's audio system.

"Bob, what is that? We were told there were no CME's even remotely in earth's vicinity," he directed the question directly to NASA's head administrator. The man was already on his phone, shrugging his shoulders and shaking his head, clearly worried.

Sulayman glanced back up at the screen. The extent of the auroral display was striking. He'd never before seen anything like it. Where it flashed and flared the iridescence obscured the surface of the earth. The lights of its cities were completely veiled.

"Unbelievable," he said into his microphone as the auroral ring flared and expanded across the globe. It now clearly extended down into latitudes it should not. Most of the United States was now covered by the shimmering light.

"They can see it outside!" someone shouted from the back of the room. In *Florida?* Unbelievable. The NASA people, his own people were all on their phones. The amount of energy required to produce a display this size was unimaginable. How could they have missed a Coronal Mass Ejection of that size? Genesis would be fried. All his plans. All of his work. It could be going up in smoke right before his eyes at this moment as he watched.

Yet—there weren't any artifacts in the live video stream. Still the earth receded slowly, still Genesis continued on its trajectory to the Moon. There should be artifacts—static, pixelation, interference with the radio transmission. There was nothing. It was clear, as clear as it could be.

"SOHO has nothing. NOAA has nothing, Abdul," Bob Hsu, NASA's head said loudly, above the noise of so many simultaneous phone conversations.

"Genesis is completely operational, Abdul," Sarah Hall shouted up from the side of the stage. "The systems aren't seeing any increased levels ... of anything."

"Confirmed," Bob shouted, adding to Sarah's update. "My people are totally perplexed. It doesn't appear to be CME related."

"Then what is it? What else could generate an aurora of that magnitude?"

"We don't know. But from what everyone is saying, it may not necessarily be a reaction to anything external. It may not be traditional auroral phenomena."

"Not external ..."

"Global communications don't seem to be affected either."

"What's going on then? What *is* that?"

At that moment he happened to be looking toward the back of the room when the large double door of the main entry opened and Fleur Romano quietly appeared. Their eyes met over and across the crowd of people anxious and waiting for something more.

She moved with a quiet grace up the center aisle unnoticed by most of the audience. Those who chanced a look saw an attractive young woman walking with a purpose, a dignity, a face devoid affectation. She approached the small stage and immediately ascended the three stairs leading up. For a moment it seemed that she didn't belong, that she was somehow crashing the event, that she might be there to protest something—or worse. But Sulayman seemed to acknowledge her with his silence, and when he stepped away from the podium and she stepped forward to take his place, it was clear that she was meant to be there.

She stood silently, relaxed and confident, looking out across the hundreds present in the room. Some had maintained their phone conversations as she entered but slowly the noise from these lessened and died until there was silence, the eyes of everyone on this strange woman standing before a screen displaying a radiating, iridescent Earth.

She remained for a few moments, holding the silence longer than one thought normal, until everyone in the room was aware of it. It became uncomfortable, each component mind of the audience becoming self-aware, self-effacing. Someone coughed. A body shifted in its seat. Someone neglected to end a phone conversation and a concerned voice on the other end demanded an update. She looked out at them and met the eyes of many with a look that promised something wordless, ineffable. It was a look of a sage, an old and wizened teacher—or perhaps the look of a child.

She turned to look up at the screen behind her and paused

in the position for a moment, the green and the red reflected in the glistening lenses of her eyes. She watched seemingly unsurprised as the massive auroral strands pulsed and shimmered and then flowed like a length of silk in the wind. A low sound was born on the room's audio system. It was at first barely discernible but rose in volume slowly. It grew in intensity and pitch and became something vaguely familiar, recognizable. Not quite music, the sound was alien and discordant—as if born from a primal thing not quite human. It rose further still until it was the only thing able to be heard, masking all other secondary noise. It took only a few seconds for most in the crowd to recognize what they heard—the music of Benjamin Janus, Zhar-Oss. It took only a few seconds further to realize that this was somehow different, and to see that with every peak in pitch, every long, deep note, every crescendo, the aurora in the image behind the woman at the podium responded in step. The lights danced with the strange music, or the music was the audible expression, the vocal counterpart to the strange phenomena now enveloping the skies of the Northern Hemisphere.

Fleur faced the audience once again. As the music faded she took a deep breath and began.

"What you just heard is a translation into audio of a recently discovered signal emitted in the area of the lower Van Allen Belt above the earth's atmosphere. The signal is not classically electromagnetic and has only recently become detectable with contemporary advancements in quantum mechanics."

As he watched her from the side of the stage Sulayman both recognized the woman, and didn't. Her left hand was held in an unnatural clutch and he saw what looked like drying blood on the back of the other. Her pants appeared to have been splashed with mud, and there were strange red marks about her neck. But still, despite these, despite the superficial blemishes to her appearance, she possessed a gravity, a presence seemingly not her own. She was utterly calm.

"Many of you undoubtedly recognize the audio translation, as it bears remarkable similarity to the music of the late musician Benjamin Janus—otherwise known as Zhar-Oss. But, as you also noticed, this song is different. It is a live feed. As the video image from Genesis is, as is the image from the observation satellite parked currently at L1. Janus did not have access to the reception and translation technology that I just demonstrated for you here. These have only been functional for the last few months. And Janus obviously didn't create his music from the images you see now. Janus *heard* it. Janus *heard* the song. And he re-created what he heard for the world with his work."

She stopped speaking for a moment, gauging the audience. Sulayman looked at them too and saw that they listened. Still the lights on the cameras in the back of the room blinked steady and he thought momentarily of the millions of people around the globe watching this strange presentation.

"Six months ago I met Benjamin Janus immediately after he opened his wrists with a razor blade on a stage in Denver. Video of that horrific act went viral. You might remember a young woman, later identified by the Denver Police Department as one of their own detectives, jumping up on stage in an effort to save the man's life. I am that woman. My name is Fleur Romano, and I'm here tonight to speak about that," she said, turning to face the image of the earth and its auroral display once again, pausing to consider it, a hint of a smile coming to her face.

"Janus' suicide triggered a series of discoveries and events in my life related directly to the ambition Abdul Sulayman has introduced here tonight. Abdul mentioned his funding model, and mentioned that it would rely on the direct participation of a measurable percentage of the world's population. Abdul mentioned a movement. I am here to tell you more about that movement—how it will come to be, and perhaps most importantly, *why* it will come to be. The movement is, as a man once said, one of *return*.

"Within a few minutes you will receive a message in the form of an email, an SMS, or a social networking private chat with both explanatory text, and a link to a video that will help to further explain what I'm going to talk about here. The distribution of this message comes about with the assistance of some of the largest technology and Internet media companies operating today. It will represent something new, and will reach every email account, every text-capable device, every social networking account in existence. The companies assisting in the distribution are also dedicating an unprecedented amount of server capacity to host the video—as billions are expected to view it in the minutes, hours and days to come."

She reached into the pocket of her jacket and checked her phone and the act was repeated by hundreds in the audience, their own devices beginning to vibrate and chirp with message notifications. The process had begun. Then she looked up once again.

"The earth, ladies and gentlemen, is not what you think it is."

Sulayman felt a surge of energy run up his spine with the anticipation of what she was about to say. Gone was his anxiety over Genesis, replaced by something else he couldn't describe.

"For millennia, since humanity abandoned the ways that had supported it since its inception and chose to settle, to grow food instead of to hunt it, to *civilize*—we have viewed the earth as something separate from us, as something to tame, to manage, to *use*. Since this time we have lost touch with essentially who we are—our bodies formed from the dust of the earth, animated temporarily by the earth's air, by the food sprung from the earth's soil. We lost touch with our own place within the system, we lost touch with the context of our lives, we lost touch with the fact that we are a part of a much larger whole, a much larger ecosystem, a much larger cosmic community.

"With this separation came an inward, insular turn. A self-obsession. A selfish myopia that has resulted in all the horrors of war, murder, genocide—justified by created things as ephemeral and ultimately fictitious as ideology, nationalism, self-identity. Many in the modern world feel detached, alone, deadened—a background emotion that cools the life within. Many of us feel as though our lives lack purpose. We see the ultimate fallacy of living for ourselves only, of living without context, of living without meaning. But most of us do not yet realize that escape from the sneaking suspicion, that background of angst is just around the corner, a simple matter of changing one's perspective. For most of my adult life I felt this way too, until everything changed six months ago when I encountered a man calling himself Zhar-Oss on a stage in Denver.

"Since his death, billions have been exposed to his work around the globe. This is not just because the man's death was the ultimate publicity stunt. Janus' popularity speaks to the universal appeal of his strange, haunting music. That appeal is primal. It is fundamental. It arises from a place deep within—a place of deep, inexplicable recognition. His music is a re-creation of the phenomena you have just witnessed, enabled by a special ability that only he and a few others possess. It is the ability to sense that phenomena without technological enhancement. But what is that phenomena? Is it simply an artifact of the aurora? Nothing but an audible transmission of a belt of radiation, itself a by-product of the planet's magnetic field? Why would so many people be so drawn to something as technical and dead as that?

"In the 1960s a British scientist proposed a theory, a hypothesis that involved a paradigm-shift in our view of the planet's dynamic systems. The Gaia hypothesis proposes that the earth can be viewed not just as a lifeless rock whose surface is covered in a thin layer of independently operating ecosystems, but as something different, something mimicking the biological functions of a single organism. In this model each biome, each ecosystem, each constituent species is part of a much larger whole—perhaps a much larger *organism*. And what if that organism had been evolving for 4.5 billion years?

"Ladies and Gentlemen, the earth is indeed a living organism. It is also," she said, pausing for a moment, "a thinking one."

She stood silently, looking out at the crowd. She looked once more at the image of the earth behind her and inhaled deeply.

"That communicates," she said. Her words were forceful, flat.

Sulayman watched as those in the crowd stared up at her. He'd expected some reaction, some resistance, some level of expressed disbelief but he didn't see any. Perhaps those of Anatoly's

Confederation were more numerous than he originally suspected. Or perhaps they anchored the crowd, they limited the skepticism of those around them. To those of the Confederation, none of this was new. What was new to them was the public forum. And him. He was new.

The sounds of various message notifications continued throughout the big room. He pictured for a moment a school girl in Japan opening the link to the video, listening to Janus' music. An old man sitting outside his dacha in Russia. A patron of a cafe in Paris. A miner in Chile, an astronaut on the aging ISS. All simultaneously doing the same. The peoples of the world were simultaneously waking up to this strange truth, as he himself had just a few weeks ago as he traveled in a plane over the Pacific.

"The earth is an organism that communicates with us," she repeated, her voice just as voluble and unwavering. She looked down for a moment, as if about to change the tempo of her speech.

"Benjamin Janus," she said. "Zhar-Oss. Zhar. Oss."

At the repeated mention of that word a few in the crowd shifted in their seats. She paused, as if giving those for whom that secret word held greater meaning time to prepare themselves for its further, public use.

"That word," Fleur continued. "Initially alien, primal, seemingly not of any modern language, yet somehow familiar, somehow not quite foreign. I learned soon after his death that it was not simply *his* name, but contained a context and a history thousands of years old. It is, in fact, a word from a language that humanity once knew—from a time when we were still at one with so much more. The word in that lost language means 'Holy Book,' or 'Holy Telling,' though the nature of what it refers to is not necessarily religious, not in the traditional sense. The word also refers to an organization."

Sulayman saw that there were a small number in the audience clearly uncomfortable, disturbed by what she was about to do. A few were shaking their heads. One old man in particular stood out, though his body was still. Sulayman had seen him earlier, unique only in his age, and by his vaguely familiar face. He was distinguished, clearly intelligent, and possessed a quiet gravity. With a moment's contemplation he placed the man's face. Of course. He was Cuban. A government official, one of the last vestiges of the old communist regime. Dias-De Santos was his name. The old man stared at Fleur with an obvious, steely resolve.

"Benjamin Janus chose his stage-name to pay homage to both that organization and the knowledge the people belonging to it protected, outlined in that ancient book, the *Oss*."

She paused again, looking down for a moment to collect her thoughts, planning her words. When she looked up once again she was no longer as calm as before.

"Zhar-Oss, as a collective entity, has existed for a little over 27,000 years. Its current membership is over 600 strong. Many of you will be surprised to learn that some of the world's most influential citizens are members. All races, all sexes, all nationalities are represented within the group. Benjamin Janus was a member. I became a member myself immediately after Janus' death. It was then that I was exposed to the knowledge that the group protects, kept secret for eons—for longer than conventional, recorded history. It was with this knowledge that my life changed forever.

"The group has survived the vast spans of time due to the obvious importance its constituents place on the knowledge they keep and protect, and also on an uncompromising tradition of orthodoxy and the refusal to act without historical precedent. This act of mine tonight is without precedent. There are many within the group who will be deeply angered at what I do now. There are divisions, deep divisions within Zhar-Oss. Some, like Janus and I, have wanted to come forward with the knowledge the group protects since we first learned of it. Others, citing the group's inherent orthodoxy and other more personal reasons, refuse.

"I direct these next words to the members of the Confederation, of Zhar-Oss, some of whom are present in this room now, some are watching now from around the world. Each and every one of us remembers our first exposure to the Knowledge, those first steps on the damp earthen floor of the cave. Each and every one of us remembers seeing the images for the first time, formed by the hands of men more than 30,000 years ago, vibrant and alive and looking as though they were made yesterday. Each of us remembers the moment we realized what the Knowledge truly was, once we relinquished our internal resistance to it— allowing that flood of implication to come washing over us. No longer did we feel alone in the world. No longer did we feel empty, living life without purpose. No longer did we feel *separate*. It is this same gift that we now give to the people of the world.

"This is, of course, without precedent. There are those who say that we as a whole are not yet ready for the Return that our Founder first spoke of. These people are wrong. We are ready. And beyond any question of *readiness* is the issue of *necessity*. We cannot continue on our present course—aimless and without purpose. Human society can not continue to expand at the rate that it has, while neglecting its development, its depth, its quality. Society is changing rapidly. This evolution is accelerating. Climate change, the coming and going of governments, rapid economic expansion, technological development—all of this is exceptional and without precedent. And as a friend of mine once said—it all leads toward one inevitable conclusion.

"Beyond the obvious, there is something else. Something most of you may not know. I can indeed translate the song our earth is singing. And I've heard within the song an update, a message for *our* time," she said to an obvious reaction by a quarter of those seated in the room now. "This message is why I am here tonight. It is why I support the ambitions of Cronos Space, Genesis and Abdul Sulayman. It is through this message that the myriad people of the earth will support Cronos as well. It is through this message that a *movement* will come about. Fundamental to that movement will be living a different way, living up to our potential, living to re-connect. We will live to create and build not just for our own satisfaction but for the *whole*; and externally—to move *up* and *out*, while gazing honestly within."

She stopped and the crowd was silent. Behind her the auroral display seemed to be pulsating like a beating heart. It had grown in intensity in simultaneity with Fleur's speech. The plasma halo of the northern pole of the earth seemed also to be her own. When she spoke next a man in the audience gasped loudly and a woman in the back of the room began to sob. Her words were low and slow.

"My children," she said. "Born of my flesh. I long to speak with you as you speak among yourselves. But time is a different thing to us. Your minds were once at one with my own as your bodies are, but this will not always be so. You will separate from me. You will seek meaning and fulfillment where it cannot be found. For millennia you will forget and during this time you will ravage my body for your own ends. Like your own mother in childbirth I will nearly be destroyed so that you in your infancy can grow. But of this body I freely give. Until you return, as a prodigal child, wiser than before. I await this day. My brothers and sisters in their dormancy await your coming too."

The words echoed for a moment in the large space. Sulayman's heart was pounding, and he didn't know why. He'd heard them before. He was struck by the fact that the world was hearing them too, and that this could not be undone.

"The last two sentences are new to many of you. They were there always, another layer, a higher note, hidden behind the rest of the song. The words are admittedly strange, maybe vague or open to interpretation. But in my mind this is not so. My brothers and sisters await your coming too. In their dormancy. A prodigal child, wiser than before. In my mind I see planets. I see the earth and then others—one now red and dry and cold and dormant. I see it as it is today. But I also see it as it once was—a primal world covered in liquid water and protected by a thick, warming atmosphere. Ladies and Gentlemen, this is why I stand beside humanity's greatest achievement and its greatest current endeavor—the earth itself wills for us to leave the womb, like children born of their mother. The earth itself is telling us to go to Mars and by the throbbing, echoing song I hear in my head right now, her words are a raging and painful necessity."

Fleur did not give any of them time to object, nor time to

consider. Her face had now reddened and there was perspiration at her temples.

"The time for Return is now," she said powerfully, her voice raised. The image of the earth behind her flared with an intensified auroral display. "We no longer hold a monopoly on this knowledge that will change the world. Your duty now is as a teacher, an older sibling teaching a younger one the truth of a reality you have always known. There is no more secret now. The Confederation is re-born into something else. It is no longer one of a few, but is now a confederation of many. Come forward with me to tell the world this story. Come forward so that your neighbors will believe. Factions, divisions are now a thing of the past, for the world now knows what we do. Stand with me as we all share it in together."

The cameras in the back of the room started to pan over the crowd as slowly members of the audience began to stand from their seats. Laura Watson, CEO of NewsGroup, was the first. She smiled shyly as she stood, and signed "thank you" to Fleur. Others immediately followed. Two more media executives. A newspaper editor. Two well-known news reporters. Sulayman was surprised when Bob Hsu, the NASA administrator, himself stood up before the crowd. Others too, whose faces were familiar but that he could not quite place, rose to their feet. Fleur looked directly at him and he felt compelled to approach her on the stage. He was surprised when she embraced him.

For the moment he held her tight as a wave of emotion took hold of them. He felt her sudden need for warmth and the touch of another; he felt her body relax into his as a child's would, knowing security, freedom and release. He could sense an intense energy in her, and also a deep fatigue. "You've done it," he whispered to her quickly, as she reluctantly released his embrace.

Fully a third of the audience now stood, most smiling, some unnerved. There came a moment when no more rose and a pause, an awkward silence took hold of the room. Then a man in the back, sitting, began to clap. Others took it up and a wave of applause rolled over them all. Fleur too began to clap, as did

Sulayman and within a few seconds the same man in the back stood, not to identify himself in any way but as an acclamation. The moment could not be resisted and soon the entire audience was standing, applauding the others, applauding Fleur Romano, applauding the earth that pulsed behind them with radiance. Most importantly they applauded a future, still uncertain but suddenly framed by purpose.

Elated, high, no one noticed the old man as he stepped out into an aisle, nor the other strange and bloodied man as he burst through the entry doors and entered the room walking with a limp. The old man, small in stature, face grim and dressed in a suit both overly formal and curiously out of date, moved calmly toward the stage. He looked around him and saw the other, moving toward him down the aisle at the other end of the room. There was a spark of recognition, a slight nod, a look of reassurance, and he continued. Reaching the stage, he slowly ascended the stairs, and Fleur caught sight of him. She knew without contemplation what was to come, and pushed Sulayman hard to the side of her.

"Get off the stage," she said to him.

The old man was reaching into the jacket of his suit and out of the corner of her eye she saw another, approaching her from the opposite aisle.

Kohl's face was swollen and nearly unrecognizable, but the blood coating the side of his head where his ear had been, his soiled clothes, his gaunt body attested immediately to his identity. His limp was severe, but already he was close enough that she couldn't escape the stage—Kohl would in a moment block one route, the old man now blocked the other. Kohl reached into his jacket and produced a handgun, the same she'd thrown into the dark water of the swamp. The old man had done the same and was now holding a gleaming revolver. He held it up and pointed it at her, now just a few yards away.

"You have profaned us enough, Ms. Romano," the old man said.

There was a scream in the audience and someone, maybe Sulayman, shouted "Stop him! Stop him!"

She closed her eyes, feeling immediately that presence now just under the surface of her own consciousness, the song, the voice—and it was singing as it always was. She went there, expecting in a moment to feel the searing heat of a bullet tear through her chest, or perhaps nothing at all save a final kind of darkness. She heard a single shot ring out, from which direction she could not tell and realized after a moment's thought that if she'd *heard* it, and not *felt* it, something was not as it seemed. She opened her eyes and saw the old man stumble backward in an unnatural collapse. The revolver fell from his hands and tumbled off the stage. She looked behind her to see Axel Kohl, arm outstretched, gun in hand. A wisp of smoke rose from its barrel.

For a moment he held her gaze with his one opened, bloodshot eye. "I hear the song, Ms. Romano," he said. "Veniamin was right. Something happened tonight. With you. I *hear* it." The handgun fell from his grasp and he turned, slowly making his way back up the aisle unhindered by the crowd too stunned to move.

Sulayman rushed to the stage and checked the old man, who was taking his last gasps of breath. A neat hole lay in his suit jacket, his vest and the clean white shirt beneath it, just above the man's heart. Sulayman rose quickly once he realized the man was no longer a threat, returning to Fleur.

"I think my work here is done, Abdul," she said, her eyes vacant and tired. He led her off the stage and out a side entrance to a waiting car. As they walked out into the open air they were struck by the brilliance of the iridescent display rippling across the sky above them.

"I've actually never seen it before in person," Fleur said. "The northern lights."

He watched the scene above for a moment before opening her door. "Tonight we've all experienced things unique to us," he said. "And somehow I know, even without that strange song in my head, that more is likely to come."

William Burcher 281

20

WARM AND WET

The beach was his, alone. It was still part of the Cape and closed to the public. He'd had to climb one barbed wire fence and stumble through a mangrove thicket to get to it. But he was satisfied that he had; it was as quiet a place as he could hope for.

There was only a slight breeze here at midnight but it was enough to rustle the long, thick grass that covered the small dunes behind him. He could see the grass clearly as it billowed gently, for the aurora still raged overhead and lit the land and the warm, calm water in electric-green twilight. He sat now just above the line where the small waves landed, his hands grasping at the sand.

When he closed his eyes the song was immediately there in his mind, like something born of the darkness, the almost-silence around him. It was not overpowering as Veniamin had described to him once, but was instead a soft and distant melody—

words spoken in a church rather than shouted on the street. Veniamin had done an extraordinary job in his recreation of it, its strange notes, its haunting discord seemed almost familiar to him. The difference was only in the sense of intelligence, depth and life underlying the notes he now heard. He knew that he would never feel alone again, even in his darkest moments, for the song would be there, always waiting for him. The connection was not just to that singular, incalculable entity singing the song—but also to other things and of course to other people.

"Veniamin," he said aloud, his voice a harsh and croaking thing among the external whispers of breeze and water. "It all makes so much sense now. So much sense." And he shook his head. A few hours ago he would have been overpowered by the guilt that came rushing over him. Veniamin. Fleur Romano. Genji Ueshiba. The repression of something so many people have wanted, have needed. But all was tempered now by the song and the connection—to it, to her, to everyone. Indeed, he could only smile at the thought of that, at how pitiful his own darkness was when compared to such a glorious thing. He shook his head again and almost laughed. To be taken in for so long by such a pitiful little falsehood!

"You knew! What it would do to me! And you tried! So hard. To get me to see it, to hear it. If only I had heard it sooner."

A wave of something else both sweet and bitter flooded his chest from deeper within and he realized that longing and loss were not of that old darkness. They were purer, lighter things. He gave in to them and saw Veniamin standing on the stage alone during his first performance in Trieste. He saw an image of the man still asleep, the morning sun on his face. And then again, Veniamin walking single-file through a dense forest with others, their clothing strange, the fog just beginning to lift.

He clutched hard at the sand beneath him. There were tears in his eyes but also a lightness, and he smiled at it all. "Danke schön," he said to the open air. "Thank you."

And rising, stepping into the water, feeling that the warmth of it was just the same as the new warmth inside him, he began wading out into the sea.

William Burcher 283

———————

Fleur awoke wondering which was the real her, the dreamer or the dreamed. She sat up, realizing that it was still early, the sun not yet risen. It would be cold, she decided, as she stood and donned her warm sweater and the ski jacket with the big hood.

She stepped out into the biting, frozen air and walked through the light snow that covered the walkway to an overlook she'd discovered the previous day. It was a kind of platform built of a dark wood for the singular purpose she sought now, she thought. It was perched on a steep hillside looking out over the valley and the village lit softly below. Above her it was utterly clear. Her breath rose in fog toward the sky as she gazed up toward an infinite field of stars and the background of the void. Two planets—Venus and Jupiter—were low in the eastern sky, just above the snow-capped mountains and the glacier that glowed with the half-light of a moon about to set.

She inhaled the cold air deeply, holding it in, warming it for a moment before letting it back out into the sky. She watched it rise and dissipate quickly, returning to the nothing from where her own lungs had brought it forth just a few seconds before.

He'd been there in the dream, of course. He *was* the dream. It had been his body, by now almost a warm and familiar thing, to enter her own. For eons, for millennia they'd drifted as a single thing in that hot place, bathed in the golden light, until time returned with the height and passing of their ecstasy. She knew then that the procedure she'd undergone the previous day had been successful; her body had accepted the embryo. Its cells would now be dividing, growing, bathed in that same golden light out of which she sometimes heard the song.

EPILOGUE

The wind is crying, moaning as it passes over and up from the crater and across the red plain. There is a valley off in the distance, a place cut once by flowing water perhaps a billion years ago. The smaller, distant sun is about to set over the western horizon and the light is bluish and clean and the shadows now are long.

Two figures stand alone in that bluish light, silhouetted against the dusty sky. One is the height of an average adult, the other is smaller, though strangely tall and thin—a child. Each is of an indeterminate sex as the suits they wear obscure personal or facial features. The suits are modern but worn from frequent use and covered in the fine red dust of this place. There are few markings, save for a curious logo seemingly not of any familiar, national organization. The logo is comprised of a strange marking, a representative character of an unfamiliar language, overlaying a stylized image of the next planet closest to the sun in this system, complete with what looks like a large auroral display at the planet's north pole. Both figures are still, gazing out at the scene, though as the adult is focused outward toward some distant hills, the child's attention is focused primarily on the adult.

There are tracks behind them in the sand and dust between the rocks and boulders strewn upon the plain. They have walked up from a depression below—the ancient remnant of a shallow crater where their vehicle is now parked.

The communications systems on the suits activate and the adult, a woman, speaks with tender seriousness to the child, a girl. The girl looks up at the woman as she points toward the south and a small outcropping of rock there. The two appear to agree to something and head in that direction, walking at an awkward half-speed in the light gravity. Minutes pass and the sun sinks lower in the sky.

They reach a large boulder, its facade sculpted by epochs of sand and wind. In the boulder's shadow is something strange. A series of rocks lies out of the direction of the prevailing wind. At first glance they appear like any other grouping of rocks but after a moment it becomes obvious that these have been placed here, stacked by someone who once had a purpose, a reason for doing so. The two maintain a distance. The comm crackles to life.

"What is this here?" the woman asks the girl, her tone a calm and patient inquiry.

There is a pause as the girl considers the question. She senses a seeming significance. Her comm crackles in response.

"It was placed here by one of us. Or by another. Its age is indeterminate, although one might be able to deduce this roughly by studying the erosion patterns of the neighboring rock."

"Yes. Good. Why was it placed here?" the woman asks. The girl considers for a moment further.

"Its placement here is conspicuous. This location was chosen. It is protected from the prevailing winds. We are also in the center of the valley, lined on both sides by higher, rougher places. It is likely that one traveling to the rim of the canyon in the distance would pass by closely and would see the placement of rock. It is meant as a message."

The woman signs "good" with her gloved and suited hand extended out and down from her helmet's visor. "What does it say?"

The girl considers this, her hands mimicking the shape of the rocks, outlining them in the air. "There can be only one message. For they don't mark any route or trail. There is one conclusion to be made. They are like the song, the one behind the others you have taught me to hear—the great one. It is a message, but it can only ever say one thing. I am here. I exist. I am. And you, seer of this simple cairn, are the same as I."

Behind her helmet's visor the woman smiles. She looks down at the girl and places a single hand on her shoulder.